D1561529

Murder on Mokulua Drive

ISBN: 978-1-932926-60-6 (hardcover edition)
Library of Congress Control Number: 2017959130

Cover Illustration and Design:
Yasamine June (www.yasaminejune.com)

Artemesia Publishing, LLC
9 Mockingbird Hill Rd
Tijeras, New Mexico 87059
info@artemesiapublishing.com
www.apbooks.net

MURDER ON MOKULUA DRIVE

By

Jeanne Burrows-Johnson

A Natalie Seachrist Hawaiian Mystery

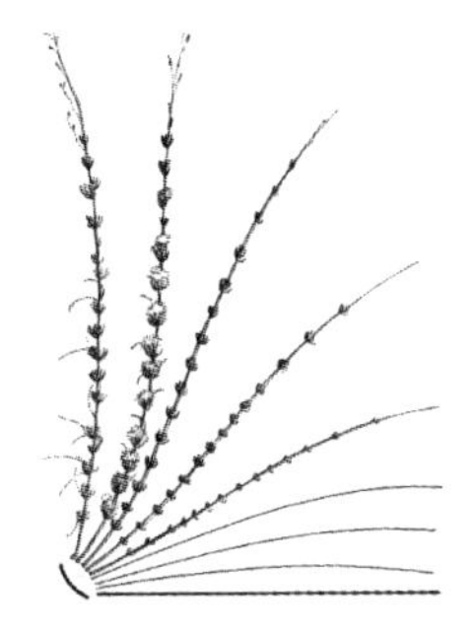

Artemesia Publishing
Albuquerque, New Mexico
www.apbooks.net

A woman's hopes are woven of sunbeams;
a shadow annihilates them.
George Eliot [Mary Anne Evans, 1819 – 1880]

CAST OF CHARACTERS

Stan Carrington	Former Colleague of Keoni Hewitt
Andre Chambre	French Canadian Tourist
Esmeralda Cruz	Housemate and former housekeeper of Miriam Didión
Monique Davis	French Canadian tourist
John [JD] Dias	Detective Lieutenant, Honolulu Police Department (HPD)
Miriam Sophia Reznik Didión	The victim; retired psychologist; wife of Henri Didión,
Ben Faktorr	Neighbor of Keoni Hewitt
Brianna Harriman	Granddaughter of Nathan Harriman
Nathan Harriman	Twin brother of Natalie Seachrist; psychologist
Keoni Hewitt	Boyfriend of Natalie Seachrist; retired homicide detective
Alena Horita	Uniformed officer, HPD
Jerry Latimer	Former colleague of Keoni Hewitt
Miss Una	Feline companion of Natalie Seachrist
James Maxwell	Uniformed officer, HPD
Ken'ichi Nakamura	Detective Sergeant, HPD
Dan & Margie O'Hara	Friends of Natalie Seachrist
Makoa Pane	Contractor and master craftsman
John Perry	Former colleague of Keoni' Hewitt
Natalie Seachrist	Semi-retired journalist
Joey Smith	Grandson of Larry and Lulu Smith
Larry & Lulu Smith	Neighbors of Natalie Seachrist
Evelyn & Jim Souza	Neighbors of Nathan Harriman; retired restaurateurs
Martin Soli	Assistant Coroner, State of Hawai`i
Samantha Turner	Housekeeper of Miriam Didión
Joanne Walther	Housemate of Miriam Didión; retired school teacher
Anna Wilcox	Friend of Natalie Seachrist; manager of her condo
Juliette Young	Cousin of Henri Didión

PROLOGUE

Each man should frame life so that at some future hour
fact and his dreaming meet.
Victor Hugo [1802 - 1885]

As in many of my visions, I look down on a sepia-toned scene. My eye is caught by a moonbeam striking the left side of a steepled structure. Even in the dark I can tell it is hewn of aged tufa travertine stone slabs, like the church where my Auntie Carrie Johansen's parents were married. In the shadows, arches frame what I know are stained glass windows, despite their being boarded to prevent the escape of light.

I now find myself standing on icy ground. I round the left corner of the building and glide down a flight of stairs. Wisps of light seep from beneath a metal-strapped oak door that creaks as it opens. I move within. Wrought iron fixtures dimly light the narrow hallway. I smell the mustiness of closed spaces. An opened doorway on the right invites me within.

Unobserved, I enter and see a small group of people seated in worn pews set in front of a partially disassembled altar. Dressed in wardrobes drawn from a mixture of seasons, these people are of varying age and features. A tall, snow-haired priest in black wool cassock with white pleated ruff at his throat smiles at his guests. He nods at a father giving his small daughter a sip of tea from a mug held securely to prevent spillage on the rounded cobble floors of the frigid stone basement room.

Outwardly, the scene is calm. But an undercurrent of nervous energy declares the imminent arrival of an unspecified something or someone. After a while, several blonde church-women in long winter coats and hats emerge from a door to the right of the altar. They set down closed boxes on the floor in front of the pews and beckon to the five seated women of varying coloring and ages. The women rise and glance uncertainly at the men and children surrounding them, then move forward in a line as though preparing to receive communion.

As the boxes are opened, most appear to hold clothing and shoes. Seeing the contents revealed, the women smile and politely examine the choices they are offered. Quickly selecting several items, they return to their waiting families. Two bend to focus on footwear for the people of their concern; the others hold jackets, coats, and heavy sweaters against their loved ones' torsos. Moving back and forth between the boxes and pews, they make decisions regarding what will prove most useful. Once the needs of every person in the pews have been met, the women turn to choosing things for themselves.

The churchwomen leave with their lightened boxes. After a while, they return with trays of open-faced sandwiches and thermoses of hot tea, brandy and chocolate. The priest moves among the non-parishioners, smiling at the women, nodding solemnly to the men, and patting the heads and faces of the children. The food is consumed with obvious restraint, but I sense the adults are wondering when they will again have the opportunity to eat or drink their fill.

Again, the churchwomen exit .They re-enter the room and pass out satchels of foodstuffs to each of the families and receive smiles of gratitude for their hospitality. Unaware of my presence, the priest walks out the main door into the hallway. The visitors earnestly pass whispered words from woman to woman, man to man and family to family. After some time, the priest returns, accompanied by three men wearing long and heavy overcoats. The light in the room increases and I close my eyes to its brightness.

When I reopen my eyes, I am standing in a forest of young pine trees interspersed with older Norway spruce and beech wood. Two families I recognize from the church basement pass close enough to have touched my arm. Bundled in multiple layers of clothing, each member of the party walks carefully, watching the frosted trail unfolding before them. They are led by a short, stocky man wearing a brown leather cap, black turtleneck sweater, heavy seaman's jacket, and leather overalls. His thigh-high boots move steadily along a worn path, until he arrives at a small clearing.

Next is a father in a Homburg hat who cradles an infant. Three women, two young and one older, follow with four children of indeterminate age. At the end of the line, another father carries a small girl. Having turned to check on his charges, the guide approaches the front of a small barn with a high thatched roof. He opens a narrow door to the left and then gestures for the people following him to enter. Hesitantly, they look at one another and then the man. Seeing their fear, he enters the doorway himself and then turns back to assure them he has no intention of locking them within. After the father and his daughter enter, I hear the door latch click shut.

Listening to the hoot of one owl calling to another, I watch the harvest moon materialize sporadically from behind cirrus clouds. When it is has crossed to the far side of the murky sky, the barn door reopens. In single file, the party resumes their silent trek along the forest path.

The small girl and baby still sleep in the arms of their fathers, who hold gloved hands across the children's faces. I do not know if this is to keep them warm or to prevent their cries from escaping. After many turns, the trees diminish in size and number. With an upraised right palm, the leader signals for everyone to halt. He gestures for the people following him to sit among the scrubby underbrush that stretches from the wind-blown tree line to a pebbled beach.

The way-shower then extracts a flashlight from his large pocket. Holding it at chest level, he transmits three bursts of light. Shortly, a similar signal flashes from above the water that laps gently against the shore. The man then returns to sit with the people who await him with fearful expectation. Soon a row-boat arrives with a young man at the oars. Beckoning to the father holding the small girl, the old seaman gestures for the family to follow him to the craft that will carry them to a trawler prepared to carry them on the final phase of their journey to freedom.

Taking the girl into his strong arms, the man in the leather overalls wades out to the boat. As he sets the child carefully on a splintered bench seat, her knitted hat comes loose and reveals a face framed with tight blond curls. In her nervousness she clutches the gold Star of David at her throat. The man reties her hat and pats her shoulder before turning back to the shore. Signaling for his remaining flock to come forward, he helps each person into the boat.

Once they are seated, the man bids farewell to his charges. Baring his white blond hair, he doffs his hat in salute and nods to the oarsman. As the boat moves outward into the bay, the small girl opens her bright green, almond-shaped eyes and whispers a few words in flawless Danish, "Farvel og tak for den lækker risengrød." While I do not speak the language of my maternal grandmother, I know that the child is expressing gratitude for the rich rice porridge that is a specialty of holiday celebrations in Denmark.

A hint of pink kisses the gun metal gray sky as the boat travels across the sound. From above, I study the mottled seascape speckled with boats of many sizes and types. The chugging of motorized fishing trawlers and speedboats registers as a soft purring beneath a symphony of bubbling water moving against wooden hulls and the flapping of canvas on boats with sails. Few people are visible and those who can be seen are mordantly silent. A distant shoreline is faintly discernible where the predawn sky touches the horizon.

CHAPTER 1

The people are like waves of sea
and I am drifting between them wherever they are blown.
The Tao Te Ching [circa 500 BCE]

The day before I had the vision drawn from a 1940s B-movie, it had seemed like life was finally moving away from deadly matters. While my family has had a higher-than-average number of death related events, my twin Nathan and I had experienced more than our usual quota in the last year. Losing both Nathan's beloved granddaughter Ariel and our Auntie Carrie had taken a high toll on each of us. I had recently retired from a career in travel and leisure journalism and had hoped to catch up with my family after so many years of being on the road. But that was not to be.

Shifting from visioning to light sleep, I heard heavy rain hitting the *lānai* doors and louvered windows of my Waikīkī condo. I was grateful that for more than a week I had been able to rise each morning without an acute jolt of loss. But in that state between sleeping and waking, I felt disoriented and continued to feel the wooing of ocean currents from my vision.

I consider my experience a *vision* because the scenes had appeared in faded sepia, rather than the hues of reality I enjoy in a normal dream. And when I view scenes in the tones of an old tintype photo, they inevitably prove to be snapshots of significant events. Usually the images come to me concurrently or before an event. At the moment, I could not see where scenes lifted from World War II would prove relevant to my life in the twenty-first century, but stranger things have happened in my fifty-plus years.

The rain continued its assault as I awakened fully. I was alone since my boyfriend Keoni had spent the night in his Mānoa bungalow, after the semi-annual gathering of his closest buddies from his years in the Homicide Division of the Honolulu Police Department. With only one more day in my condo, I knew I needed to get started on a final to-do list, if we were to be ready to clear out the next day. But despite the need to up my momentum, I lolled in bed a bit longer.

In some respects, Keoni's maintaining his own place reminded me of the handful of years I had been married to Bill Seachrist. As a young naval officer, Bill had had twenty-four hour duty fairly frequently when he was assigned to a ship. While some wives complained, I used the time to get together with single girlfriends, wax floors, or luxuriate in a tubful of hot water...with a clay mask on my face, oil in my hair and a champagne glass on the floor beside me.

I tried to shake off images of boats of any kind since the sight of them usually makes me queasy. Instead I thought about what I had seen in the stone church and the little girl who was bundled in a warm jacket for a journey at sea. Experience has taught me that I will learn the importance of these vignettes eventually. In the meantime, I should hit the shower and launch the final day of preparation for my move to Auntie Carrie's cottage in Lanikai.

As I sat up and swung my feet to the floor, my valiant feline companion Miss Una arrived to announce her desire for breakfast.

"Yes, you've been a very good girl, this morning. You actually let me to sleep in until seven-thirty. Did you eat all of your dry food? Whatever would you do if you had to face an empty bowl for more than a couple of hours?"

Staring at me with suspicion, Miss Una turned to lead the way into the kitchen. After meeting her loud demand for immediate satisfaction, I started a pot of Kona coffee for myself. Moving into my normal routine, I looked at the kitchen phone to see if the light was blinking to announce I had voicemail. As I expected, I found a message that had been left after I had switched off the ringer of my bedside phone to ensure a good night's sleep.

"Hi Natalie," said my twin Nathan. "I'll bet you're getting one last peaceful night of rest before the big move. I was just wondering if you and Keoni would like me to bring over some chop-salad and a pizza from Zia's Caffe tomorrow night? And maybe some crispy calamari? You know how to find me if you like the idea. Also, have Keoni call me if there are any tools or supplies you need. I can always run down to your condo, if you want something before getting to the cottage."

Great. That was one less item to think about. Keoni has a good appetite. After moving my entire household and some of his belongings, I wanted to be able to offer him a decent meal—without our having to clean up the kitchen, or drive over to Kailua. Not that I did not appreciate the windward town's great restaurants. Their abundance had helped tip the scale in my decision to move into the old Lanikai cottage which is just southwest of Kailua.

For the last two weeks I had been using up as much of my fresh food and refrigerated staples as possible. So, my morning coffee was lightened with ice cream and my breakfast consisted of the carton of Tillamook yogurt a friend had brought from the mainland plus the last apple banana from Nathan's yard. Until I wrote an article on agricultural specialties of Hawai`i, I had no idea there were several varieties of apple bananas. I think Nathan's are sweet dwarf Brazilians.

After the impact of my vision, I allowed myself a leisurely second cup of coffee spiced with a dash of organic cinnamon that my grandniece Brianna had brought over from Portland, Oregon, during the holidays. After the death of her twin Ariel the previous summer, we were glad to be reunited as a family, if only for a short while. This had proven especially significant since Auntie Carrie had died before Bri's return to college.

Finally, I reached for my list of things that had to be done before tomorrow morning. Unlike my last move, this one was not temporary. As Wayne Dyer often said, it was *The Big Enchilada*. All of my belongings were being moved out. Once the condo was empty, I had to have the unit cleaned and painted before converting it into a rental property.

Fortunately, I would not be playing landlord. I had decided to have Anna Wilcox (my friend and the manager of the building) handle every aspect of the rental. My decision to give up control of this area of my life was made while substituting for one of Anna's colleagues at the weekly mahjong game held by several Waikīkī property managers.

With four tables running, I am often invited to join in the fun. Each hostess provides the entrée and drinks, while guests bring side dishes and desserts. I am a happy girl anytime I can enjoy a good meal with minimal effort, and this was one activity that I would try to maintain after the move to the Windward District of O`ahu.

Listening to the conversations of those powerhouses of all things condominium, I had realized I did not want to undertake responsibility for keeping a tenant happy. Since I was not relying on the rental income to sustain myself, I decided to let Anna make a couple of dollars and save myself the agony. The condo's appliances were almost new and I would be leaving the unit in good condition, so hopefully there would not be much drama on the landlord front for a while. When one emerged, I would follow Anna's advice and simply write a check for what needed to be done.

After a bit more packing, I planned to catch a ride with Keoni to pick up my parents' old Chevy Malibu from Nathan, as temporary transportation until my new hybrid Kia Optima arrived from the mainland. Once I had left college, I relied on my husband Bill's MG. If he was on shore duty, I simply dropped him at the office. When he was on deployment, I had the use of his car whenever I wanted. After Bill died, my fledgling career as a journalist had moved into high gear and I spent most of my life travelling. With the MG remaining parked for extended periods, it had only eighty thousand miles on the odometer when I finally sold it.

Since I had never bought a new car before, the adventure of selecting features for the Optima seemed as daunting as it was exciting. The easiest decisions were the Snow White Pearl finish for the exterior and gray leather for the interior. I could not believe how many trim options I could select from. Loving classical music, as well as Hawaiian slack key guitar, I was delighted that SiriusXM Satellite Radio was available in Hawai`i. With an upgraded sound system, I would be getting the best of all things audio.

Beyond those choices, I let Keoni talk me into several features for safety as well as comfort, including auto-leveling headlights and folding outside mirrors. With the hybrid's fabulous mileage, onboard navigation and communication systems, he said he would not have to worry about my being stranded some night when he was not with me. And given our climate, I was thrilled at the thought of air cooled seats!

It seemed appropriate that I would have a new car to go with my new—at least to me—home. When our Auntie Carrie passed, Nathan and I decided he would continue to live in the waterside Kāne`ohe home built by our parents in their retirement and I would move into Auntie's White Sands Cottage. Admittedly there's quite a disparity between the value of the large up-to-date home in Kāne`ohe and the modest old bungalow in Lanikai, but surprisingly, the difference in valuation is not based on size or amenities. That is because the land near the rocky, unwelcoming Kāne`ohe Bay does not have the value of the cottage that lies near one of the most glorious beaches in Hawai`i. The address itself puts the Lanikai cottage in one of the most affluent real estate markets in the world.

While the cottage is not large in terms of square feet, it seems like a palace after all my years in apartments, condos, and hotel rooms. Counting the small attic, there were three levels to the house and many old fashioned built-ins plus odd little nooks and crannies. These features would certainly provide Miss Una with a very active life. And, of course, there was the great out-of-doors to which she was about to be introduced.

The lot was over a quarter of an acre, which is fairly large for Hawai`i. Most of the streets are narrow in Lanikai and the house is set near the front of the property to maximize enjoyment of the backyard and ocean view. The house, or cottage as we always call it, is a *kama'aina*, an Island interpretation of the classic bungalow. The balance of traditional Arts and Crafts design with a touch of Asian and Hawaiian styling shows in the foundation, chimney and porch columns of lava rock, upturned eaves, and use of local woods like *koa* and *`ōhi`a*.

Eventually both properties will pass to Brianna, Nathan's sole remaining granddaughter. At the moment, she is not interested in real estate, no matter where it is located. She has slowed the pace of her studies since her twin's death, but is still on track to complete her Bachelor's degree in psychology and then enter a Master's program in social work.

While Nathan and I try to focus on the present, it is difficult for us to control our emotions about her twin's murder. We had envisioned the girls marrying and having families that would surround us as we aged. Unfortunately, half of that dream will never materialize, because the machinations of a crazed drug user caused Ariel to fall to her untimely death.

After I had returned to my condo from a short period of sleuthing at the apartment complex where the girl had died, I had turned to putting my own affairs in order. When Ariel's murder was followed by Auntie Carrie's quiet passing on the second of January, I forced myself to begin sorting the clothing, personal effects, and household goods of both my beloved grandniece and aunt.

Although Brianna had returned to the Islands for spring break, she was still too distraught to sort her twin's belongings. Selecting a few items for herself, Brianna had asked Nathan and me to disperse her twin's favorite pieces of jewelry and clothing among her friends and then to donate the furniture and remaining accessories for the benefit of families of women and children who had suffered or died from violence.

Nathan, a semi-retired psychologist, had just been elected to the board of Hale Malolo, a women's shelter at the time of Ariel's death. Since they were always in need of a variety of things for their clients, there was no debate on how to utilize Ariel's and Carrie's earthly possessions. Although I have never had a vision of Ariel since her passing, I had a dream about her as a young girl the night after we delivered the last of her belongings to the shelter.

* * * * *

In my dream, I stand at the side of the garden in our parents' former home on an early Sunday morning. The sun shines vibrantly on the leaves of hibiscus bushes that are still wet with morning dew. I look toward the back of the property, where palm trees sway in a gentle breeze. Around the house and along the sides of the garden, plantings of Song of India and monstera provide a backdrop for pops of yellow from ginger and rattlesnake plants. At the base of the flower bed, lower-growing orange and white lantana ground cover creep onto the edge of the lawn. The garden is especially lovely because of the blooming annual flowers Nathan has planted recently along the lava stone path leading from the lānai down to the rocky edge of the bay.

The previous night, Ariel and Brianna invited a couple of their closest friends for a slumber party. Always early and on target, Auntie Carrie arrives to add a few of her special touches to the girls' brunch that morning. She always loved any excuse to turn a simple supper into a pā`ina *or a casual Sunday breakfast into a festive Island-style brunch. Although a beachside gathering of young girls does not require it, Auntie Carrie wants to make the day a memorable one for both the hostesses, as well as their guests.*

Her menu includes shrimp quiche, ambrosia salad with fresh pineapple and tiny sandwiches with crusts trimmed as the old gracious Waikīkī hotels do for their famous high teas. The beverage du jour *is cinnamon tea that has steeped for hours in a glass jar set out in the yard. For dessert, there is a festive coconut cake with* haupia *filling. On top of the cake are two hula girls painted to look like Ariel and Brianna.*

What is truly amazing is that Auntie Carrie has devised a small mechanism for making the cake toppers perform the hula at the press of a button. Well, I should be honest and say that the dolls are not performing the hula. *The shimmy they perform has been known to evoke ribald jokes at adult gatherings.*

The ambience is also per Auntie Carrie's recipe. Nathan has been instructed to set up the patio with a large buffet for the varied food selections and a large round dining table set with straw mats and yellow linen napkins. Even beneath the extended roof, there are bright splashes of color, with hanging baskets of bromeliads and large red ceramic pots with red ginger and pineapple plants.

With the stage set, I watch as the girls rush out the back door to "ooh" and "ah" over everything set before them. After Nathan pulls out a chair for each girl to be seated, Auntie Carrie pours sun tea into tall glasses and inserts stalks of pineapple core as stir sticks. Gesturing to the elegantly printed menus in front of them, she then describes highlights of the meal they are about to eat. Nathan begins the event by passing a tray of miniature bagels, fresh whipped honey butter and guava jelly. He then announces that the girls may help themselves to the buffet any time they wish.

To ensure the longevity of joyful memories, Nathan had taken many photos and even created a photo album for me since I was gone on assignment overseas. I remember laughing the first time I saw a picture of the foursome of teens toasting each other, as well as the providers of this rare treat. I think my favorite shots are of the girls pulling on rubber slippers and dashing out to the water for a casual game of water polo in the late morning surf.

* * * * *

My reminiscing ended with the chirping of my cell phone. I saw that the caller was Keoni.

"You're up earlier than I would have expected," I observed.

"What are you saying? I keep to my usual schedule, even when the guys and I have been out. I was up promptly at six-thirty and had my morning constitutional walk, as your Auntie Carrie would have said. According to my pedometer, I put in four miles today in spite of my bum ankle."

"I'm proud of you. The only things I've exercised this morning are my fingers—entering a couple of items in my to-do lists while consuming two cups of coffee."

Keoni groaned, guessing correctly that I had increased the number of issues for him to address during the move.

"Don't worry. All I need from you is an 'Okay' for Nathan to bring us a catered supper tomorrow. By the way, he said for you to call him if you need to use of his tools or other supplies."

"Well that's easy. Yes and yes. I'll give him a call with a *yes* to the offer of dinner at the same time I plead for the use of his hand truck. I know you've got access to furniture moving equipment at the condo. We're going to need more than the low dolly I use for maintaining the truck once we get to the cottage. And I think he's got an electric drill that's newer than mine."

We hung up after I made a few suggestions for his last-minute supply shopping. I then returned to surveying the mess that greeted my eyes as I moved from room to room. I was glad that I would be able to leave Miss Una at play with her mother Mitzy at Anna's condo while Keoni and Ben were loading the moving truck. Fortunately, Waikīkī is not thronged with traffic very early on Sunday mornings. But by the time we were heading across the Ko`olau Mountains on the Pali Highway, there would be crowds of tourists as well as locals coming into the resort area for Sunday brunches and other forms of R and R.

After tossing in a few last items, I began closing and taping every box I could. Hoping to ensure easy access and prioritization at the other end, I quickly labeled each before I could forget what they contained. Having been on the road for much of my life, the extent of my normal packing routine had consisted of simply ensuring I had enough underwear, cosmetic and first-aid supplies, as well as batteries for assorted electronic gadgets.

Most of my overseas assignments had been as a travel writer, and my schedule sometimes changed without notice and I had to traipse from one dream vacation locale to another without a break. Sometimes I ended up in the wrong place at the wrong time; instead of reporting on ways to spend one's leisure time and discretionary funds, I had had to pinch-hit for broadcasters unable to cover an unforeseen event.

Now that I am semi-retired I usually work as a free-lancer. This allows me to select the subjects I explore personally and control my work schedule. Sometimes I am contracted to write about a specific topic. Occasionally, I perform research for an individual or organization—as I did last year when Keoni asked me to research his family home in Kaimukī.

Although it had brought us to our current romantic relationship, the launch of that assignment had coincided with Ariel's death. Looking back, I do not know how I would have made it through the experience of looking into Ariel's murder without Keoni's guidance and active support.

We now spend nearly every night and most of our days together, despite having kept our separate residences. With Keoni's bungalow in Mānoa and my condo in Waikīkī, it has been relatively easy to merge our schedules. Now that we will be living together in Lanikai, it may take a bit more planning for some of our activities. However, since I will be just a half-hour drive from downtown, it will still be easy for me to get to the research resources I need periodically.

Generally, I am ecstatic about this move. But through my years of ownership of the condo, I have become very close to Anna. Through her, I have made friends with other property specialists in the area. Thankfully, my spiffy new car will allow me to drop into town for an occasional mahjong gathering, but it will not be as easy to enjoy a spur-of-the-moment shopping spree, or a glass of wine at the end of a day. If only our cats were kids; Anna and I could schedule regular play dates!

CHAPTER 2

All changes, even the most longed for,
have their melancholy; for what we leave behind us
is a part of ourselves; we must die to one life
before we can enter another.
Anatole France [1844 - 1924]

By the time Keoni arrived, I was nearly finished with the packing of all things small and personal. To minimize Miss Una's potential insecurity regarding a third move in the last two years, I had scheduled a morning playtime with her mother at Anna's condo.

"Honey, we're home," called out Keoni in his rich baritone voice, as he and Nathan strode through the door.

While Nathan is my brother, and has seen me in all states of dress and undress, I was glad I had changed from my occasional housework uniform of tatty unmentionables and into a shortee sundress and flip flops. After hurrying to kiss my two favorite men, I stood back and looked them over.

Although Keoni has a fuller body, Nathan and he are about the same height—just over six feet. It has always seemed unfair that Nathan got the tallness gene from our Nordic heritage. As the elder twin, you would think I might have been blessed with the wherewithal to ensure my younger brother would always look up at me. At least most of the time I had managed that figuratively, if not physically.

Looking back and forth at them, I recognized an uncanny similarity in their wardrobes. "What is this? Same shirt, shorts and sandals? Just who are the twins around here?"

"Can I help it if we both have great taste," retorted Nathan.

"Besides, we're not really duded up as look-alikes," amended Keoni. "My Cooke Street Hawaiian flag print shirt has a blue background. His is gray. My Scott's sandals are brown. His are black."

I laughed, glad that my two favorite men were fond of one another. "Well, try not to make a habit of dressing in unison. What brings you to my faint reminder of a home today, Nathan?"

As Keoni moved into the kitchen, Nathan explained. "Keoni reminded me that you had to pick up the Malibu. He also said he needed my hand truck and a couple of tools. So, it seemed best to team up and bring everything over here this afternoon."

Continuing, he said, "I'm having dinner with the Souzas at PF Chang's tonight and they can drop me home afterwards. In the meantime, I figured we could load the cab of Keoni's truck and the car with items you need to access when you first get to the cottage."

"Good thinking," I responded. "But some of those things are going to get used tonight."

Keoni re-entered the living room with a tray with glasses of tea for all of us. "To make things easy tonight, I think we should do something simple for dinner, and put the must-haves for the cottage's kitchen in the Malibu's trunk. And, while Nathan's here, we can take the bed apart, and put the mattress on the floor for tonight. Think of it as indoor camping."

"Or a slumber party," I laughed, remembering my dream of Ariel and Brianna. "Okay. Let's get this show ready to take on the road."

With three of us to share the work, we quickly disassembled the bed and secured drawers and doors of large furniture pieces. Miss Una was not sure if we were playing a game, but she tried to participate in the action whenever there was a loose piece of twine or an unexpected open cabinet. Within a couple of hours we had put a quick change of clothes for Keoni and me in the car, along with kitchen essentials like the wine opener, and a few boxes of goodies I had purchased for the master bedroom and bath.

The guys finally collapsed in the living room, where I had left the loose cushions in place on the koa furniture. A moment later I announced the final cocktail hour in the condo. "Here it is boys, the last of the kippers, cheese and crackers, plus a pitcher of margaritas. And that, as they say, is all there is to this chapter in the story of entertaining at this address—at least by me."

Surrounded by stacks of boxes, cord-wrapped lamps and skewed furniture, I surveyed the landscape. "Looking pretty good for the day *before* a move."

"You're right about that," said Keoni. "Do you remember what it was like the day you moved to the Makiki Sunset Apartments?"

"I remember it all too well. It was notably stressful because that was the site of Ariel's death. Since it was a temporary move, I worried about what I'd forgotten and might need immediately."

The room remained silent for more than a theatrical beat, as we each thought about the circumstances surrounding that move.

Keoni then cleared his throat. "Well, you certainly didn't forget the food. That's one thing both you and Nathan are great at—providing excellent food. Your helpers never go away hungry."

"That's courtesy of our Auntie Carrie. What would she say—bless her spirit—if we ever allowed someone to depart hungry?" observed Nathan.

"Speaking of her, let's lift our glasses to her memory, and to what I suspect will be her continuing presence in the cottage," I said.

"Hear, hear. I met her just once, but she seemed like a grand old gal," remarked Keoni.

"You have no idea," started Nathan.

"We'll probably never know the full details of her life," I

said, jumping in.

"You're right, Natalie. I'm sure there was more to Auntie Carrie than she revealed to us," summed up Nathan, extending his glass to clink against Keoni's and mine.

Following up on the theme, I said, "When we hired her caregivers, I thought we might discover details of her life. Patients with dementia often remember facts from their early years, despite forgetting nearly everything of their current day-to-day existence. But that wasn't the case with our Auntie. Oh, sometimes in cleaning and positioning furnishings for easier access, they'd unearth some letter, photo or keepsake with a note taped to the bottom. I guess note-writing was an art form practiced by both our mother and her sister Carrie."

We all laughed and got up for another round of sorting through the few open boxes poised for departure. After touring each room and pronouncing our work complete, we called it quits. While I sat consolidating my final short checklist, Keoni walked Nathan down to the lobby to chat until the Souzas arrived to take him to dinner.

It was too bad Keoni and I did not have time to join in their night on the town, because Evelyn and Jim Souza are two of my favorite people. They had been Nathan's neighbors for about ten years prior to Ariel's murder. I do not know how we could have managed her memorial celebration without their assistance.

They had been successful restaurateurs in California, Oregon, and Washington before moving to Hawai`i. To keep themselves busy while their Kāne`ohe Bay shore home was being remodeled, they opened one last bistro in Kailua. With all their experience and connections, Nathan's every need was quickly met with such style that I know Ariel looked down with delight at how her family and friends were *fêted* in her honor.

Evie had offered to help with a similar event when Auntie Carrie passed this last winter. But with Carrie's friends having predeceased her—or being on the mainland in nursing homes—we kept our gathering small and simple. Despite our designated honoree, we could not help thinking about Ariel, as we realized the last time some of our attendees had gathered together was for *her* memorial. I smiled at the thought of the two of them flitting about the Universe in delighted tandem as they shared new discoveries.

Although I had taken possession of the property several months earlier, tomorrow would be my first night in what had been my Auntie's home for many decades. The time has passed quickly with the sorting of her belongings and renovating the cottage. The most important work had been strengthening the structure's integrity after removing termite-damaged wood. Then we had updated the windows and doors, modernized the kitchen and two bathrooms, and repainted every room.

Tomorrow Keoni and I would be able to sit on the back *lānai* at sunset. I could already picture us toasting Auntie Carrie with champagne, in thanks for the opportunity to live in her wonderful little home. Now where had I put that new *peignoir* set I had gotten at Neiman Marcus during their July Fourth sale?

As the door opened and Keoni came in, I realized I had been off in a romantic daydream for a while. Noticing a large cooler in his hand, I commented, "It looks like you've brought more than Chinese takeout for supper, honey."

"I confess you're right. You're so organized, I thought we could just laze about and enjoy a picnic and the condo's amenities for one last evening."

"Good planning, Prince Valiant. What's on the menu?" I asked, following Keoni and our dinner into the kitchen.

With everything in closed boxes and sacks, I could not get a good sense of the tasty treats awaiting me. But with Keoni coordinating the meal, I knew I would be delighted.

Concentrating on finalizing arrangements for our dinner, Keoni stood with his back to me as he unloaded nearly everything from the hamper into the refrigerator. Turning around, he cleared his throat.

"Let's begin with our agenda. It's a little before five o`clock. To ensure you can enjoy the evening, are there any calls you need to make before we shut down business for the day?" he asked with a quizzical mischievous look on his face.

I paused. "Mmm. I guess I should check in with Anna to verify when I should take Miss Una down to play with Mitzy kitty—and to make sure nothing has come up to interfere with our use of the freight elevator between eight and eleven in the morning."

Gesturing around the kitchen crowded with boxes, he said, "My, aren't you being optimistic. Do you really think we can get all this down the elevator in three hours?"

"As you said, we're very organized. It might take longer than three hours to get it in the truck, but I think we can get everything down to the loading area. And if no one else has booked it, I'm sure Anna will give us some leeway. That is, if your buddy is here on time."

"Hey, Ben's already proven himself reliable. Remember, he's the one who picked me up at the hospital after I damaged my ankle last year."

"Don't misunderstand my questioning his arrival time. I'll be grateful for his help, whenever he gets here. I'm just thinking he could get caught in traffic, since Waikīkī is brimming with locals as well as tourists late on Sunday mornings."

Leaning against the sink, he looked me in the eye with a reassuring smile. "Ben and I have already taken timing into our considerations. We're renting the moving truck from another ex-cop who's pretty flexible in helping friends. Ben will be picking up the truck tonight so he can get an early start in the morning."

"Uh, not *too* early. Remember the condo rules; the loading bay won't even be open 'til eight."

"You're worrying too much. It's like the story of Goldilocks and the Three Bears. It won't be too early and it won't be too late; it will be just perfect. Trust me."

"I just want the move to be complete. I wish I were a genie who could snap her fingers and this move would be over."

Keoni looked serious as he said, "It would be nice if everything in life could be done that way. But you seem especially anxious about something. What's really bothering you?"

"It's Miss Una. I'm really concerned about her. You know those stories where a cat or dog escapes from their new home and walks hundreds of miles in search of their old one?"

I paused, picturing my little tortoise shell colored kitty trudging all the way over the Pali and down into Waikīkī, only to stare up at all the high rise condos.

"I don't think you have to worry about her," Keoni reassured me. "She had a great time when we took her over while we were drawing up the plans for the master suite. Remember how she loved running up the stairs to the attic and opening every closet door she could hook her paw under?"

"That may be true. But I also recall how she scooted outside when the Italian tile for the master bath was delivered. It took us half an hour to woo her back to the *lānai* with some dried *`ahí*. I don't know what she was doing in the neighbor's garden, but she was staring at that house intently—even after she was back in the kitchen. She knows she's not supposed to be on counters, but there she was—up in the garden window above the sink."

"What's a girl kitty to do, when there's no furniture to sit on? Like I've said before, Natalie; a good scout is always prepared. You never know when you or someone you care about might get hungry. I have an entire glove compartment of turkey jerky at the ready."

"My, you *do* think of most everything."

Pulling me toward him, Keoni hugged me and whispered, "Yes, I do. And I have planned a lovely evening for all of us tonight."

With a brief squeeze of my *derriere*, he drew me to what I thought was an empty hamper. Pulling back the top, he tipped it over until two cans of Danish herring dropped onto the counter.

"You see? I wouldn't forget Miss Una. One can for bedtime and one for tomorrow when we take her to Anna's. She and Mitzy will have a great time fighting over who gets the lion's share. Then, if there are any complaints in the truck, you'll just pop open some turkey jerky and pacify her until we get to Lanikai. Okay?"

I laughed and agreed that he had done well in planning for my favorite feline.

Keoni led me by the hand into the living room. After gesturing for me to sit on the sofa, he handed me my cell phone and sat down beside me. Before I knew it, he had pulled my legs up onto the sofa and was rubbing my feet.

After I finished talking to Anna, we walked back through the condo and took a final inventory of our toiletries and clothing for the next morning. Although Keoni still has his bungalow in Mānoa, he keeps nearly half of his clothes with me. That way we are ready for any spur–of-the-moment occasion that arises.

"You didn't pack your swimsuit did you, Natalie?"

"No dear. This morning you told me not to. What are you planning? A quick jaunt to the old Waikīkī *Natatorium* for a moonlit swim?"

"No, that sounds like too much effort. I was thinking we'd have our picnic down by the pool and enjoy the spa one last time."

"That's a lovely idea. Once the place is rented out, I'm not supposed to be using the amenities....Of course I could be a guest of *Anna's* from time to time. Like when we come into Waikīkī before dinner on the town."

"Have you run these ideas past Anna? She might have some qualms about letting you obliterate the rules of the house."

"She's done it for other off-site owners. And besides, I don't think there will be that many occasions when I would ask to impose on her good will." I then grabbed my swimsuit and cover up from the chair which was piled with clothing I might need in the next fifteen hours.

"I've already got my suit on, so I'll pull our dinner together while you change," said Keoni with a large grin across his face.

I could tell he had more than supper on his mind as he kissed my shoulder before walking out the bedroom door.

That inspired me to take a couple of moments to tidy the mattress and dress it with some clean sheets.

When I joined Keoni in the kitchen, I found Miss Una was enjoying her fresh *`ahi* supper. In a couple of minutes, we were on our way to the pool, hamper and towels in hand. As the elevator doors opened onto the pool deck we were greeted by Anna.

Holding a beach bag in one hand and a travel mug in the other, she looked at us and said jokingly, "Well, how are you two doing? It seems like ages since we last spoke."

"If we'd known you were coming down for a little play time, we could have come earlier," I said.

"Don't worry yourself about it, honey. I barely got in three laps before I got a call about some stopped-up plumbing. No rest in the condo business, you know."

Looking at the hamper, she added, "I have it on good authority that there's a pool party scheduled to celebrate the engagement of Kenny and Diane on the seventeenth floor, so you two enjoy some peace and quiet before the crowd arrives."

Keoni smiled and said, "Isn't that the couple that won the grand prize on some kind of reality show?"

"That's right. So now they've bought their dream home in Hawai`i and are planning their platinum wedding. I just hope they can get through the party without damaging anything around here. If you're lucky, all their guests will be out of your way by tomorrow morning."

Thinking about my condo being on the sixteenth floor, I saw Anna's point. Even though Keoni and Ben would be using the freight elevator, I was planning to use the regular elevators for smaller loads of personal items.

"Have a nice evening. I'll see you and Miss Una in the morning."

While I spread out our towels on a couple of loungers near the pool, Keoni took the hamper over to one of the tables under an umbrella. Turning on the sparkling LED lights in advance of sunset, he started pulling out the mysterious packages he had hidden from me.

"I hope you're hungry, Natalie. I've got several of your favorites here."

"Am I allowed to come and look yet? Or are you planning to hand feed me, one morsel at a time?"

"Very funny," he said, pulling out a chair. "If you'll start serving, I'll open the wine."

"Lovely," I replied. I realized Keoni really had thought of everything to make our meal and even the cleanup as delightful as possible.

As I began opening the packages in the hamper, I saw that he had bought large and sturdy sectioned paper plates and even deluxe over-sized flatware. It was nearly as good as china and silver.

Within a couple of moments, Keoni handed me a stemmed plastic glass, brimming with my favorite bubbly, Mondoro Asti Spumante.

"This really isn't appropriate for all of our dishes, but it should go well with the strawberries on top of our chocolate fudge cake."

"Mmm. You really outdid yourself," I congratulated him on his shopping. "Where all did you go?"

"I simply worked my way along Ala Moana Boulevard. Actually, I should be honest and confess it was just one pit stop at Ward Warehouse. The Patisserie had the pastrami on pumpernickel sandwiches for tonight and cake and blueberry scones for the morning. Kincaid's provided crab and artichoke dip with artisan bread, plus seafood Louie salad to share, and, ah..."

"You didn't forget the Horatio's Burnt Cream did you? The best interpretation of a crème brulée I've ever had!"

"You know me better than that. This meal is rather heavy on the carbs, but I figure we'll work it off tomorrow."

"Now that's the man I adore!"

Keoni listed the key ingredients of each menu item as he unboxed them with great fanfare. Without further delay, we dove into our meal with enthusiasm, if not finesse. Between sips of my bubbly, he fed me bites of bread with crab dip and I offered him forkfuls of shrimp from the Louie salad.

Soon we had finished everything—except the second sandwich and half of the cake. We were definitely well satiated, at least in the food department, and sat back to enjoy the last of our bubbly.

"That was *`ono* my love, but if you continue to spoil me with such delights, I may never learn to use that fully-loaded kitchen you've installed at Auntie Carrie's cottage."

"I'm not going to let you off that easily, Natalie," he said with his blue eyes sparkling in the twilight. "With all the work you're expecting from me tomorrow, I'm hoping for a five-course dinner on Sunday."

He then patted his *`ōpū,* to indicate how full he was. We agreed we were not up to any Olympic diving or racing. But before going back upstairs, we enjoyed soaking in the spa. Almost on cue, half an hour later, the doors of the elevator lobby opened and about two dozen partiers emerged, holding drinks and beach towels. Wishing them well, we gathered up the remains of our delightful repast and exited the scene quickly.

After dropping off items for the recycling bin, we tossed our perishable leftovers in the refrigerator.

"And now, my dear, what do you say to a warm shower before turning in early?" he leered with an all-encompassing hug to inspire me. "I only hope there's enough hot water!"

CHAPTER 3

Let him who would move the world first move himself.
Socrates [469 BCE - 399 BCE]

With the brush of a playful feline paw, I came to consciousness, just before the alarm was to ring at six-thirty on the first Sunday in August. I looked up and saw that my dear tortoise shell kitty was enjoying the rosy morning light from the top of the headboard that rested against the wall. Realizing Keoni was already in the shower, I surmised I did not need to turn off the alarm.

"So, what do you think about all this, my little cutie?" I asked, reaching up to stroke her silky fur.

Wrapping her tail around herself, she sat up regally and looked down her nose at me. She then jumped down to the floor and pattered over to the bathroom door.

"Okay, Natalie, it's your turn," called out Keoni. "I let you sleep in a bit, but now that I see your bitty buddy, I'm guessing you're among the vibrantly awake."

"Why didn't you wake me when you got up?" I could have washed your back," I said teasingly.

Coming out of the bathroom with just a pair of shorts on, Keoni observed, "You know where *that* would have led, and Ben is due here in about half an hour."

"Why so early, if we can't use the freight elevator for another hour?"

Pulling on a University of Hawai`i aloha shirt, he said, "Because I figured we'd share some coffee with the blueberry scones I picked up yesterday. Then I thought we'd plan how we're going to load the truck. Satisfied? So hit the shower, honey, or you'll be sharing my favorite views of you with a near stranger."

Running past him into the bathroom, I began my morning routine. I emerged twenty minutes later with my short hair pulled back in a scrunchie and wearing a tank top, tennis skort and my new zippered walking shoes. It might not do a lot for diminishing the size of my tush, but I could move without worrying about providing a floor show.

The fragrance of a medium-blend Kona coffee, with a hint of cinnamon, wafted through the air. Pulling off the sheets and pillowcases from our makeshift bed on the floor, I tossed the linens into the washer. Next I went into the kitchen and poured some coffee into a travel mug. When I walked out onto the *lānai*, I found Keoni flicking a bird-on-a-line toy at Miss Una. He barely looked up as I slid into a chair across from him.

"It's a good thing Miss Una likes people. It'll make the move to the seaside a lot smoother."

"I hope so," I replied, munching on a fresh strawberry and reaching toward a paper plate filled with scones. As I spread on some *lehua* blossom honey, I expressed my sincere gratitude for another sweet gesture on Keoni's part. "Thanks for the lovely breakfast. You thought of everything. These paper plates and cups and plastic flatware are the best I've ever used."

"Well, I didn't think you'd want to run the dishwasher."

"You're right. Doing laundry is bad enough."

At that moment, the entry buzzer alerted us that Ben had arrived. Keoni quickly picked up his cup and plate and went inside. Within a couple of minutes, I had finished my breakfast and tidied the table for our partner in manual labor for the day.

The door opened and Keoni and Ben came in, laughing as usual. "Hi, beautiful lady. Are you ready to rock 'n roll?" asked Ben.

"As ready as I'll ever be. It's been a long process to reach this point—with all the remodeling, cleaning, and shelf lining."

Seldom without a reply, he quipped, "You know what they say…always low and slow."

Keoni piped up, "That phrase isn't applicable in every case. We may be going to a cottage, but I wouldn't call any roofing job *low* or *slow*. I nearly broke my neck on the first day of that task."

"All right guys, enough banter. Ben, the coffee's in the kitchen; scones are on the *lānai*."

"As you can see, I've already visited my favorite barista, but I won't say no to a refill." As Ben settled into a chair with his renewed hit of caffeine and a plate of fruit topped by a scone, Keoni arrived with a clipboard.

"Here's the layout of the cottage," he said, holding up his diagram. "I thought we could strategize loading the truck, based on balance and how soon we need to access things."

Between sips of coffee and continuing punches of humor, we arrived at a game plan. By the time my second load of laundry was finished and folded into large garbage bags, the men had lined up boxes from the front door to the back guest room.

Glancing at his watch, Keoni pronounced, "On time and ready to launch. Natalie, why don't you take Miss Una down to Anna's? If you'll pull the truck into the loading dock, Ben, I'll call up the freight elevator."

Fortunately, Miss Una likes her carryall because it usually means she's about to have an adventure. Within a few minutes, I was ringing Anna's doorbell.

She quickly answered. "Good morning, Natalie. Come in and sit for a minute; it'll probably be the only break you get today. Are you and Keoni ready for the next phase of your lives?"

"Yes, indeed. Keoni and his neighbor Ben are set to begin loading the truck. We should be ready to leave in a couple of hours. Here's Miss Una AND a treat of Danish herring for her to enjoy with her mummy. Speaking of her, how is Mitzy doing since being neutered?"

I opened the pet carrier for Miss Una to jump and gave Anna the can of fish. "As you can see, Mitzi's romping like a kitten. I think the girls and I will be having more fun than you and the guys for the next couple of hours."

"You're probably right about that," I concurred and made my exit.

Back in my condo, I found that a considerable dent had been made in the boxes lined up like soldiers in formation. I was glad when the auspicious momentum of the beginning continued for the next couple of hours. Per orchestration, at ten o`clock the last of my worldly possessions were assembled on the loading dock and the truck was nearly filled.

After checking the condo one last time, I returned to Anna's and gave her the keys for my former home. Putting Miss Una back in her carryall, I headed to Lanikai in my parents' old car. Waikīkī was now crowded with tourists and locals looking for a good Sunday brunch. The delay in my departure from Waikīkī meant that when I reached Kailua, traffic would be backing up on the road to the beach park and Lanikai. At that point, Miss Una was serenading me with pleas for freedom.

In the long run, it was good that it took me longer to reach the cottage, because the guys had already unloaded the patio table and chairs, as well as several boxes of things for the bathrooms and kitchen. With the food and drink I was ferrying, we would be able to survive comfortably while moving in. I parked on the street behind Keoni's fully loaded Ford F150 truck with extended cab. Then I got out and went to the passenger's door for Miss Una.

"Here we are sweetie. Our new home."

Without missing a beat, Miss Una continued to wail her displeasure.

"Hi, Natalie. Welcome home to White Sands Cottage," Keoni said expansively as he emerged from the front door.

Taking the carrier from me with his right hand, he wrapped his left around my waist and leaned down to kiss me.

After settling Miss Una in the guest bath, I did a walk-through with Keoni, while Ben continued bringing in boxes that had been wedged around the furniture in the truck. By noon, we needed a break and were lounging on the back *lānai* with plate lunches ordered ahead from Kalapawai Market.

Sipping a glass of the sun tea he had brought, Ben said, "A cold beer *sounds* good, but one becomes two and that would lead to a nap we don't have time for."

"Amen to that," responded Keoni. "If we laze around much longer, we won't get the truck back on time."

Reminded of my good fortune, I said, "Thank you so much, Ben. I really appreciate your giving up your Sunday to help with our move."

"No problema, Natalie. And *I* really appreciated you researching my family's name."

"I love looking into anything related to Ellis Island. So few Americans realize how many of our surnames were changed for the convenience of pencil pushers, let alone their ignorance. Your family's name was one of the easiest research projects I've ever worked on. Finding that your family is related to Max Factor—the famous Hollywood makeup artist and founder of the cosmetic company—was a fluke. I didn't connect the dots until I saw the original name. The odd spelling, *Faktorr*, indicated a misspelling at Ellis Island. After a little digging, I found your name resulted from the shortening of your grandfather's original surname, *Faktorowicz*."

Recalling translation challenges closer to home, I thought of the Hawaiian language. In the late eighteenth century, Europeans and Americans wrote lists of their interpretations of Hawaiian words. Later, Protestant missionaries reduced their seventeen letter Latin-based Hawaiian alphabet to twelve letters. Then they moved on to translating the Bible, hymns, and other Christian texts into Hawaiian. As they, and then Roman Catholic missionaries, opened schools across the Islands, words were added to the various Hawaiian dictionaries.

Analyzing these early records is hard, since early transcriptions did not include diacritical marks. Conflicts in interpretation were further complicated by variations in how Hawaiian was spoken on the different islands. Even without distinct dialects, variations in translation can indicate the origins of some names and words. Thank goodness my research seldom dealt with foreign languages.

"It's amazing what can be unearthed with a little effort—yours not mine, that is!" Ben affirmed.

We all laughed and moved into high-speed to reach the finish line in as timely a manner as we had begun. While I was grateful for Ben's help, I could barely wait for him to leave with the truck. Then Keoni and I could slip into our swimsuits and head to the beach…or take a shower.

While I completed putting things away in the master bath and worked on bringing initial order to the kitchen, Keoni and Ben assembled beds together in the guest bedrooms. About three o'clock, I heard the deep classic chimes of the doorbell. It was too early to be Nathan, so I dabbed at my face with a paper towel and smoothed back my sweaty hair as I trotted to the front door to greet our first company.

Standing side-by-side on the porch were two women obviously north of sixty years of age. Each was wearing a short floral print *mu`umu`u* with flip-flops. One had her long blond hair pulled to the side with a beautiful tortoise shell comb, and the other had a tight afro with silver streaks.

"*E komo mai*," I said in greeting.

"Hello, I am Miriam Didión," said the blond with a slight accent I could not identify.

"And I'm Joanne Walther," said her companion."

"We live just down from your *lānai* at Mokulua Hale. I think you met our third housemate, Izzy, when you began your remodeling this spring," offered Miriam.

"Why yes," I said, recalling the petite Filipina. "She brought us the most delicious *malasadas* one weekend."

"That's our Izzy…Esmeralda Cruz. She's always filling the kitchen with the fragrance of luscious treats, for the neighborhood as well as for us," continued Joanne.

"As she probably told you, we were very fond of your Aunt Carrie. We hope you'll enjoy our little corner of paradise as much as she did," said Miriam.

"Oh, I'm already in love with this house. I've visited here since I was a teenager."

Extending a tinfoil covered pan, Joanne said, "You've

probably planned your entrée for tonight, so we brought a potato salad that will go with most anything. I hope you like it Hawaiian style."

"I adore potato salad, especially local style: potatoes; macaroni; slivers of carrot; tops of green onion, and mayo. Did I get it right?"

"Pretty much," replied Joanne. "Though I confess, I add a tiny bit of finely minced Maui onion plus a dash of Dijon mustard and seasoned salt."

At that moment, Keoni came around the side of the house. Stepping forward, he shook hands with each woman. After another round of introductions, he continued on to the truck and I invited the ladies into the living room.

"We do not mean to take you away from your work," said Miriam. "But we have been dying to see what you have done with the cottage. You know our two homes are among the few historic bungalows left in Lanikai. Nearly all of the others have been replaced by McMansions."

I agreed with their observation. "Yes, it's sad to think of the spirit of the old neighborhood disappearing. I'm proud to be the new keeper of White Sands Cottage. That's how I see it. I'm merely the caregiver of this lovely home until it's my turn to pass it on to the next generation."

"I know what you mean, my dear. That is why I invited Joanne and Izzy to join me. No matter *whom* we are or *where* we live, I believe we are merely keepers of small patches of earth for a short while. And hopefully, we leave our corners of Mother Earth in better condition than we found them."

"So true, my dear Miriam. And now I think we'd better leave Natalie to complete her tasks for the day," added Joanne in a warm contralto voice that spoke of Louisiana.

"Well, sometime in the next few days, you must come back for the full tour. And bring Izzy," I invited.

As we stood up, the front door opened and in walked Nathan.

"I just couldn't wait...oh, hello..." he said, seeing the visitors.

"This is Miriam and this is Joanne. They're our seaward neighbors," I announced.

"Delighted to meet you. I've heard this is a very friendly neighborhood. I'm Nathan Harriman, Natalie's brother."

"No one could miss seeing that you are brother and sister. Am I right that you are twins?" asked Miriam.

"Yes, the pairing of siblings in the womb runs in the family," he replied.

"Well, it is nice to meet you, Nathan Harriman. Are you *psychologist* Nathan Harriman?" Miriam inquired.

"Why, yes. Have we met before?"

"I do not believe so. But I read your recent article in *Professional Psychology: Research and Practice,* about bringing creativity into the workplace. I found it on target for therapists, as well as for innovative employers. I especially appreciated the extensive list of potential activities to boost the morale of employees. I believe it will heighten awareness of the benefits of recreational activities, as well as the overall productivity in the workplace."

"That's quite a review. May I quote you?" asked Nathan with a grin spreading across his face.

"You may indeed. Allow me to formally introduce myself. I am Dr. Miriam Didión, a former advisor to the National Center for PTSD."

"Now it's my turn to be surprised. Before being with the National Center for PTSD, you were at UNICEF and the United Nations. I've followed *your* work since college."

"This is when I should blush and think about all the gray hair I would have if it were not for Miss Clairol."

Just then, we heard the crashing sound of metal meeting brick coming from the back *lānai*. Hearing the back door open, I went to see what was up and put the potato salad in the refrigerator. Entering the kitchen, I found Ben putting a handful of paper towels under the faucet.

"What was all that noise, Ben?" I asked.

"Nothing much. Keoni's okay, but he scraped his hand when the frame of the porch swing toppled over."

I quickly grabbed a towel and ran outside. "Are you all right, honey? I appreciate everything you're doing, but you don't have to donate your blood today."

"I'm fine, Natalie. There's nothing wrong that won't be cured by getting this little task completed," he replied. Taking the kitchen towel from me, he brushed off his forehead and used the wet paper towel from Ben to dab at the back of his hand.

"Have our guests left? I thought I heard the doorbell a while ago."

"Nathan just arrived with our dinner. He and Miriam are sharing professional perspectives. If you're okay, I'd better return to my duties as a hostess," I said.

As I re-entered the living room, everyone was laughing at something Nathan had said about his work with a windward shelter for abused women and their children. As a new board member, he had been focusing on providing new avenues for expanding clients' self-awareness and empowerment.

Continuing his explanation, he said "As I watched a few of the women and their teenage kids experience *aha* moments, I realized that simply providing shelter wasn't enough. In addition to physical and psychological support, we need to provide opportunities for them to obtain and refine skills that are directly applicable to the work place. I'm hoping to develop a program to help the women find jobs that will evolve into successful careers."

Joanne glanced at me with the polite look of a non-participant in a technical conversation. After a few minutes of the continuing discussion of effective programs for helping battered women, she spoke up.

"Miriam, you've said you want to remain active professionally. Maybe you could be one of Nathan's motivational guest speakers. And, perhaps there's a way for all of us to help Nathan's program. When Izzy's arthritis worsened, she shifted from being part-time housekeeper to fellow housemate. The maid's quarters have been empty for years and we've been talking about getting some additional help around the house.

Why don't we have one of the women from the shelter join us. I think it would be wonderful to help women needing to make self-empowering changes in their lives."

Miriam responded immediately. "That's a wonderful idea, Joanne. It would free up a bed at the shelter, and help a woman build skills that can lead to a permanent job. Selfishly, it will ease things for us. The position wouldn't require any heavy work, Nathan; just general housekeeping and coordinating with gardeners, maintenance staff, and repairmen. With one or more of us travelling frequently, we really need someone to stay on top of the cottage's day-to-day operations. After six months or so, the woman would have experience as well as references to list on a resume. Then, if she wanted to move on, we would begin the process all over, providing shelter and entry-level work to another woman in your program."

"I thought I was bringing supper to the work-weary," he said, handing over several paper bags to me. "Now I've found a solution to one of our major concerns at Hale Malolo. This fits in perfectly with my networking with community staffing agencies. If I can find several sites for our clients to intern, I can provide potential staff to employment agencies. That's a win-win in my book. I'll check in with the staff and find out which of the women are ready to move back into the community. I should have one or more candidates lined up in a couple of days for you to interview."

"That would be wonderful, Nathan," responded Miriam. "And now, as Joanne said some time ago, we should move on to our home and let you finish your work."

"I appreciate your positive reinforcement, Miriam," I said, "but it's going to take a lot more one day to finish settling in."

While I escorted the women to the door, Nathan went outside to see what Keoni and Ben were doing. Before joining them, I put the bags with our dinner on the kitchen counter. As I opened the back door, I heard a *right on* and quickly saw that the challenge of the porch swing had been conquered.

Keoni declared the mission of the day complete and went into the kitchen for a round of drinks, as I settled on the swing.

Soon after, the men were passing around a bag of sourdough pretzels to go with their Fosters beer and I was downing a tall glass of iced tea before deciding which wine to serve with dinner.

"Now *this* tastes smooth," said Ben.

"And it's truly deserved," agreed Keoni, clinking bottles with him.

I jiggled my glass. "Here's a toast to friendship that has survived the test of another move."

Adding a quick rejoinder, Keoni said, "And after all the work and money you've put into the place, may this be your *final* move."

"Hear, hear," chimed in Nathan.

"Well, this has been fun, kiddies, but it's about time for me to hit the road," declared Ben.

Ever the gentleman, Nathan was quick to invite Ben to join us for the Italian dinner he'd brought. "You don't need to rush off. I brought plenty of food for everyone."

"I'd love to stay any other time. But by the time I return the truck, I'm barely going to make my hot date with Viki—she lives in that big old craftsman across from me."

"Whoa. What's Viki got planned for tonight?" asked Keoni.

"Who knows? With her creativity, it's definitely not subject to questioning."

"Viki sounds like my kind of woman—leaving a few things to your imagination," I commented. "But don't be a stranger, Ben. You—with or without Viki—have a standing invitation anytime you'd like a swim or a little something from the grill."

While Keoni and Ben gathered up scattered furniture blankets and the hand truck, Nathan and I moved into the kitchen. After reheating a few items, we laid out a buffet on the island.

"Believe it or not, Nathan, I have something to add to tonight's feast—homemade potato salad."

"Now don't try to pull a fast one on me. Isn't that the container you were holding when I met Miriam and Joanne?" asked Nathan.

"I cannot tell a lie. This is Joanne's potato and macaroni salad, complete with slivered Maui onion."

By the time Keoni returned from seeing Ben off, it was time to eat. "That sounds wonderful, honey. And what all did *you* bring, Nathan?" Keoni asked, moving to the sink to wash his hands.

"You don't need to worry about anyone leaving the table hungry. As promised, I went by Zia's and was inspired anew. I picked up some crusty calamari, a large portion of Tuscan chicken salad and some eggplant parmesan—which I think will complement the potato salad."

"And don't forget that fabulous chocolate fudge cake we have left from last night," I added.

CHAPTER 4

Home, home at last.
Thomas Hood [1798 - 1845]

As planned, by sunset we had filled our plates and settled around the table on the back *lānai*. We watched the approaching twilight with champagne glasses lifted in unison to celebrate Auntie Carrie's life and thank her again for this lovely home.

Looking at the remaining portion of Italian bread, Keoni noted, "I think that'll make an excellent base for crostini or maybe *bruschetta* tomorrow. Some garlic, a little seasoning, a sprinkle of parmesan and Romano cheese, and we'll be good to go."

"Sounds great, but right now, I'm simply relieved there are no dishes to wash."

"Getting a bit spoiled aren't you," Nathan said. "I saw that great new dishwasher. You won't get any sympathy from me about doing the dishes—especially not with Keoni planning, if not doing, all the cooking for you."

"Hey, I've earned a break from Kitchen Patrol," I said to Nathan. "Do you remember what it was like when we were kids? A lot of military housing didn't have dishwashers, so Nathan and I flipped coins to see who would wash and even learn to cook."

Nathan looked at Keoni shaking his head. "I suggest you have a backup plan whenever she's trying a new recipe. Did she ever tell you about the year she was in 4-H. Most of her *food* was awful, although she did win a blue ribbon at the county fair for her *demonstration* of making muffins."

"I'll have you know I eventually perfected that recipe," I countered. "The only problem was that I had to make it so many times, that I can't stand the smell of corn muffins."

"Well, no matter *who* does the cooking, you've got a great setting for *eating*—indoors or out. Yes, this really is the life. You may not have the ocean lapping at your doorstep, but it's a great beach home nonetheless."

Looking around, he continued. "I think you could really improve your ocean view if you trim the oleander hedges."

While I appreciated Nathan's suggestion, I had one concern. "I'd only want them trimmed a bit, because we're going to put in a hot tub and we don't want to lose our privacy."

"That won't even be on the agenda until I've finished extending and tiling the patio," stated Keoni. "One project at a time's my motto—or you end up with a mess everywhere."

We all groaned at the truism. Nathan yawned and announced it was time for him to go. Kūlia, his new mixed-breed dog, needed to go for a walk. After seeing him to his car and clearing the remains of our dinner, Keoni and I went back outside to enjoy the evening sky. I sat down on the porch swing and Keoni sank into one of our new patio rockers.

As we enjoyed the bliss of our first night together in Lanikai, I thought about the many blessings in my life. Close to one of the world's most beautiful beaches and surrounded by elegant multi-million dollar homes, I could not imagine a better place to live—especially with all the upgrades Keoni and I were adding. I sighed and looked down for a moment so he wouldn't notice the tearing in my eyes.

"Natalie, you seem a long way off. What are you thinking about?"

"I was just wishing Ariel and Auntie Carrie were here to enjoy this phase of my life. Except for missing them, I think my joy is hovering somewhere between the moon and the Mokulua Islets in the bay. I'm so grateful for everything in my life right now—especially you."

"Ditto, my love," he replied, moving to join me on the

swing.

We sat silently holding hands for a moment, before he reached to turn my face up to his. "I can't think of another evening that could top this one," he said, before kissing me gently.

Leaning back, he looked me over from my head to my toes.

"What are you staring at?" I asked.

"I'm debating which end of you needs more attention—your head or your feet?"

"Do I have to limit my pleasure to one or the other? How about ALL of me."

"Now there's a note on which end the night," he said, standing up. Taking my hand, he led me into the house.

The next morning may have been the beginning of a heavy work week for most people, but Keoni and I could afford a lazy start since we are semi-retired. The bulk of our current bout of remodeling was nearly complete and it was wonderful to savor the joy of opening a new chapter in our lives together.

The dawn of life in my paradise by the sea featured a round of blueberry scones and Kona coffee with a hint of cocoa. After that, we took an early morning walk on the beach. With the sun already bright against the white sand, I wished I had put on a swimsuit instead of shorts.

"When do you think we should give Miss Una her freedom?" I asked Keoni, who was busily looking at pebbles and small shells in the sand.

"Well, she's been to the cottage before. And after a night of being reassured that all of her belongings (including *you)* are here, it should be safe to let her out on a leash later today."

"Maybe she'll learn to enjoy going for walks with us. Auntie Carrie had a cat who loved to do that. The only problem was that he sometimes took off mid-way through a promenade and stayed gone for a couple of days."

Keoni snorted, before saying, "There's probably a simple explanation for *his* absences—entertaining the ladies feline along his path. I don't think you'll have to worry about Miss Una in that regard. But there are dogs in the area who frequent the beach, and *they* could scare her into scooting off.

Let's take it a day at a time and try not to worry about problems that haven't even presented themselves."

Returning home, we enjoyed a second round of coffee and discussed enhancements we were planning for the house and yard. For once Keoni held the checklist.

"Aside from hooking up the grill, I think it's worth putting in a cooking island complete with running water and a refrigerator."

"That sounds wonderful. I'll even help you build it."

"And how do you plan to help with the brick and mortar side of the project?"

"That's easy. I'll keep your glass filled with cold tea or beer and hand you each tile with a kiss and a promise of personal reward at the end."

He nodded with a big grin, "That sounds like a fair division of labor. And what kind of *personal reward* do I get when I'm through?"

"Oh, I'll think of something to make it worth your trouble," I said, rubbing his shoulder. "Maybe in that hot tub you've been discussing? Have you thought about where to put it?"

"I think the master bedroom *lānai* would be ideal. The upstairs balcony provides a roof. And we can plant bougainvillea against a trellis for additional privacy. Speaking of which, I should be finished with the security system in the next day or so."

At that moment, Keoni's phone rang, and he indicated he needed to take the call inside. When he returned fifteen minutes later, he had a bemused look on his face.

"What's up, honey?" I asked.

"Well, you know I don't necessarily have to work?"

"Mmhm."

"But until I met you, I didn't have a lot going on in my personal life. To keep busy, I let my business float and my assignments expand or contract depending on my mood. Now that we're together, I'm trying to decide how to position myself professionally."

"Well, thank you. I'll take that as a compliment."

"You're welcome. Until recently, my work with insurance brokers has been perfect—enough to keep me busy, but easily put on hold when I want to go fishing or travel. But when the economy saw a downturn, discretionary spending by both businesses and individuals dropped. Even insurance companies cut back. And although things are on the upswing, many business owners aren't expanding their staffs, so they require fewer background checks. Couples that may have sought divorce at an earlier time are remaining united despite whatever suspicions either partner might have."

I nodded at that reality.

"The big question I've been facing is deciding whether to enlarge my business or let it continue to float. With this call I just took, I've made the decision to shift the focus of my business. I'm teaming with a national company to provide security systems to both commercial and residential clients.

"If you're okay with it Natalie, I'd like to make White Sands Cottage a prototype for the new hard-wired and digital equipment I'll be offering my clients. When I'm through installing everything, I'd like to video isolated parts of the system for a new website. Of course, no one will know where the property is or who owns it."

"It sounds like a good plan to me."

"With me here most nights, a security system might not seem important, but I'll feel better about you when I'm not here. And if we start traveling, security will be really important if we leave the house empty for very long."

"I know you're right about that. Even at the condo, we had some cases of burglary when the owners were on extended holidays. So, what do you think the cottage needs?"

Keoni then pulled out a diagram of the cottage and a number of brochures from the folder he was holding and began outlining ideas for maximizing our household security.

"Could any of this equipment hurt Miss Una? Could she set off any of the alarms by mistake?" I asked.

"Unless she's addicted to biting into wire, I don't think we'll have a problem."

"The closest she comes to playing with wires is playing with the creatures that dangle from her fish-line toys."

"There's a big difference between plastic fish line and the wire I have in mind," he chuckled in response. "And the motion sensors will not be at ground level."

For the rest of that day, we rearranged furniture and determined how to use our closets and built-in cabinets efficiently. Throughout the week, my partner in love addressed matters of security, while I pulled the kitchen, bathrooms and dining room together. Room by room and cupboard by cupboard, the cottage was coalescing into a beautiful retreat. Best of all, the collectibles from my world sojourns were showcased to their greatest advantage.

On Friday, our new king-size bed was delivered. Finally, we were ready to move into the master suite, with its glorious bathroom and customized walk-in closet. Even Keoni's tall frame was easily accommodated by the large shower. I found the classic claw-foot design of the whirlpool bath equal to the luxury of spas I have reviewed through the years.

As we worked on our various projects, we met several of our neighbors. Across the street in one of the new mansions lived the Ho family. Maya's antecedents had been in the Islands for over a hundred years, but Ming had come to the United States as an exchange student from Taiwan. Once the couple was married, he was offered a great job in the burgeoning field of software design and later became a proud citizen of the United States.

Next door to us were Larry and Lulu Smith. He had been a general in the U.S. Army. When he was approaching retirement, they bought one of the last small bungalows in the neighborhood. Since then, they have renovated it to the point of non-recognition. But to be fair, it was not entirely by design. They had simply continued adding square footage to accommodate their grandchildren who wanted to visit during school holidays and summer breaks.

Then there were Miriam and her roomies, who were the closest to us in many ways. With a simple latched gate separating our back yards, it was easy for us to visit one another frequently. When I broke my salt shaker one night, it was a quick sprint to their home for a few tablespoons to tide me over until I could go shopping. And when the electricity was off for a few hours, the Ladies joined us for an impromptu barbecue.

Izzy had just returned from visiting relatives in Portugal and was getting back in the flow of manning her kitchen. After checking to see if we had set up our grill yet, they showed up with the ideal additions to the pork ribs we were planning to cook. In addition to chicken legs and a pot of rice, they brought a salad of mixed greens and tomatoes from their garden. The crowning glory was a sauce for the pork and chicken that Izzy had thrown together with odds and ends from the refrigerator she had been cleaning out.

As Miriam laid out their additions to our menu, Izzy presented us with a bottle of Portuguese port wine she had brought home from the hillside vineyard of her relatives. "I hope you like your port smoky and strong," she said.

"I'm thrilled with any variety of wine from Portugal," Keoni replied, taking it from her hands to place alongside the other elements of our meal.

Knowing The Ladies were hoping to see what we done with White Sands Cottage, I gave them the grand tour. By the time we reached the front yard, I was grateful it was still light enough to see the stepping stones to the fountain. Periodically, Miriam commented on our changes to the home she had known from her years as Carrie's neighbor. After we returned to the kitchen, Izzy went outside to help Keoni grill the meat and poultry.

"I think everything you've done to the house is wonderful," remarked Joanne, picking up a stack of plates and flatware.

Joining the procession to our dinner on the patio, Miriam grabbed the pot of rice and salad bowl. "Many people could take a lesson from what you have done here. You have struck the perfect balance in modifying this lovely old home without ruining its charm," she observed.

Heading out the door with a tray of glasses and a few last items, I found everyone standing around Keoni at the new grill.

"Obviously, I haven't quite finished the outdoor kitchen, but this table will get us by. In a couple of days, the island will be finished and I can drop this grill into its permanent home."

Just as we were serving dinner, the electricity came back on, and we all laughed about the social benefits of a periodic power outage. After dinner, I sat back in the swing, enjoying some of Izzy's port and watching Miss Una make the rounds in hopes that one of our guests would share a tidbit from their plate. As I looked around at the smiling faces surrounding me, I thought about the joy I felt in being a homeowner. There is no going back in life. I never would have given up my years of trotting to exotic corners of the globe. However, I was glad to be settled in a cottage I could claim as my own.

That night, Miss Una failed to show up at bedtime. I tried not to panic. I wondered whether we should have installed a doggie door. But when we realized that any small animal could enter the kitchen, we had discarded the idea. Instead, we had opted to install a hinge on one of the small panels in the garden window above the kitchen sink. Since there did not seem to be any other cats in the immediate vicinity, we hoped Miss Una would be the only user of the small passageway. I was pleased when Keoni declared this simple solution should not interfere with the security system he was installing.

Eventually I went to bed with little comment, since I did not want Keoni to know how upset I was about my wandering animal companion. But once he was asleep, I got up several times to see if she had returned. Shortly before dawn, I awoke to a soft patter of rain punctuated with a crash of thunder. Keoni turned briefly to reassure me all was well and fell back asleep. Slipping out of the covers, I moved quickly back to the kitchen.

Although she had not come inside, I was pleased to see Miss Una perched under the umbrella on the *lānai* table. As I opened the back door, I again wondered why she was intently watching Miriam's home. When she disregarded the snapping of my fingers, I called out softly to ensure I would not awaken Keoni—or any of the neighbors.

"What are you doing, Miss Una? Don't you think it's time to call it a night?"

She continued to ignore me for a moment. Then she unwound her tail from around her body and turned toward the house. After gracing me with a brief look, she daintily jumped from the table to the window ledge and darted inside her private entrance. Before escorting me to the bedroom, she ate a few bites of dry food and had a long drink of water.

The next morning Keoni and I stayed at the beach longer than usual, enjoying a swim after our walk. We found a note taped to our back door when we returned.

"Miss Una is paying us a social call. At least one of us will be home throughout the day, so come whenever it's convenient," wrote Joanne in a finely scripted hand.

"It doesn't sound like there's any crisis," said Keoni. "Why don't we clean up and take over some of the bagels from San Francisco for Miriam and her ladies?"

"That's a neighborly idea," I replied. "But there's no need for you to interrupt your schedule, dear. I've been dealing with Miss Una's antics by myself for quite some time."

Soon I was heading next door with a bag of bagels in one hand and the cat carrier in the other. As I opened the gate into Miriam's yard, I looked with appreciation at the garden. The rows of fragrant herbs, vegetables and even strawberries were laid out in two beds in the center. Running along the edges of the house and below the hedges of deep red oleander were numerous varieties of beautiful flowers.

I had barely arrived on the *lānai* when Izzy opened the classic Dutch door with flour across her apron. "Well, good morning. I guess you got the message Joanne left on your door."

"Oh, yes. I would have been here earlier, but I didn't think you'd want me tracking in sand from our morning at the beach," I said, setting the bag on the counter. "It may be coals to New Castle, but I brought you a few of the bagels we have flown in weekly from Noah's New York Bagels in San Francisco."

"Lovely. We always enjoy a new taste treat. Your timing is perfect. Just let me wash my hands and I'll take you upstairs where Joanne and Miriam are holding our invader at bay."

Continuing, she said, "I'm especially glad to have the bagels because I've been a little slow to pick up the pace since I got home from Portugal."

I followed her into the hallway and up a flight of stairs. "I know how it is when you return from a long trip. Although you've had a break from your normal living, you need a rest after your vacation."

She nodded. "You're so right. I finally put my empty suitcases on the balcony outside my bedroom to air yesterday. When I went out to bring them in this morning, I found a tortoiseshell cat napping. I guess I scared her, because she sprang up and dashed inside."

"That's Miss Una—always making the most of any opportunity for adventure. Unfortunately an open door would be all the invitation she'd need to get into mischief. I'm sorry for any trouble she's caused."

"Oh, she hasn't been a problem; it's really been rather fun."

After climbing the first set of stairs, we looked up to see Miriam and Joanne standing in a doorway at the top of another stairway.

"Hello, Natalie," greeted Miriam. "We've been getting organized and bagging items that may be of help to the women at Nathan's shelter. While I was downstairs emptying out a dresser in the old maid's quarters, I heard a disturbance up here. When I reached the first landing, I saw a ball of brown, cream and white dash from Izzy's room to Joanne's doorway. I guess she felt blocked by the mound of clothes we've been gathering for Nathan's clients, because the little dynamo turned around and ran up the stairs into my attic suite. When

I got to my bedroom, I found the stepladder I had left in front of the closet swaying slightly. Even though I could not see her, I knew where she was hiding."

Continuing the saga, Joanne said, "At the time, I had a headset on and was in the living room transferring some old jazz pieces from records to my MP3 player. When I saw Izzy run from the dining room into the hallway, I figured I'd better see what was going on."

"After I spoke to Izzy and got a description of the culprit, I realized it must be Miss Una who had dashed into the house," said Miriam.

As we stood crowding the front of the room, I heard a faint mewing.

"All right, you little intruder, I'm here to take you home," I called out. Opening her carrier, I set it on the bed and climbed up the ladder.

"Come on, Sweet Pea."

My empty hands must have looked inviting, because she crept out from behind a hat box and walked over serenely for me to pull her into my arms. Although she saw all of the ladies, Miss Una remained calm and allowed me to move down the ladder and put her into the carrier.

"I'm sorry for all the fuss. We're still trying to get her settled," I apologized again.

"We're just flattered Miss Una wanted to continue our chat after last night's party," said Joanne with a broad smile.

"Speaking of parties, I'm planning a surprise birthday party for Keoni and I hope all of you'll all be able to come."

"That sounds like fun. None of us plan to travel any time soon. Just let us know what we can bring, said Izzy."

"Well, I wouldn't say *no* to more of your potato salad, Joanne," I remarked, remembering how delicious it was.

CHAPTER 5

Good fortune is what happens when opportunity meets with planning.
Thomas Alva Edison [1847-1931]

The period of transition from city to seaside living was a grand time enjoyed by all of us. While Keoni might have to travel farther to see clients and friends, he was excited about completing his many projects at White Sands Cottage. My own days were filled with such delight that I barely missed my friends in Waikīkī. I had so much to do that I did not even notice the absence of research or writing assignments. As to Miss Una, there is no way to describe the joy with which she dashed around the house and yard during the days. Mysteriously, her evenings were spent in guard duty stance on the table on the back *lānai*.

After a week of settling into White Sands Cottage, it was time for Keoni to catch up on the demands of his own home—and his business. To launch his *marriage* to a large security company, he was training on their hardware and digital systems for a couple of days. Therefore, he would be staying at his bungalow above the University of Hawai`i for at least one night a week. Once he was familiar with the products, he would begin analyzing the existing security systems in a downtown office building in which he already had several clients.

Although I would miss his presence, I had a lot to keep me occupied that second week in August. My first chore was the blending of art from my condo with that of Auntie Carrie. Most of my art consists of framed travel posters and photographs from my years traversing the globe. Carrie's ranged from architectural line drawings of old buildings in downtown Honolulu to shockingly bright oils of Island scenery.

Next on my to-do list was the office. There I needed to re-shelve the books of my substantial reference library and cull decades of neglected files. While Keoni's preference is for computerized recordkeeping, I maintain both hardcopy and electronic versions of everything I have researched and written. For once I was glad that many of the newspaper clippings I have kept are so old that they could be tossed into the recycling bin.

* * * * *

On my first night alone in the cottage, I treated myself to one of my favorite bachelorette dinners: veggies with dressing; Havarti and sharp Vermont cheeses with rice crackers and taro chips; sliced deli meats (no nitrates, of course); and a split bottle of Ayala Brut Majeur. With a blend of Pinot Noir and Chardonnay, its fruitiness was a great compliment to my menu. With the use of a special tray, I was able to eat dinner while soaking in my new whirlpool tub. I brought an assortment of Miss Una's treats into the bathroom, where she joined me in listening to some vintage Emma Veary recordings of Hawaiian songs with her classic vocal styling.

When we moved on to the bedroom, I pulled out several magazines and my current suspense novel about an old woman endeavoring to find the murderer of her childhood friend. After reading for a while and saying goodnight to Keoni over the phone, I turned on my side and thought about the party I was throwing for his sixtieth birthday. He is a couple of years younger than I am and does not seem to care about marking the chapters of his life. But with everything that has occurred in the last year, I think this is a great excuse to hold a major celebration.

Thank goodness we were nearing the end of the alterations to the cottage. With all the cupboards and closets now available, I would be able to squirrel away the necessary decorations and supplies for the event. First of all, I needed to plan the guest list. I had not seen my friends Margie and Dan O`Hara for a while and this would be a great chance for them to get to know Keoni. If I told Keoni they were coming for a vacation, it would give me an excuse for scurrying around...and that would be a great cover for party preparations.

Keoni did not talk about his years in the military, but he had several buddies from his years with HPD. He had mentioned having a half-sister somewhere in Washington State, but they did not seem to have any contact and I did not want to go fishing in waters that might be polluted. I felt confident that with the help of the friends I knew, plus Keoni's electronic data base and his little brown book, I would be able to figure out the most important invitees from his perspective. Surprisingly, there were few old girlfriends mentioned anywhere.

Once I had determined the number of guests, I could move on to having the Souzas help me plan the food and drink. For entertainment, I decided to have one of Brianna's friends play classical guitar at the beginning and a DJ spinning Golden Oldies afterward. As to everything else, I had been so busy with the move that I had not video-conferenced with Brianna for a while. I was sure she would have suggestions beyond music.

Before falling asleep, I thought about what I could give Keoni as a unique gift. He would not expect a party and I wanted to give him a tangible reminder of the event. He certainly deserved it with all that he's done for me and my family. He does not wear much jewelry, although he enjoys the watch he was given at retirement. I could not think of any other personal items he would use on a daily basis. That left clothing. Maybe an aloha shirt, new or vintage. But how could I compete with his own Internet cruising for the classics he loves so much?

With that thought, I fell into a state of dreamless sleep. In the morning, I pulled on a pair of shorts over an old swimsuit in anticipation of another great day in my cottage by the sea. While I waited for a pot of mint tea to brew, I put some tinned fish on a plate for Miss Una. I then chopped a peach into a container of yoghurt and stirred some agave syrup into my tea. After I had eaten and rinsed out my teacup, I addressed my animal companion.

"So what do you say to a little walk this morning? Just us girls. I'll put on your harness so I can swoop you up if a canine dares to come close."

Absorbed in her breakfast, Miss Una did not even look at me. Lifting her harness off a hook by the back door, I reached over and slipped it onto her when she sat up to wash her whiskers. Fortunately, she does not mind the harness, as long as we are going out of doors. She knew I was serious when I stepped into my sandals and walked toward the door. Once outside, we strolled through the back gate and onto the path leading toward the beach.

I could tell she was enjoying the scents in the air, but was not thrilled with the texture of the sandy footing. I picked her up to cross Mokulua Drive and we sauntered along the final stretch of walkway to the open beach. There, Miss Una sat down and we both looked around for potential threats.

"What do you think?" I asked. "Are you ready for a surf-side adventure?"

The answer was a silent negative. Getting up, she promptly turned around and pulled at her lead to start walking toward home.

"Oh, well. It was a start on walksies," I said to myself.

We retraced our steps and once we were through the back gate, I took off the harness. After springing onto the table, she quickly turned to study the cottage of the women I had come to think of collectively as The Ladies. Grabbing a towel from the short laundry line behind the garage, I turned around and returned to the beach for a quick swim.

After showering, I began gathering some permanent press items for a load of laundry. I grabbed a couple of Keoni's things and checked every pocket for anything he might have forgotten to remove. I noticed that one of his aloha shirts had a Cooke Street label. I was pretty sure it was a Beth Surdut design and that reminded me that I still needed to find a special birthday gift for him. Why not a custom hand-painted shirt?

I remembered that day when I had met Beth in her Punalu`u studio. I was driving along the windward side of the island when I saw her evocative sign at a beachside art gallery. It was magical watching her laying down outlines in gold resist on a long piece of luscious white silk. Then a fantasia of tropical flowers, birds and sea life came alive as she filled in their forms with rich French dyes. I vividly remembered the recording of Hawaiian falsetto singing by the Ho'opi'i Brothers and the Siamese cat grabbing at her long Chinese brush, as she applied gold resist on the edge of a purple orchid.

Inspired by my memory, I moved into the office. I turned on my computer, Googled her name, and within a couple of keystrokes I was at Beth's website. It was my lucky day, because she quickly responded to the email I sent. We were soon visiting on the phone, while I continued looking at images of her beautifully detailed work in several media.

Listening to her sultry voice, I again thought of our brief visit in her studio. This was indeed the ideal gift for Keoni. She said she could create something new, but I could not see any reason to interfere with the perfection of work she had already created. After describing Keoni and his sparkling blue eyes, I said I wanted the shirt to be elegant and we agreed that a black background would be optimal. Once I decided on a short-sleeved shirt, Beth gave me a quote. She then asked me to send her one of his best-fitting shirts to use as a pattern and said she would send a few design samples that afternoon.

I was disconnecting from Beth when I received a call from Nathan. He informed me that he had a potential housekeeper for Miriam. To keep things casual, he suggested we get together at my house initially. Depending on Miriam's response, the women could adjourn to her cottage. If it was a *no-go*, it would be less awkward for everyone concerned. I followed up immediately and scheduled a meeting with The Ladies at three o'clock that afternoon. I might not have fresh cookies, but there were a few blueberry scones in the freezer I could heat in the toaster oven in case anyone was hungry.

The timing was perfect since Keoni would not be returning until the end of the day. By then I hoped he would have the tile for completing the *lānai* outside of the master bedroom. It would match the work he had finished on the back patio that now extended beyond the covered porch I had enjoyed since childhood.

With a moderate temperature and slight breeze to keep us cool, I decided we would sit outside. I wiped down the furniture and set out a tray with glasses and napkins plus iced tea and a variety of sodas and declared myself ready for today's gathering. Although I did not have a stake in its outcome, I was hoping the woman Nathan was bringing would be a good fit for all of The Ladies' needs *and* their personalities. I was glad when he and the candidate for the housekeeping position arrived first.

"Hi, Natalie," my brother called out, letting himself in with the key I had given him.

Moving into the hallway, I replied, "Well, 'Hi' yourself."

"This is Samantha," he said, introducing a beautiful, tall blond woman in her thirties. She was dressed in a spaghetti-strapped sundress in blue vertical stripes. Although she was staying at a women's shelter, her engraved gold bracelet and enormous engagement and wedding rings projected wealth. As a client of Hale Malolo, I wondered about the appropriateness of the word *ku`uipo* on the bracelet. Of course, she could always have the Hawaiian word for *sweetheart* replaced with her name.

"How do you do, Samantha? Welcome to White Sands Cottage," I nodded and shook her hand. Beckoning for them to follow me, we moved through the hallway and kitchen and out the back door.

"What a lovely home, ma`am. It seems both new and old at the same time," she remarked.

"That's because we've been carefully remodeling for several months," I answered. "The work actually started with my Auntie Carrie, who lived here for decades."

Shortly after we sat down, the back gate opened and Miriam, Joanne and Izzy entered. Following a round of introductions, everyone settled down with their beverages.

Always alert, Miriam noticed that we had completed the enhancements to the *lānai*.

"Your new kitchen island looks wonderful."

"Thank you. Or perhaps I should say that I accept your complement on behalf of Keoni, who did all of the work out here."

"You've even got a sink," observed Izzy with a wistful sigh.

With that remark, we moved on to the topic of the day. Miriam and her companions explained their united front for economical living in the modern age. Then they politely encouraged Samantha to talk about herself.

"I guess you could say I'm starting over. I've been at Hale Malolo for a couple of weeks, and I think I'm ready to move on. I don't really know what I'm going to do with my life. I never finished college, and since I don't have kids, maybe I'll take some classes to help me decide what to do."

No one asked about Samantha's motivation for going to Hale Malolo. Nathan had told me she was married, but that things had reached a difficult spot and she needed to leave the relationship.

When it was clear that Samantha had volunteered as much about her circumstances as she wished to, Joanne spoke up. "I was in a similar position when I was in my twenties in rural Louisiana. At the time, the military was the best option for me. After one hitch in the Army, I had the GI bill to help put me through school. That's how I ended up becoming a teacher. In fact, you could say I joined my two careers, because I was a teacher on military installations around the world for more than two decades."

"That's how we met," volunteered Miriam. "I was touring the Pacific, giving talks on women's rights. After addressing public school teachers and counselors on Guam, Joanne came forward to discuss her concerns for the women and children with whom she did volunteer work. We stayed in touch through the years and after my husband Henri died, I invited her to join me here when she retired."

Izzy then said, "And I was originally Miriam and Henri's housekeeper. After my husband passed on, bless his soul, and Joanne had joined Miriam, I was diagnosed with rheumatoid arthritis. I couldn't handle all of the housework anymore, and that's when Miriam offered me a home."

Looking at each of her housemates, Miriam summed up. "So, Samantha, that is *our* story. You can see Mokulua Hale from here. It's not too big. We keep things picked up on a daily basis and twice a month, I have cleaners who come in to perform normal maintenance. I also have a wonderful gardener who does the heavy work in the yard. Do you think you would be interested in joining us? Shall we say as a supervising housekeeper? You would not have to do a lot. Your primary work would involve keeping our schedules straight and ensuring everything is done that needs to be done."

Samantha immediately nodded. "Oh, I'd be pleased to join you, ma`am. The one thing I have to confess is that I'm not much of a cook."

"Oh, you don't need to worry about that—at least not when I'm in town," responded Izzy with a smile. "And if I'm going on vacation, I leave plenty of meals in the freezer."

"Izzy's quite the cook and baker, my dear. So I hope you don't have to keep to a strict diet," said Joanne. "I provide fresh produce from our little garden and she whips everything into mouth-watering delights."

"As long as my hands hold up, there will be fresh malasadas every week," promised Izzy.

Just then, the house phone rang and I went inside to answer it. I was pleased at how things were working out for the women. It looked like a real win-win. Being uncertain what I had in the refrigerator for dinner, I was glad that Keoni had called to suggest he bring home a pizza around sunset. When I returned to my guests, Nathan was explaining the goals of Hale Malolo.

"We try to provide a lot of support to the women and children in our care. One topic we cover is stranger-danger. In the case of the families at the shelter, we have to emphasize that it's not enough to be concerned about strangers. Friends, neighbors and even family members who were once in their lives can't be relied on *not* to reveal something the women or kids might say. It's not so much that the intentions of these people are suspect, but anything someone says or does can have an unexpected impact."

"It must be hard on the kids. Deciding who they can talk to or play with," commented Izzy.

"There's really no one who's safe for them to visit with outside of the shelter. That's why most of the children are home schooled. If they do meet someone, they can't refer to the shelter, or describe it in any way—let alone tell anyone where it is. Most importantly, they can't let anyone give them a ride back to the home," clarified Nathan.

"That's quite a lesson for a little person to handle," said Joanne, shaking her head.

"You're right about that. It's hard on everyone. The staff, the moms, and even those of us who are on our own," added Samantha.

Shortly after confirming that Samantha would move in the next day, Nathan and she left to return to the shelter for an appointment Nathan had scheduled with the director. Switching to the topic of party planning, The Ladies and I continued chatting for a while.

"I'd like to keep it a surprise, if I can," I said. "I've decided to hold the party the Saturday after next. That should give me time to invite everyone he'd like to see."

"That sounds wonderful. I'll make sure there's plenty of room for any supplies and food you need to keep out of sight," suggested Izzy.

"Oh, thank you. That means I won't have to be sneaking around wondering where to hide things. I'll just call you when I have a few things ready to stash away."

"There won't be any problem with space, Natalie. You know how these old cottages are; they may look small on the outside, but they're full of surprising nooks and crannies," said Joanne.

"I could make a cake, if you'd like," offered Izzy.

"Oh, that would be great. His favorite desserts begin and end with chocolate, so any variation on that theme would be fantastic," I answered, mentally licking my lips at the thought of whatever she would bake.

"Well, I think we have a plan for moving forward," concluded Miriam. "And now we should return home to prepare for Samantha's arrival tomorrow."

After saying goodbye to my guests, I tidied up and went into the bedroom for a brief rest. With so many delectable scents, not to mention all the choices of activities both inside and out, I was surprised that Miss Una still showed up whenever I took a siesta.

"Hello, my little bunny. Have you had a good day? Where were you when The Ladies were here? You're always so interested in their doings and you missed their visit."

Calmly washing her whiskers with her paw, Miss Una did not seem concerned with my questions. Within a couple of minutes, we were snuggled together and I fell asleep thinking of her soft fur. I wondered if a pet shampoo might soften my sometimes bristly hair.

Awakened by the abrupt sinking of a heavy body next to me, I opened my eyes to see Keoni had brought me a sliver of pizza.

"You looked so peaceful, I didn't want to disturb you when I came in, Honey," he said. "But if you'll put on a little something so we aren't putting on a floor show for The Ladies, we could eat in the dining room."

Rousing myself after a couple of bites of the delicious mushrooms, tomatoes, garlic and onions on the cheesy crisp crust, I put on a short *mu`umu`u*. The menu was hardly what I had envisioned for our first meal in the formal room. But when Keoni escorted me to my seat, I caught my breath at the charm of the room with its glass-fronted corner cabinets and a credenza. It was a very romantic place to dine at this time of day. The scenery of the backyard was highlighted by the waning twilight showing through the new French doors and with the dimmer set low, light sparkled on our plates from the crystals of the classic chandelier.

Sitting beside me so that we could both enjoy the view, he raised his glass of Chianti and said, “Here’s to another wonderful night in your private corner of paradise. You’ve worked hard your entire life, Natalie, and now you even get to enjoy pizza in a grand setting. I’m just sorry it isn’t from your favorite Peppino’s Italian Food, but they’ve been closed for a couple of years!”

I raised my glass in turn and looked into his eyes. “You know how rough the last year has been, Keoni,” I said. “There’s no way I could have survived it without your support and... and I just want to say, that through it all, my love for you has grown.”

As we looked at each other deeply, the movement of a swirling ball of red light caught our attention to the left of Miriam’s home. Always alert to his surroundings, Keoni broke eye contact with me and moved swiftly to the doors. Opening them, he strode quickly onto the *lānai*, where he stood watching the light move out of the driveway and turn onto the road.

“It’s an ambulance leaving Miriam’s house,” he said, with a frown of obvious concern. “But there’s no siren and there are no police or other official vehicles.”

“Should I call?” I asked.

“Mmm. Not knowing the situation, I think we should wait. If they needed us, we would have heard from them already.”

He hesitated for a moment before adding, “I’m sure they’ll call as soon as things calm down. And if we don’t hear from them tonight, we’ll call them in the morning.”

Feeling there was nothing we could do, our dinner continued in a silent and restrained atmosphere.

CHAPTER 6

May your home always be too small
to hold all of your friends.
Irish Toast

Despite our efforts to return to our romantic meal, we both remained on edge as we finished our pizza and wine. As we cleared the last of the dishes from the dining room, the landline phone rang. I dashed to set the glasses down and answered the call on the second ring. It was Izzy, out of breath and quite stressed.

"You probably saw the ambulance. I'm just calling to let you know we're okay," she said.

"Mmhm," I answered, putting the phone on speaker so Keoni could hear.

"She's going to be fine, but Miriam fell and broke her leg and had to go to Castle Hospital. *Graças a Deus*, it's not too bad. It's what they call a "hairline fracture. They're putting on some kind of cast and she'll be ready to come home in another hour or so."

"I'm glad you called, Izzy. We didn't want to bother you by barging in, but Keoni and I were worried when we looked up from dinner to see the lights of an ambulance."

"Thanks for your concern, but you couldn't have done much…except watch the EMTs. Joanne went with Miriam to the hospital. I'm about to drive over to pick them up."

"We appreciate your letting us know she's okay," said Keoni. "Is there any way we can help?"

"There might be something tomorrow, but I think we're

okay for tonight. The only problem that's come up is that we need to change our arrangements for Samantha. Until Miriam can climb stairs, Samantha will be upstairs in Miriam's suite."

"Are you sure you want to go ahead with having a new person in the house?" I asked.

"It might be confusing for a couple of days, but we need the help even more now."

After telling Izzy that I would update Nathan, I reconfirmed that Keoni and I were available for whatever the women might need. As we tidied the kitchen, my love and I discussed windward O`ahu's good fortune in having an excellent hospital. Although nothing traumatic had occurred in *our* lives that day, we both felt exhausted and turned in early. I fell asleep wondering if Miss Una was watching over The Ladies' home from her usual vantage point.

Later that night I awoke with a start. Hearing Miss Una mewing from afar, I pulled myself from another dream of the girl in the boat. All that I remembered clearly was her father's arm holding her tightly as her small hand stroked the Star of David at her throat. Wandering through the house, I found my darling feline sitting on the kitchen table looking out the door.

"What're you up to? You know the rule. No cats on the table, even to admire the view."

It was mid-morning before we had an update. Miriam called to say she was home and doing fine, but would appreciate our helping to reposition some furniture in time for Samantha's arrival. Joanne met us at the backdoor soon after, saying Izzy had gone to get a few supplies before Nathan and Samantha were to arrive. She escorted us into the living room, where we found Miriam ready to hold court from the sofa. Her leg was in a walking cast that she had raised on a footstool. With a cheery smile she greeted us.

"Good morning. I am so grateful for your help. Even without my accident, I was thinking of doing a bit of rearranging, now that there will be four of us in the house."

"That's what neighbors are for. Just tell me what you need done, and I'll get right to it," said Keoni.

"Joanne and I have gone over several issues. She'll show you what we have in mind. However, if you think of something else we should consider, please speak up."

With that, he and Joanne left the room and went upstairs. Soon after, we could hear furniture being moved around.

"You seem pretty chipper, Miriam," I said. "But how are you *really* feeling?"

"It hurts," she replied. "I won't lie about that. But what's worse is my breathing. I have had congestive heart failure for some time, but the accident put me over the edge. It is frightening to feel you cannot breathe. But if I take it easy while adjusting to my new meds and add a few seated exercises, my doctor thinks I should be able to return to my normal routine."

"I'm so sorry. Thank goodness you'll have Samantha to help out here and run errands."

"Indeed. I am very grateful that that young woman needs our help, because we certainly need *hers* now!" Miriam confirmed.

"Well, don't hesitate to call on *us*, if there's anything else we can do," I offered.

"I assure you I will. With my limited movement, I will not be doing much on my own for a while."

"How *did* you break your leg?" I inquired.

"It was the silliest thing. I was on my stepstool, trying to finish organizing my closet—which I was doing when Miss Una came calling. I had just picked up a hat box when Izzy called me to dinner. I do not know why I was startled, but when she pushed the door open, I fell off the stool and hit the corner of the chair I had positioned for stacking things."

Just then, Keoni entered from the hallway. "Okay, Miriam. Joanne and I adjusted the upstairs bedroom per your instructions. She's now making the bed. Where would you like me to put the recliner? In here?"

"No, I think the best place is the maid's quarters. I did not rest very well last night. If I cannot sleep in the bed, I may as well be able sit comfortably."

As Keoni joined me on the sofa, Joanne arrived with a tray

with tea for us, plus a glass of pineapple juice and a couple of prescription bottles.

Laughing, Miriam said, "As you can see, I am well supervised. I am not allowed to miss my meds by as much as a quarter of an hour."

"That's right, Miriam. I'm not going to have your health decline because one of us failed to keep you to your schedule," Joanne said with a nod as she returned to the kitchen.

"I have a feeling these next two months are going to be awfully boring. Maybe you two could encourage Miss Una to visit us on a regular basis."

"That shouldn't be a problem. I'll bet if you sit out on your back *lānai* and called her, she'd come running," Keoni reasoned.

"She certainly seems concerned about your welfare. There isn't a night I don't see her perched on the table watching your back door," I announced.

"That brings up a matter I have been meaning to discuss with you, Keoni," said Miriam.

Immediately on the alert, Keoni looked down at her with concern.

"I have heard via the grapevine that you are not only a private investigator. I believe you also help clients with security systems."

"Why yes. High tech equipment is a new aspect of my security business."

"Well, now that we are getting organized, I think it would be good to update my old system. What do you think?"

"It's a very good idea Miriam, especially with your helping women from Hale Malolo. Even if you select candidates for 'housekeeper' carefully, neither you nor they can be sure that the circumstances that led them to seek help from the shelter wouldn't impact them here."

"You're right about that," commented Joanne, who had returned with a plate of Izzy's latest batch of chocolate chip and macadamia nut cookies.

"How do you recommend we proceed?" asked Miriam.

"Being neighbors, I think we can bypass the pitch I'd give a new client," responded Keoni. "I'll give you a survey to fill out while I inspect the house and grounds, and we'll go from there. I assure you I won't be trying to talk you into anything over the top."

"That sounds great. I trust your judgment, but I should remind you we're not exactly electronic wizzes."

"You've got a landline phone, cell phones and computers, right?"

"Yes," said Joanne, passing the cookies. "I've got an old clunker of a tower, but Miriam has a top-of-the-line laptop and tablet."

"I got them for my last overseas speaking tour," explained Miriam.

"Before I get that survey, is there anything else I can help move?"

The Ladies looked at each other before Joanne responded. "Izzy might have something in mind, but I can't think of anything right now."

"Well, if you're okay, I'll run home for a couple of tools, the survey and some product brochures for you to look over."

"I don't think I'll be much help in this discussion, so I'd better get back to further organization at our house," I said, following Keoni out the door.

After a brief call to update Nathan, I turned to files in the office. I became so engrossed that I failed to notice Keoni was gone most of the day. Late in the afternoon Nathan surprised me by standing quietly in the office doorway, just as he had when we were kids.

"So, what's up, Sis?"

"Oh, you gave me a start, Nathan" I said, looking up from the floor where I was sorting through a pile of papers in front of the shredder.

"Sorry. You looked so intent, I hated to interrupt your concentration."

"The neighbors should be grateful I'm not screaming bloody murder. In the back of my mind I knew you were coming. But with Keoni strategizing how to update Miriam's security system, I assumed I was alone for a long time."

"What time do you think it is, Natalie?" queried Nathan with a smile.

"Okay, I get it. It's after five o'clock somewhere in the world, and you'd like a 'wee dram as my favorite old Scotsman used to say."

"Actually, I came over because Keoni and I just finished moving a couple of things for Izzy and Samantha. We're thinking it might be a good night to run to Buzz's for dinner."

"Samantha is settled in?" I asked.

He nodded.

"Your suggestion is greatly appreciated. I keep meaning to get into the dinner thing, Nathan, but it's hard to break the take-out habit," I said laughing. "Help yourself to a beer and chill out on the *lānai* until Keoni's home and we're ready."

"Sounds good to me," he said.

With so many restaurants in Hawai`i looking like they belong in L.A., it was great to be in an old style beach-side restaurant. Buzz's is noted for its fresh food and island preparations. Its patrons are a blend of locals plus visitors—like the President and other members of an international cadre of the rich and famous. Of course, being near one of the most celebrated beaches in the world, the influx of tourists often makes it difficult for a Kailua resident to make it onto the veranda, let alone into dining room.

As I bellied up to the salad bar for a plate to pile high with local tomatoes, avocados and bamboo shoots, it was the first time I really felt like a resident Kailuan. While the men stayed with their favorite beef entrees, I opted for shrimp cooked on the *kiawe* stoked grill.

Allergic responses can be odd. I am unaffected by the burning of *kiawe*, but when it is blooming, look out. During a short-term assignment at a resort in the Southwest, I had the misfortune to learn first-hand that our tropical *kiawe* is a cousin of mesquite.

* * * * *

Keoni and I continued our walks most mornings. We were often escorted by Miss Una, who had been freed from her halter. Usually she would stop at the open beach and after watching us for a few minutes, she walked herself home. But occasionally, she sprinted ahead to explore and would return to escort her people to her findings. Once she found a dead Portuguese Man of War. Fortunately for all our sakes, she recognized the danger and we avoided the poison within its stingers.

Having set the date of Keoni's party as the deadline for completing house beautiful, I continued to spend the bulk of my energy indoors. During this time, I was glad that Keoni was involved with his security project for Miriam. On the days when he worked on The Ladies' cottage, Miss Una walked him to the gate, and then moved back to our *lānai* to observe as much of the activity as she could from her tabletop perspective.

Although I was busy with the house and party planning, I was glad to hear about his work at dinner each day. In his initial analysis, Keoni told Miriam it was good that she was updating her security system, since her old outside control panel served as an open invitation to burglars. Nevertheless, he advised her to continue with the moderate level of monitoring she had with her current security company until the new system was in place.

Another suggestion Keoni made was for her to have her hedges trimmed to ensure no one could sneak onto her property unobserved, Miriam said she would have the work done the following month when she was having her palm trees trimmed. When he encouraged her to install solar lights along the pathways and edges of the flower beds, all of The Ladies got involved. I watched as they piled into Joanne's mini-van for a trip to Costco. I could picture them free-wheeling Miriam around the warehouse as they emptied it of decorative solar lights. They wasted no time in implementing their vision when they returned. That night their backyard glowed after their generous sprinkling of solar-powered elfin figures and flowers. Their only disappointment was that they would have to wait for another shipment of lights in order to complete illuminating their front yard.

While Miriam looked forward to a reduction in insurance rates, she was in no rush to complete the work. This made it convenient for Keoni to do the installation in stages. He began by ordering a few custom sunscreens for windows and doors incorporating alarms that function even if the system is on standby. Next, since Miriam had opted for a combination of wired and wireless components, he put in new smoke and fire alarms throughout the house. The most complex part of his work was updating door and window contacts and motion detection devices at strategic points around the house and grounds.

I was glad that Keoni was busy working next door. It made my preparations for his party easier, especially determining who would be attending. After sending out invitations, I called people on the neighbor islands and the mainland who were likely to come. When Keoni's buddies alerted me that he and his half-sister did not have a positive relationship, I bypassed inviting her. After a lengthy chat with my grandniece Brianna, we realized her schedule precluded her taking time off from her studies for a single weekend. Instead of the live Brianna, we decided to have her to send a fun video on the night of the party.

My primary cover for the polishing and heavy-duty shopping for the party was the forthcoming visit of the O`Hara's from San Diego. Saying they had air travel miles to use or lose, I announced they were coming to see our handiwork in the cottage and then continuing on to visit their daughter in Australia. Since they were staying in a Waikīkī time-share, I told Keoni we would join them in town for dinner on the Saturday night of the party...and that they would be coming to brunch the next morning.

One detail I enjoyed finalizing was the order for Keoni's custom aloha shirt. Fortunately, Beth Surdut is accustomed to dealing with clients who are overwhelmed by their choices. She talked me through several options and I chose a mountain scene with a waterfall surrounded by Hawaiian flowers, birds, and geckos. Without concern for geographical accuracy, I asked her to include a blue parrot to complement his eyes.

As to the menu, I constantly checked in with the Souzas. Eventually we decided that with so many guests wanting to share their personal specialties, I would prepare trays of fruit, veggies and cheese, and order just a few catered dishes. That still forced me to do a little sampling at caterers, which dovetailed with Izzy's plan to introduce Samantha to Kailua. Being a newcomer myself, I was delighted to be included in one of Izzy's all-day shopping expeditions.

We began our outing with a classic Hawaiian breakfast of Portuguese sausage, fried rice, and eggs at Times Coffee Shop. Next, we browsed through several stores that demonstrated there was no need to go into Honolulu very often. My favorite stop of the morning was Heritage Antiques, where I arranged to have Auntie Carrie's silver tea service repaired.

After a couple of hours of power window-shopping, we took a break at the Coffee Bean and Tea Leaf Shop, where we each made selections for our future drinking delight. At Whole Foods Market, we concentrated on replenishing our pantries and I placed a couple of orders for the party. After a stop at Foodland for bulk paper goods, I declared my party planning complete—except for having the Ladies pick up my orders on the afternoon of the party.

I was thoroughly exhausted by that afternoon, but better acquainted with our neighbors and my new community. And, in keeping with my vow to enter the world of culinary experience more fully, I brought home a couple of Cornish game hens. They seemed like the ideal way to inaugurate use of one of the new ovens Keoni had insisted on having installed.

The following days whizzed past as I continued to personalize our home and take a few baby steps in the realm of cooking. My greatest accomplishment was making a raspberry vinaigrette. I poured it over chicken salad (not homemade) set on fresh greens from Joanne's garden.

One afternoon I felt incapable of making any decisions regarding dinner and was delighted when Joanne called to announce the arrival of Keoni's shirt. I opened it in front of all of them and they agreed unanimously that it was a thing of beauty.

"It's lovely," cooed Izzy. "Like something you'd see an artist painting in a jungle."

"Well, actually, Beth does paint on location—most anywhere in the world," I noted.

"No wonder her work is shown in museums," commented Miriam. "I should suggest her art to some of my friends with UNICEF."

* * * * *

"Careful coordination" was the theme of the day of the party. Miriam told Keoni that she was getting ready to have company, so she could not have any work done. I plotted to have Ben call Keoni for help with planting a couple of trees in his front yard. Since the actual date of his birthday was a couple of days later, there was no reason for Keoni to be suspicious. While he was gone, Miriam supervised her Ladies and me as we gathered all the party supplies and non-refrigerated food I had stored at their house. I was lucky that everything fit in the dining room credenza and cupboards.

When Keoni arrived home, I rushed him into the bathroom and then scurried around bringing out a banner and other decorations. Although it would have been fun for him to open my gift at the party, I decided to have him wear it instead. So while he was in the shower, I hung it on the back of the bathroom door with a big bow with one of Beth's cards hanging from it.

Shortly after that I heard a whoop of joy. "Natalie, where are you?" he called out. "How on earth did you get such a perfect fit?" he asked, buttoning the shirt.

"Oh, a little bird with a paint brush suggested I send your best fitting shirt. I also said you've been walking and swimming so much lately that your waist has shrunk a bit."

With twinkling eyes, he grabbed my hand, "What time are we *really* due in Waikīkī?"

After a long kiss, I pushed back on his chest. "Actually, this shirt is just the first of tonight's presents. We've got to finish dressing now, and I don't mean for a trip into town."

For a moment, he stood looking at me quizzically. "Oh, Natalie. You didn't."

"I did. In fifteen minutes Izzy will be here. In half an hour, the World According to Keoni will be arriving for your sixtieth bash. Now come here and let me present your birthday *lei* and then we need to get with the program sir, or we'll be giving tours we weren't intending."

I then reached into the closet and brought out a *maile lei*. Bending forward, he accepted my kiss and the long open *lei* I placed over his head. As he stood looking in the mirror to adjust its position, I put on a classic Tori Richard *mu`umu`u* in white on black. After another quick embrace, we dashed out of the bedroom ready to greet our guests.

Soon Izzy arrived with Keoni's red velvet cake, which she had decorated with tropical birds and flowers to harmonize with his new shirt. Next, wheeling in a full complement of electronic equipment, was the DJ dressed in a straw hat, flashy shirt and slacks dating from the 1960s. After him were Miriam, Joanne and Samantha, all wearing short *mu`u`mu`us* that had to be from the Hilo Hattie Collection. With Miriam walking carefully with a cane, we sat her at a small table near the front door where she could be involved with greeting each guest with a name tag.

I was delighted that Marge and Dan O`Hara were in the next group to arrive. As they moved into the living room, I enjoyed relaying the details of my plotting to keep the party a surprise. I had missed a rendezvous with them when Ariel was murdered, so it was especially good to have some time with them, even if the room was crowded with other well-wishers.

Although she usually avoids strangers, Miss Una pranced

in the front door with Anna Wilcox who sported a sleek peach toned caftan. "Obviously she hasn't forgotten me. So even if she's enjoying life in the country, we should schedule a few play dates with her mother," Anna observed.

Most of Keoni's friends and former colleagues live on O`ahu, but I was also glad to see several from the neighbor islands. One surprise was John Perry, who had worked with Keoni at HPD before taking a job on Maui with the State's Narcotics Enforcement Division. Although I did not have his contact information, John Dias had made sure he received an invitation. It also looked like he might have spread the word that all the men should wear their own favorite vintage aloha shirts in honor of Keoni.

The house soon filled with guests from the neighborhood clamoring to see the changes in Auntie Carrie's cottage. As I made the rounds, I caught snippets of conversation as old-timers and new comers offered their perspectives on the last century in Kailua. Their stories ranged from vacationing Victorian era Hawaiian Royals, to the establishment of residential housing developments and cows grazing on the hillside above late twentieth-century restaurants.

When the DJ played a drum roll, everyone gathered together for the presentation of Keoni's birthday cake. Izzy was known for her fantastic desserts and no one wanted to miss the red velvet chocolate cake filled with red-tinted ganache she had prepared.

Looking at me before blowing out his candles, the man of the evening said, "Thank you, everyone, for making this gathering so memorable." He then insisted on serving each guest personally with both cake and a personalized greeting.

The rest of the evening passed in a blur of smiles, stories of the past, and projections for the future—all set to the tunes of Golden oldies. My breath caught briefly when Lulu Smith talked about barbecues with her family and members of the outrigger canoe club that had carried Ariel's ashes to sea. No one seemed to notice my response and I was able to regain my composure as everyone offered recommendations of windward attractions we needed to see.

As I passed Keoni with the last tray of *teriyaki* chicken sticks, I heard Ming Ho ask whether he played golf.

"It seems like every time I start to take it up, life has interfered," responded Keoni.

"Well, even if you don't need a golf course on a regular basis, you might want to think about a social membership up at Mid-Pacific Country Club."

"Wasn't that founded as a retreat for Honolulu's business leaders in the nineteen twenties?" I asked.

"Yes. It was only the third golf course on the island. Boy, did they pick the ideal spot for the clubhouse. The views are stupendous from every room. It's a great place to take guests and they even have a monthly bingo night with dinner buffet."

Another neighbor chimed in. "They give away some great prizes and the food's good. Years ago, the Ft. Ruger Cannon Club up on Diamond Head was the place to take out-of-town guests. The views of the ocean and the lights of Honolulu were gorgeous and the meals superb. It was always good to know at least one active duty or retired officer who could sponsor you into such a club for special occasions."

"I know what you're saying. My dad was a naval officer. As children, Nathan and I loved to run around the back patio and hide under the Cannon Club's tables during special events."

As always, Ming's wife, Maya looked elegant in a blue and white silk *cheongsam*. "Now don't write that place off—at least that location. You should know that Kapiolani Community College took over that Diamond Head site and built its fabulous Ka `Ikena Restaurant up there."

"We'll have to try it some time," I said.

CHAPTER 7

...the midnight murderer... invades the sacred hour
of silent rest and leaves, unseen...
Samuel Johnson [1709 - 1784]

The party had been a great success with friends coming from across O`ahu, the neighboring islands and even the mainland. Not only had we celebrated Keoni's sixtieth birthday in grand style, but we had established ourselves as a sociable couple concerned with maintaining the integrity of the Lanikai neighborhood of windward O`ahu. Therefore, it was gratifying to hear several guests comment on the balance we had struck between preserving the design aesthetic of my Auntie Carrie's bungalow and the conveniences of modern living.

Although there was no strike of lightning to announce her presence, I was sure my darling auntie had dropped in that night to see if my new love and I were doing justice to her home and neighbors. Throughout the evening we heard stories about her varied holiday hijinks. Several people chimed in to tell me about one significant night in the neighborhood.

Carrie had loved Halloween especially, when she could dress outrageously and offer unique treats to her neighbors' children and grandchildren. One year, when she had volunteered in experiments with dolphins at Sea Life Park, she transformed the classic bobbing for apples into a bobbing for baby dolphins event. Unfortunately, the carving of the apples had removed the fruit's peel, so the caramel topping slid off into the tub of water that had warmed during the preceding daylight hours.

With the night sky occluding a clear view of the tub, no one realized there was a problem until the first round of kids sat up from their attempts to capture the wee dolphins with caramel smeared all over their faces and worse yet, in their hair. To say their mothers were less than pleased was the understatement of the evening. This was at a time when neighbor Henri was still living, so he and Miriam had helped remove the tub from center stage. By the time they were finished, Miriam was the last fatality—with her Gypsy costume covered in a reddish film. After that event, Carrie took an oath to offer only store-bought Halloween treats in the future.

Another story related to a home just up the road. By this point in the evening, most everyone knew I was a writer who gathered stories like other people collect antique dolls. As with many historical tales of Hawai`i, this one included complexities of characters. Evidently the house had been owned for decades by relatives of royalist Robert Wilcox, who had tried to preserve the Kingdom of Hawai`i and its last monarch, Queen Lili`uokalani. The first of the Wilcox owners was one of Robert Wilcox's nieces, who frequently hosted her sister, Niau Johanna Wilcox, the first woman registered to vote in the Territory of Hawai`i. This was ironic since with the demise of the Kingdom and annexation by the U.S. in 1898 (the year of Johanna's birth), women had actually *lost* the franchise they had enjoyed in the Hawaiian Kingdom.

Evidently, Johanna Wilcox's voter registration was planned as a media event to inspire Island women to participate in the political process. Escorted by governmental powerhouses of the day, Johanna registered to vote shortly after midnight on August 30, 1920. I already knew several stories about the Wilcox family. This one reminded me of my grandmother who had given up the right to vote when she emigrated from Denmark at the start of World War I. Shaking my head, I thought about how casual young women are today about the precious rights their forbears fought so hard to win for them.

For a moment, I lost track of the conversations around

me. Thinking of Denmark, I remembered the recent vision I had interpreted as a young Jewish girl's escape from Denmark to Sweden in World War II. I still could not see any connection between the vision and my grandmother...or any other person in my life. Ah, well, eventually the significance of each of my visions is eventually clarified.

Turning back to the people standing in the dining room, I was pleased to see Keoni visiting with Marty Soli. I had been delighted when he accepted my invitation. He was a medical examiner with the City and County of Honolulu and had been very supportive during the investigation of Ariel's death.

One of the highlights of the evening was meeting several of Keoni's buddies from his years in law enforcement. In addition to John Perry, a couple of Keoni's former partners had retired on O`ahu and he saw them on a fairly regular basis.

Unfortunately, I only met one of their significant others. Jerry Latimer's wife had died a couple of years earlier. Lenny Kojima's second wife had departed on a vacation with her daughter. Only Stan Carrington's girlfriend Tamiko Sato was in attendance. She was a delightful woman he met recently at the annual Sapporo Ice Festival, on the Japanese island of Hokkaido. Until she retires, they will be enjoying all the romance and trauma of a long-distance courtship. At this point, their romantic adventure was in its infancy and their mutual adoration was a pleasure to see.

One thing I've found especially endearing about my own love, is his desire to be part of every aspect of my activities—including the clean-up from an event like this. Once the last of our guests had wandered into the beauty of the tropical night, we began clearing the remains of our first event in Auntie Carrie's remodeled home. I carried a small waste can around to catch the odds and ends, while Keoni juggled a tray on which he stacked the last of the glasses and dishes. We alternated between companionable silence and sharing our observations of what we had learned about the neighborhood and Carrie.

Although Keoni only met her once, he is as dedicated to my auntie's home as I am. Always on the lookout for sources of unique materials to enhance White Sands Cottage, he was excited to tell me about an upcoming opportunity for further home improvement.

"You won't believe what Makoa Pane said tonight. Not only is he a contractor, but he's actually a master craftsman, working in exotic woods. As such, he gets invited to harvest fallen trees on government land. He said he was impressed with the work I've been doing around here and the next time he gets a call, he's going to invite me to join him. That means we'll probably get enough wood to embellish the porch posts and the dining room's cabinets."

"That's great dear. I've told you I think your work is wonderful."

Another popular topic that night had been home security. Larry Smith and Keoni had spent several minutes discussing electronic security systems. The General said he had experienced several incidents with their dog or grandchildren setting off motion sensors.

"I told him he probably had the lights focused too low to the ground. If you position the sensor too low, a stray cat walking by can set them off," Keoni observed.

As we compared conversations about area restaurants, I contemplated taking classes at a nearby gourmet culinary school. The master chef who owned it had worked at world class resorts and on a cruise line about which I had written. I might never be a true chef, but I longed to learn how to make some of his appetizers. Given my track record in the gastronomic department, I decided to keep the idea under wraps until I had some tangible results to offer.

"Did you catch the funny exchange between Samantha and Makoa?" I asked.

"I don't think I saw those two together at all," replied Keoni.

"Well, the conversation started when I was introducing them and Samantha heard me pronounce his last name, "pah-neh." She giggled slightly and told him that when she had stood in for Miriam at the door earlier. She had scanned the guest list to see who was yet to arrive. When she saw his last name spelled, p-a-n-e, she had assumed it was the English name "Pane." We all laughed and talked about other Hawaiian names that have led to innumerable misunderstandings."

Another topic in our summary of the evening involved points of environmental and historical interest for numerous day trips we might take. Over the years, I have stopped at the Pali Lookout several times, but had not realized the scope of the history and archeological remains at Kawai Nui Marsh below its jagged peaks. And despite the many articles I had read about Queen Lili`uokalani, I was surprised to learn of her links to the area.

I was familiar with aspects of the last Queen's final years, since researching possible connections between Keoni's family home in Kaimukī and a school founded in her honor. In fact, that project was part of what had shifted my relationship with Keoni from one of friendly acquaintanceship to romance.

After everything I learned at the party, I was especially pleased with my decision to move to this splendid corner of O`ahu. As I contemplated the many adventures awaiting us, I only regretted that Keoni and I would not be skinny dipping in the swimming pond I was told lay at the end of a hiking trail along one of the marsh's streams. But with it being on a public path, I did not think my by-the-book ex-cop sweetheart would agree to that form of recreation any time soon.

Finally, with essential cleanup completed, Keoni and I collapsed on the porch swing on the back *lānai*.

"Hey, honey, I've got one last story from tonight. Did you hear about your Aunt's attempt at scuba diving? It was in the eighties."

"That's a new one for me," I answered.

"I guess she was getting ready to take a vacation in Papua, New Guinea, where she heard that deep-sea diving is preferable to merely snorkeling. She took a diving course and then, having purchased all the equipment the salesman could unload on her, she decided to practice in what we might call her own back yard."

I laughed, trying to picture my never-slim auntie crammed into neoprene or whatever they used for scuba suits back then.

"No joke. Well, it sounds like a joke. But she had her diving suit on, and was carrying a bag with a tank of air and her fins and mask. She'd almost made it to the ocean when one of her flip flops caught on some roots in the beach access path, and she took a tumble.

"Luckily for her, Joanne and Izzy came along. They helped her up and carried her equipment. But when Carrie tried to dive into the water, she found the fins weren't suited to the rocky bottom at this end of the beach. She ended up taking another nose dive—no pun intended. While she was struggling, her mask came loose, dislodging her oxygen tank. Sitting up, she looked as helpless as a little kid who hasn't even learned to float."

Shaking my head, I inquired. "After that auspicious beginning, how did the diving in New Guinea go?"

"Well, according to Miriam, the mainland friends who were to join in her South Seas adventure had their vacation time cancelled and Carrie ended up with some very expensive scuba gear in the attic."

"That's got to be one of the few categories of junk I didn't find when I inherited the cottage."

"Well, according to Miriam, that junk eventually proved useful. Several years after her adventure, Carrie was visited by a couple who were actually going to New Guinea. They were on their way to where the woman's father had died in World War II, while serving on a U.S. Navy ship that sank in the area. Carrie offered them the equipment, and they had it checked out by a dive shop. I guess the couple had a great time diving on the old shipwrecks that have provided homes to new coral reefs."

I chuckled and said, "That's a great ending to one of Auntie Carrie's less-than-successful adventures. Like most events in her life, I can tell there was laughter and joy in it for *someone*, if not her."

Settling into a corner of the swing, I extended my legs to

Keoni's lap. Recognizing my plea for ministrations for my aching extremities, he set down his glass of sun tea and applied his strong fingers gently to my feet.

"Now that's what I call the ideal ending to a perfect evening," I purred.

"What do you mean, 'the end of the evening?' This is just the warm-up to our private celebration of my birthday," countered Keoni, with a leer.

I shook my head in response, and on that note, we decided it was time to go inside if I wanted a full body massage. First I took my nightly stroll around the outside of the house, calling for Miss Una to come in for her nightly portion of kitty treats. Once she was happily munching some dried *`ahi*, I joined Keoni in his methodical closing of the house. Despite our new security system, he insists on shutting all the doors and windows, except for those in the master suite.

As I took off my dress, I glanced out the French doors and noticed the cloud swept moon had moved far across the night sky. Pulling my hair back with a barrette, I moved into the master *en suite* bath where I found Keoni replacing our regular bath towels with the fluffy bath sheets he had bought after installing a new steam shower.

"Hi, beautiful. Ready for another adventure in the finer points of cleanliness?"

Later, I fell asleep snuggled in the arms of a very happy birthday boy. Unfortunately my peaceful sleep did not last through the night.

* * * * *

When you think of Hawaiian beaches at night, the images that come to mind often showcase bright moonlight, undulating ocean waves and swaying palm trees. The images I was viewing were presented in sepia tones—alerting me that this was no simple dream. Evidently I was having another of my visions that usually present uncertainty, and too often lately, death.

I knew where I was because I could see Nā Mokulua, the

two islets that dot the waters out in Lanikai Bay. The first scene of this vision did involve sand, water, and moonlight. But the palm trees along this part of O`ahu's shoreline are at a minimum and there was no breeze to stir the few I saw.

As I watch the idyllic scene from a vantage point in Miriam's front yard, I catch a movement along the walkway across the street leading from the beach. Suddenly, my vantage point shifts and I am hovering somewhere above the waters of the bay. I watch as a tall, erect man in a black diving suit and booties walks up from the beach toward Mokulua Road with the precise footsteps of someone who knows where he is going. As he strides up the center of the walled pathway, he looks neither to the left nor the right. Reaching the roadway, he pauses briefly. At the approach of a speeding vehicle, he steps back into the shadows. As a Jeep passes, a blast of rap music with the cadence of Jamaica punctuates the otherwise silent night.

After a moment, the man returns to the edge of the empty road. He then crosses the street and moves up a few houses. Instantly, my position changes to the gate between my backyard and Miriam's. Looking to the left, I watch the man in black approach "My Ladies' Safe Haven," as Miriam refers to her home. He pauses at the arbor framing the gate on the front walkway and releases the latch to move under trailing vines of bougainvillea. He reaches into a pouch I have not noticed at his waist. With cloud cover passing across the moon, I cannot see the details with clarity. From the movement of his hands, I know he is putting on gloves.

As he rounds the left side of the house, I surmise he is going to the electrical panel that covers the wiring of the old security system that Keoni is in the process of replacing. Within a couple of moments, the man reappears at the front of the house. After glancing around, he walks decisively to the front door.

A moment of dark void passes and I find that I am standing in Miriam's kitchen looking down the main hallway. I watch as the front door opens silently and the man in the diving suit enters the house. Previously his face has been wholly in shadow. I now realize his head is covered with a scuba hood that reveals only his eyes, nose, and mouth. All that I see is that he is Caucasian and that his eyes are dark. There is no visible jewelry, birthmark, or tattoo by which I might identify him.

Unlike previous visions when I have been isolated from the unfolding scenes, I am now in the center of the action. I want to get up from my bed and scream for help. But there is nothing I can do. I am paralyzed with fear, as though the man can see me standing there watching him.

Bypassing what I know is a coat closet, he goes directly to the second door on the left. After placing an ear against it, he carefully turns the knob and pushes forward into a bedroom. Reaching again into his pouch, he brings out what looks like a bolo tie.

Without any conscious effort, I suddenly stand behind him at the open doorway. I watch as the man inches past a single bed in a seamless motion. He then halts at the back of a wing-back chair positioned in front of a large mullioned window. Following his downward glance, I can see the long, blond hair of a woman's head resting in the crook between the back and arm of the chair.

As I try to force air into my lungs, I feel my heart pounding rapidly. The pace of the action in front of my eyes changes and begins to unfold in slow motion. As the black garbed figure reaches forward, a bright moonbeam pierces a diamond-shaped window pane. I stare in disbelief at what the man holds between his second and third fingers—two small sticks attached to the ends of something dark and smooth—like the black wire you find in an old piano.

Abruptly the scene reverts to normal time. Crossing his hands, the man drops the gleaming loop over the woman's head and then, with a jerk of the dowels, the man's task is completed. With little struggle, I see the body slump forward while the wire flips backward with a flick of the man's wrist. After placing the lethal device into a clear plastic bag, he puts it in his pouch and pulls out a second plastic bag.

Remaining frozen, I view the eerie ballet's last act. As the man yanks a few strands of hair from the body doubled over below him, the chair shifts slightly and dislodges a cane leaning against the wall to the left of the chair. When he has dropped the long pale hairs into the plastic bag, he zips it closed and replaces it in the pouch. Next he bends over to pick up the cane, and repositions it against the wall. Standing back, he pauses to analyze the deathly vignette before pivoting rapidly on the ball of his foot and turning toward me.

Inhaling sharply, I stand as still as I can. Without a second of hesitation, the man walks through me. I then watch as he moves back along the short distance to the front door. Opening it, the nocturnal diver turns to close it with the same quiet precision with which he has accomplished everything else.

* * * * *

Panting from the horror of what I had seen and the exertion of trying to remain invisible, I awoke sweating and shaking with fear. I looked to my right side, but I was alone in the new king-sized bed. I did not know where Keoni was. If he had been present, I am sure I would have disturbed him as I flailed about tossing off the covers. As often happens when I have a vision, I felt disoriented. I have seldom observed a crime in progress, and the enactment of the murder I had just seen left me questioning the source of each component of my vision.

After swinging my feet over the edge of the bed, I sat upright for a few minutes to collect myself. Once my breathing eased, I began to analyze what I had just viewed. My first thought was that although the experience had been in the usual tones of my visions, I had never been so involved in the enactment of one. Then there was the fact that many of the elements of what I had seen were related, at least in part, to recent events or conversations.

Consider the man in the scuba suit. Just a couple of hours earlier, Keoni and I had been laughing over my Auntie Carrie's adventure with scuba diving. And, with the expansion of Keoni's business, residential security systems have been a frequent topic of conversation lately. As to the woman in the chair, I knew that with her broken leg, Miriam could not maneuver up and down the stairs of her home. In fact, she had mentioned she was having trouble sleeping, and often sat up through the night in her favorite chair.

In short, there were seeds of reality in the nightmare I had just watched....except for the fact that the scenes had been in sepia tones. Finally, there was the issue of the piano wire. I could not begin to think of any source from either the party or my life in general that would explain that aspect of the scenario.

As my pulse slowed, the solid features of my home displaced the lingering images of the murder sequence. Perhaps I had merely had a bad dream. Shoving my feet into my house slippers, I rose to use the bathroom. With a splash of water on my face, I felt somewhat renewed. I then went to the kitchen. After drinking a glass of cold water, I began to feel my normal self.

Deciding I had merely experienced a nightmare, I set out to find Keoni and Miss Una. Keoni is sensitive to my being a light and easily disturbed sleeper. On evenings that he's not sleepy, he frequently stretches out with a book or magazine on the new leather sectional in the living room, or the hammock he's strung up on the *lānai*. But after our long evening, I did not want to disturb *him* if he had fallen asleep, thinking he had allowed me to have a peaceful night's rest.

Wandering through the house, I continued to feel agitated. I tidied a few things in preparation for the Sunday brunch we had scheduled with Nathan and the O`Haras. Then hearing Keoni's soft snoring, I entered the living room. Sitting down quietly on the chaise lounge extension of the sofa, I picked up his ever-present glass of tea and took a deep sip. Sensing my presence, he stirred and turned around to lay his head in my lap. Without awakening fully, he hugged me and immediately fell back into a deep sleep. I stroked his hair and gradually my uneasiness subsided. Within a few minutes, I joined him in the Land of Nod.

CHAPTER 8

Now comes the mystery.
Henry Ward Beecher [1813 - 1887]

With the sun's rays warming my face and Keoni's arm around my shoulder, I floated at that delectable point between sleeping and waking. Reluctantly, I moved toward consciousness and reached out to stretch. I then realized we were lying on the living room sofa, here we had been since my horrible dream.

As I moved closer to wakening, an inner dialogue began, as the dark hold of nocturnal vagaries and potential terrors returned to gnaw at me. The night before I had talked myself into believing that what I had seen was merely a nightmare. But now, I was not so sure. Was I in denial of another *true* vision? Why do I have these visions at all, if I cannot help the people I envision in dire circumstances? Regardless of what I called it, this particular dream or vision had been different than others I have had. Perhaps for the first time, it was a premonition and I would have an opportunity to help someone avert dire events.

My emotions were raw with indecisiveness. I rose and looked down on Keoni blissfully snoozing. Swallowing the taste of fear in my mouth, I strove to shake off the disturbing images that continued to grip me. In my current state of mind, I would not be very good at explaining myself. I decided to make a pot of coffee and calmly prepare for a discussion of what I had seen with Keoni as soon as he was awake.

Just as I hit the button to start the brewing cycle, the

kitchen phone rang. It was Joanne. She was so distraught that I could barely understand her. Some of the words may have been Cajun.

"I, I can't believe it. She was fine last night."

"Joanne, calm down. I can't understand you. *Who* was fine last night?" I asked, in as composed a voice as I could muster.

"Miriam! It's Miriam! She's...she's dead! She's just sitting in her chair, and there's blood on the floor! Samantha's really out of it! You've got to come! You and Keoni!"

Gruesome images from my terrifying vision immediately flooded into my mind's eye. "Okay, Joanne. We'll be there in a few minutes." Trying to think logically, I said, "And, don't do anything. Do you understand? Don't touch anything and don't call anyone else until Keoni's had a look."

Quickly disconnecting, I dashed back to the living room to alert Keoni to the situation. I was making enough noise as I ran into the room that he was already half awake.

"Honey, you've got to get up. Joanne just called and...Miriam's dead. We've got to go over there right away," I said.

There's nothing like a crisis to bring a retired cop to attention. After sitting up and rubbing his eyes, Keoni gave me a hard stare.

"What do you mean, Miriam's dead? She had a heart attack, or what? Who's there?"

"I think it's just Joanne and Samantha. Let's talk while we get ready. Joanne mentioned blood on the ground. That doesn't sound like a heart attack and I don't see how it could be related to her broken leg."

In a moment, I was in the bedroom, pulling on a swimsuit and shorts. As Keoni continued to pepper me with questions from the bathroom, I debated whether to mention my vision. It did not seem vital to the moment and I simply answered with the little information I had received from Joanne. As Keoni made a bee-line for the office, I went into the bathroom to put some allergy drops in my eyes and swipe a comb through my hair. Not knowing what the day might demand, I stuffed my cell phone, keys and a package of tissues into my pockets.

I entered the hallway just as Keoni emerged from the office with a look of concentration I had not seen since the previous summer when he helped me to solve Ariel's mysterious death. At his waist, he was securing a small pouch that triggered another unwelcome memory from my vision.

Despite anything Keoni might be feeling, I knew he had moved into his resolute detective mode. I was almost jealous of his ability to separate personal anguish from the need to function professionally. It was certainly the best way to help Miriam's Ladies and I would try to mimic his behavior—even if I did not have his inner strength.

Rushing toward the kitchen, he said, "As soon as I take a quick look at the situation, we've got to get HPD to the scene."

I nodded. It was going to be a very long day. I checked Miss Una's supplies while Keoni armed the security system. Leading the way out the back door, he strode toward Miriam's cottage. Approaching the gate between our properties, Keoni stopped, opened his pouch and pulled out disposable vinyl gloves, as I knew the CSI team would when they arrived.

I shivered, suddenly thinking of the man in the diving suit who had done the same thing the night before in my vision. As we passed through the gate, I called Joanne from my cell phone to alert her that we were almost there. I looked around at the peaceful garden briefly and thought of the contrast with what awaited us within Mokulua Hale.

The nightmare Miriam's roommates were experiencing would never be erased from their memories, but I resolved to support their emotional survival. Pulling on the gloves Keoni had given me, I paused and watched him scanning Miriam's home from its roofline to the ground with the camera on his smart phone. He then moved forward along the path, glancing across the windows and door.

At this point, I was not sure when I should mention my latest nocturnal event. I had never before interacted so closely with the company of players I saw. Normally—if there is anything "normal" about my visions—I merely float above or at the periphery of the scenes I am presented. But last night

I had stood in the midst of everything as an unknown man garroted Miriam and then turned to walk right through me. Despite being rooted within those images and badly shaken after, I had been in denial of the reality of what I had observed.

Approaching the cottage's back door, I was called out of my confusion by a keening that was reminiscent of ancient Hawaiians receiving news of the death of a close relative or prominent person. Keoni and I paused and looked at each other for a moment. He then glanced through the window of the top half of the Dutch door, and signaled me to enter while he continued along the side of the building toward the garage.

Opening the door into the kitchen, I found Joanne kneeling in front of Samantha, who was seated on a chair pulled away from an old oak dinette set. I patted Joanne's shoulder. She glanced up at me as Samantha continued to emit a shrill moan. Shortly, the sounds softened and Joanne soothingly said, "Shush now, Samantha. There's nothing you could've done."

The young woman then looked up, and seeing me, started to breathe more steadily. Standing she came to me, obviously wanting a hug.

"Oh, Natalie. Thank God you're here! Is Keoni with you?"

I nodded and opened my arms to pat her shoulder carefully to avoid disturbing any trace evidence that might be on her clothing. I looked over her at Joanne, who stood shaking her head in disbelief about the entire situation.

At that moment, I heard Keoni arrive behind me at the doorway.

"Morning ladies. I'm so sorry for what has happened," he said softly. "Shall we all go out on the *lānai*?" he asked, beckoning to us as he held the door open widely.

Gesturing toward a gliding rocker, he spoke reassuringly. "You're going to be okay, Samantha. Right now I need you to sit down and breathe slowly, all right? Please remain here until I come back, or someone comes for you. Can you do that?"

As he looked her over thoroughly, she nodded and collapsed on the edge of the chair like a crumpled piece of tissue.

Signaling me to stay with him, he said, "Joanne, can you bring Samantha some water?"

Joanne nodded and went back into the house.

Pulling me to the side, he said, "While I take another look at the front of the house and street, I want you to keep everything calm and untouched. Okay?"

I nodded and watched him walk away slowly, taking in every detail of the property. By the time Joanne returned with a glass of water, Samantha was rocking slowly, her eyes staring straight ahead but clearly seeing nothing. She looked up at us with a wan smile, but said nothing as she sipped the water.

"Will you be all right alone for a couple of minutes, Samantha?" I asked.

"Uh-huh," she replied meekly.

Somehow I managed to control my own feelings and motioned for Joanne to follow me out into the garden.

Looking back at Samantha, I said, "I've been thinking about the fact that Izzy doesn't know what's happened here. I'm concerned that with her own health challenges, it might be hard on her to arrive to face a street filled with official vehicles."

"You're right, Natalie. I thought about that a while ago. But I took your words to heart when you said for me not to call anyone else until you and Keoni had come. And since I know Izzy leaves her phone off during services, I thought I'd have time to figure out what I should say in a voice message."

Thinking fast, I responded, "Why don't you go into the house and call her now. If you get her personally, you'll have to decide how much to tell her over the phone. If you have to leave a message, why don't you say there's been an emergency here and you need her to call you before she comes home. While you do that, I'll cancel brunch with Nathan and the O'Haras."

Agreeing with me, Joanne turned to go inside the house. I called Margie and Dan first, since they were likely to leave their hotel in Waikīkī fairly soon. As usual, their response was understanding and generous. They asked if there was anything they could do to help. Not knowing how the remainder of the day would develop, I declined their offer and said I would check in with them again when I had some news. At the moment, it looked like our plans for a beach party would have to wait for another one of their vacations.

As I dialed Nathan, I debated whether to have him come over, since I did not know how soon Keoni would be able to rejoin me. Even though Samantha was now subdued, without knowing her history, I was uncertain about whether something unexpected might cause her to erupt again. Once I gave Nathan a thumbnail description of what had occurred, I asked him how he thought Samantha would handle the situation. He said he believed she would be all right, but offered to come over if I wanted his support. After considering a couple of scenarios, we decided he would remain on standby at home in case it developed that he was needed.

After verifying that Samantha was calm, I went into the kitchen. Joanne said she had not spoken with Izzy personally, but had left a message asking her to call Joanne's cell phone as soon as possible. She said that without explaining the circumstances, she had also called to cancel an appointment with the gardener who was scheduled to come the following morning.

Knowing we did not have long before a world of public safety officials descended on Miriam's cottage, I suggested Joanne show me the maid's quarters. Walking through the kitchen, I went down the three steps to the front hall and on to the room that held the body of the woman I had hoped to know as a close friend.

With careful attention, Joanne used the edge of her robe to open the door fully. "I'm so glad you and Keoni are here, Natalie. I've tried to keep Samantha calm, but it's been very hard."

"I can tell. You've done a remarkable job. Now that we've got her settled, I think she'll be okay for a bit. When Keoni rejoins us, we're going to have to call the police."

"I know. I wasn't sure who I should call first, but I thought maybe there might be something that Keoni would find significant."

I did not reply. For a moment we stared at the *tableau* of death before us, overlaid with a contrasting scent of lavender. Sharing the experience, Joanne commented, "Miriam always loved the scent of lavender. She once told me that lavender sachets had been the last gift her mother had given her. She had treasured them for many years, keeping them in her suitcases so a piece of her childhood accompanied her wherever she went."

At that point, I nearly broke down as I looked into the room that had promised shelter for an abused woman. I thought of how it had become the final scene in the life of a woman I had been told was renowned for helping people find safety from crimes beyond imagination. How ironic that *she* had met her end in an abrupt and horrific fashion.

Shaken from our private thoughts and shared sorrow, we watched the front door open and Keoni move into the hallway. Glancing from my face to Joanne's, he announced, "You won't believe it, but Miss Una's up on the roof watching the front door, which I found unlocked."

Joanne shook her head. "Boy, that cat seems to get everywhere. That door shouldn't be open. With everything you warned us about, we've been very careful about closing and locking all the doors and windows—and setting the system's alarms every night and whenever we are all going to be gone. And this morning, knowing the rest of us were sleeping, Izzy should have reset it when she left for church."

"It's all right, Joanne. I don't think there's anything you or the others could have done to prevent this. Someone wanted in and they seem to have had no trouble in disabling the security system. I'd now like you both to wait with Samantha on the *lānai* while I call 911."

Knowing that nothing could be done for Miriam at the moment and Miss Una could take care of herself, Joanne and I moved toward the back door. Glancing around, I watched Keoni pull out his phone. In addition to making the official call to the police, I was pretty sure he would be checking in with his former partner with the Homicide Detail of the HPD Criminal Investigative Division.

After assembling a tray with some glasses and a pitcher of iced tea, Joanne and I rejoined Samantha, who continued to look like a zombie. Keoni came back outside shortly. He accepted a glass of tea and caught us up on his official notifications. "A unit from the Kailua station should be here in a few minutes. We have to be careful not to disturb the...scene. I'm going back out front and wait for the blue and white. I've also called my former partner Lieutenant John Dias who happens to be up the hill at Mid-Pacific Country Club. He'll be here as soon as he can get off the golf course. His partner, Sergeant Ken`ichi Nakamura, will arrive later since he's coming across the Pali. If you're okay Joanne, I'd like to show Natalie something." After Joanne nodded, he opened and held the back door for me to enter the kitchen.

Walking a couple of feet into the front hall, he turned to face the back door so he could be sure we were speaking privately. "How do you think The Ladies are doing?"

"Samantha is really rattled," I responded. "Joanne's upset, of course, but I think she's got a grasp on things, if only to keep a lid on Samantha."

"That's the best we could expect. The house is now secure, so while you rejoin them, I'll check things out here in the hallway and then take a look into the maid's room. But we don't want anyone else to walk through the hallway or the room where the body is until JD gets here. I'm going out front to direct everyone around the side of the house to the back door."

A minute later I sat down beside Joanne. "So, when did Izzy leave this morning? Where does she go to church?"

"She converted from Roman Catholicism several years ago and is now a member of Kawaiaha`o Congregational Church. She'd made fresh *malasadas* for the coffee time following the nine a.m. service. I guess she would have left early enough to help arrange things in the fellowship hall before going into the sanctuary. "She would have departed about seven-thirty or so, if she wasn't running any errands, or picking someone up along the way."

Filling in the gaps, I asked, "So, Samantha is the one who found Miriam?"

Looking over at the woman who continued to rock silently, Joanne told me everything that had occurred that morning. "I was having a cup of coffee on the *lānai* about nine o`clock. I looked up and saw Samantha's banging against the kitchen window....and then she came running out. She was hiccupping and I couldn't understand her. She said I had to come with her to her room. Then, she said she meant the maid's room. I followed her to the doorway, where she stopped and simply pointed inside."

Reliving her own discovery of the death, Joanne was becoming agitated.

"All right, Joanne. Take a deep breath and tell me what you saw." I was already shivering from what I knew she would tell me, even though I had not stepped into the room…in the flesh that is.

"It was terrible. I saw Miriam slumped down, with her head resting on the arm of the chair. There was blood on the ground…little drops of blood. She didn't move and I knew she was dead."

"Okay."

"And something looked wrong. Miriam's cane. It wasn't facing her chair. It might seem silly that with everything else going on, that's what caught my eye. But she was so precise about positioning the cane, so it faced her wherever she was."

So far, we had been speaking as though Samantha was not present, but she stopped rocking and shifted in her seat. I decided it might be good to try and engage her in conversation before the police arrived.

"Honey. Samantha. Look at me, Samantha."

Putting my gloved hand on her shoulder, I repeated myself. "Samantha. Look at me, please. Before you…opened the door and looked in the room, did you see anything out of the ordinary? Did you see Izzy this morning?"

Like a snowman thawing in a desert sun, the woman let loose with a torrent of tears. She then rose and started to pace while emitting garbled words and phrases.

"No, I...I didn't see anything, anyone. I just...I just opened the door...needed....bag...in the closet...saw she's, she's dead. But I touched nothing; nothing at all."

"That's good, Samantha," Joanne said with a false tone of calm. "We mustn't touch anything. That's why we're staying out here until the police arrive."

Suddenly, there was a shift in Samantha's demeanor and she stood very still. "Yes, Joanne. I've been through this before with Luke," she revealed. Seating herself again on the rocker, she continued. "Of course, that was different. I mean there was no one...dead. And it was different each time. Either the police came without any warning, or Luke's lawyer was there to make sure we didn't say or do anything without his approval."

Not knowing whether Samantha's revelation of frequent interaction with the police in her marriage referred to spousal abuse or criminality on the part of her husband, I remained quiet. Hearing cars pulling into the driveway, Joanne sighed deeply, tucked a strand of hair behind her ear and looked down to make sure her housecoat was snapped completely closed. As she glanced toward the garage, a uniformed police woman came around the corner of the building. I stood and silently watched as she presented her badge in its case.

"Good morning. I'm Officer Alena Horita. I met Keoni Hewitt at the front of the property. My partner, Jim Maxwell, is also on the premises. He is now taking Mr. Hewitt to the... scene of the...death."

Glancing down at Samantha, who had returned to a non-responsive pose, the woman again addressed Joanne. "If you'd be seated with the other ladies, I need to take some initial information from you all."

Once she had sat down, Joanne took the lead. "I'm Joanne Walther, roommate of Miriam Didión. This is our new roommate, Samantha Turner. She's just joined us from Hale Malolo...to be our housekeeper.

Seeing that Samantha was not in a state to be interactive, the officer next turned to me. "And you, Ma'am?"

"I'm Natalie Seachrist. Keoni Hewitt and I are neighbors," I replied, gesturing toward the gate between the two cottages.

"Ah, yes," responded Officer Horita, as though my two sentences summarized all that needed to be said about me.

Turning back to Joanne, she continued her questions. "Is there anyone else living on the premises?"

"Yes. Izzy. That's Esmeralda Cruz. She used to be Miriam's housekeeper and then became one of our roommates."

"And where is she now?"

"She's at church this morning. As I was telling Natalie, she probably left here around seven-thirty or so."

"Who found the victim?"

"Samantha did. And then she came to tell me," said Joanne.

We all looked toward Samantha, who continued to look blank.

"I see. As you may expect, the EMTs will be here shortly. After they've ...seen you all, we'll speak again. At this time I need you to remain out here on the *lānai*. I'll be back as soon as I check in with Officer Maxwell."

Within moments, sirens filled the air. Soon Officer Horita rejoined us, accompanied by three male EMTs. Evidently, they had been informed there was nothing to be done for Miriam, but I knew they were also on-site to care for the possible needs of those surrounding the recently deceased.

With the EMTs clearly alerted to the situation, two of them began trying to engage Samantha in conversation, while taking her vital signs. The remaining tech glanced at me, and when I shook my head slightly, he turned to Joanne, who was gazing toward the bird bath in the center of the garden.

"So, how are you doing, ma'am," asked the tall man who had identified himself as Tony Connors.

"I'm fine," responded Joanne. "Well, I'm as well as anyone could be."

"May I take your pulse and other vital signs?"

"Sure, that's fine. I know you have to do your job. My concern is Samantha; she's the one who, who found...our friend."

The next few minutes passed quickly as Officer Horita and I watched the evaluation of the two housemates of Miriam who had observed her deathly repose. I suspected that once the EMTs had completed their procedures, they would have a consultation with whomever was checking the numbers on their readings of Samantha and Joanne. Until Keoni entered the garden from the garage with a short, stocky, *haole* with gray hair, we sat in awkward silence.

CHAPTER 9

One step at a time is good walking.
Chinese proverb

Since he had been nearby, I was not surprised to see John Dias arrive so quickly. With immediate recognition that this man was in charge of the crime scene, Officer Horita seemed to grow two inches as she stood to attention. Springing forward, the young policewoman greeted the man with her notebook and pen in hand.

"Sir," she said. Gesturing to Samantha and Joanne, she announced, "These are the roommates of Miriam Didión and this is Natalie..."

"Hi, Natalie," said John, cutting off Alena Horita's introduction.

"Hi, John. Long time no see." In the morning daylight, the grooves and pock marks in his face had intensified. And it looked like he had more salt than pepper in his hair than he had the night before.

"Yeah. I sure didn't think I'd be seeing all of you again, so soon—and certainly not in a professional capacity."

I nodded as he turned to my companions with honest sorrow.

"Joanne, Samantha, I know we only met briefly last night, but I'm very sorry for your loss. Miriam seemed like a delightful person."

They both nodded, and as Samantha gazed at John Dias, she seemed, to consciously recognize the reality of the situation facing her. After looking me in the eye, John continued.

"I've taken a look into the ...room. Since neither of you witnessed anything unusual last night—and didn't see Izzy this morning—I don't need to take your statements immediately. It might be best if you both went next door for a while, if that's all right with you, Natalie?"

"Uh, yes. That'll be fine. I'd originally planned a brunch for Nathan and some out-of-town friends, so there's plenty to eat. I'll see there's plenty of coffee, tea and bagels, and anything else you and your team might need, John."

"That would be great Natalie. It will allow us to minimize disruption at the crime scene, and keep the team working steadily," he replied. "Will it be satisfactory with you ladies to wait at Natalie's home?"

"Of course, Detective," replied Joanne. "Can we take our purses? And before we go, I should tell you that I've left a message for our third housemate, Izzy, to call before she comes home. She should be leaving Kawaiaha`o Church in Honolulu at any moment and I'm concerned about her driving up and seeing all the cars and ambulances."

"Thanks for reminding me about Izzy. Why don't you try calling her again and ask her to park over at Natalie's. If she doesn't ask too many questions, it would probably be best for you to delay informing her about Miriam, until it can be done in person. Once she's arrived, please give me a call on my cell phone," he said, gesturing to a number on his business card. "I'll need to speak with her as soon as possible, since she was the first up this morning. Officer Horita will now escort you into the house to get your purses, meds, and anything else you'll need in the next few hours."

John nodded to the young officer. She then walked inside with Joanne. Once they had departed, he looked at me over Samantha's hunched shoulders. At the moment I was debating when and how I should reveal my vision.

Seeing the consternation on my face, a look of realization passed over him. "Natalie, I sense there's...something you want to share with me? Right?"

"Uh, yes. I, wasn't sure what to say about my...my..."

"Dream?" John offered.

"Yeah, my *dream*," I said with a sigh. Samantha seemed to hear what was transpiring, but she was obviously confused by my obtuse dialogue with the detective.

"Mm. Well, Natalie, as you can imagine, I need to get the CSI team going. Let's say you and I will have a little...*tête-à-tête*...after Sergeant Nakamura arrives?"

I was already emotionally, if not physically, exhausted, but I knew the demands of this day would continue to escalate. At the moment, I needed to get Joanne and Samantha away from Miriam's home.

"Okay, John. I look forward to talking with you later." Shortly after he went through the garage door, Officer Horita and Joanne returned. Joanne handed Samantha a large straw purse, sunglasses and placed a lace shawl around her shoulders.

"Thank you, Joanne," said Samantha, getting up.

After bidding farewell to the diminutive policewoman, The Ladies and I headed across to my house—which I realized had become their refuge. Walking into the cottage, I felt both conflicted and relieved. I was glad to be out of the atmosphere of fear that had permeated Miriam's house. However, I knew that for the foreseeable future I would be involved with trying to help reset the lives of the ladies Miriam had cared for so intently.

When in doubt about anything, I tend to write lists. At the moment, my list-writing needed to be mental, since I did not want Joanne or Samantha to see the scope of what I had on the immediate agenda for all of us.

"Well, ladies, you may not think you're hungry, but I've been through enough emergencies to know that the old adage about eating for strength in a crisis is valid. In a short while, you're going to be facing questions from the authorities about all kinds of topics you may not find relevant; you're also going have to deal with Izzy's homecoming. You know how devastated you were earlier. Even if Izzy is not going to be in Miriam's home any time soon, I'm sure you can imagine how she'll feel when she's told what happened."

At these words, Samantha began sniffling. I opened a drawer and brought out a tissue box. As I turned back, I found Joanne hugging the young woman and smoothing her hair out of her face.

Placing the tissues on the kitchen table, I gestured toward the chairs. Joanne took the hint. She seated Samantha and knelt beside her, much as I had found them on my arrival at Miriam's cottage. Chattering, as much to calm my own nerves as theirs, I said I would put the kettle on for tea. I pulled out Auntie Carrie's prized Spode teapot and began filling a small basket with an assortment of tea bags. Just then Joanne's cell phone chirped an electronic sequence of tones.

She glanced down at caller ID and gave me a sickened look. Turning, she spoke briskly into the phone. "Oh, Izzy, I'm so glad you called. Yes, there's been an emergency here and I need you to park at Natalie's and join us in her cottage as soon as you can. Uh, we seem to have a poor connection and I can't really talk right now. Just get here as soon as you can, okay?"

She quickly disconnected with a deep sigh. "I know I'm being a coward, but I just couldn't tell her about Miriam on the phone."

Trying to console her, I responded, "You weren't being a coward, Joanne. Lieutenant Dias has dealt with these situations for a long time, and he *wanted* you to be able to tell Izzy in person. That way, no matter how she responds, we'll be here to support her."

"I guess you're right, Natalie. I'm just so grateful that you and Keoni were home this morning. I don't know how I would have handled things without you."

At that moment, we heard the kettle whistling. Looking over at the stove, we were both surprised to see Samantha taking charge of making tea.

"How strong do you like your tea? I put in three bags of Earl Grey, but I'm not sure how long they should steep," said Samantha with an unexpectedly intense look on her face.

After sharing a quick glance with Joanne, I said, "Just leave them in for the time it takes us to pull out a few items from the refrigerator." Opening the door, I polled my companions. "How about some bagels, fruit salad and salmon pâté?"

"That sounds wonderful," Samantha replied, obviously relaxing about her tea-brewing dilemma. "I didn't think I'd want anything to eat, but I guess I really am hungry."

"I don't feel very hungry myself," said Joanne. "But Natalie's right. Today is going to be draining in every way and we don't know when there'll be another chance to eat. I think it's best to do it before Izzy gets here. That way, we can focus on *her* needs."

Within a few minutes, we were seated, quietly munching on small portions of the leftovers I had set out. Once we were through, we all pitched in to tidy the kitchen. After that, I prepared trays of sliced fruit, cookies, bagels, hot and iced tea and coffee for the dining room table. Looking at the art deco clock above the china cabinet, I realized that Izzy was not the only person due to arrive momentarily.

Keoni and members of the Crime Scene Investigation team could show up at any moment in search of food and drink. After settling The Ladies in the living room with the flat screen TV turned to Sunday talk shows, I called Keoni to compare notes on how the day was progressing.

"I don't mean to pull you from anything important, Keoni, but I thought you and John should know that Joanne spoke to Izzy and she'll be arriving soon. Also, I'm sure you must be starved. I've set up some refreshments in the dining room for you and any of John's team who need to take a break."

"Good planning. You're right about my being hungry. And, with Ken`ichi, the CSI team and the ME's wagon having arrived, I'm not needed. I'll see you as soon as I tell John your news. Once Izzy has been told what's happened—and she's calmed down—he can come over and interview her and the other women."

"That sounds good. Joanne and Samantha are in the living room watching TV for the time being. Unfortunately, even Sunday programming is agitating, and I haven't any idea of how to soothe their nerves before Izzy arrives."

"Don't put so much pressure on yourself, Natalie. Just take it one thing at a time; that's all any of us can do. At least you got them out of Miriam's, yet they're close enough for JD to question them whenever he needs to. And it's nice they've got easy access to anything they might need from Miriam's cottage. That's more than most people have in a crisis like this."

Soon I heard Keoni come in the back door. After he greeted Joanne and Samantha, he settled in the kitchen with a plate of food so we could have a few minutes to speak in relative privacy.

"So what would you like to drink?" I asked.

"I think this is a day for three-alarm caffeine, Natalie."

I went into the dining room to prepare a couple of cups of dark roast Kona coffee—his black, mine loaded with vanilla almond milk and cinnamon. Returning to the kitchen, I settled down with him at the old Formica kitchen table that had belonged to my parents. I touched the chrome corner I had nicked with a spoon as a child, seeking to feel grounded as I prepared to reveal my vision of Miriam's death.

As Keoni loaded a bagel with cream cheese topped with a slice of blackened *`ahi*, I thought about the joy we had felt just the night before. Taking advantage of his preoccupation with food, I launched into a preamble for what I had to tell him.

"So, how are things next door? Does John have all his team in place?"

"It's actually several teams, you know."

"I know, but they're all coordinating through him, right? Do you think he'll have a report today?"

"Yes, and later. All the teams report to him, and their department heads, but until each unit is through with their work, there won't be a consolidated report. You must remember how it was with Ariel's case?"

"Well, at least John will be watching the puzzle pieces come together. And speaking of those pieces, he'll be coming over this afternoon to put several into place."

"Yes. He's asked that we set up a room for him to interview each of The Ladies."

"I figured the office would be best for that. I've already cleared off my desk for him and set up Auntie Carrie's old *koa* card table."

"Good thinking. We can use the living room for everyone else who arrives—invited or not. But what if one or more of The Ladies breaks down?"

"I think our bedroom would be the most peaceful place for them to rest and recover."

"Okay. I'll pull out a couple of things from the office and bedroom and we should be set for the rest of the day."

"Well, almost, Keoni. We don't know when Izzy is going to arrive...or anyone else...but I really need to tell you something before John gets here."

Looking up from his plate, Keoni's eyes met mine. "Okay."

"You know how crazy everything has been all day?"

"Mmhm."

"Well, I didn't get a chance to discuss much with you earlier...You know how you left me to have some peaceful sleep last night? Well, it didn't last very long."

"If that means what I think it does, you had another *vision*. Right?"

"Yes, and I'm afraid it was about Miriam. But I didn't realize it at the time."

'How much of the...event...did you see?" he asked, reaching to pat my hand.

"Oh, Keoni, it was terrible. For the first time, I was right in the middle of everything. I was even afraid the man would see me...and...."

"Whoa, Natalie. Take a breath and tell me what you saw, from the beginning."

I paused and drew several cleansing breaths, like I had been taught in the yoga class I had not been attending very regularly. "At first I sort of hovered between the beach and Miriam's yard. I saw a man in a wet suit walking up from the beach."

"Okay," said Keoni, now holding both of my hands.

"He went in Miriam's gate and around the side of the house to where the old security system box is. Then he came back, walked up to the front door and opened it," I said in escalating tones.

Keoni maintained eye contact with me as I recited what I had seen. With his hands continuing to caress mine, I managed to maintain control as I recounted the horror of the scene of what I now knew was the murder of Miriam.

"I stood in the doorway and watched the killer take out a loop of wire from a pouch. Then he dropped it over her head... and...jerked it...Her body slumped. I watched, sickened as he pulled a golden strand of hair from her head and put it in a plastic bag drawn from his pouch. He then picked up the cane that had fallen and put it back up against the wall. After that, he left the room, walking right through me, out the bedroom door, down the hall and out the front door. Oh, Keoni, I was so dumb. Even though everything was...was like in my other visions, I mean, in that pale washed-out color of old photos, I thought maybe it was just a bad dream because..."

"It's okay, Natalie. It's okay," said Keoni, in a soothing voice.

I gulped a bit and tried to explain my confusion after waking up. "You see, some of the elements in my vision echoed things from the party—like Miriam's security system being worked on... the story of Auntie Carrie and the diving suit... and Miriam using a cane. I just thought maybe my vision was a jumbled up nightmare.

It never occurred to me that it might actually be a premonition. Maybe after having this, *dream*, there was something I could have done to *prevent* something awful from happening. I was just about to tell you when Joanne called announcing that Miriam was dead."

Shoving back his plate and coming around to my side of the table, Keoni hugged me and tried to assure me that there was nothing I could have done to prevent Miriam's murder. "Even if you'd awakened in the middle of your vision, by the time we could have gotten to the cottage, Miriam would have been dead."

At the sound of something dropping in the living room, I knew that Izzy must have arrived. I wiped the tears that streaked down my face and stood up. "I've already let John know I had a vision. He said we'll talk about it after he interviews The Ladies."

"Okay, honey," he said touching my cheek. "Why don't you handle things with Izzy and I'll tidy up in here. Not knowing what might happen later, I'll grab my phone, keys and wallet and wait in the office until you tell me to call John over. We should do that as soon as possible."

"Sure. The sooner they've been interviewed, the faster the women will settle down. But what about tonight? We've got a couple of spare bedrooms; maybe we should have them stay here."

"Let's just deal with one issue at a time. We don't know if the women will want to remain together. Or, maybe Izzy will want to stay with her niece down the road."

As I entered the living room, it looked like a play staged in an arena theatre. Evidently either Joanne or Samantha had pulled my wingback out of the corner and positioned it to face out the front window. Izzy was seated in the chair. Joanne was standing over her and Samantha was kneeling in front of her. Dumped on the coffee table were Izzy's purse, a couple of empty Tupperware containers and a potted orchid that had become dislodged from its bark when it was dropped.

Approaching Izzy gingerly, I expressed my condolences and then sat quietly on the sofa in front of her. When her sobs had subsided to murmurs of disbelief, I heard what I assumed were Keoni's approaching footsteps. I looked up and with a slight nod and a spread of five fingers, signaling him to call John. Hearing Izzy repeat the phrase, "Miss Miriam," I knew she had reverted to thinking in terms of her years as the woman's housekeeper, rather than as her companion.

Izzy was clutching a glass of water and staring out the window at the fountain when John arrived. Joanne and Samantha had moved to join me on the sofa. Even though only a couple of windows were open, the sound of bubbling water seemed to have a calming effect on us all. I was truly glad Keoni had been motivated to revive that old curiosity that featured three Art Deco nymphs circled by butterflies.

With Miriam's Ladies settled in the living room, I went into the kitchen for a brief consultation with John. Taking the lead, Keoni said, "I know we discussed doing your interviews in the office, but may I suggest you do Izzy's in the living room since she's finally calmed down?"

"I agree. So, Natalie, why don't you bring Joanne and Samantha in here for a little tea time. Keoni, how about you run interference with any of my team who show up needing a break? I don't want to introduce any unknown factors, so if anyone other than Ken`ichi insists on seeing me, just pop in the room to let me know."

"Sure, JD. Natalie can put together anything they'd like and I'll serve them outside to keep the noise at a minimum."

With our plan in place, John approached Izzy's chair with clear deference for the fragile state of her mind and emotions. I beckoned to Joanne and Samantha. Soon we had positioned ourselves for a prolonged period in the kitchen. I began pouring a round of iced tea while we listened to a soft murmuring start up between John and Izzy. Personally, I was glad we could not decipher the details. I did not want anything to cause Samantha to return the hysterical state she had been in earlier. Perhaps it was the presence of the police that affected me, but despite my continuing disbelief, I found myself moving to Keoni's stance of resigned acceptance of the grim reality facing us.

Fingering our cups more than drinking our tea, Joanne, Samantha, and I passed the next quarter of an hour without significant conversation. Hearing noise outside the back door, I went out to greet a couple of members of the CSI team. Fortunately, I had some thick paper cups and plastic plates, so I was able to prepare their requests for coffee and a couple of bagels to go.

Soon after, John joined us. As we looked up expectantly, he

immediately calmed our concerns.

"I'm through taking an initial report from Izzy, who's obviously shaken like you are," he said to Joanne and Samantha. "Nonetheless, we have to go through our normal procedures."

We all nodded solemnly.

"I'm going next door for a few minutes, so you all might as well go and keep Izzy company for a while. When I return, I'll need to take statements from each of you, okay?"

Again, we all nodded and John exited through the back door. We then picked up our cups and moved to rejoin Izzy, who sat quietly watching doves splashing in the fountain.

As the afternoon wore on, the flow of people in and out of my home reached a rhythm that was almost serene. Miriam's Ladies spent their time in the living room, watching the usual Sunday television programming with little comment. Mid-afternoon, John returned through the front door with a polite but formal demeanor.

After establishing himself in the office, he began his interviews. Between each, he conferred quietly with Keoni in the kitchen or visited with the members of his team who arrived for refreshment. Until he chose to speak with me about my vision, I continued to follow his directive to keep everything tranquil.

Phones rang periodically and I handled the myriad questions from neighbors as briefly as I could. With all the blue and whites, unmarked detective cars, emergency vehicles, and the ME's van in plain view, it was obvious to everyone that there had been an emergency—and one that ended in at least one person's death. When the volume of calls dropped noticeably, I knew the police had begun their house-to-house inquiries.

Finally, in the late afternoon, John entered the living room with an intent look on his face, by which I knew the time for my revelation had arrived. At his signal, I rose from my seat. "Mm, Ladies, are you needing anything to eat or drink?" I asked.

Looking up at me in unison, they shook their heads. "I'm going to be visiting with Detective Dias for a while, so help yourselves to anything in the kitchen or ask Keoni, who is on the back *lānai*."

They assured me that they were fine and I moved to follow John into the office. I sighed softly at the thought of what was to come, for often the retelling of a vision is more disturbing than the actual experience.

CHAPTER 10

And there was the last nightmare touch....
G. K. Chesterton [1874 - 1936]

As I entered the room, John was arranging himself at my desk. Knowing I was ill at ease, he rose and came to seat me as though I were a visitor to *his* office. After sitting again, he turned to a new page in his notepad and adjusted his voice recorder.

"I can't imagine how this is affecting you, Natalie. I'm very grateful for the assistance you and Keoni have given me and my team today."

Choking back the effects of the tightness in my throat, I swallowed deeply. "I'm glad to do anything I can to help. I still can't believe what has happened. It seems even worse than Ariel's death. I just can't imagine anything Miriam could have done to invite this attack."

"From what we can tell so far, I tend to agree with you. She's a retired person with no enemies known to her housemates. There's no overt sign of wealth to have attracted a burglar. She hasn't remodeled to the degree you have and there's no signs of valuable art or collectibles that would invite special attention. From our quick glance through her legal papers, there's no one who stands to benefit from her death."

"It's funny you mention that last point. In one of our conversations, Miriam remarked that her home would remain available to her housemates throughout their lives. She also said that she and Henri had set up an irrevocable trust with the bulk of their assets going to UNICEF."

"Well, since she already told you that, I'll confirm that what you've said is borne out by the papers in her desk. With her work for the U.N. and other agencies, I was surprised she had no filing cabinet. But I guess she'd reached that point in life where she'd gotten rid of all but her personal papers, so Ken`ichi was able to go through everything fairly quickly. Of course, we'll have to confirm results we've found in our preliminary search, but that leaves our list of leads for this case rather blank.

"Frankly, the lack of motive may make your ah, dream, vision, rather important. You've already proven yourself a valuable resource—not only to me, but to the Department in general. With the mix of so many cultures and beliefs in the Islands, we see a lot of unusual things in the cases we handle. On top of that, I had a most unique grandmother. Please don't repeat it, but she came from Ireland and had what her people called "the gift." As a kid, I learned there was no point in fibbing to her. She always knew what was going on, even when she wasn't there to see it. So you see, I don't have any problem in examining your little visions. It's just too bad you can't call up them up on demand. If that were the case, my closure rate might be a lot higher."

I smiled bleakly at his attempt to put me at ease.

"Before we get started, do you want anything to eat? Do you need to take a break for a moment? Once we start, we could be quite a while, because I need to ask you about details you may not even know you've observed."

"I'm fine, John, I planned ahead—I've eaten already and here's my cup of tea. What about you? Do *you* need anything?"

With a chuckle he said, "You're always the perfect hostess, Natalie. I don't need a thing. I'm full thanks to your delicious leftovers from last night and I'm coffeed out. On my last run to the kitchen, I got this mug of water, so I'm set for the duration."

With the niceties over, we settled into our chairs and John gestured toward the digital voice recorder. "If you're ready, I'd like to record your memories and even your speculations, in case I can't keep up with my note taking."

We laughed lightly and I indicated I was willing to be recorded for posterity. After citing the date, our location and identities, John began his questioning.

"Although I was present, I'd like you to recount your recollections of last night's party at which Miriam Didión and her roommates were your guests. If possible, please include the times they arrived, their appearance and any conversations you had with them, or you overheard taking place between them."

"Mmm. I know Keoni's birthday party started at six o`clock. I guess I should clarify that Keoni's last name is Hewitt. He's my boyfriend and a retired detective with HPD. I remember being glad our long-distance guests arrived first, so they could spend some time alone with him. I'm not really sure how many people came, since I'd invited quite a number of our neighbors. I just know the house was full until the end, and there didn't seem to be anyone strange, anyone who wasn't known by at least one other person."

John nodded, but remained silent, so I would not lose my train of thought—or, I suppose, slant the direction of my reporting. "Izzy must have come in officially about four thirty, because she was bringing the last of the food she had prepared. Miriam arrived with Joanne and Samantha after Izzy, but before any other guests. That would have been five forty-five or so," I said, feeling renewed sorrow at her passing.

"I remember those three came in as a trio. Because, as I said, Izzy... Esmeralda Cruz...had been back and forth with food items since late afternoon, when Keoni was gone for a while. They all had on lovely, almost formal, *mu`u`mu`us*. Joanne Walther...that's the retired school teacher Miriam met in Guam during a speaking tour many years ago...was holding Miriam's elbow. Samantha Turner...who had just joined the household from Hale Malolo...came in the door next. Izzy came out from the kitchen about that time, balancing some cupcakes she'd made from the leftover batter for Keoni's birthday cake."

As I took a sip of tea, John paused the recorder and glanced at his notes. "As you can imagine, I'm trying not to make personal comments about the party, but that cake was great!"

John then raised his index finger to indicate I should hold my words until he had turned the recorder back on.

"Everything Izzy bakes, or cooks, is fantastic. It's just too bad about her hands."

"What do you mean, Natalie, about her hands, that is?"

"Well, she has rheumatoid arthritis and it's really affected her hands. That's why she had to stop working as Miriam's housekeeper. But by then, Henri had died—that was Miriam's husband—and Joanne had been a roommate for several years. Miriam was very fond of Izzy and asked her to remain as another housemate."

"So you're saying that Izzy has limited use of her hands?"

I nodded, and then seeing John point to the recorder, answered aloud. "Yes, that's right. Thank goodness for all the appliances in their kitchen; but sometimes she still has to ask for help in moving large containers or pouring ingredients. In fact, that's one of the reasons Miriam decided to have Samantha live with them and function as their part-time housekeeper."

"I believe you mentioned that Samantha had moved to Miriam's home from Hale Malolo. That's the women's shelter in Kāne`ohe?"

"Yes. I don't know her personal story, but when Nathan—that's my twin brother Nathan Harriman—met Miriam the day we were moving in, the two of them got to talking about their individual work in psychology. Nathan told her about his serving on Hale Malolo's board of directors. Somewhere in their conversation, he mentioned that he was looking for job training positions to help the residents plan for their futures. Before the women left that day, Miriam said she'd like to interview someone from Hale Malolo to become their housekeeper."

"If Samantha was to become the housekeeper, why is Izzy still cooking?" asked John.

"Well, the day Samantha was interviewed, she mentioned

she wasn't much of a cook, and Miriam said that wasn't a problem. Izzy made it clear that she loved to cook whenever she felt up to it...and wasn't traveling. In fact, the main reason for Samantha joining the household was that one or more of The Ladies are often on the road, and sometimes the scheduling of maintenance for the house or yard gets confusing. That reminds me, I don't know if it's important to your investigation, but Joanne mentioned she cancelled an appointment with a gardener who was scheduled to come this week."

"Hm. Thanks for that information. I'll be putting together a list of the individuals and companies who provide services to the household." After looking over his notes he continued. "Is there anything in particular that Joanne is responsible for in the house?"

"Not exactly. But I've noticed she does most of the driving and she watched over Miriam. I think she has some kind of background in first aid—maybe from her stint in the Army, or her years as a teacher overseas on military bases. That's how they met. Miriam was on some kind of lecture tour about the welfare of women and children, and they started chatting after the Q and A. I guess they corresponded for some time and eventually Joanne visited Hawai`i. After Henri died and Joanne retired, Miriam invited her to move in."

"So Joanne is retired from a career with the Federal government?"

"I think so. I don't know if it's part of the Department of Defense or the Department of Education."

"Mmhm," he said, scribbling down the information. "And what about Izzy's retirement income or assets? Have you heard anything mentioned about that?"

"Miriam was open about most everything in her life. I know Izzy worked for Henri and her for a long time. I heard something mentioned about a pension they had set up for her. That wasn't surprising because Miriam often spoke of women being taken advantage of in the workplace. I'm sure she would have been set up a retirement fund for anyone working for *her*."

"Mm. Returning to the party last night, what did The Ladies do? Initially? Did they stay together as a group?"

"Well, the party was rather lively from the beginning. I do remember Izzy walking through to the kitchen with the cupcakes. Knowing it would be difficult for Miriam to get around with her foot in a cast, and that she knew a lot of the invitees, we seated her at a table in the front hall, where she could greet everyone and hand out name tags. I think Joanne stayed with Miriam for a while. After that, I saw her visiting with various neighbors from time to time.

"And, Samantha...well...you've met her, John. She's a bit shy. At first, she stayed at my side. Then when she saw the empty glasses in the room were piling up, she began bussing. In general, I guess I was so busy that I lost track of The Ladies. So many other people were coming up to me and asking about our remodeling. And when I wasn't running tours, a lot of the neighbors cornered me with stories about my Auntie who had lived here in the cottage for decades."

"That's your Auntie Carrie died recently?"

"Yes. Carrie Johansen. She passed away just last winter, on January second. She was always the great partier. Even when her reasoning was gone, it was as though she knew there had to be a party somewhere in the area and didn't want to check out too soon."

"When did you take possession of the house?"

"Oh, it was right after her passing. I'd been co-owner for many years, so there wasn't much paper work to process. But you know we didn't move in until August first, because we've been redoing most everything."

John nodded and asked, "Were you already friends with Miriam and her roommates before you moved in?"

"No. We'd met them a few times. It seemed like one or another of the women was often traveling and we were pretty busy ourselves. I knew them primarily from Auntie Carrie's stories about the neighborhood. You see, until I retired officially a year and a half ago, I wasn't on the Island very much, because most of my assignments as a journalist took me overseas."

"I see. I know you had a lot to do last night, but do you recall any conversations between the women that you might have overheard?"

"Not really. When I think about it, it's almost as though I got catering staff without having booked it. Izzy kept filling platters and Samantha was constantly carrying dirty dishes and glasses to the kitchen. And someone ran the dishwasher at least once during the evening."

I paused for another drink of tea and John looked at me with a questioning gesture toward the recorder.

I nodded and cleared my throat.

"Are you okay to continue?" asked John.

"Yes. It's just been a long day already, and my throat's getting a bit dry. But I'm good to go again."

"All right, if you're sure," he said.

Knowing that the smallest detail could be a turning point in John's investigation of Miriam's murder, I tried to put myself back into the swirl of Keoni's party.

"I guess I should emphasize that I'd invited a lot of the neighbors to the party. Most of them had known Auntie Carrie for years and had expressed interest in seeing what we'd done with her home. That meant there were many people I don't know except as faces, addresses or vehicles in the neighborhood."

I closed my eyes and thought of the people who had come through the house. "I really can't think of anything anyone did or said out of the usual range of, 'Nice to get to know you,' 'Looks great,' or, 'Come and join us for....'"

"Okay. I know you and Keoni have concentrated a lot of your efforts on beefing up your cottage's infrastructure...windows and doors, the roof, your security system...."

"That's right. Keoni wants to make sure that when he's not here, I'm safe and the house can withstand anything from heavy rain to a hurricane or break-in.

"Speaking of that last item, I know he's been working on updating the security system at Miriam's."

"Yes. Of course, you'll have to speak with him about the technical aspects."

"I'll follow up on that. Did you hear home security systems discussed? Was anyone especially interested in the topic—maybe talking about it with one of Miriam's roommates?"

"No. I do know Keoni and our neighbor General Smith were talking about security lights and the General's grandchildren setting off timers and alarms by mistake. That's the only time I heard anything dealing with security."

"Before we leave the topic of the party, did you hear any conversations referring to Miriam, her home, or the ladies living with her?"

"Uh, regarding Miriam…everyone expressed concern for her health. But everyone left the topic once she reassured them that, aside from her leg, she was fine. They all laughed as she told the story of Miss Una. That's my cat. You know her from the day Ariel's death was solved. Well, one day, she ran into Miriam's bedroom suite from the balcony and interrupted Miriam's attempt to reorganize some things before Samantha arrived. It was when Miriam returned to that project that she fell and broke her leg. As to the rest of her *entourage*, I didn't hear anything, other than Samantha being welcomed to the neighborhood."

"Okay, Natalie. Let's stop for a couple of minutes and when we resume, I want you to tell me about the end of the evening…and the vision you had."

With that, John switched off the recorder and we took a break. Knowing how tense the next segment of the interview would be, I brought in a pitcher of water with lemon to keep my voice as clear as possible. One thing I have learned from on-camera and voice-over work is never to drink cold water, so I looked at the remaining ice in his glass with envy.

"Ready, Natalie?" John asked.

At my nod, he resumed the recording and asked me to summarize the end of the party.

"I know Miriam and Joanne left about nine and I scooted Izzy and Samantha out of the kitchen at eleven. The party finally broke up around midnight, and Keoni and I spent about a half hour tidying up. Then we went out to sit on the *lānai* for a while. After sharing a few stories from the evening, we went inside for the night. I'm not quite sure what time we went to sleep. Later, when I awoke after...my vision...I was alone in bed."

"All right, Natalie. You know I'm not trained in interpreting dreams, let alone visions. As you tell me about this latest vision, I want you to close your eyes and walk through it. Just as it happened originally."

"Okay, John. I'll try. But before I start, I want you to know that this one was different, somehow. That's why I didn't quite trust that it was one of my...usual visions."

"How was it different?" asked John, pausing in his note-taking to look me in the eye.

"Well, everything was the usual color of an old photo. You know, sepia, kind of purplish brown. But this time, instead of being on the periphery, I was right there, in the middle of everything when it got bad. It really scared me...but...there were several elements that seemed like they came from the stories I'd been hearing all night about my Auntie Carrie..."

"It's okay, Natalie. I already know that it's not like something you can control or put on pause or slow motion."

With a thin smile, I responded. "Actually, sometimes scenes do go into slow motion."

"I'm glad you can still smile, Natalie. Why don't you explain the aspects of this vision that seemed unusual."

"Mmm. Let me think. One of the stories I heard from Keoni, was my Auntie's learning to scuba dive. So, of course she was in a diving suit. Then there's the topic of security systems. Like you and I discussed earlier, Keoni was updating Miriam's system, as well as our own here at White Sands Cottage. When Nathan & I were kids, Auntie Carrie had a piano, and I remember looking inside it once when the piano tuner was at her old apartment...the black wire in the murderer's hands looked like what I saw inside Auntie Carrie's piano. Oh, there was the wingback chair facing the bedroom window. You see, Miriam had had Keoni move her favorite chair downstairs because she couldn't climb up to her bedroom suite...and she talked about sitting up at night, just napping all night long...."

I had been rushing my words to keep up with my thoughts and my throat had tightened again.

"Okay, Natalie. Drink some water and we'll get started with the vision itself when you're ready."

I took a sip of water and nodded. He then directed me to close my eyes again. "So, you're in bed, right?"

"Yes. I don't walk around during my dreams, or visions. As in most of my visions, this one started with me being on the fringe of things. I was standing in Miriam's front yard when I saw a man coming up from the beach access path. Then suddenly, I was hovering above the water watching him from the rear."

As I began re-experiencing the vision, I calmed down and managed to scrutinize the images objectively without being riveted on the horror of the murder itself.

"That's good, Natalie. I'm with you. You're watching the man move up the path toward...toward Mokulua Drive, right?

"Yes. He's in a black diving suit. He's all covered up, from his head to his feet. He reaches the road and stops. I hear a car coming. There's loud music playing and the man steps back into the shadows until it passes."

"Hm. What kind of music?"

"Some kind of rap, with an Island rhythm—I mean Caribbean, not Hawaiian style.

"Okay. Can you see the car?"

"Yes, it's a Jeep. It's open; no roof. I know what kind it is, I saw one on TV, it's a 'C' something."

"That's good, Natalie. Don't worry about the exact model. We'll figure that out later."

"After the Jeep's gone, I see the man cross the road and walk toward Miriam's. Next, I'm in front of her cottage, watching him enter the front gate. He goes around the house on the left. Somehow I know he's going to the old security system box that's on that side, near the garage."

I paused, trying to picture details from the scene.

"Go on, please."

"He's back at the front almost immediately. He lets himself in the front door, after looking to make sure no one sees him. Now I'm in the hallway, near the kitchen, watching him come inside. He's very quiet. He's wearing what I think is called a skullcap; it's kind of like a ski mask. It covered up everything but his eyes, nose and mouth."

"All right, Natalie. I want you to freeze the scene. Look at the man carefully. What can you tell me about him? How tall he is...his race...any distinguishing features."

"He's not terribly tall. Somewhere between my height and Keoni's. Maybe five foot ten. He's pretty slim. His skin is fair. He's probably not a resident of Hawai`i or a tourist, because he's not tanned nor is he sunburned. Just a pale *haole*. His eyes are dark, I can't tell the color because there isn't much light in the hall. There's a little bit of hair showing by his right temple; it's light brown, not quite blond, kind of mousy. I don't see any marks, like a birthmark, scar or tattoo. I can't see any jewelry—except, now that I look closely, there's a watch, on his right arm."

"What can you tell me about it. The color? The face? The numbers?"

"Mm, it's black and silver. Well, it's probably stainless steel with a black band. The face is white and the frame is steel. The face is white. The numbers for the hours are black Roman numerals. There's a circle inside the face itself with smaller numbers I can't make out.

"Is there anything else that's unusual about the watch?"

"Uh, there are little points on the part that joins the band to the watch itself. Two on each side, so that's four altogether."

"That's excellent, Natalie. Go on now. Tell me what the man does next."

"He looks around, but doesn't see me even though I'm right in front of him. He takes a walks down the hall and passes the coat closet. Next he listens at the door...the door where Miriam is. But I didn't know it at the time. He turns the knob slowly and goes right in."

My breathing was quickening, and I could again feel the terror I had experienced during the vision itself.

"I'm standing right there, in the doorway. He pauses. Then he pulls out a plastic bag from a pouch at his waist and extracts what looked like a tie. You know, like those bolo ties cowboys wear?"

"Mmhm, I think so. But tell me *exactly* what it looks like."

"Well, what I'm calling a tie is more like a single piece of old black piano wire with wooden sticks on both ends."

At this point, I heard the Lieutenant inhale deeply. "Okay. What does the man do next?"

"He walks forward to a wingback chair that's facing the window, with...with Miriam's long, blond hair covering her face. She's lying sideways in the crook between the chair back and arm. The guy drops the wire over the chair and I see his hands cross over...then he jerks the sticks...Miriam just... slumps down. And it's finished. Except that he puts the wire away in the plastic bag in his pouch. Oh, he yanks out some strands of Miriam's hair and puts them in another plastic bag. Finally, he looks around and sees something on the floor; he puts her cane against the wall. Then he turns and walks right through me, out the door, down the hall and out of the house."

I opened my eyes to see John's deep brown eyes staring at me. I sighed and licked my lips which were very dry. Silently, John reached over to hand me my water.

"Thank you Natalie. Let's break for today, unless there's anything you want to add?"

"No, no. That's my vision. All of it.

Signing off with the time, John turned off the recorder.

"Thank you very much, Natalie. You may not realize it, but you've brought up several points that may prove useful in finding Miriam's murderer. I know this has been a long day for all of you. Let's figure out where Miriam's roommates are going to spend the night. Then you and Keoni can get some rest. We'll pick things up again tomorrow. Okay?"

CHAPTER 11

Nothing has such power to broaden the mind
as the ability to investigate systematically...
Marcus Aurelius Antoninus [121 - 180]

I had not realized how exhausted I was from retelling my vision of Miriam's murder until I tried to get out of my chair. Not wanting to look foolish, I bent over and acted as though my foot needed rubbing.

"You all right, Natalie?" questioned John.

"Yeah, just a little tired. But I can't imagine how drained *you* must be from spending an entire day—let alone weeks—with this kind of intense investigation."

He laughed. "With this second round of seeing the life of a homicide detective, you probably understand why there are high rates of alcoholism, divorce, and suicide."

"So how did *you* avoid all those pitfalls?"

"Oh, don't kid yourself. I'm separated from my second wife and I can't say I don't tip back one too many bottles of beer on occasion."

"I know Keoni has really cut back on his intake of alcohol, but I don't understand how *he* managed to avoid the cycles of marriage and divorce."

John looked at me blankly for a moment. I worried I had crossed the line of my friendship with him. "Well, I don't mean for you to give me details. He and I discussed his first serious girlfriend being a nurse who died in Vietnam. And I know he's been engaged a couple of times."

"Let's just say Keoni has a pretty accurate meter for measuring the likelihood of success in relationships. Plus, I think looking at the rest of us caused him to put the brakes on whenever he wasn't sure about things."

"I guess that's one reason we get on so well. We both played the avoidance game for a long time and we're happy to enjoy each other without all the youthful baggage of whether to marry, have kids, *et cetera*. It's also great to be able to avoid all the awkward family situations that can mess up a relationship," I observed.

John nodded and squeezed my shoulder as we walked out to the living room. I found my guests sitting out on the front porch while Keoni watched a television sports talk show. Looking up he gave John and me an inquiring look.

"I think Natalie's vision is going to be a great deal of help," announced John softly. "I'm going check in next door. Then, unless something unexpected has come up, I think it's time to call it quits for today."

"Sounds good, JD. I haven't heard much vehicular traffic. Ken`ichi was over about half an hour ago. He said for you to give him a call when you and Natalie were through. He didn't sound stressed, or like anything major had come up. "

Keoni and I looked out at The Ladies, and then each other. I knew we were both thinking, "What now?" Neither of us wanted to be inhospitable, but with only one designated guest bedroom, I was debating my neighbors' short-term living arrangements.

Turning to John, Keoni asked, "Are you going to need access to The Ladies tonight, or in the next day or so?"

"I'm not sure. I've got their initial statements, but until we've had a chance to go through the evidence we've gathered, I won't know what will require follow-up. One of the first things I need to check on is how the murderer knew about the security system. From what Natalie has shared from her vision, the man knew exactly where to go to disable it. This means someone did their homework."

"The security company Miriam uses is one of the oldest in the state," observed Keoni.

"Yeah, but obviously someone provided the perp with the information he needed. As I see it, there are a couple of scenarios that make sense. The perp could have checked things out personally in advance. If he didn't, then the intel was provided to him—either through someone's on-site analysis, or from info gained through the security company. I've never dealt with a case involving leaks from that company, but you know how many employees a company like that goes through, even in a single year."

"You're right about that. How many cops retire in a year and end up looking for a job in security?" added Keoni.

John nodded. "So far, no one in the neighborhood has reported seeing or hearing anything out of the ordinary last night—except to confirm the loud music Natalie reported occurring when the Jeep pass by. That reminds me, I need to have Natalie identify which Jeep model she saw."

"Don't worry about it, JD. It's one thing I can do without interfering in your work. She can go on-line or I'll swing by a dealership for a couple of brochures with color samples."

"Oh, the color is simple. It was red. Bright red," I offered.

"That's good to know. With the way our sun fades finishes, if the color was that bright, it's probably a newer model. First thing tomorrow morning, Ken`ichi and I will be at Miriam's security company to greet the powers that be when they arrive at work."

"I think you already know they run a 24/7 schedule," Keoni said.

"Yeah, but the big boys won't be there for the graveyard shift, and I don't want to tip our hand in case there's something funny going on at that office—let alone with their people out in the field."

"So, what about our guests?" I asked.

"I don't know, Natalie. There's no ideal solution. I don't have any serious doubts about their intentions where Miriam is concerned. Granted, they all had the opportunity, being in the house, but none of them has a motive—quite the reverse. All three women would benefit from Miriam's continued well-being and generosity. Furthermore, even without your vision, I doubt that any of them has the tactile strength required to have garroted Miriam—certainly not Izzy, if she has RA," John summarized.

"Then I guess it doesn't matter where they stay for tonight or the next few days?" I asked.

"At this point, I think we need to ask what *they* want to do," said Keoni.

"Is it okay for them to get some clothing and toiletries, John?" I asked.

"Yes," agreed John. "But I'd prefer to take them over to Miriam's one at a time."

As though on cue, my cell phone rang. I had turned it off during my talk with John, and although I had turned it back on, I had not had a chance to check for messages.

"Hi, Nathan. What's up? We're winding down here. That's a good idea. None of us is in any mood to face cooking a meal tonight. Why don't you bring three pizzas with a variety of toppings, plus a salad? We've still got plenty of appetizers and wine."

Ending the call, I turned back to Keoni who had already said goodbye to John. With a nod toward the front porch, Keoni led the way to the fountain where The Ladies were now seated.

"So, who's ready for some wine and cheese, until Nathan arrives with pizza and salad for our supper?" I offered.

At the suggestion of food, Samantha smiled and Izzy stopped playing with the blue glass pebbles that line the bottom tier of the fountain.

"I take it the police are finished for today...at least with us?" asked Joanne.

Keoni nodded. "Yes, they still have some work to do at Miriam's home, but they won't be back today."

Izzy sighed. "*Auwē,* I still can't believe what has happened. We were all so happy last night...talking about the trips we were planning...after Miriam's leg healed."

Joanne added, "I just can't believe anyone would want to

hurt Miriam. In all the years I've known her—knew her, she never said anything mean about anyone. Even when she'd read about some despicable crime against women or children, she'd comment on the terrible things that must have happened to push someone into doing something like that. When she was giving speeches, even the small one I attended in Guam, you'd be amazed at the people who would come up to her and hug her and thank her for what she had done to make their lives better."

Trying to reassure them, Keoni said, "I want you all to know that John Dias and his team will do a thorough job of looking into Miriam's death. And with their success rate, there's every reason to believe they'll bring her murderer to justice."

"I hope so," added Samantha. "I don't like to think that such a horrible person is wandering around the island."

Not wanting to prolong the discussion that was making all of us feel a renewed sense of sorrow and anger, I called for everyone to regroup in the house.

"Why don't you all freshen up in the guest suite upstairs, and I'll start laying out the last of the odds and ends from last night. You'll find towels, soaps and creams in the medicine cabinet and vanity drawers. Call me if there's anything else you need."

With that, I turned to preparing for an early meal. When Nathan arrived, he had brought the basics for our supper, and a couple of items for our pantry.

"I thought that with the company you're having, you might be able to use some fresh produce," said Nathan, setting down several grocery bags, in addition to his gift of dinner. "Here are some papayas, lemons and avocados from my yard and I stopped by Agnes's Bakery for some cinnamon rolls."

Always glad when anyone helps out in the food department, I quickly expressed my gratitude. "Oh, Nathan. Thanks so much. We're still not sure about where everyone's staying tonight, but I know this will all be eaten in the next couple of days."

With a number of officials still visibly busy at Miriam's home, I repositioned beverages and snacks for them on the *lānai* table while we ate indoors. Izzy then helped me reset the dining table. In the center we set trays with pizzas with a range of local delicacies: Maui onions; shiitake mushrooms; artichoke hearts; luau pork; and, teriyaki chicken. By the time we added a large bowl of *niçoise* salad and the last of the party leftovers, we were ready to sit down. With two bottles of Nipozzano Chianti and a pitcher of water, our gathering was an unsettling echo of the festivities of the previous evening.

We were all rather quiet as we seated ourselves around the table. Before placing her napkin in her lap, Izzy crossed herself and looked down for a moment. Realizing she was saying a prayer, I waited until she looked up to begin passing the wine.

"This may not be a time of joy, but I think it's appropriate to toast the memory of your dear friend, Miriam Didión, who dedicated her entire life to supporting the cause of peace around the world," said Nathan.

The simplicity of these words seemed to bring us all to a moment of reflection. As Keoni chimed in with a supportive "hear, hear," The Ladies smiled slightly, with their thoughts turned inward at their various memories. In honor of both Miriam and my Auntie Carrie, I lit the large tuberose scented candle in the center of a protea arrangement. Perhaps, as we were feeling the sorrow of loss, Carrie was welcoming her friend Miriam to a new adventure on the other side.

Raising her glass once more, Joanne added, "And we want to recognize the kind support of Nathan, Natalie, and Keoni who are helping Izzy, Samantha and me get through this."

"And the police who are helping resolve Miriam's...death," added Samantha.

As I looked around the *koa* table, I was glad I had been in a position to have Miriam's Ladies seated together for at least one more meal. While no one seemed especially hungry, we spent at least an hour in the dining room.

As the room grew quiet, I announced, "There's still quite

a bit of Keoni's cake."

While the women demurred, Nathan and Keoni's eyes lit up. "Nathan, why don't you and I cut some cake. The rest of you can take your beverages into the living room."

Once we were alone, I asked Nathan's opinion on where The Ladies should spend the night—and for whatever days it took for the police to complete their investigation of Miriam's property.

"As you know, Nathan, I only have the one guest room, plus a daybed in the office. I just don't know whether it would be best for the women to remain together or not?"

"You're being very generous to offer them shelter. But they're adults, Natalie. I think you should leave it up to them. And speaking of that, don't forget that I can take one or more of them over to Hale Malolo for at least tonight," he responded.

Despite their earlier declarations of not wanting it, Nathan and I cut several slices of cake. In the end, everyone but Izzy opted to have a piece. Having glimpsed her baking habits, I knew she was not watching her slim waistline. She had probably had her fill when sampling each stage of her rich concoction to ensure the cake, filling and icing all came out perfectly.

As I re-entered the dining room, Keoni gave me a certain look. He and I had reached a point in our relationship in which we were developing a private non-verbal system of communication. Clearly, he knew I had had a conversation with Nathan about The Ladies' circumstances and nodded once to indicate his support for whatever I had decided.

"I want you ladies to know that before he left, John Dias said that he may not need to speak with you again for a couple of days. So, once you've gathered whatever belongings you need from Miriam's cottage, you're free to go wherever you wish—as long as he knows how to get in touch with you. Keoni and I have one guest room and the day bed in the office to offer you, but I don't know how you would feel about staying with us."

Nathan added, "Before you decide, please know that the women of Hale Malolo will also be glad to offer all of you a place of rest and recuperation."

Izzy, who was usually the last to speak, replied immediately. "You know I was getting ready to spend a couple of weeks house-sitting for my niece Malia down the road. I gave her a call before we sat down to dinner. She'd already heard about what happened from another neighbor and has suggested I move in a couple of days early. So I'll just get a few things from Miriam's and go over to Malia's for a while."

"Well, if you're sure you'll be comfortable and it won't be a burden for her," I replied, relieved to learn I'd have one less houseguest to care for.

"I'm sure one of the Lieutenant's staff can help your get whatever you need," affirmed Keoni.

"I'd just as soon go back to Hale Malolo. I already know most of the women and their kids, and it doesn't look like anyone will need me here any time soon," declared Samantha in a wistful voice.

Obviously not wanting to inconvenience us, Joanne offered to move to a B and B. "Oh, no, Joanne. Our guest room is sitting empty," I hurried to say. "It might be good if you were here—close enough for John Dias or his sergeant to ask any questions that might arise."

"Well, if you're sure I won't be a bother. I'll gladly help in any way I can to find out who did this to Miriam," she said.

With living arrangements completed, Keoni called John to have an officer escort each woman to Miriam's cottage. The first to go was Samantha, since Nathan was going to take her to Hale Malolo. Given the lateness in the day, she did not take all of her things. Despite knowing she would be returning at some point in the future, her departure from Izzy and Joanne was tearful. Next, Izzy went to gather some personal things, and with John's permission, her favorite frying pan and a couple of cooking utensils. With Joanne staying with me, there was no need for her to bring very much.

Soon Izzy and Samantha had departed and Joanne was getting settled in the guest room. Keoni and I then collapsed on the front porch with tall glasses of cinnamon tea to enjoy the lingering lavender hues of twilight.

"Oh, Keoni, I can't believe the day is finally over. How did you ever live through decades of days like this?"

"I never thought about it that way. It's like anyone's life; you live each day as it comes. Bit by bit, you find your groove and the days just meld together, one into the next. I'm sure it was the same for you, my love."

Shaking my head, I squeezed his hand in continuing admiration for the life he had lived as a homicide detective. Clearly we had both known tragic moments in our lives, and I was so glad to have him there beside me, sharing in this one.

Soon darkness enveloped our corner of the world, and we watched a blanket of flickering stars fill the sky. With the fragrance of flowers surrounding us on nearly every side, it almost seemed possible to turn Life's clock back. As I reviewed the day, I thought about my latest vision. I realized that most of the time, usually only two or three of my senses are present in my visions—sight and hearing.

In the case of my vision of Miriam's murder, there was an additional element at play—the cloying aroma of a lavender candle. By the time I stood with Joanne in the doorway of the murder scene, the candle had burned almost to the end. However, the sweet fragrance lingered on, as though Miriam were offering me a flower.

When wispy clouds occluded our view of a perfect quarter moon, we decided to go back inside. Taking our glasses into the kitchen, I looked around and realized I had not seen Miss Una since setting out her morning food. When there was no response to my calling her, I began checking all of her favorite hiding spots on the ground floor. Next I went upstairs where I checked the linen closet and behind the claw foot bathtub in the bathroom.

Just as I had given up my quest and prepared to join Keoni in the bedroom, I saw a faint light coming from the slightly opened door of the guest suite. I approached on tiptoe to keep from disturbing Joanne if she was asleep. Hearing the beautiful strains of a Frédéric Chopin concerto for viola and piano,

I nudged the door gently. Directly in front of me, Joanne was sleeping upright in bed with a book lying across her chest. Above, on the headboard, Miss Una lounged with a front paw extended downward onto Joanne's head. Opening one eye to bid me good night, my darling kitty made it clear she was on personal guard duty for the night.

Pulling the door close to the jam, I went to join Keoni who was already asleep. I crawled into bed, grateful to lie down snuggled against the man I had come to love. It seemed I had barely fallen asleep when I felt Keoni rubbing my arm briskly and realized I was moaning.

"Natalie, Natalie, wake up!"

Shaken to some awareness of my surroundings, I turned into Keoni's arms.

"Mm. Mm."

"It's OK, Natalie, you're OK."

"Mmhm. Mmhm," I murmured again, trying to rouse myself to full consciousness.

"What were you dreaming about, sweetheart? You kept say, 'the smell…the smell…. How am I going to describe the scene if I can't mention the smell?'"

Coming fully awake, I rolled onto my back. "Oh, that. Well, sometimes I have dreams about places I've reported about."

"Like a rock climbing wall on a cruise ship at Rio de Janeiro's Carnival, or the *Mo`ai* on Easter Island? What's that got to do with smells you find frightening and can't report about?"

I touched the line of his jaw with my index finger. "Well, you're right about my reporting on Carnival…from nearly everywhere in the world… and things like the *Mo`ai* . But you know that's not *all* I used to cover. Every once in a while I ended up in places that didn't fall under the category of travel and leisure."

Wrapping a finger around a lock of my hair, he merely said, "I see."

I shivered slightly as he blew my hair off the nape of my neck and traced the curve of my tricep to the crease on the inside of my elbow.

"And sometimes, I even had a brush with history."

"Okay."

"Like Nairobi, August 7, 1998."

The movement along my arm stopped.

"I was scheduled to cover a pair of celebrity tourists who were supposed to spend a couple of weeks volunteering at the renowned Masai Mara Game Reserve in Kenya. There'd been some kind of snag with their visas, and I was accompanying them to the U.S. Embassy to help straighten it out. I've never been so grateful for a flat tire. You see, our cab hit a sharp pothole about a quarter of a mile from the embassy's gate and because we were delayed, we missed being victims of the late-morning bombing."

"Oh, God, Natalie."

"Just a few minutes and a several meters, and instead of reporting *on* the news, I would have been a footnote *in* the news. As it was, I went from writing a two-part fluff piece on the growing popularity of eco-tourism, to live coverage of a world-shifting tragedy."

As I continued my story, Keoni returned to massaging my arm soothingly.

"The event kept me in that country for an extended period, as I covered the aftermath of the event for cable news. I never did make it to Masai Mara, where I'd anticipated getting paid to enjoy some extended R and R."

"I had no idea Natalie. You're always so upbeat about your career as a travel journalist."

"Well, most of the time it *was* a big holiday, for me, as much as the tourists I was covering. But occasionally there was an unexpected change of schedule."

I paused and sighed, gathering the energy to continue. "It really was the smell, you know. That mix of burning buildings and furnishings; chemicals... and... the bodies."

"No wonder you're familiar with police and government ops."

"Mmhm. But I don't understand what Nairobi has to do with my seeing a man taking aim at Samantha in a forest.

There wasn't any forest near our Nairobi embassy," I muttered, already falling back to sleep in the safety of his arms.

Knowing there was an abundance of cinnamon rolls and fresh fruit available to Joanne, Keoni and I slept in the next morning—at least until Miss Una came scratching at the door to reaffirm that locked doors were not acceptable. Once we were ready to face the day, each of us spent nearly an hour calling everyone who had left voice messages on our cell phones or the landline. Some of the calls came from friends who wanted to express their delight with Keoni's party. Others came from neighbors who conveyed their shock at the murder in our neighborhood.

With Keoni being a retired homicide detective, quite a few of the callers in the second category were hoping to learn inside details about Miriam's murder. Since we had missed most of the news broadcasts in the last twenty-four hours, we did not know what information was already public knowledge. Clearly, neither of us wanted to reveal facts that John Dias, or other officials, preferred to keep under wraps. Therefore, we kept our comments on the tragedy to a minimum, claiming that we, like our callers, were dependent on reports provided by the media.

Sensitive to our concern for her, Izzy had left a polite message assuring us she was fine and helping Malia pack for the family's upcoming vacation on Kauai. When I got around to touching base with Nathan, he informed me that Samantha had passed a peaceful night at Hale Malolo. While horrified by what had happened to Miriam, she had commented she was back to square one in determining what she would do next.

CHAPTER 12

The time will come when diligent research over long periods will bring to light things which now lie hidden...
Seneca the Younger [4 BCE - 65 CE]

Eventually I entered the kitchen in search of something to eat. Looking out the window, I found Joanne sitting on the *lānai* with a magazine, as she did mid-morning at Miriam's home.

"Hi. How did you sleep last night?" I inquired as I walked out the back door.

"Wonderfully...once I had settled in with a book. With everything that happened yesterday, I didn't think I'd be able to sleep at all, but that wasn't the case. In fact, I slept so soundly, I never noticed Miss Una was keeping me company 'til this morning."

"Oh, she has a way of keeping her paws in everything that takes place in the house. Have you eaten yet?"

"I'm a fairly early riser, so I've been enjoying some of that wonderful fruit Nathan brought over—and one and a half of the cinnamon rolls. I think that'll keep me going until noon or so."

I laughed at her obvious guilt about eating more than one cinnamon roll. "I've found that nothing from Agnes's Bakery remains in the cupboard long enough to go stale."

At that point, Keoni joined us with his tall mug in hand. "All I ask is that I get two of them for myself."

"That shouldn't be an issue, Nathan brought three dozen," I observed.

"Speaking of food," said Joanne, "I thought I'd call Lieutenant Dias and see if he'd allow me into Miriam's kitchen. While prepping for Keoni's party, Izzy overstocked our pantry. The refrigerator is full of fresh veggies, some leftover chicken *adobo* and I don't know what else. She was planning to do some batch cooking and freeze a lot of meals for us for while she is house-sitting for her niece for a couple of weeks.

"With Samantha having returned to the women's shelter and Miriam....We might as well bring a few food items over here," said Joanne, wiping a single tear that had appeared on her cheek.

"I'm sure that will be fine with John. I don't think any of his people are going to be preparing any meals in Miriam's home. We'll just verify his approval and find out when it would be good to go over. Maybe you could do that, Keoni."

"Sure. It's going on eleven and I was ready to check in with him. He's probably about finished with his follow-up investigations for the morning."

Keoni then went inside to use the land line. Through the window I could overhear his responses to John's comments on the case. Shortly thereafter, Keoni opened the back door and beckoned me inside.

"It's your turn, Natalie. JD has a few questions for you and then he'll be on his way to Miriam's." Passing me the phone, he went into the garage.

Not knowing what we might discuss, I remained in the kitchen and kept my voice at a low volume. Aside from a warm greeting, John was all business. "Natalie, you said that the wire you saw in the hands of the perpetrator was dark, even black. Is that right?"

"Yes. It definitely made me think of the wires in Auntie Carrie's old piano."

"Okay. Now I want you to picture the wire in the man's hands. What color were the wooden pieces at the end of the loop of wire?"

I closed my eyes and forced myself to view again the murder scene. "Well, it was awfully dark in the room and there wasn't much contrast with the wire, so I guess I would say the wood was dark."

"So, if I offered you golden oak, cherry, or walnut finishes, which would you say was the closest in color?"

"The sticks were closer to walnut. The fact that I could tell the pieces were made of wood, and there was *some* contrast with the wire, makes me sure they weren't black. But it's not like they were finished like a piece of furniture. I think they were rougher, worn—like they were plain wood that darkened with use, from oil and dirt on the man's hands."

"On a more general note, I want you to picture the killer the first moment you saw him, coming up from the beach. Are you sure he was in a scuba suit—not just black pants, shirt, and maybe a ski mask?"

"No, John, he definitely wasn't wearing black street clothes. First of all, everything was form-fitted, close to his body. And there were the shoes—I've seen those booties fairly often—especially here at this end of our beach, where it's a bit rocky."

"And his headgear?"

"Again, it was really close-fitting, like a glove. I think it's called a skullcap."

"One thing we haven't discussed is odor. Are you able to smell things in your visions?"

"Sometimes."

"So, was there any scent emanating from the man?"

"Not really. The primary scent in the room where Miriam died was lavender. I don't remember seeing fresh flowers, but she seemed to have candles in every room. Besides that? Well, when he passed through me, I think there was a slight smell of...I guess it was a combination of rubber and sea air—like from his scuba suit and the ocean. And when I was in the back yard, I could smell dirt and strawberries and vegetables—what you'd expect in a garden."

"Okay. At this point I think I only have one more question. Was there anything the man looked at with particular attention, or touched? Or, maybe there's something that one of The

Ladies has said is missing?"

"I don't think so. The Ladies haven't mentioned anything being different or missing. I've been thinking about anything I might have overlooked. But nothing new has come to mind. It's horrible to say, but the man came for just one thing and he did it...he killed Miriam."

"Mmhm," he said. "When you first revealed your vision, you said you hadn't realized the victim *was* Miriam. So, let's say for the moment that there hadn't been a murder and you were just walking through a stranger's home. How would you describe the person sitting in the chair?"

"Well," I said, closing my eyes again to picture the scene. "As the man walks into the room, I don't have a clear view of the figure in the chair. What I do see is the long blond hair—so I know it's a woman."

"What was she wearing? Never mind what you saw when you looked in the room with Joanne the next morning. I want to know what you remember from your vision regarding what the woman wearing when you saw her slumped over the chair's arm?"

"Hm. I can't tell what *kind* of garment she had on. But it was patterned with several colors on a vanilla background."

"All right, Natalie. I think that's all we need to talk about, unless you have something else for me."

"I can't think of anything else, John. Keoni and I should be here most of the day. Let us know if you need anything else."

At that moment, Keoni came in from the garage and reached for the phone. "Hey, JD. I forgot to mention I'm about to pick up those Jeep brochures we talked about, so you might want to go through them with Natalie sometime later today."

The volume on the phone was set so high that I could hear John's response. "Good idea. Right now I'm going to Miriam's to catch up with Ken`ichi who's checking on the forensic team's final sweep for additional evidence. We've already got Miriam's computer, cell phone, and legal papers. With the house being such a immaculate crime scene, I don't think there's any reason to keep it in lock down much longer."

After I hung up the phone, Keoni came to me with an uncertain look on his face. "Well, that brings up the issue of The Ladies. It sounds like they might be able to get back into the cottage sooner than I thought," he said.

While Keoni was gone on errands, I began reorganizing a few kitchen cupboards. With the party over, I had more available space. And with my having provided my limited input to the investigation, it seemed like a good way to keep my hands busy. I was not overly interested in domesticity at the moment, but the mechanical decisions of where to move pots, pans and pantry items kept my mind off the tragedy burdening so many in our community: How had one of our dearest neighbors come to meet such an unlikely death? Hearing the noise I was creating, Joanne came in and offered to assist. Obviously, I was not the only one who needed a break from the tragic circumstances surrounding us.

With our little project completed within a couple of hours, Joanne set off on errands of her own. When Keoni returned, we sat down with the Jeep brochures he had brought for me to consider. As predicted, what I had seen was a recent model, complete with an enhanced sound system. When John dropped in, I was able to identify the vehicle I saw and heard by make and model.

"It was a 2011 Jeep Wrangler Unlimited Sport Utility in a deep Cherry Red color. From the sounds I had heard, it seemed like the vehicle had an automatic transmission. And it did not have a top. If it was a rental, it was the soft-top model.

I invited John to join us for a late lunch but he declined. "Thanks, but I don't want to slow the momentum next door, or delay returning to the office. We may not have gotten anything useful from the security company this morning, but with the info you've provided, we can start checking licensed owners of that Jeep model, plus rental companies that have featured it. It's a long shot, but there's always a chance the driver may have seen something that will add detail to your vision. You did say the driver was alone, didn't you?"

"Yes. It was a single guy. I could tell he was dark skinned

and I got the impression he was young. But the car went by so fast. I couldn't see anything else—it was just a flash of red and a guy enjoying his music."

Keoni jumped in, "That begs the question of why a young guy would be out here alone? That is, if he's not a resident of the area. We haven't seen the vehicle around here before and there's nothing public at this end of the beach to attract a solitary tourist…or any guy by himself."

"Maybe he'd just dropped his girlfriend at her home and was heading back to his house, a B and B, or even a hotel in town," I suggested.

"Good point. All right, kids, I'm going to take off. Ken`ichi and I'll be in an out of Miriam's home for a bit longer. To be honest, there's not much of a paper trail in Miriam's life. But we still have to go through everything, if only to fill out our own paperwork. We've got one unit working on the financial institutions she dealt with. Another is going through her phone and credit card records. But like I said, since the perp wore gloves, brought his own "tools," and came and went from only one room, there's not a lot for us to pursue in terms of on-scene forensic evidence. Tomorrow we'll be dropping in for a consult with Miriam's attorney, but I'm not expecting anything unusual to pop up."

Since it looked like we were not needed at the moment, Keoni and I took off for a swim. When we came back, Joanne had already gone over to Miriam's to clean out her refrigerator.

"I put things away as best I could. It's good the party leftovers are gone, or there wouldn't have been room for what I brought. I hope you won't mind, I went ahead and fixed a salad and seasoned some chicken for grilling tonight...with just a touch of Louisiana hot sauce."

"Thanks so much, Joanne. I hadn't thought about dinner, but it sounds perfect."

By the time we had showered, the day was pretty much over. Thanks to Joanne's preparations, we had an easy supper and enjoyed an evening of summer re-runs on TV. The next morning our guest announced she would be gone most of the day, having both doctor and dentist appointments. Since Keoni needed to check out potential clients downtown, Miss Una and I were on our own for several hours. Although we set out for a walk together, she parted company with me in Joanne's garden.

"You're right, little one. It's a great place to hang out. Even the smell of the dirt is nice, let alone all the foliage."

Demonstrating her concurrence, she plopped down in the shade cast by a large tomato plant and I sauntered to the beach alone. On my return, I found no sign of Miss Una, Keoni or Joanne. With no looming deadlines, I luxuriated in the multi-head shower for several minutes longer than necessary. At least the new rain catchment system made up for the few times I took a long shower.

Refreshed in mind and body, I checked both my landline and cell phone for messages. With all the activity surrounding Miriam's murder, I was glad that Margie and Dan O`Hara had found something to do with their time in the Islands. Rather than idling at their O`ahu timeshare, they had opted to trade a few days at another timeshare on Maui.

"Hi. It's Margie. We've had a great time on the Valley Isle. Since we haven't heard from you, we're going on to the Garden Isle of Kaua`i for a little fun in what passes for a river over here. I don't mean to be too light-hearted about why we're not getting together, but you and Keoni need to avoid being around crime—especially murder. Haha. Give a call when you get a chance."

Well, that was one phone call I could not make until I had a firm proposal for scheduling some R and R with them. One call I did make was to Anna Wilcox. After I caught her up on the murder investigation, she gave me a profile of the tenants who were moving into my old home. The only other call I needed to make was to Izzy. She seemed to be holding up emotionally, but was already tired of her stint as a house sitter.

"Oh, Natalie. It's good to hear your voice. I'm settled in at Malia's and the biggest challenge I face is walking the two dogs several times a day. I don't know how my niece manages to do that, plus taking care of her home and husband and kids. I can't wait for the next week to go by. God forbid I should sound snoopy, but is there any news on, on Miriam's...murder?"

I did not want to give Izzy false hope that there would be an official proclamation any time soon. "I'm sorry to say there's nothing tangible to report. The police are finishing up their analysis of the cottage and Miriam's personal affairs. Until that's completed and the initial autopsy report comes in, we won't know anything more."

With the afternoon half over, I did not think I would be hearing from John. But I was wrong. About three-thirty he called and asked if I was available to come over to Miriam's for a short meeting with him and Nathan.

"Keoni's out on business calls and we've got leftovers for dinner, so there's nothing I need to do for a couple of hours. When's Nathan coming over?"

"To be honest, he should be here shortly, since he was already in Kailua. Until I spoke with him, I hadn't thought of including you in the project I have in mind. Why don't you come over in about fifteen minutes? Officer Horita will let you in the back door."

We hung up and I wrote a note telling Keoni and Joanne where I had gone. By the time I had filled a metal bottle with water, it was time to head over to Miriam's. As expected, Officer Horita greeted me and escorted me to the living room. There I found John and my brother in conversation. After we all said *hello*, the detective turned to the purpose of our meeting.

"I'm glad you could join us, Natalie," he said. "As I was telling Nathan, the CSI team is through with its final sweep of the house. On the outside, it looks like the perp interacted with only the front gate, the security system, and the front door. Inside, it appears the only contact he had was the front door, the hallway and the room in which Miriam was murdered. Despite that, we had our videographer shoot the entire property in case anything else comes up. But since nothing seems to connect to Miriam's housemates, we couldn't see disrupting their lives any further. So depending on what Curtis Leighton—that's Miriam's attorney—says about disposal of her property, I'll be telling The Ladies they can move back into the house."

"Nothing will bring them peace about Miriam's death, but I'm sure they'll appreciate having access to all their belongings and being able to settle back into a routine. Of course, I won't say anything until you give it the green light," I responded.

"The reason I wanted you two to come over this afternoon is actually upstairs. So, if you'll follow me, I'll explain what I mean."

Walking up the stairs, I thought of the last time I had been there—retrieving Miss Una, during her social call. Moving forward into Miriam's suite, I saw that most everything was as I remembered it. But with some items, like her chair, having been moved downstairs to the maid's quarters, it seemed a bit empty. Also, the bed had been stripped of linens and like much of the house, there was evidence of fingerprint dusting.

"You've been here before Natalie, right?" John asked.

"Yes."

"Does anything look different to you?" he asked.

"No. Well, of course her chair has been moved. By Keoni. He put it down in the maid's quarters after Miriam broke her leg."

While John and I were visiting, Nathan looked over Miriam's extensive library.

Glancing at him, John said, "You're getting ahead of me, Nathan. Part of her collection of books includes Miriam's own work—published and unpublished. You see all those blue binders on the shelves under the window and on the shelves to the right?"

We both nodded.

"Well, those are Miriam's journals. They cover nearly every day of her life, from college on. I guess that's something a lot of you shrinks, uh, psychiatrists, do, right, Nathan?"

"Mm, yes. By the way, I'm not a psychiatrist, John. But you're right that a lot of analysts, regardless of category, journal as part of their continuing study."

"Correction noted. To be honest, we're nearly at a dead end in this case. I'm wondering if there might be some hint of discord in her personal thoughts that could help us in solving her murder."

"What do you mean—you're at a dead end? I asked. It's only been a couple of days?"

"Natalie, you've been through this before, with Ariel's case. As you know, the first thing we look at is the victim's family and inner circle. When we looked at *your* family, it was small, but your grandniece had a wide range of activities and contacts among family, school, and work. But despite all those potential persons of interest, we didn't get anywhere with Arial's case. To be honest, it really was only through an accident of circumstances that we learned the truth about her demise.

"With regard to *Miriam's* family, we've only found one of Henri's cousins. She's actually a second cousin living on the mainland who only met Miriam a couple of times. The victim was retired and had a heart condition that prevented her from continuing her public speaking. Regarding other interaction, nothing has materialized from the list of gardeners, cleaners, and other service providers, including the security company she'd used for more than two decades. In short, there's only a small circle of people in her life for us to consider.

"The next issue is motive. We can't find any reason for someone to off her—recently or in the public record of her past. Unless something shows up in the autopsy, or microscopic evidence in her clothing, the yard, front hall or maid's room, there's not much for us to pursue.

"Her housemates' lives are just as sanitized. Although I told you Ken`ichi and I are going to drop in on her attorney tomorrow, we already know the details of Miriam's will. As far as we can tell, there's no way the women benefit individually from her death. Miriam's irrevocable trust *does* provide a home—including all expenses and upkeep—for any and all of her unspecified housemates for as long as they choose. When the last of them moves or dies, the property will be liquidated and all the assets remaining in the trust will be given to UNICEF. Her attorney has confirmed that Miriam has had no contact with him in the last year, so nothing has occurred that would indicate she was in the process of changing her will or altering the trust.

"And so, here we sit with no apparent reason for Miriam to have been killed. That brings me to the favor I'd like to ask of you two."

"Anything," said Nathan. "The papers she published and Henri's photojournalism were influential in my becoming a psychologist focused on abused women and children."

"I'm happy to help in any way I can," I concurred.

"I'm grateful you're willing to help out. I wish I could offer you a consulting fee as the psychologist you are Nathan. But unlike when you've helped us in the past, we've had so many cuts in funding, that I can't this time," said John.

"As to you Natalie, well, as you already know, you're my pocket resource for inspiration. Nothing you say can go on the record, but you've pointed me in the right direction on more than one occasion and I'd really appreciate your focused input now. In short, I think you're the perfect pair for a little project I have in mind. Simply stated, what I need is for you to go through all of these binders and see if there's anything that might be pertinent to Miriam's death that I can turn our Department analysts on to."

We agreed, and after a few instructions regarding the importance of maintaining possession of the journals, the flexible Lieutenant left us to decide how we would approach our work. Clearly, the project was under Nathan's direction. I was there merely as his assistant.

Since the CSI techs had determined that the only fingerprints on the shelves or journals appeared to be Miriam's, there was no problem with our handling them. Believing that it was unlikely that Miriam's death was related to anything from her distant past, Nathan chose to begin with the most recent journals and work backwards.

Although I am not a counselor, I am good at reading masses of material in a short space of time, while seeking information on various levels. Therefore, Nathan asked me to concentrate on examining the first half of the journals for an overall sense of Miriam's life. He then gave me some colored stickers that could be inserted on pages to indicate specific topics Nathan and the Lieutenant had determined were of interest. These included her likes and dislikes, as well as personal concerns and fears. In addition, I was to note any individuals or organizations she mentioned repeatedly.

As I looked at the volumes before me, the first question was whether I wanted to examine them from the more recent to the beginning, or vice versa. Knowing that Nathan was seeking the most blatant reasons for someone to wish to kill Miriam, I decided to look instead at the origins of the young woman who would grow into such a staunch advocate for alleviating human suffering.

To facilitate our project, John presented both Nathan and me with keys to Miriam's home. Since I was not going to begin my work on the journals until the next day, I helped Nathan pack the last shelf of journals so he could begin analyzing them in his office.

CHAPTER 13

As a small child, I felt in my heart two contradictory feelings, the horror of life and the ecstasy of life.
Charles Baudelaire [1821 – 1867]

The next morning, Keoni and I decided to take a long stroll around the neighborhood. Except for the remodeling of one of the last vintage cottages, we did not find anything remarkable. We returned to find Joanne busily at work in her garden.

"Even though we don't know what will happen to the cottage, I would hate to let the garden go to ruin," declared Joanne. She then bent to dump her handcart of yard clippings into the composter.

"It's great that you're taking such good care of the garden. I'm not officially in the loop, but John Dias has indicated things are winding down in the analysis of Miriam's home. I'm pretty sure you're about to receive a status report pretty soon," volunteered Keoni.

"With that end in sight, I should go inside and begin the assignment John's given Nathan and me," I said. "We've been asked to read Miriam's journals, to see if there's anything that might be relevant to her murder."

"Good. I hope you'll learn something that'll help the police," responded Joanne with a weak smile.

Soon Keoni was on his way into Honolulu to follow up on his new clients and I sat down at the computer. I then spent several hours online, researching Miriam's career in international affairs. Mid-day Joanne and I met in my kitchen and prepared a lunch salad with vegetables from the garden, Italian bread and tea. Just as we were setting the table, the doorbell rang. When I opened the front door, I found John Dias staring at Miss Una perched on the fountain's edge.

Turning around, he said, "Surprise. I'm about to do a final walk-through at Miriam's and thought I'd return the keys to The Ladies. Is Joanne around? I can fill her in on what I've learned."

"Good timing, John. In fact, why don't you have a bite of lunch with us while you do that?"

"Thanks for the invitation. I'll accept, since it'll keep my time in Kailua fairly short."

After adding another place setting, we all settled down for a working lunch. Confirming that the women could move back to Miriam's cottage, John handed Joanne the keys she had given him after the murder.

"Maybe it would be a good idea for both of you to join me in my walk-through. Ken`ichi and the CSI team have already cleared out, and it could be useful for us to look things over together before I leave. I have to inform you that while you, Izzy, and Samantha are welcome to return to the cottage, something might develop that will require another official look at the property. Also, Natalie and Nathan have keys so they can complete their study of Miriam's journals, so I trust you can find a schedule that will work for all of you."

Joanne glanced over at me, before answering him. "Of course. And, with all the talk in the neighborhood—let alone the news coverage—I know it's important not to leave the house empty because of the possibility of thieves or vandals. I'll be glad to move back in today; Izzy should be able to join me at the end of this week, when she finishes housesitting for her niece."

"That's good, Joanne," responded John. "You're certainly right about keeping the cottage occupied, now that the police will be gone. Before I leave, I should also mention that you and Izzy will be hearing from Miriam's attorney, Curtis Leighton, in the next day or so."

On that note, we carried our dishes to the sink and trooped out the back door. Within a half hour, we had completed looking over Miriam's property with John. After a few final instructions for safety, he checked that all the doors and windows were closed and locked before leaving Joanne and me alone.

"While you gather your things at my house, why don't I put together some food for you to restock this refrig and pantry?" I suggested as we walked out of Miriam's kitchen.

"Thank you so much for your hospitality. I know I speak for Izzy as well as myself when I say we really appreciate everything you and Keoni've done."

"We've been delighted to help out," I replied. "With no disrespect to Miriam, I'm so glad you and Izzy and Samantha have remained safe through everything that's happened."

"Maybe there's something to be said for those candles that Izzy lights every night."

"There's a lot to be said for faith of every kind," I noted.

After I called Nathan to announce that Samantha could return to Miriam's, I assembled some basic supplies for reopening Miriam's kitchen. Meanwhile, Joanne called Izzy with the news they could have full access to the cottage. Izzy decided that while she needed to walk the dogs and do a few chores at her niece's during the day, she would spend her nights at the cottage with Joanne.

By the time Keoni arrived home that afternoon, White Sands Cottage was again our private haven and Joanne and Izzy were settling back into Miriam's home. Since he was determined to complete his downtown assignment the next day, I checked in with The Ladies to make sure it was all right to begin my journal analysis in the morning. Accordingly, I arrived at the open Dutch door at nine a.m., where Izzy greeted me with an offer of freshly brewed tea.

"You're welcome to most any variety of tea you'd like. Our tastes are so different that we just keep adding to the varieties in the pantry. Name one and I'll see if we've got it."

"I'm easy. What do you have brewing?"

"Oh, that's Earl Gray."

"That'll be fine," I said.

"Would you like cream or sugar?"

"Both, please." I requested, taking the teacup and spoon she offered.

Although I needed to begin my project, I thought it would be rude not to visit with her for a bit.

"How are you and Joanne doing? It must seem strange without Miriam here."

"You're right," agreed Izzy, gesturing toward the table. "It almost feels like we shouldn't be here without her."

"Oh, Izzy," I said, walking around to hug her. "You know that isn't so. Even the police have said you should be here. I know there's been no official announcement by Miriam's attorney. However, a little bird confirmed that a copy of Miriam's will has been found. It specifies that you and Joanne—and any other women living in the home at the time of Miriam's passing—are to continue here in the cottage as before."

"My mind tells me you're right, but my heart tells me this is no longer our home. It's just not the same."

I nodded and sat down. I knew what she meant. I remembered what it was like when my husband Bill had died. The condo we had lived in had been leased in both of our names, but somehow it did not feel like my home without him. As I headed up the stairs to Miriam's suite, I experienced similar feelings of being out of my element. Opening the door, I looked around Miriam's airy and beautifully appointed sanctuary. While I knew that I was helping the authorities solve a murder case, I also had to recognize that I was invading the space of a woman whom I had only recently come to know and respect.

Ahead of me was the infamous double closet above which Miss Una had hidden during her unannounced visit. To the right, was the bathroom finished in glossy white subway tile that reached from floor to ceiling, plus a claw-foot tub and pedestal sink. Under a dormer to the left of the closet sat a nightstand of well-polished walnut. Next to it was Miriam's double bed, that someone had returned to its normal state with a crisp white lace duvet and pillows embroidered with birds and flowers. To the left of the bed was a small dresser that matched the nightstand. Beside the dresser was an empty space where her blue leather wingback recliner had stood until she fell and broke her leg. On the left wall sat a small kidney-shaped desk in burr walnut to the left of a long narrow window.

From that point, the bedroom was dominated by books. At the end of the room, mullion-paned windows were framed by tall bookcases filled with volumes in English, French, German and Swedish. Below, a large window seat with tufted blue cushion invited one to curl up and read. Underneath the window seat were two more rows of bookshelves. In front of it, a Bentwood rocker sat waiting for me.

Dispersed across the walls, photos of laughing children looked out at me in frames of every kind and size. A multi-hued sampler, in what looked like Swedish or Danish, hung above the dresser. To the right of the bed was a classic blue photo of the earth taken from space, matted with the flags of the members of the United Nations. Above the desk were three revealing pictures: One featured Miriam as a young woman seated beside Eleanor Roosevelt at a conference table. Besides that, another showed her standing with Dag Hammarskjöld. A third showed her in an ecru colored lace wedding dress with a small gold Star of David at her throat.

I stared ahead at the bookshelves containing the work I had been assigned. While Nathan was analyzing the journals to the right of the window, I was to skim those to the left of the window and running horizontally below the window seat. With his work at Hale Malolo and his part-time counseling practice, he was smart to take the first shelf of books with him. I had opted to come to Miriam's room each morning, after my time of exercise and reflection at the beach.

For the most part, the room looked as though Miriam had just stepped out and would return momentarily. Except for a blotter with a calendar of the current year, her desk was neat and bare. On a table to the left of the window sat her final reading materials. I paused for a moment to page through the three books.

An ebony bookmark shaped like a bird in flight lay in an open book of poetry by Maya Angelou. A blue enameled butterfly stuck out from a French text by Voltaire. Last was a well-worn gold embossed black leather thong bookmarking an illustrated book of children's poetry. Each selection was presented in both English and the original languages of the youthful authors whose words cried out in joy and sorrow from distant corners of the earth.

I knew that nothing could be changed or removed from these rooms for the time being—certainly not until Nathan's and my work was completed, and the reading of Miriam's will had officially declared the disposition of her personal effects. As I sat in the rocker and sipped tea from a cup in her collection of Royal Copenhagen cobalt-blue and white porcelain, I felt all the more that I was embarking on a final invasion of Miriam's life and personal space.

In fact, I almost felt overwhelmed by the enormity of the task I was facing. It seemed the delightful and diminutive woman whom I had barely gotten to know could not be the human dynamo whose voluminous work and sometimes fiery words had lit the lives of so many people, including my twin.

Thank heavens I had done my homework as a researcher before undertaking the assignment to help review the life of Miriam Sophia Reznik Didión. Born in Russia, she and her family had fled to Sweden during the Second World War. While she had taken some undergraduate courses in European languages at La Sorbonne in Paris, most of her collegiate studies were in England. Her bachelor's degree was from St. Anne's College at Cambridge; her eventual doctorate was obtained at Bristol University. Although her official accreditation was as a psychologist, she had taken varied courses in medicine and international law.

After initially meeting in Paris, she and freelance photographer Henri Didión had married in London. They had then spent many years travelling to war-torn places of the world as freelance photojournalists. Combining her text and his photography, they generated newspaper and magazine articles spotlighting situations that might otherwise have been overlooked by the mainstream media.

Considering her academic record and demonstrated eloquence in both print and speech in several languages, it was not surprising that she came to the attention of the United Nations. Through the years, she had worked with them in several capacities. Initially, she was a researcher and analyst with the International Court of Justice, dealing with cases stemming from the horrors of World War II. This connection might sound like a possible origin for a motive in her murder. But since it was so far in the past, it seemed unlikely to me.

At that phase of her life, her strong words were concealed behind the work of prominent public figures. Later, she became an advisor to the U.N. Secretariat. She remained there until she accepted a final full-time position with UNICEF. During those years, she and Henri had lived in New York. Following her official retirement, she had served as a consultant to the National Center for PTSD, spending most of her time touring as a public speaker.

After she retired from even public and private consultation, she and Henri continued travelling. Along the way they continued writing meaningful articles, as well as two books, highlighting both the travails and the accomplishments of humankind in Third World nations. Periodically, they had visited Hawai`i, usually on their way to some country in Asia. Prior to his death, they purchased the Lanikai cottage and enjoyed a few years of quiet retirement. Always well-read, they continued to speak out in letters to newspaper editors and annotated photo essays in noteworthy national and international publications. Occasionally, Miriam was asked to speak at conferences addressing the rights of women and children.

I soon realized why John had thought that analysis of her private thoughts might provide a potential line of inquiry. But there seemed little in her public life to link her to any murder, especially her own. What was visible throughout the journals was her signature calmness and use of gentle persuasion in her argumentation of myriad causes. I felt certain that these qualities had helped to harmonize situations that appeared headed for regional turmoil, if not nation-wide warfare.

Since I was to develop an overall perspective of her as a person, I decided to start at the beginning and skim through each journal until I found something of interest that warranted further investigation. Opening the first volume, I noted flowing penmanship that spoke of another age and place. I had only had a couple of years of French in high school, so there was no way I could fully understand the thoughts of a sophisticated writer of that language.

I did not know what languages were spoken in Miriam's childhood home. Since she had been born in Russia and grew up in Sweden, English must have been her third or fourth language. I suspected that the material at the beginning of the journals had been recopied from a childhood diary. With no surviving family members to ask, we would never learn the language of the original text. That meant that readers of Miriam's journals would never understand any linguistic subtleties she might have included naturally, or even inserted intentionally.

With my limited understanding, I began skim reading as quickly as I could. I was glad that about a third of the way through the collection, the entries shifted to English—except for marginal notes written in what looked like a form of French shorthand. Slowing my pace, I was able to pursue my original plan to read her words with several specific topics in mind. While some of the entries were mere itineraries, others were a blend of gentle but poignant prose and poetry. I found that although she had spoken English with a soft lilt from her early years in Sweden, her passages of English prose displayed her mastery of the language's artistry, as well as syntax.

Fortunately, she had drawn occasional sketches and although I might not understand the text of early entries, I recognized her cartoon-like interpretations of popular product advertisements and even book titles from the late forties and fifties. In addition, I found carefully inserted clippings from world publications that had impacted her. It was clear that much of what she offered in her journals was an abbreviated view of life in Europe and across the globe in the mid-twentieth century. At first, the headlines were linked to the hunting of Nazis who had escaped the Allies—and the spreading technology of atomic power and warfare. In later volumes, I found references to regional warfare and atrocities of many kinds, especially against women, children, and ethnic minorities.

Appreciating the essence of the woman Miriam grew to be, I gently turned the pages of each volume, being mindful to look for materials she might have inserted between the pages. Although I had missed being able to read about the specifics of day-to-day activities in her early life, Miriam occasionally referenced her childhood. Those entries, combined with the preliminary research I had done, provided me with an overall sense of her youth.

Growing up in Sweden during and after the Second World War, my life as a child provided little excitement. But, as Jews fleeing the horrors of Hitler's Third Reich, my parents and I were grateful merely to be alive and to openly greet the sun each morning. Although disturbed by the continuing warfare when we first arrived, my family gleaned a positive perspective from the horror of newspaper photographs and blaring radio broadcasts. Unlike others with less personal involvement, we were very appreciative for the generosity of our host country and Jews in America who sent what money they could to help sustain our community. Of course, until I was an adult, I did not recognize the significance of the sacrifices so many had made for our benefit.

Having been home schooled during her early years, it was not surprising that most of Miriam's reflections on her childhood centered on activity with her parents. The one thing I found surprising was the lack of any reference to searching for Reznik family members at the end of the war. This may have been because her parents already knew that none of their family was left alive. In discussions of her life following her mother's death in 1948, Miriam sometimes mentioned her father, who had resumed his own academic career as a professor of classical languages until his death in 1952.

Throughout the post-war period, she occasionally referred to people who had been friends and colleagues of her parents. I did not recognize see any names I recognized, but I could sense the relief her family had felt at learning someone they cared about had survived, despite the millions who had not. Sometimes Miriam's references seemed odd. There were stories of Allied soldiers and airmen who had miraculously escaped the Nazis for whom I could see no connection to the Reznik family. There were also scraps of newspaper articles about events in the Middle East that I imagined must somehow relate to people involved in the founding of Israel. And interspersed, were heroic sounding tales of women and children being saved from dire circumstances by shady sounding tales of women and children being saved from dire circumstances by shady sounding men of the *Unione Corse who participated in the La Résistance Française.*

From Miriam's curriculum vitae, I knew she had begun her collegiate studies in European languages at La Sorbonne in Paris. She never mentioned why she had left La Sorbonne and moved to England. As I explored her university years in England during the 1950s, I found many parallels to my own college experience. While my IQ was not on par with hers, I too remembered enjoying the richness of the intellectual stimulation. And, although I am sure the dampness of Great Britain must have been far more biting than the dry cold of Sweden's winters, the cold rain of Portland Oregon, was a shock to *me* after the warmth of California and Hawai`i. More importantly, for both of us, there had been the sense of being an outsider, with no family near to whom either of us could turn when challenged or disheartened.

* * * * *

In 1953, I was privileged to enter St. Anne's College in Oxford, England, for my undergraduate studies. It was one of the first colleges open to women at Oxford, and I was glad their com-

mitment included providing financial support to those needing it. Although thrilled to be in such an esteemed institution, I was uncertain about what the future would offer me—or anyone. With the doom and gloom atmosphere created by fear-mongering gun and flag-waving proponents of nuclear warfare, I had little faith that we could avoid another world war.

During my years at St. Anne's, Mary Ogilvie was the Principal. Under her ambitious and creative tenure, the school grew in it its number of faculty, students, and physical structures. They were also noted for innovative measures, such as building a dining hall and instituting nursery services for its staff with young children. Despite her title and many personal and professional obligations, Lady Ogilvie was accessible to even foreign students like me who sought her advice.

Despite this supportive atmosphere, I struggled to find direction in my studies. Fortunately, I did not have to narrow my focus beyond the arts and science of Classical Studies in completing my baccalaureate. When I moved on to advanced studies at Bristol University, my tutor, I was informed that I had to commit myself to a specific course of study or face expulsion.

When I left his office that afternoon, I was still pondering the realities of my life. As I walked through the beautiful and peaceful commons, I again turned to an image that will remain with me to my dying day. It was nearing dawn and I was with my family in a small boat floating over the waters to freedom in Sweden. It was the fall of 1942, and although I was a small child, I knew that this was the day that would determine the rest of my life. Staring back toward the shore of Denmark, I thought about the last meal I had been given in the dark and mysterious basement of what I now know to have been a Lutheran church.

The women of the church had taken turns bringing the refugees who had sought shelter within their sacred space the food clothing and toys they could spare from their own homes. I now know that with its agricultural economic base, the people of Denmark did not suffer from a lack of food for the most part during World War II. But I had known hunger, for my parents, my baby brother and I had traveled from the Ukraine to Den-

mark by a circuitous route that I still do not understand. By the time we reached Denmark, my little brother had succumbed to death and I had known many days and nights of fear and hunger. After several weeks of hiding in attics and basements, my family was given the opportunity to escape to Sweden.

As I sat rocking in a boat watching the steel gray waves undulate around me, I thought of the kindness we had been shown by our Danish hosts, even during our last day in their country. We had enjoyed a meal of smorgasbord sandwiches and hot cocoa in the basement of the church where we were hidden during the daylight hours. Later, the man in leather cap and trousers who led us to a barn in the forest treated us to a delicious holiday rice porridge. It was he who placed me on the boat and wished me well on my journey across the waters. With my father on one side and my mother on the other, I felt, if not warm, at least as safe as I could be.

After a time, my mother leaned in across me to place her head against my father's shoulder. Remaining vigilant to the insecurities surrounding us, my father looked constantly across the horizon. Like any child, after a short rest of my own, I began to look with interest about me. On the seat in front of me, was another Jewish family. I believe that they were also Ashkenazi *Jews, but I do not know for certain. As during our walk in the woods, the father of the family cradled the baby in his left arm, with his right hand placed over the baby's face.*

I have been told the journey would have been a short one. But to a young child, even that can be an eternity. Without the sound of a human voice, the incessant sound of the waves and the oars slapping against the water became almost unbearable. And then, in the distance, far off to the left, there came the sound of a puttering motor. While several of the people on our boat remained asleep, others anxiously looked to the source of the sound. With stern glances, the man who seemed to be in charge of our journey looked about with a finger to his lips and a shake of his head; clearly there was to be total silence.

I was old enough to understand the silent command and felt reassured by the gentle squeeze of my father's arm. In rigid stillness, we all sat wondering if the sound of the motor would increase in volume, indicating a movement of the craft toward us. At that moment, the baby in front of me whimpered slightly. As all eyes turned toward him, the man rocked the bundle in his arms and pulled it toward his chest. When the distant motor began sputtering, the eyes of the people on our boat shifted toward it. At that moment I saw a struggle between the blanketed shape in front of me and the man who held it. The motor gave one final gasp and I saw that the movement of the father's arms had ceased. As though he felt my eyes upon him, the man stared at me. With his mouth set in a straight line, the steel of his eyes uttered a stern command for me to maintain my silence.

Being a child, I was not certain what I had seen. After our boat reached Sweden, everything moved so quickly on the wharf that I did not have a chance to voice my concerns. And to whom would I have said anything? As quickly as we had arrived, the boat and its two-man crew departed. And, with the pressure of people greeting the boat, our fellow refugees quickly dispersed.

* * * * *

I was stunned. A shiver went through my body. I rubbed my arms and found I had actual goose bumps. I now realized that the dream vision I had had of the little Jewish girl crossing from Denmark to Sweden in wartime was of Miriam. The significance of the event was not in the danger she faced, but rather the impact it had in shaping her future life and career. For the renewal of *her* life had come at a very high price—the life of another child, sacrificed so that Miriam and the others in the boat could achieve personal freedom.

CHAPTER 14

Through every rift of discovery
some seeming anomaly drops out of the darkness,
and falls, as a golden link, into the great chain of order.
E. H. Chapin [1814-1880].

I was so disturbed by what I had read that I had to take a break. Rising, I walked to the windows so I could look down at the flowers whose beautiful fragrance I had been smelling. In a few minutes I was calm enough to return to reading Miriam's journals.

* * * * *

The years of my life in Sweden were bland. My family had been taken in by successful Swedish Jews, who were able to offer us rooms that had been used previously by their housekeeper and chauffeur. My parents and I spent most of our days within the small apartment, for without proper work, there was no money for shopping, eating in restaurants or going to the cinema.

Although my father maintained some practice of his religion throughout his life, I noticed that after we arrived in Sweden there were changes. Being a child I could have been wrong, but it seemed like the intensity and depth of his observance had lessened. On high holidays and other special occasions, we would gather with other Jews who had found safe haven in Sweden. Sometimes I saw that father from the crossing and I watched his son grow up during the years that our families lived in Sweden. But never did I hear reference to the baby in the pink knitted hat that he had held in his arms during our journey. Perhaps she never existed in the consciousness of others, but what I observed has remained with me throughout my life.

When next I sat with my tutor, I decided what to do with the life granted me. I might never be able to shake the guilt I felt as a young adult for failing to speak of what I had seen in that morning's dawn. But I did know I could, and would, explore the conditions that had brought about that tragedy. And so I began my exploration of the world of psychology.

* * * * *

Within a short span, I had found confirmation of my initial response to Miriam. She was definitely a person who lived life fully: She had put into practice her beliefs that the world could be a good place—if we would all invest ourselves in maximizing the opportunities we are given.

Although nothing I had read seemed connected to a motivation for killing Miriam, I was mentally and emotionally drained. Kneeling, I replaced the last journal I had analyzed horizontally to mark my place in the bottom bookshelf below the windows. Glancing around the room, I noted the shadows of trees in the garden had shifted and realized I must have been working for a couple of hours.

When I went down to the kitchen, I found Izzy preparing lunch and Joanne finishing a centerpiece she had made from cuttings in the yard. After I complimented her creativity, Joanne informed me she had received a call from Miriam's attorney. Both she and Izzy would be meeting with him the next morning. In addition, I learned that Samantha was authorized to move back into the cottage later in the afternoon. Not knowing what Samantha might be doing, The Ladies said that if they were not home, I was to enter the cottage using the key John Dias had given me.

Declining an invitation to join them for lunch, I returned home and had a quick bite of leftovers. Next I called Nathan. He, like I, had found nothing in the journals relating to Miriam's murder. However, in the most recent volumes, he had found that some pages had been carefully cut out. It appeared the removal covered a span of several months, indicating that Miriam may have self-edited. Since Samantha had been sleeping in Miriam's bedroom at the time of the murder and my vision gave no indication that the man in the scuba suit had detoured upstairs, it was unlikely that anyone but Miriam had performed the removal of those pages.

When it comes to murder, there is no way to predict what might agitate someone enough to cause them to take another's life. We were not through with the project. A motive of passion could still materialize from the pages of these journals. But in Miriam's case, I felt that the time and the mechanism of her murder made it unlikely that it was a spontaneous crime of passion. Financial or other gain remained possible motives for hiring a hit man. The careful planning and precise delivery of murder by garroting made it look like a professional job to me.

Since neither Nathan nor I had found anything worthy of a personal show-and-tell, he decided he would continue with his analysis in his home office and have someone from Hale Malolo drop Samantha off at The Ladies' cottage. With a clear afternoon, I expanded my notes on Miriam's life. Then, inspired by her methodical selections of news items she found pertinent to her work, I returned to analyzing my own files of newspaper clippings. It seemed almost eerie that many of the stories that caught her attention were ones I remembered from news broadcasts in my youth.

Mid-afternoon, the Kia saleswoman called to announce my Optima had arrived on the island. I could pick it up in a couple of days after it had been detailed. I felt like a kid getting their first vehicle. Would it be as fun as promised by the advertising hype? Would it be too silent for people to hear me coming? Would it have any get-up-and-go, or would I feel like the grandma-aged person I was becoming?

Between organizational details after the move and Miriam's death, I had not needed to do much driving since moving to Lanikai. But with the prospect of my new car at hand, I was determined to clear the decks on the home front. When Ariel died, I had great plans to put my legal affairs in order. With the passing of Auntie Carrie and the remodeling of her home, I had gotten side-tracked. The current discussion of Miriam's estate made it clear that it was time to make some end-of-life decisions for myself.

By the time Keoni arrived home, I had completed my personal filing chores, with the exception of a few projects that would require the attention of an attorney. In recent years, several of our family's lawyers have died, and while Nathan and I know several members of the Bar, their specialties do not align with the tasks I had in mind. So, knowing Izzy and Joanne would be visiting with Miriam's attorney in the morning, I thought I might follow up their meeting by inquiring whether they would recommend him.

With a pitcher of fresh sun tea, Keoni and I settled down on the back *lānai* for our nightly summation of our day's events. Like many law enforcement personnel, Keoni tries to separate his professional life from his personal. However, since I have known him through several years of his career—and he is trying to be sensitive to my new position as his girlfriend—I have noticed him making a conscious effort to bridge his two worlds.

Our mutual brevity rendered our catching up a relatively short process. On his side, it looked like he would be servicing quite a number of new clients in downtown Honolulu, which meant he would need to stay at his home in Mānoa from time to time. Therefore, we were both glad he had completed the security system for White Sands Cottage.

I shared my initial analysis of Miriam's journals and the news that The Ladies would be seeing Miriam's attorney in the morning. Then I considered how to broach the topic that was foremost on my mind. "I know we've only been together a short while, Keoni. But with everything emerging about Miriam's life, and the choices she made regarding her estate, I've been thinking it's time I got organized in the end-of-life department."

"I don't think it's ever too soon to think about issues dealing with one's passing," responded Keoni. "With no family of my own, I've been considering several non-profits to which I might leave my small estate. For me, the big decision is whether to choose an organization focused on education, or one directly involved in public safety. In the long run, an educated public actually reduces the need for the latter."

"You're certainly right on that issue. While Nathan and I have Brianna to consider, he's got an irrevocable trust to cover whatever monetary issues she and her future family may have. And since she'll be inheriting both this cottage and our parents' old home in Kāne`ohe, I'm thinking of designating a non-profit to receive any cash that might be left when I go. You know Miriam worked for UNICEF during part of her career and they're the recipient of the residual of her irrevocable trust, once the women die or move on."

"Does that mean they'll be staying in the cottage?" asked Keoni.

"It looks like it. I think they'll know for sure after their appointment tomorrow. But I doubt that Miriam's attorney would have told them to have Samantha move back in with them if that were not the case."

"I'm sure that's a relief to them—if anything can be—after Miriam's murder," observed Keoni.

We continued our discussion of our legal issues and decided to fill out forms to set up living wills. Then I said I would ask The Ladies for their perceptions of Miriam's lawyer. Fortunately, we had reached the point in our relationship where we knew we could rely on one another to make decisions in accord with our mutual desire to be released from this life if we had reached a vegetative state. We were lucky that with proper paperwork, the state of Hawai'i is reasonable about unmarried couples being able to make end-of-life choices for one another.

The next day, after what Auntie Carrie would have called a "constitutional walk," we returned from the beach for a little morning delight in the shower. Later in the morning, we embarked on our individual assignments for the day. With Keoni facing a couple of long days in town, we agreed he should spend the night in Mānoa and I would enjoy a girls' night with Miss Una. It reminded me of when my husband Bill had had twenty-four-hour duty. I have never minded having time to myself, and the current situation suited my desires perfectly.

With a thermos of chocolate Kona coffee and notebook in hand, I went over to Mokulua Hale, where I found Miss Una asleep under a plumeria tree.

"Well, I see you've got my schedule pinned down. I can't really let you into The Ladies cottage unless they are there. I left fresh water on our *lānai* and plenty of food in your bowls in the kitchen."

She looked up at me with complete disinterest and stretched before turning to lick her tummy. As expected, there was no response to my knock, so I let myself into Miriam's home with the key John had given me and went upstairs. With our beautiful weather, it was no surprise that someone had left a window open and the fragrance of Miriam's beloved lavender wafted up from the flower bed below.

As I again settled into the rocker, I pulled a small footstool over to hold my coffee, notebook and the last of the journals from the shelf below the window seat. Before beginning my work, I paged through my notes to put my mind in tune with Miriam's thoughts in the last volume I had reviewed the preceding day.

As I thought about her life as a young adult, I realized that growing up in war-devastated Europe had given Miriam a great deal of sensitivity to the challenges faced by many people around the world—even when they were well mentally and physically. Like so many people of her generation, Miriam had been forced to mature at a younger age than most of us after World War II. It made me feel rather spoiled.

Looking over my notes, I considered life experiences that Miriam and I had in common. A major component that separated us from most women in the twentieth century was that for very different reasons, neither of us had had children:

As time passed and my work assignments with the International Court changed, I had many occasions to review innumerable films recording Nazi life. It has always amazed me that the National Socialists never thought a day of reckoning would come when they enacted the Nuremberg Laws in 1935. I might have become numb to the vocabulary they used to excuse their policies for achieving lebensraum *and to attain and maintain a "pure" Aryan race. But, what* rassenhygiene *led to in their avoidance of* rassenschande, *cannot be denied: Their own maniacal need for keeping flawless records delivered the most damning evidence of their war crimes.*

I was appalled when I realized that if the Nazis had achieved world supremacy, any children my gentile husband Henri and I might have had would have been declared michlings. *In fact, for even marrying me, Henri would have been charged with* rassenschande, *a grievous crime against the state. And that was without his converting to Judaism (another horrendous crime in the eyes of the Nazis), which I know he would have done if I had wanted it—for he had no religious affiliation, or even a firm philosophical orientation.*

Once we knew I could not conceive a child, the issue of religion was a moot point. I do not know the level of my parents' religious practice in Russia, but growing up in Sweden we paid only superficial homage to the high holidays. And when I was young, we celebrated Purim, *a holiday mistakenly considered by some gentiles to be parallel to All Hallows Eve, since children usually dress in colorful costumes. Throughout my childhood, we nominally celebrated* Chanukah *within our home. After my Mother died and I had moved away from my father to attend college, it had been easy for me to slide into non-practice of any faith, other than my innate belief in the goodness of the human spirit, when it is nurtured.*

Miriam and Henri may have hoped for children. But when it was clear they would never have them, the poor and suffering of the world became the focus of their personal, as well as their professional lives. Henri's photos of conflicted regions and Miriam's work for several committees of the United Nations brought attention and resources to the plight of those who could not plead their cases directly to global leaders.

I continued to examine her life for anything that would have caused someone to want her dead. I found nothing she had done professionally to bring her into the spotlight as a threatening individual. None of the relationships she discussed indicated a level of animosity that would have generated hatred or jealousy...let alone a motivation for a coldly-calculated execution order. Beyond the absence of an individual or event begging to be red-flagged, Henri had been dead for nearly a decade and he and Miriam had been retired for several years before that.

With each journal, the pace of my reading sped up. Eventually I reached the bottom shelf to the left of the windows, where entries focused on her later career, spanning the 1970s. I may have been tired by that point, but I was riveted by many of her remarks. Besides addressing the end of the Vietnam War and the horrible discoveries of Pol Pot's Khmer Rouge regime in Cambodia, she noted uplifting events like Nixon's visit to China and the launching of Skylab, America's first space station. In passages long and short, Miriam laid down her inner feelings about the headlines that had dominated each of her days. Through her cogent and sensitive words, I continued to explore the world I had known as a young adult.

Around noon, I was finishing my thermos of coffee. As I reached over to set my cup down, I was startled to look up and see a hummingbird tapping its beak against a mullion paned window from its perch on the Hawaiian wedding flower vines that climb a trellis on that side of the house. As I shifted in the rocker, my knee edged into the bookshelf and dislodged several journals. When I bent to gather them, one fell open to reveal an envelope of fine linen paper.

Two lines of small print in black ink declared the contents' topic: *Some Thoughts on My Passing; Miriam Sofia Reznik Didión*. With a sharp intake of breath and shaking hands, I opened the thickly stuffed envelope and removed the personal stationery featuring wildflowers and birds.

* * * * *

If you are reading these words, I have passed beyond this plane of existence. I cannot, of course, know when or how I have made my transition. Nor can I begin to guess who you may be. Are you a stranger to me? Or, have we known one another? If so, in what capacity might that have been? Are you a professional acquaintance, or perhaps a long-time friend? Our single known bond lies in your reading of these words. Although you may eventually share my thoughts with others, it is with you *that I am now communicating.*

The most important thing I wish to share with you, is that regardless of what may have triggered my transition to the next plane, **,** *I have enjoyed a rich and satisfying life. There are, of course, events that arise in every life that cause momentary anguish and a desire that one's thoughts, words or actions might be recalled and negated. But that can seldom be done, and I have no desire to recall any of my words or actions.*

Therefore, I am affirming that both my personal and professional living has been fully satisfying. Indeed, my academic, marital, and career choices have all proven to be rewarding and as full of joy as I, or any other human being, could possibly expect within a single lifetime. As to other, less public activities I have undertaken, each has been considered with circumspection and executed with concern for achieving the greatest good for those who may be impacted.

Even within the unpredictable events in my life, I have been saved from the disasters that have devoured many around me. From the dim morning when I sat with my parents in a small boat watching the receding shores of Denmark, I knew that I was a person destined to have luck as my constant companion. Snuggled between the love of my father on one side and that of my mother on the other, I knew that I was safe, despite the fear I could sense in those who surrounded us.

Lulled by the lapping of water against the boat, I dozed through most of the short journey to safety. I awoke only once, sensing an intense wave of fear spreading through my companions. Looking to the family in front of me, I saw what would become the beacon of reality that guided the direction of my studies and career. In that fog-filled moment, I heard the sound of another, motorized vessel across the waters and then, to my horror, watched in slow motion as the hand of the father in front of me tightened across the face of the baby in his arms until the bundle lay limp like a sack of rags.

Frozen in fear and uncertainty, I knew that no one else had observed what I had. I closed my eyes and mind to the most terrorizing sight I had seen in my years of war. Through my family's escape from Russia, across Germany, and on to Jutland, I had never seen such savagery up close. No, this event was my first agonizing experience of war, my personal encounter with the inhumanity of mankind. Perhaps it was triggered by the most understandable of causes. As I discovered through the writings of authors like Pearl Buck, it was the need to sacrifice the life of one person in order to preserve the life of one's entire family, as well as the lives of everyone in the boat.

I have never told this story to the public, only vaguely citing my experiences as a refugee as a motivating factor in my inspiration to find a way to help bring peace to the lives of those who have suffered the most from war, torture and other mayhem. During studies in England, I met my beloved Henri, and was only too glad to leave my personal angst behind me. Together, we highlighted ways in which leaders of business and nations could work to bring greater harmony to people who suffer across what can be a truly beautiful world. Through Henri's camera lens and the writing and personal consulting I provided, we passed our years together in personal peace and harmony, despite whatever evil may have been circling around us.

Today, I sit in my chair at the top of a wonderful cottage in the beach home of my dream retirement. I am content with all that has gone before in my life and only wish I could have stretched my years of active involvement in certain things a bit longer. At this time, my only desire is to have a little more time to enjoy the occasional bird who visits at my window and the nearby blue sea and white sands.

In recent years, I have opened my home to two women who

join me in this phase of my latter-day living. In proper legalese, I have ensured that they, and any others who may have joined us in our haven, shall be taken care of until they too pass beyond the light of this good earth. Thereafter, any assets remaining in my estate shall pass to UNICEF to continue their vital work in the world.

As to how I may have passed, I cannot know at the time I am writing this. If there is something in my passing that is disturbing to you, let me assure you that I will have been at peace with myself and any fellow travelers at the time. Further, I would not have knowingly shortened my life—as I have many friends in the medical community who will ensure I have not suffered inordinate pain. And I could choose to go to a state like Oregon, if this journey truly became unbearable. If my demise has not been through peace-filled dreams in the night, perhaps I have simply been in the wrong place at a wrong time.

And so, having shared these thoughts from before my passage to another plane of consciousness, I wish you, my final reader, as pleasant and peaceful a life as I have known.

Good night and good morrow, Miriam

* * * * *

Again I was shocked. Miriam had confirmed that the infant in the boat had been smothered by its father. I sat in silence for a while. I pictured her sitting in this very chair looking out at the view she had loved so much. Growing tired, my eyes closed and I found my thoughts returning to the sepia-toned images of my first vision of Miriam as a little girl fleeing with her parents before the Nazis could snatch their lives from them. Then I pictured her as she might have been as a young woman, with her long, blond hair flowing around her as she and her beloved Henri danced at their wedding.

In a second, my eyes opened to the stark realization of the truth behind Miriam's death. For at the clearing of a throat, I looked up to see Samantha standing hesitantly at the door with a question forming on her lips. Previously, I had always seen Samantha's hair braided or coiled on the top of her head.

In bright sunlight coming in through the panes of the window between the tall bookcases, I saw her long, blond hair hanging straight down, well below her shoulders.

With the clarity of line and light, my mind flashed to the moonlit image of my horrific vision of Miriam's murder. From the doorway into the maid's quarters, my eyes again followed the moonbeam from the window to the blond tresses that spilled over the arm of the wingback chair. In silent shock I sat for several moments, simply staring at the real target of a murderer's hands—the mild-tempered woman standing before me. Here was someone who was supposed to come to a secure place, a veritable haven in which she could put her life in order and plan for the future. How on earth was I going to put what I had just realized into terms that would make sense to *her*, or either Joanne or Izzy...let alone to Lieutenant John Dias?

CHAPTER 15

...Explanations take such a dreadful time.
Lewis Carroll [Charles Lutwidge Dodgson, 1832 - 1898]

Difficult as it was, I think I managed to keep the shock I was feeling from showing on my face. Rising, I swallowed my desire to blurt out what I was thinking and said, "Uh, hi, Samantha. It's good to see you."

"I didn't want to bother you, but I know you've been working for a couple of hours, and I wondered if you'd like something to eat?"

"Oh, don't worry that you're interrupting. I think I've finished my work for the morning, and I really couldn't eat a thing right now."

I picked up my coffee carafe, notebook, and keys and exited the room. As we descended the stairs, I was grateful she did not ask any questions or try to make small talk. Entering the kitchen, I sought a closing remark with which I could quickly exit. I needed to get home immediately to call Nathan and John Dias.

"Have you heard from Joanne or Izzy?" I asked.

"Yes, Izzy called just before I came upstairs. She said they had good news and would be home to share it with me shortly."

"That's great," I replied. "Why don't you have them ring me after you've heard their news."

"Okay."

Walking home quickly, I thought about how it all made sense. Samantha had left her previous life to find shelter at

Hale Malolo. I wondered whether she had withheld something about her past life, with or without awareness that someone in her past might want her dead. In terms of sheer logistics, had Miriam not broken her leg the previous week, she would have been upstairs in her suite at the top of the cottage. Samantha would have been in the maid's quarters the night the man in the scuba suite entered the house.

As I entered the backyard, I again found Miss Una perched on the *lānai* table, intently watching Mokulua Hale, as she had before Miriam's death.

"What's up doc?"

She looked up at me for a split second and immediately reverted to her stakeout stare over the back gate. I moved on to my kitchen and picked up the landline to place a call to Nathan. After I apprised him of my theory about Samantha being the real target of the man in black, he agreed that I should call John Dias without delay.

Unfortunately, I got no answer at John's cell number and had to leave a message. "Hi, John. Natalie Seachrist here. No news to report on Miriam Didión's journals, BUT there has been a major development. Please call me ASAP."

Next, I called Keoni, but he did not answer. Knowing he was probably enjoying a working lunch with a client, I did not leave a message. I had barely assembled my own lunch of Caesar salad with crumbled boiled egg, when John Dias called.

"I'm so glad you could get back to me so fast."

"No problem, Natalie. I was consulting with Marty Soli about Miriam's autopsy when you called. Nothing unexpected to report on that front; her body will be released for burial in a day or so."

"That's good. I'm sure that will help to bring some closure to her Ladies, along with whatever the attorney has told them this morning."

"You know that the issue of 'closure' is overrated....There really is no such thing. Now, what's come up where *you're* concerned?"

"Listen John, before we get into that, I want to clarify that what I'm going to say is *not* connected to my vision, or anything I've found in Miriam's journals."

"Okay."

"And, if I hadn't already established some credibility with you, I don't know how I could tell you what I think really happened to Miriam."

"All right, Natalie. I'm ready for whatever you've got to tell me."

"Simply put, it was a mistake: Miriam was killed by mistake. *She* wasn't the target. *Samantha* was."

After a sharp intake of breath, John asked, "And what makes you think that's so?"

"Well, before this morning, I've always seen Samantha with her hair in a braid or coiled on top of her head. But today, just as I finished reading a letter Miriam had left in case of her death, I looked up to see Samantha standing in the doorway of Miriam's bedroom, with her long, blond hair flowing over her shoulders...and it just hit me."

"Hmm," said John, after a pause. "I'll have to say there's nothing about Miriam that has emerged to make her a likely target for a hit man. And it's clear that the killer *was* a pro. I've run all of The Ladies through preliminary background checks and nothing of interest emerged, except that Samantha's husband is a scumbag."

"I was pretty sure that was the case. She's never divulged anything about her situation, but she wouldn't have been at Hale Malolo unless she needed to get away from him."

"I'd better set some things in motion here regarding *him*. Then I think I need to hurry over your way for a little chat with Samantha about her marital situation. I'll give you a call when I've got everything set. Do you have the time to join us this afternoon? There's no telling what might emerge and I want you present for several reasons—if only because of how emotional she can get."

"That's no problem, John. I only left Miriam's because I was afraid to say anything to her without talking to you first. Call me when you've decided what you want to do."

"Okay. I'll check back with you soon. By the way, what's up with Joanne and Izzy? When was their appointment with Miriam's attorney?"

"This morning. They're due back now and I'm sure they'll be home by the time you get here," I replied.

Disconnecting, I quickly ate my lunch, checked Miss Una's supplies and tidied my hair and makeup. Knowing that some serious details regarding Samantha's life and marriage would be discovered that afternoon, I called Nathan to check on her mental state.

After telling him what was on the agenda, I said, "I know you can't divulge anything Samantha may have said in consultation with you, but do you think she's strong enough to undergo an in-depth interview about her marriage?"

"I can easily answer that question, since she's not a client. From what I've observed of her, both before and after Miriam's death, she is emotional and subject to abrupt tears, but she's really quite stable underneath. She's solid in her decision to leave her husband Luke and she hasn't been overly secretive about his being a creep who is a borderline criminal at best. Yes, I think you and John can interview her. But, I'm appalled to think that Miriam's death may have been a total mistake."

After John called to confirm a meeting with Samantha at Miriam's cottage that afternoon, I tried calling Keoni again. When he did not pick up, I left a message telling him what I had learned and where I would be for the rest of the day.

When I arrived at Miriam's cottage, Izzy and Joanne had returned from their morning of legalese and were excited to tell me about what they had learned.

Not knowing what John had revealed to Samantha, I thought I should be careful about what I said. "I see I'm ahead of John."

"Yes," returned Samantha, with her usual lack of detail.

"Why don't we all enjoy a cup of tea or coffee until he arrives," suggested Izzy, who was bustling about the kitchen.

"I had more than my quota of caffeine this morning," I said. "But I could go for an herbal tea."

"Hm. I know we've got mint and maybe chamomile as well," she offered.

"Okay, mint it is. I'm not big on chamomile, even though it's supposed to be good for you."

"That's for bedtime," said Joanne entering the kitchen with a laundry basket. "I'll have mint as well when I get back from hanging this to air," she said continuing on out the back door.

Within a couple of minutes, the four of us were seated at the kitchen table with Miriam's beautiful blue and white cups in hand.

"I don't usually use Miriam's good china, but I think we deserve a celebration," said Izzy, passing a plate of her yummy macadamia and white chocolate cookies.

"Good call, Izzy," affirmed Joanne. "We have a lot of reasons to celebrate, and Miriam is, of course, at the center of it all."

"It's so exciting. She always told me that I'd be taken care of," said Izzy with a big smile on her face.

"Yes. Caring for women and children was Miriam's great goal in life, and it appears she has continued to do so past her death," said Joanne. "We've been declared official tenants of Miriam's home for as long as we wish to remain. It even includes Samantha, since she was here prior to Miriam's death. The maintenance, upkeep and monthly operational expenses are paid for by the trust Miriam set up."

"That's wonderful," I said in honest admiration for what Miriam had done.

"I still can't believe it. I'd just come to join them," chimed in Samantha.

"New, or long-term, it didn't matter to Miriam. She wanted all of her Ladies protected, throughout their lives," explained Joanne.

"And whenever we have all left or passed, the remaining assets will be gifted to UNICEF," said Izzy.

I paused for a moment, trying to absorb the enormity of Miriam's generosity. "I'm so happy for all of you. It looks like her Trust encompasses everything Miriam believed in."

"Yes. Graças a Deus," said Izzy. "When Lieutenant Dias called about coming over, he said the Medical Examiner's office is releasing Miriam's body soon. So we need to start planning for her funeral or memorial."

"We're so glad you're here, Natalie. We sure would appreciate your helping us with the memorial arrangements," proposed Joanne.

"Could you join us for lunch tomorrow?" asked Izzy.

"I'd love to, but I'm waiting to learn if my new car is ready for pickup and I may not know about my schedule until the morning," I answered.

"That shouldn't be a problem," said Joanne. "We're still getting resettled, so just let us know if you can come, even if it's at the last minute."

"And if tomorrow isn't good, why don't you and Keoni let us take you out for margaritas and pūpūs at Haleiwa Joe's Seafood Grill at Ha`ikū Gardens at sunset tomorrow," offered Joanne.

Not knowing where they stood financially, I hesitated to accept the invitation.

"We even get a monthly stipend for entertaining," announced Izzy. "It begins immediately, so you'll be our first guests."

Obviously, with The Ladies' life-changing—or perhaps I should say *stabilizing*—news, the cost of cocktails and hors d'oeuvres would not be a problem. Therefore, I accepted the double-pronged invitation on the proviso that Keoni did not have a scheduling conflict.

At that point, the front doorbell chimed, and Joanne left the room. Evidently there had been some discussion of our meeting between John and Joanne. After greeting all of us, he immediately asked Samantha and me to follow him up to Miriam's rooms without explanation.

I was glad John had suggested interviewing Samantha at home. If there was reason to worry about her husband looking for her, it was good that we were not downtown at police headquarters. And, if she needed physical reassurance, I would be there to comfort her.

In Miriam's bedroom, John gestured for Samantha to sit in the rocker and for me to sit on a chair someone had set next to it. After placing a few items on the desk, he pulled its chair out for himself. Striving to put her at ease, he said, "Thanks so much for helping us, Samantha. There's no way of knowing how the tiniest piece of information might help us in solving Miriam's murder—let alone any other crimes that might surface as we go along. So I want you to feel comfortable to say whatever comes to mind."

She did not respond verbally, but nodded and stared straight ahead as she rocked slightly back and forth.

"While facts will aid us in running down the specifics, your inner thoughts and feelings can also be useful—not to mention any *suspicions* you may have."

"I'm glad to help."

He nodded. "Now, before we begin, is there anything I can get for you ladies to be comfortable for might be quite a while?"

"Uh, maybe some water would be good," I suggested.

He rose to go back down to the kitchen and I looked at Samantha. "Are you okay about this, Samantha," I asked.

"Yes, Natalie. With everything Miriam did to help all of us, I'll do whatever I can to help."

John reentered the room with a couple of bottles of water. Accepting one with a simple "Thank you," Samantha eased back into the rocker. I set mine on the floor beside my chair, where I was glad to see a box of tissues at the ready.

"Well, then, we'll get started," said John. "I'm going to be recording our talk, Samantha. That way I can concentrate on our conversation and not worry about taking notes."

"Okay."

As he prepared to turn on his voice recorder, John said, "I don't know where your information might lead the investigation. But I'll be grateful for anything you can give me now, or even after our conversation today."

Samantha nodded and he proceeded to enter the day, time, location and our three names. Although I had to be identified as being present in the room, we had agreed ahead of time that except for offering Samantha a supportive nod or pat on the shoulder, I would remain silent during her interview.

"To put things in perspective, I think it would help for you to tell us about how you first met your husband, Luke Turner."

Samantha looked confused. John looked calm; like he was accustomed to interviewees who said nothing. I wondered how I could help to get things on track.

"My husband? I don't understand. I thought you wanted to talk about Miriam."

"That's right, Samantha. Miriam is our focus. But I need to understand a little bit about everyone in her life. I know that you came to her home from Hale Malolo, where you sought shelter from your, ah, husband."

"Yes."

At the rate we were going, it would be midnight before John learned anything that might help his investigation. "Samantha,why don't you tell the lieutenant what you told me about Luke...and how you came here."

"It seems so long ago."

"I first met Luke, when I left a detox program.

John's left eyebrow went up, but he continued to write notes in his little blue book.

" I tried to make my parents happy most of my life, but college was very hard for me."

Samantha paused and drank some water. She then placed the bottle on the floor. Looking down, she began to rock slowly back and forth. With a sigh, she stared into space and resumed her recollections.

"I'd been sick as a teenager, and was late in getting a high school diploma. After a couple of years of jumping from job to job, I studied really hard to make it into the University of Denver. Even though I really tried, I barely made it to the end of my freshman year. Stubborn as always, I didn't want to confess that I couldn't keep up. But from the beginning of my sophomore year, I just kept slipping—one class at a time...one beer at a time.

"After two months, I had dropped all but two classes. That weekend I joined my roommate for a weekend party at a frat house. About the last thing I remember is her leaving with her boyfriend and me remaining at the party with one of his buddies. I don't know what happened after Chantel left. Eventually, I woke up at the door of a hospital's emergency room. Without any ID, I ended up staying two days until someone noticed I was missing. Finally my mother showed up to claim me.

"Unlike other weekends when I'd simply had too many beers, someone decided it would be funny to give me roofies. Not only had I never done any pharmaceuticals, I'd never even smoked pot. I'd done binge drinking before, but the combination I had that night was too much. The doctor told my Mom that my system also had an large amount of tequila on top of the beer and drugs. But the main reason I was in the hospital was because I'd been raped multiple times and had wounds of several types I won't mention.

"It was painful, but my parents recognized I wasn't college material—and that my drinking had gone beyond the weekend party scene. They insisted I go into rehab. After that, I went home and spent some time just chilling out. I'd never been much of a party girl in high school and was so embarrassed about all my failures that I didn't want to see any of my friends.

"I spent a couple of months of doing nothing except helping the staff with the cleaning and gardening. Then, one day, an unusual opportunity came up with a family in the neighborhood. I had always thought my good friend Bethany had lived a life that was fairytale perfect. She had been a cheerleader; was high school homecoming queen; and had gotten an associate degree in culinary science. Finally, she had married Doug Adams, her longtime sweetheart. Recently, she had moved to Japan where Doug had a job with an international conglomerate. Unfortunately, Bethany was lying in a coma after a car accident caused by her being drunk. Her husband declared he couldn't care for their son and was calling relatives stateside to find someone to assume responsibility for the boy.

"Since Doug's parents were on a mountainside in South America, Bethany's Mother was looking for someone to bring the child to her. I agreed to play escort to the toddler, and within a day I was in Hamamatsu, Japan. The next morning, I boarded a high-speed train to Tokyo. Travelling in any foreign country can be a challenge. Travelling with a two-year old is even worse. That day I was lucky to meet Luke, who insisted on our joining him in his limo for the trip from the train station to the airport. I don't know how I would have managed all the toys, bags, and the child without Luke's help.

"Mid-day I was on a plane with a boy I'd only met once as a baby. Because I was a Caucasian and an American, everyone thought he was my son and Luke was my husband. Except for the fact that my days of drinking champagne were over, I enjoyed the perks of flying first class. By the time we reached Honolulu, where Luke deplaned, he'd promised to call about a job he thought I might enjoy—involving lots of first-class travel, and no toddlers.

"That's how I became a courier for Luke. At first it was like the job I had performed for Beth's mother. My first assignment was to escort the teenage daughter of Luke and his wife Renée to boarding school in Switzerland. Their need may have been real, but on the way back, a man identifying himself as one of Luke's colleagues took me to an elegant lunch in Paris. As we parted, he gave me the traditional kisses on both cheeks, plus a surprise birthday gift for Renée that I was to pass on to Luke to on my return to Hawai`i.

"I believed everything Luke told me without ever checking on him, his business, or anything he told me. He described himself as the CEO of an international firm specializing in a wide range of services for clients investing in art, jewelry, and antiques that often needed to be picked up or delivered by courier. I asked why they didn't use one of the large international shipping companies. He said that would draw too much attention. His clients preferred discreet and personalized delivery services.

"It was all very exciting for several years. I got to go to exotic places and meet beautiful people. My parents thought I'd found the ideal job for a young woman without a college degree. I remained clean and sober, had a great wardrobe and frequently showed up for family celebrations. I even had money to give nice gifts to my relatives and friends.

"Since I was on the road most of the time, I never fully settled in one place. What I didn't keep at my parents' home in Denver, I put in a studio apartment in Pearl City, near the Honolulu airport. Although their Wai`alae Iki Ridge home was quite a distance from my apartment, I was happy to attend the gatherings Luke and Renée invited me to whenever I was in the Islands.

"The Turners' staff and guests were multi-ethnic, reflecting the nations of my overseas junkets. I often saw the same people at their home that I met when on assignment. At the time, it didn't seem unusual that Luke's clients repeatedly showed up on his A-list for social events. The one thing that did seem odd was that I made a lot of trips to a single destination in Marseilles, France. Since Renée was French, I thought the Marseilles clients might be friends of her family. As I look back today, it seems surprising that *all* the clients I met were men—since I've found that women are usually the purchasers of jewelry, antiques, and art.

"Several years after joining the team, I received a text from Luke informing me that Renée had drowned at their estate in Playa de Carmen in Mexico. I immediately expressed my condolences and asked how I could help him. Overnight, my schedule changed drastically. I was spending a lot more time in Hawai`i, where Luke often asked me to perform as the hostess of his social gatherings. In less than six months, I'd gone from being a minor member of an international organization to being the wife of its chief executive.

"I don't mean to sound superficial, but the escalating gifts of jewelry, sunset suppers on his yacht, and the supportive words of his friends, combined to make me feel I was the ideal answer to the loneliness in this successful man's life. Our wedding was a blink in a getaway weekend at the base of a tropical waterfall near Hilo. Although it greatly disappointed my parents, our only attendees were two of Luke's right-hand men who served as our witnesses.

"My fairytale in paradise lasted for eighteen months. Then I opened a drawer and learned everything I had assumed about Luke's life was a sham. The home on the Hill was heavily mortgaged and owned by the company, not Luke. Closed meetings held before and after the frequent parties were the real reason for the festivities. The final revelation about my marriage came when I asked about having kids. 'No way' was all he said. At first I thought his refusal related to his daughter Naomi; yet he never spoke of her after I dropped her in Europe.

"It was a sham of a marriage. After a while, keeping my hair, nails and wardrobe perfect became the focus of my life. One night, when I thought Luke was alone in his study, I went in with a tray of his favorite brandy and interrupted one of his private meetings. I'd seen the man before, but only in Marseilles. Within a minute, I was strong-armed out of the room and told I was never to mention seeing the man that evening.

That night I slept in a guest room. In the morning, dark and painful bruises had developed around my right wrist and arm. After two more incidents of his physical violence toward me, I heard a conversation between two of the newer servants. Neither of them, nor any of the staff, knew I understood Spanish and I did nothing to let them in on the fact that I knew exactly what they were saying. The man and woman were new to me. Evidently they were from the house in Playa del Carmen, where Luke's previous wife had died. I say *previous* wife because I'd learned she was actually his second wife.

"Between his growing hostility, and the servants' speculations about Renée's drowning, I was starting to doubt everything in my life. In fact, this incident marked a shift in both my marriage and Luke's overall affairs. After that point, I grew accustomed to his black moods and got used to periodic visits from the police. There were times when he must have been expecting them, because his attorney was present, but sometimes they just showed up and interrupted whatever event was going on. I'm glad to say that after a while, Luke seemed to lose interest in my existence and practically ignored me. Although he never grabbed or bruised me again, I didn't feel safe and I knew I couldn't go on with things as they were.

"One afternoon I delayed going home after a hair appointment, so I could call my mother. When she learned the truth about my life, she told me to get out without delay. Since my Dad had recently had a stroke, and Luke had threatened to kill me if I ever left him, I decided not to go home. Later, while Luke was at a business dinner, I went through my drawers and closet to see what might be valuable. In the morning I parked my car on a side street in Chinatown and pawned some jewelry. Then I checked into a low-end hotel. Sitting on the sagging bed, I picked up a phone book and called several government agencies. That's how I learned of Hale Malolo.

"There's not much else to say. Except for abusing me, I never saw Luke commit a crime. But in addition to lying about his property, when I tried to pawn them, I learned that a lot of the jewelry were fakes."

With a disgusted shake of her head, Samantha reached for the water bottle sitting beside her chair.

CHAPTER 16

The real voyage of discovery is not in seeking
new landscapes but in having new eyes.
Marcel Proust [1871 - 1922]

Clearing his throat, John Dias said, "Samantha, you may not think you've told me anything important. But we both may be surprised by where your information leads. I know it's been a couple of years since you were couriering for Luke, but do you remember any of the dates when you travelled on behalf of him?"

"Yes, I do. I've always kept my day planners. Until recently, they've been reminders of the high points in my life since leaving home. There's one interesting thing I can tell you about my trips for Luke. A lot of them were on days following holidays. Not the big ones like Thanksgiving or Christmas, but St. Valentine's Day and the Fourth of July. One year, it was on January third."

"That's interesting because some of those days are low-volume travel days with the airlines. Also, ones like Valentine's coincide with the giving and receiving of gifts," observed John.

"I guess you're right. There were a lot of times when the first-class cabin wasn't all that full."

"Also, you've said you met a lot of people through Luke. I think it would be good to have you look through some photos I can access. It won't be right away, because I need you to provide me with a list of your travel dates.

Samantha nodded and took a sip from the bottle of water in her hand.

With Samantha's story told, we got up and headed downstairs. After the prolonged look John gave me, I knew he agreed with my assessment of Miriam's death being a mistake. Earlier I had wondered how to handle my realization that Samantha, and not Miriam, was the intended murder victim. Now I wondered how *John* would handle making an official declaration of that possibility.

"How do you feel about continuing our conversation in the living room," John asked Samantha.

"That's fine, but I need to run to the bathroom for a minute."

As she turned toward the powder room in the hallway, John pulled me to the side. "When I have Samantha's information, I'll check in with Federal agencies like the F.B.I. and I.C.E. I'll look also look into anyone that comes up on the radar of Interpol, Europol and the French National Police. Like I told her, depending on what I learn, I'll be checking back to see if she recognizes anyone those agencies turn up from the underworld of major criminals. After that, I'll have to decide whether there's a need for her to go into witness protection."

I nodded. "Despite the information that's emerging, you've done a great job of keeping everything calm and smooth for Samantha."

"Well, it's not like I'm new to this. The key was simply to get her talking about a topic she was relatively comfortable with—herself."

When we arrived in the kitchen, I could tell that Joanne was curious about Samantha's meeting with John and me. Trying to remain non-intrusive, she continued rinsing dishes and casually mentioned that Izzy had gone to her niece's home to check that everything was ready for the family's return that night.

"You must be wondering what's happened, Joanne" said John. "I'm sorry Izzy isn't here, but it's time to look at where the evidence is leading in the investigation of Miriam's murder. I'm going to lay it all out when Samantha joins us, but the short story is that it's looking like Samantha may have been the intended victim."

Sagging against the edge of the apron of the sink for support, Joanne moaned and said, "Oh, no. Don't tell me Miriam died by mistake! How could anyone confuse Miriam with Samantha?"

John shook his head in understanding. "I'm sorry to be so abrupt, Joanne. But Samantha will be back in a minute. I think we should all sit down, either here in the kitchen, or in the living room so I can explain everything."

I had been trying to control my natural tendency to blurt out my thoughts, but now I rushed into a spur-of-the-moment response. "I think it would be best to go into the living room. We can spread out a bit, and there'll be room for Izzy to join us."

"Good idea," said John.

Joanne looked solemn as Samantha came into the room. The former teacher quickly put on her take-charge smile. "You all look kind of tired. Why don't we go into the living room until Izzy gets home. I've got some fresh grapes and a fresh pitcher of iced tea with lemonade."

Soon we were all seated. Obviously John wanted to set a casual tone and refrained from bringing out his recorder. He did, however set a small black notebook and pen on the coffee table. Seated in a wingback chair, he looked at each of us as he cleared his throat. At that moment, the front door opened and Izzy dashed into the room breathlessly.

"I'm sorry to be late in returning. I didn't want to miss out on whatever you have to report, Lieutenant."

"You haven't missed anything, Izzy."

Quickly sitting beside Samantha on the couch, Izzy dropped her handbag and a carryall on the floor beside her and turned to face John.

Speaking slowly and evenly, John engaged us in his findings. "As you all know, there have been very few leads for the CSI team, Ken`ichi, or me to pursue. There's simply nothing in her life—at least in the last forty years—that we can find to have provoked such a crime.

"It is true that her initial work with the United Nations dealt with crimes stemming from the Second World War, but she was a minor cog in a huge wheel. She had no public voice; she was merely working behind the scenes as a researcher and analyst. The only other issue we examined in her professional life was her serving (with her husband Henri) as an expert witness in a few international high profile cases of human rights violation. This could have made her a target. But in all probability, anything arising from those cases would have occurred years ago."

"What about her finances? This home is worth a lot, and both she and Henri had successful careers. They must have acquired quite an estate," said Joanne.

"That's all true. But as you and Izzy learned this morning, all of Miriam's assets are in an irrevocable trust. Aside from providing for your living in this home, and a small gift to one of Henri's cousins, the balance of the trust goes to UNICEF to benefit women and children around the world," replied John.

Continuing, he moved toward the bombshell announcement of the day. "One of the reasons I wanted Natalie to be here today is that she has some results to report from her time analyzing Miriam's journals. And while it's not directly related to their contents, I think you'll understand her concern when she's explained what she may have uncovered." With that brief introduction, he turned to me with a cautionary look.

As always, I tried to reveal my thoughts without discussing my vision. "Do you all remember when we were chatting at Keoni's party, and Joanne made the remark about Miriam's only vanity being her hair—maintaining both its color and length throughout her life?"

They nodded blankly. "Well, when I looked at the scene of her death, it was that long, blond hair that I saw from outside the room. And today, when I was finishing my morning of reading her journals, I looked up to see Samantha standing in the doorway of Miriam's bedroom."

I took a deep breath. "And what did I see? *Her* long, blond hair."

I paused for a moment. "Think about the night of the murder. There were no lights on in the room where Miriam died, only muted light coming in the windows from a cloudy sky. The murderer would have looked into the room as I did. And what would *he* have seen? The long, blond hair of a fairly slim woman seated in the room where he'd been told his target would be.

"But what if Miriam *wasn't* the target in the first place? She wasn't even supposed to be in that room. It was to have been Samantha's room until Miriam broke her leg and couldn't get up the stairs to her suite."

There was dead silence. Even though Joanne had known the gist of what would be revealed, my words produced tangible disbelief among all three of Miriam's Ladies. In the middle of the heavy pause, John's cell phone rang. After glancing at caller ID, he signaled that he needed to take the call and left the room.

Reaching forward to refill our glasses, Joanne said, "That was the only thing Miriam was vain about—as she aged, she refused to give up keeping her hair long and blond."

Unconsciously, I touched my strawberry blond hair that has had more than a little assistance from bottled colorant through the years. I wondered if I too was being vain...

At that point, Samantha had returned to the dazed pose she had on the day she discovered Miriam's body. Seeing her glazed eyes and rounded posture, I was not sure how much of what John said would register with her. When he returned, I could tell he had absorbed the state of everyone's mood and knew he needed to address the situation quickly.

"I'm sorry for the interruption. This development has to be a shock to all of you, but I thought it was important to take that call."

"That was Sergeant Ken`ichi. He's completed a cursory look at Luke Turner's record. It's worse than I first thought, Samantha. You said the man has grabbed you on more than one occasion. Would you describe him as a violent person, in general?"

Finally looking up, Samantha said, "Well, uh, yes he was. Following the incident where he jerked me around because I'd seen that man in his office, there were more occasions when he got rough and only stopped when someone walked in on us. That was enough to make me pay more attention to his moods and behavior—you know, because I was afraid something would set him off again. Like I said, that was a turning point in every aspect of our lives. He seemed to be on edge all the time. Maybe he'd always been that way. Before then, things seemed so wonderful and I thought he was just being controlling to make sure everything was perfect for us."

"You've mentioned social gatherings and private meetings with some of the men you'd met in Europe. Did any of *them* seem violent to you?" John continued.

"No. But thinking back, it seemed like *they* were kind of afraid of Luke too."

John contemplated that for a moment. "Is there any reason you can think of that would have motivated Luke to want to have *you* killed?"

"Not that I know of. Of course, I don't know whether he was ever violent with Renée or if he might have been involved in her death in some way."

Except for the dialogue between John and Samantha, the room remained still. After adding to his notes, he asked, "You've said that his previous wife, Renée, died in Mexico. What do you know about Renée? Did you ever see any documents about her life…or her death? Perhaps her maiden name?"

"No, John. I only know she was from Marseilles."

"Hm. Well, I'll be checking in with Interpol about Luke's European business operations. I'll add checking on her background to my list of inquiries."

"Except for Luke's not wanting me to see that man from Marseilles, I can't think of any reason why he'd want to hurt me. I never saw anything really bad happen—like a drug deal, or murder or anything. But he did threaten to kill me if I tried to leave him. That's why I went to Hale Malolo. I would have left the Islands, but I didn't have much money and I was afraid to put my folks in danger. I mean, he knows who they are and where they live."

"I guess the next thing we need to explore is how he found out you were here, in Miriam's home. You don't have a car of your own, do you?"

"No. Since going to Hale Malolo, I've been relying on other people for transportation."

"And who's been driving you, Samantha?"

"Well, first there was the lady who took me to the shelter. I don't remember her name, but I'm sure Nathan or one of the staff would know who that was. Then there's Nathan. He brought me here to meet Miriam, Joanne and Izzy; then he helped me move in. After that, Joanne has done most of the driving, the few times I've gone anywhere."

"Have you been back anywhere near your home, in Waikīkī, or maybe out near the airport?"

"No."

Breaking her silence, Izzy said, "What about the day we were out in Kailua. You were with us, Natalie. I needed to do some shopping, and thought it was a great way to introduce you and Samantha to our community. We parked the van and walked all over Kailua Town. We went so many places. I don't think I could name them all. There was Times Coffee Shop for breakfast, and Heritage Antiques, and clothing stores, and A Cup of Tea, and Whole Foods."

"That's right! I ordered some items to be catered for Keoni's party," I remembered.

"With all that activity, I doubt you would have noticed anyone paying attention to you, what you were saying, or whether they followed you back to the cottage," commented John.

"No. You're right. We were having too much fun to notice anyone around us," replied Izzy.

"I sure wasn't thinking about Luke. After all, I wasn't anywhere near where he or his friends would be," Samantha added.

"But there's no way of knowing how many people he might have put in place to look for you. O`ahu isn't that big, and if he thought you were still on the island, it would have been easy to stake out shopping areas where you might show up."

"That's why Hale Malolo tells the women not to go out—at least not until it looks like they're safe. Even then, only when they're with people who can be on the lookout for any sign of trouble. I just didn't realize I was in any real danger," said Samantha with a sniffle.

"That's how it is in these situations. Most people never think they're going to be the target of an attack. There's no way of knowing *how* you were discovered. It won't do any good to worry about the past. We simply have to make sure no one can get to you again."

"Should I give Nathan a call and see if Samantha can return to Hale Malolo tonight?" I asked.

"Okay, Natalie. That may work in a pinch, but I want to put her in a more secure location as soon as possible," said John.

As Izzy and Joanne comforted Samantha, I went to the kitchen for my phone. When I returned, I found that John had gone out to his car for a moment and that The Ladies were helping Samantha pack her bags again. As I entered the maid's quarters, I found Joanne staring out the window as she folded some of Samantha's clothing while Izzy and Samantha were in the bathroom assembling the young woman's toiletries.

"There's been a change in plans," I began. "Hale Malolo is full for at least tonight, so I think you'll be coming to White Sands Cottage with me."

"Okay, Natalie," replied Joanne. "We'll finish up here and meet you and John in the living room in a few minutes."

When I re-entered the living room, I found John scribbling something in his notebook. I apprised him of the situation at Hale Malolo and told him of my idea to take Samantha home with me.

"That's probably better than the shelter. There are so many people coming and going from a place like that. We don't know how the initial discovery of Samantha's location came about. And with all the police vehicles coming and going in this area, I doubt that Luke and his associates know Samantha has returned to Mokulua Hale. Also, we're going to take her out the back gate, so no one will see her from the front of either property. I've got a call into a couple of sources for securing a safe house, and I'll let you know if there's going to be a change tonight. Is Keoni at home now?"

"I'm not sure, but he's due back by this evening."

"I'll give him a call and fill him in. We need to make sure the front of your house is secure, and if he's not back yet, when I walk you and Samantha over, I'll check to make sure everything is clear before I take off. You do know where Keoni's gun safe is? Do you have access to it? And can you fire a gun?"

"Yes. Yes. And yes. And even though I don't like firearms, I know how to use them."

Within a short while, Samantha was settling into my guest room and John was on his way back to police headquarters to put several things in motion. I called Keoni to catch him up on our status.

"JD's given me an overview. I can't believe what a day you've had," said Keoni. "I'm glad my work has wrapped up and I'll be home fairly soon."

"Are you sure?" I asked. "We're fine here, with the new security system and all."

"Yeah," he said sarcastically. "Like there's no concern there's been a hit man in the neighborhood—or that Miriam was murdered by mistake. Whatever triggered the hit hasn't been dissolved by a little error like that. In fact, whoever's behind all this may be all the more motivated to see the job completed!"

I could not argue with that line of reasoning. After promising to remain indoors until he got home, I turned to planning an early cocktail hour with heavy *pūpūs*. Thank God I had discovered the fabulous deli offerings of Whole Foods and the freezer was full of several items I had been looking forward to sampling.

Startled by her quiet footsteps, I greeted Samantha's entry to the kitchen with a small squeal. "You'll have to forgive me. I get jumpy when I think I'm alone and someone startles me."

"I'm sorry. I didn't mean to frighten you."

"It's not you. I'm jumpy because Keoni expressed concern about our safety until he returns. Why don't we go into the family room to enjoy some nibblies and a little liquid refreshment. I think we've earned it, don't you?"

"Anything you'd like is fine with me. I'm still so shocked by everything that I'm numb."

As we sat down on my folks' old *koa* furniture, I thought about the other times when it had brought me comfort. The cushions may have changed every decade or so, but the old sofa and chairs still held the warmth of family.

Samantha and I may not have had much to celebrate—except for the fact that she was alive—but we were soon well nourished and somewhat relaxed after drinking a bottle of Asti Spumante. When Keoni arrived, I was glad things were winding down without any disturbing events or revelations. Exhausted by the day and lulled by the wine, Samantha declined dinner and retired to the guest room for the night.

Keoni and I opted to enjoy the view from the back yard during our twilight supper, so Samantha had my cell phone number programmed into the bedside handset. That way she could speak to us without exposing herself.

Once again, I was spared from routine cooking by the continuing gifts of fresh produce and frozen delights. In addition to ample salads, I served some of the appetizers left from earlier, with a bottle Pinot Grigio. I was feeling no pain by the time we finished, but still appreciated the back rubs we shared before drifting into dreamless sleep in one another's arms. Around eleven thirty, I heard the soft buzzing of Keoni's cell phone. Within a minute he had hung up and turned to tell me John would be taking Samantha to a safe house in the morning.

The next concern was my new car. Not knowing how

long it would take to finalize everything with the dealership, I called Miriam's home in the morning. The Ladies and I decided to follow through on plan B for a sunset cocktail hour at Hale`iwa Joe's at Ha`ikū Gardens. Before Keoni and I left to pick up my car at the Kia dealer on Nimitz by the airport, Samantha had called The Ladies to thank them for everything they had done for her and departed with John.

Since Keoni was free until the afternoon, I had him remain with me for the introduction to my new means of transportation. While I am comfortable with basic computer and cell-phone technology, some of the accessories on the Optima were difficult to absorb within so short a time.

"The cool thing, Natalie, is that when you're in doubt, you can call for help. If it's a personal problem, you call me with the hands-free cell phone setup. If you're lost or having trouble with the car's equipment, you can use the on-board navigation and communication system to get help."

"That's easy for you to say. I still have to remember which buttons to push for any of the systems to work."

"Well, are you comfortable enough to drive home? We can play with all your new toys when I get there this afternoon."

Feeling slightly offended, despite my own salvo at myself, I pushed back. "Of course I can drive myself home! I'm not *that* much of a basket case."

I could tell the saleswoman was not sure how serious our banter was, but she clearly wanted to complete delivery of the car and get me off the lot. After making sure my seat was adjusted for my height and the steering wheel for my arm length, Keoni gave me a quick kiss and waved goodbye. I did not have any challenges on the drive home. And since there was nothing on my schedule until sunset, I buzzed by Mokulua Hale to show Joanne and Izzy my new wheels.

After expressing their congratulations on my pearlescent car, we talked about scheduling some all-girl day trips when Keoni was busy with clients. When I arrived home, I realized I had forgotten my garage door opener and had to get out of the car to manually key the control panel on the wall to allow me drive into the garage. Opening the kitchen door, I found Miss Una waiting by her empty food bowl. The expression on her face announced I was again remiss in my duties. I certainly had a lot to share with Anna. Maybe I should plan a play date for Miss Una at the condo with her mother Mitzy.

CHAPTER 17

All is flux, nothing stays still.
Plato [427 BCE - 347 BCE]

My current to-do list was rather short: feed the cat; make a smoothie for me; and, return calls to anyone who had activated my voicemail since I had left the house. Aside from that, I had several hours in which to beautify myself for a night out with my sweetheart. With all the commotion regarding Miriam's death, not to mention the semi-final touches we had been putting on the cottage, we had not had time to enjoy the offerings of our new community. Following our outing with The Ladies, I figured we could take in a movie or maybe some live music at one of the local bars.

The rest of the afternoon passed by easily, while I enjoyed a soak in the whirlpool bath, followed with a facial and recoloring of my mani-pedi. I cannot deal with blue or green nail enamel, but I put a dazzling copper color on my toes instead of my usual vanilla frost. Slipping into a vintage Tori Richard's dress, I pulled back my hair with a couple of antique amber clips. Then I fastened strands of Auntie Carrie's chunky coral at my throat and wrist.

Overcoming his initial disappointment that I had not waited to bathe with him, Keoni gave me a whistle in greeting and completed his toilette in record time. With him dressed in his birthday shirt and a pair of tan chinos, I felt we made a stunning couple. I had not gotten this dressed up since the last governor's inaugural ball. Keoni might not be in a tux, but he looked very handsome and I was anticipating a wonderful evening.

By the time we arrived at Haleiwa Joe's Seafood Grill at Ha`ikū Gardens, we had devised a strategy to depart politely from The Ladies early. This was the first time Joanne and Izzy had done anything social since Miriam's death, and we hoped they could enjoy the evening. As though on a military operation's timeline, the women were already seated in grand style with slice of a view of the gardens at a table that would put us in the front row for singer Ellsworth Simeona's performance.

Inviting us to sit, Joanne gestured toward a platter of coconut shrimp accompanied with the restaurant's signature sauce of plum and honey-mustard, plus a pitcher of margaritas.

"Not knowing how you like your drinks, I ordered both plain and salt-rimmed glasses," she declared with a grin.

"I hope you'll like the *pūpūs* I ordered," said Izzy. "In addition to the shrimp, there'll be Thai fried calamari and ahi spring rolls."

"It sounds divine," I responded, growing hungry at her recitation.

"Shall I do the honors?" offered Keoni, nodding toward the pitcher.

As Joanne and Izzy smiled with pleasure, Keoni served our drinks, with me being the only one who chose a glass without salt. Just as he finished pouring, another platter of food arrived. After Izzy toasted us for our assistance in meeting the Ladies' latest challenges, Joanne made another in honor of Miriam. By the time we were half way through the delicious food, Ellsworth Simeona had taken the stage.

With his delightful sense of his audience, quick-paced delivery of Hawaiian lyrics, and a falsetto many women singers would envy, we were hooked for the duration of his performance. Any thoughts of our going somewhere else that evening evaporated. After a while, Keoni ordered *tempura* crab rolls, blackened *`ahi sashimi* with pickled ginger, and a ranch dipping sauce. To accompany this, Joanne ordered another pitcher of margaritas and some hot sauce.

During an intermission, Joanne leaned over and said, "I know we were going to discuss Miriam's memorial, but I don't think it's going to work tonight. Why don't you come for tea with Henri's cousin Juliette Young tomorrow and later we can discuss Miriam's service."

"That's a good idea, Joanne," I replied. "Maybe she'd like to help with the planning."

"We already asked her what she'd like us to do, and she didn't seem interested in anything except what she could have to take home with her," said Izzy.

"Once she's at Mokulua Hale, she may feel more connected to Miriam," suggested Keoni.

"I hope you've both followed what Miriam wanted you to do—select some things you can enjoy in memory of her before Juliette takes anything," I said.

"At Christmas, Miriam gave us jewelry she had acquired during her years of travel. But except for a couple of shawls and sweaters, none of her clothes would fit me," said Izzy, with a giggle in her voice and a tear in one eye.

"What about you, Joanne? You're taller. There must be at least one *mu`umu`u* that would fit you?" I suggested.

"To be honest, we just haven't been able to go through anything yet. Why don't you come over early tomorrow and help us look through Miriam's things before Juliette arrives?"

I agreed and we continued to enjoy the music a while longer. After Keoni escorted The Ladies to their mini-van, we drove to Kailua Beach Park for a romantic stroll before the ten p.m. closing time. At that hour, parking near a beach access was easy. We locked my purse and Keoni's wallet in a hidden compartment, then took off our sandals and headed toward the water. With his pants rolled up mid-calf and my short dress, we thoroughly enjoyed the soft wet sand between our toes and the star-studded sky overhead.

Pausing to hug me closely, Keoni asked, "So, what do you think of life in windward O`ahu?"

"I love it! I don't know how I ever thought living in Waikīkī was Island living."

"Honey, you were never in Hawai`i long enough as an adult to get bored with the fun of living in one of the world's best tourist spots! Plus you had Nathan's family and your friends to remind you of *real* Island living whenever you were in the mood to venture outside Waikīkī."

"I guess you're right. And since I've retired, there's been so much going on. First I was getting settled into my condo full time. Then there were Ariel's murder, Auntie Carrie's death, and remodeling the cottage...not to mention Miriam's death."

"Well, things are settling down now. We'll soon get our lives into an enjoyable groove. With your new car, you can zip into town to see Anna and your other Waikīkī chums whenever you want. Before long, we'll start taking advantage of all the great things there are to do on O`ahu, as well as the neighbor islands. You'll see; everything is starting to come together, sweetheart."

* * * * *

When I arrived at the back door of Miriam's cottage in the morning, I found Izzy scurrying around to make sure everything was ready for the upcoming eleven-thirty tea time.

"Except for making the tea itself, everything is laid out in the dining room. The china looks so lovely with the flowers Joanne cut this morning. I hope Juliette feels as though she's sharing a part of Miriam's life," said Izzy.

I smiled and tried to support her positive expectations. "Of course I hope you're right, Izzy. But you told me Juliette was Henri's second cousin and that she's a lot younger than Miriam. If they only met a couple of times, she may not relate to Miriam's life at all."

"I know we need to be careful not to judge her. Miriam's death may have caught her by surprise. Imagine waking up one morning and being given a trip to Hawai`i to learn about a relative you barely knew. Miriam may have been a part of Juliette's mother's life, but she probably wasn't part of Juliette's," added Izzy.

Concurring, Joanne said, "You're right. After all, her mother was Henri's *younger* cousin who came to the U.S. as a war bride when she was barely twenty years old."

"Well, it seems to me that you've done all you can to make her feel welcome. Even if she didn't know her cousin, Juliette might treasure some of Miriam's belongings and pictures of the life she and Henri built together."

In the short time we had, Joanne and Izzy took me on a tour of the house. As we went through Miriam's suite of rooms, Joanne commented on her friend's recent bout of household organization.

"You know, it's almost as though Miriam knew she didn't have long to live. She'd been going through all of her pictures, keepsakes and files. It seemed like every week she was sending off packages of her memories to former colleagues and people like me, whom she'd met briefly during her travels."

"Several packages went to the United Nations Archives and some to non-profit organizations," added Izzy. "Miriam told me they contained photos and notes on work she'd done through the years she had been with them." Obviously proud of the woman she had known as an employer and friend for decades, she concluded, "And I know there were also newspaper articles and film and videos of her speeches."

Working quickly, we soon completed going through the closets, dressers, and other drawers that held Miriam's personal belongings. I was glad to help Joanne and Izzy select items they could enjoy throughout their twilight years.

"I think you both know I've had to go through this process myself in the last year, so I know how hard it is. You mustn't feel like you're invading Miriam's privacy or being greedy or self-centered. She wanted you to have some of her favorite things, so you'll remember her with joy."

When the front bell sounded, everything was ready for the day's main event. After introducing herself to the middle aged, and pursed lipped woman, Joanne said, "And this is Natalie Seachrist; her Aunt Carrie was your cousin's neighbor for many years."

The woman smiled blandly and shook my hand limply. As

the three of us moved into the living room, I saw Juliette surreptitiously wipe her hands on the sides of her double-knit suit. Joanne politely tried to interest her in the albums Miriam had assembled so carefully throughout her life. There was little response and clearly no interest. Fortunately, Izzy arrived with her teapot in hand, saving us from an embarrassing gap in conversation. Inviting us into the dining room, Izzy tried to make each of us feel the warmth that was the hallmark of every visit to Miriam's home.

For the most part, I sat back and watched as The Ladies tried to engage Juliette in explorations of Miriam's life. But their efforts were to no avail. The only responses they garnered were incomplete answers to their questions about Juliette's family...delivered through a pinched mouth. The woman's dull eyes scanned the room, but gave no indication of appreciation for anything she saw. At least she was polite enough to thank them for their hospitality, but she might as well have been eating week-old packaged goods and tea brewed from used tea bags.

After Juliette declined a second cup of tea, Joanne looked across at me, registering that she had finally gotten the unspoken hint. "Perhaps you'd like to see some of Miriam's personal things that have been left for you to consider taking home."

"Yes. That would be good," responded Juliette, with the first sign of enthusiasm since her arrival. "I thought maybe I could use her suitcases for whatever I might, uh, take home."

"That's a good idea. Those bags carried Miriam around the world so many times, it seems appropriate for you to use them to carry mementos from her life back to your own home," agreed Joanne.

While Izzy cleared up our tea things, Joanne and I escorted Juliette through the rooms of Miriam's cottage.

"Would you like some of the albums Miriam filled through the years?" I asked, as we passed the living room.

Juliette's response was simple and summed up her visit in general. "I think not. They wouldn't, um, mean much to my family."

Most of her other comments fell into categories of, *rather old-fashioned, more suited to Hawai`i`*, and *doesn't harmonize with my style.* After expressing her clear disdain for books, she asked pointed questions about Miriam's lack of "good" jewelry and furs. In a mere hour, she had departed with a single suitcase that I was sure would be on its way to the Goodwill soon after her arrival home. Juliette's foraging through the decades of her cousin's life had yielded little: two framed pictures with signatures of political heavyweights; a hand-tatted lace table cloth with matching linen napkins; one Italian inlaid burl wood tray; a small leather jewelry box with a few vintage pieces of costume jewelry; and one Chanel handbag.

She was gone and we were glad of it. Without a word, the three of us turned from the front door and walked in a straight line to the living room, where we spread out to enjoy Miriam's well-used and comfortable furniture.

"I don't think she was pleased with the reading of the will," said Izzy.

"That's putting it mildly. I think that if Curtis Leighton had seemed like a light-weight attorney and UNICEF wasn't named as the primary beneficiary, that woman would be contesting the trust and everything in Miriam's will," mused Joanne.

"I don't think she even cares whether there's a memorial," lamented Izzy.

"She might not have said much, but I know you're right about her disapproving of Miriam's legal arrangements," I said in accord with both of them.

"If she'd managed to get her hands on the estate, you know there wouldn't have been anything left for the causes Miriam cared about," summarized Joanne.

"I agree," I declared firmly. "And despite her self-control, I saw a seething anger behind that mask of cool politeness. If she'd been given free reign, you would have seen an even colder person. As author C.C. Benison might have said, we would have found that Henri's cousin is an 'unrepentant bossy boots' when put in charge of anything. I can't imagine what it's like to live with her."

"We should be glad she's disinterested in both Miriam *and* Hawai`i. I'm sure we'll never have to see her again," said Joanne firmly.

"Heaven forbid. No wonder Miriam never spoke of her. So, since none of us had much to eat with our tea, let's raid the refrigerator," proposed Izzy.

I never argue with the offer of good food. And good food is all that ever emerges from the kitchen that is now Izzy's for life.

"I've been doing a little harvesting in the garden, so let's make a large salad," suggested Joanne.

I had a feeling that all of our emotions were as worn out as Joanne's hands must be from the continual weeding of her beautiful rows of produce.

"And there's leftover *`opihi* sautéed in butter and garlic from yesterday's lunch," said Izzy.

"It sounds delicious, as are all of your offerings. I must say I'm feeling rather spoiled with all the food I've been receiving from you and Nathan. Today's luncheon menu is making me feel guilty. I really should do something special for Keoni tonight!"

"I may have a solution for that. You know that even with nutrients added, our sandy soil isn't great for growing fruit. But my strawberry baskets are doing just fine, so we'll have a couple to top off our lunch and you and Keoni can have some for your dessert tonight."

"Oh, thank you, Joanne. Keoni's been experimenting with making ice cream. The berries should go perfectly with his latest creation, a variation of the Horatio's burnt cream recipe from Kincaid's Restaurant. If he's got the proportions right, we'll have some for you to sample tomorrow."

"Now that's a treat *I* can look forward to," said Izzy with anticipation.

Within the warmth of our growing friendships, the unpleasantries of the morning had evaporated. It was time to approach the issue of planning Miriam's memorial.

"I'm disappointed Juliette has no interest in joining in

your plans to honor her cousin," I said, sighing. "But at least she won't be here to interfere in whatever you wish to do."

"You're right about that, Natalie," said Joanne, joining me in an honest appraisal of the situation. "Looking at everything *you've* been through recently, where do you think *we* should begin?"

Since our last conversation, I had been thinking about the complexities of a life celebration for a world renowned person. "Why don't we take a page from my mother's playbook and write out a list or two," I suggested.

"Excellent. That's right up my alley," said Joanne getting up to get a yellow legal pad from a nearby drawer.

I paused to try and organize my thoughts. "It's usually the family of the deceased that makes the arrangements."

"You're right," said Izzy. "Whenever I pass, even though the people in my family belong to several churches, they know I want my service held at Kawaiaha`o Church, and, of course, to be buried beside my darling Freddy. I've even written out a list of the hymns, songs, and *Bible* passages I'd like included in my service."

"You're the dream parishioner of every minister who performs funeral services," I responded with a laugh.

"And then there are people like me. I have no plans beyond my purchase of a cremation policy. Whenever I pass, I'm glad to know I won't be responsible for any pollution. I don't really care about anything else. Have a party for me if you'd like Izzy, but that's all. I'm just a 'dust to dust' kind of girl. I have no expectations of an afterlife, but I don't want to leave the planet worse than I found it."

At this point, both women turned to me.

"Given what everyone has done to the earth in the last two hundred years, I think you're expecting too much," I countered. "As to my own beliefs and desires, I guess I'm somewhere between the two of you. My parents raised Nathan and me with Jewish and Christian principles, although I don't have a particular church and haven't gotten around to thinking about a memorial service.

"Regarding Miriam, I'm happy to offer a few suggestions, but I don't want to interfere with anything you may have planned to do."

"You're not interfering with anything," assured Joanne. "We've been too upset to do any serious planning—especially since we thought Juliette would be giving us some input. But like you said, we should be thankful for her *non*-participation, if she's not going to make a positive contribution."

Continuing on, I said, "Well, unless someone else materializes soon, the issue of family is moot. As to Miriam's friends, it's not like she belonged to a synagogue or large organizations, so I think you can feel comfortable about making all the decisions."

They nodded in unison.

"One thing you may need to research is Jewish customs," I said.

Busily writing, Joanne replied, "That's true. We need to learn how those customs are applied to couples of mixed background, since we should refer to Henri in some way."

"I know that as a child she was raised in Judaism. Then, as a young adult she drifted away from religion. I saw a *menorah* in the dining room," I observed. "Did she light the candles for *Chanukah*, or observe any of the high holidays?"

"Not as long as I've lived here," answered Joanne.

Izzy looked into the distance for a moment. "I remember her lighting the *menorah* for *Chanukah* the first couple of years I was here. Maybe that's because there was a Jewish family living next door that they enjoyed having dinners and outings with. The first year they all spent *Chanukah* together, and everyone gave presents to the couple's little girl after lighting the candles and saying prayers. I can still picture the little *keiki* smiling when she opened the box of child-sized gardening tools Miriam gave her."

Returning to the topic at hand, Izzy asked, "Once we've decided on the details of a ceremony, who should we invite?"

I thought about her question for a moment. "How about looking in her address book? If John Dias has hasn't released it yet, I'm pretty sure he can give you a copy so you can notify her friends and colleagues about her passing and invite them to whatever celebration you plan. Next, what about social media? Did Miriam have any listings on popular networks?"

"Oh, no. In spite of all the people Miriam knew around the world, the Internet didn't interest her," said Joanne shaking her head. "When I was setting up a couple of pages for myself, I talked to her about it. She said *Everyone who needs to find me, already knows how to*. You know, even the landline is an unlisted number because she didn't want to be bothered by solicitors. She certainly didn't make it easy for someone to breeze into town and try to look her up."

Izzy's eyes lit up. "Once a month, she called someone at the U.N. to see if there were any letters, packages, or calls for her. "I don't think I mentioned that to John Dias. It's been about a month since her last call and I should notify him about that."

"Good idea. She probably called the same number each time, and if it was at the U.N., it's most likely got a New York area code. John can check that by looking through her long-distance records," I suggested.

"And what should we do about the people who knew Miriam, but aren't able to come to Hawai`i?" asked Izzy.

"Hmm. That is a serious issue. Maybe instead of merely placing a single obituary in the *Honolulu Star-Advertiser*, you should place several in European newspapers…with details of the work she and Henri did," I suggested.

"Excellent," responded Joanne. "You've mentioned social media, Natalie. Maybe we should set up a website where we can display Miriam's obituary and some pictures documenting her life's work.

"And we could take pictures of her life in Hawai`i…of Mokulua Hale and the garden and even the beach," suggested Izzy eagerly.

Joanne nodded. "You've been looking at her journals, Natalie, is there anything you think we could put on display or some of her words that we could quote?"

"Oh, yes. You know Miriam inserted copies of newspaper

accounts of her speaking engagements. You could make digital versions of them with some of her comments as captions under the pictures. Even though John Dias doesn't need Nathan or me to do any further work on them, I'd like to finish going through the rest of the journals."

Looking at the clock on the mantle, I said, "There's still time for me to get to a few today. And, if it's all right with you, I'll come back and finish tomorrow. Also, I'll ask Nathan if he's found anything we can use for memory boards at the memorial, or to digitalize for the website. With Miriam's focus on Stockholm and Post Traumatic Syndromes, and the universal rights for women and children, it would be a poignant memorial to her life—and perhaps provide a wake-up call to people in pivotal positions across the globe."

"That would be wonderful," said Izzy with a wide smile on her face.

"What's next? I know planning food and beverages for the guests won't be a problem with Izzy in the kitchen. I guess the last major issue is Miriam's ashes. I think one of you told me Miriam wanted hers put next to Henri's, but you never mentioned where that will be."

Joanne sighed. "That's something we're up in the air about. The urn with Henri's ashes is up in Miriam's closet. I don't whether they can be put in a Jewish cemetery. If not, I guess we could scatter both of their ashes at sea."

She paused to look down at her notes. After glancing at Izzy, she concluded, "Oh, Natalie, thank you so much for helping us get organized. There's a lot to do, and this list puts it all in perspective."

The three of us smiled through our sorrow and I went upstairs to continue looking into the inner life of Miriam Didión. After a final session on Saturday morning, I emerged from Miriam's bedroom with a notebook half filled with quotes and a stack of photos for Joanne and Izzy to go through. Despite the purpose of my work, I felt invigorated—and all the more grateful for the stage of life I had reached. I only hoped that at the end of my days, I could say I had had a meaningful life.

CHAPTER 18

Through every rift of discovery some seeming anomaly
drops out of the darkness, and falls, as a golden link,
into the great chain of order
E.H. Chapin [1814 - 1880]

This proved to be a day for finalizing several projects related to Miriam and her Ladies. Keoni had cleared his calendar to be available for the arrival of the custom security screens he had ordered for Mokulua Hale. As usual with contractors and deliveries, there was no telling when the product would actually arrive. When I came home at noon, Keoni was happily playing with some of the new electronic toys he had obtained for Hewitt Investigations. After kissing him, I zoomed into the kitchen to prepare tuna wraps with some of the produce Joanne had given me. As the can of fish popped open, Miss Una arrived to announce she wished to join us for lunch.

After we ate, I was torn between doing something meaningful—like unpacking the last couple of boxes from the move—or just lazing around and reading for a while. Even the second option seemed too much like work, since I would be choosing between a book on Shànghǎi during World War II and a recent release from a world class chef.

The dilemma of time management was solved for me when Keoni emerged from the office with his cell phone ready for transfer to my hands.

"It's JD. He'd like to schedule a meeting this afternoon. He's got Miriam's initial autopsy report and the CSI overview."

I took the phone. "Hi, John. Sure, today's fine, but you know I don't do well with the technical, and um, more gruesome side of your job."

After assuring me he simply wanted me to skim through some written text, we agreed to meet in an hour. I knew that the main purpose of his visit was to consult with Keoni, who would be reviewing everything in depth.

"What about your delivery, Keoni?" I asked.

"As long as one of us can sign for it, we're copasetic. It's too late to begin the project today. The most I would do is compare the delivered items with my plans, and maybe verify that I have the supplies I need for the installation."

"Well, let's have our meeting with John here in the kitchen. I don't want The Ladies to see us on the *lānai* and realize what we're looking at. That would definitely be *un*cool."

In a short while, I had laid out a tray with refreshments on the counter. In addition to the end of last week's bagel order, I was ready to offer John a glass of our most recent batch of sun tea, this time with a kiss of orange and clove.

With time to spare, I joined my partner in the living room. He was sitting on the recliner, scrolling through some apps on his new tablet. Above him sat Miss Una, who was peering over his shoulder clearly entertained by the bright colors and moving objects.

Lying down on the sofa facing him, I said, "I see you're well supervised in your endeavors to conquer this century's technology." He laughed, and I considered broaching a topic that had been on my mind for some time. "Keoni, I've been meaning to ask you something ever since Ariel was murdered."

Knowing I was launching into a serious topic, Keoni closed his tablet and looked at me.

"I don't mean to cross into areas I shouldn't. I was just wondering how things are with John. I mean, he sometimes discusses his cases with you and I wondered how that works. How it compares to when you were actually partners at HPD?"

"Well, that's a sensitive issue. You know I'm no longer a team player. I've got no official standing. I have to be careful about a lot of boundaries. JD tells me what he chooses to. If he wants something specific, I try to accommodate his needs—without crossing the line. That means I have to be vigilant about what I say, and where I say it."

"I was just wondering if you, mm, discussed me with him at the beginning of Ariel's case?"

At that point, he got up and crossed the room and set his tablet on the coffee table. After gently lifting my legs, he sat down on the sofa next to me. He rubbed my feet for a couple of moments before responding, "Well, honey, you and I weren't involved at that point—beyond our friendship of several years. When he asked me about you, I verified that you were trustworthy and a straight shooter. Beyond that, he already knew your brother from a couple of cases he'd helped out with previously."

"What about my, ah, dreams? Did that come up in conversation?"

"Not until you spilled the beans yourself, that day at the ME's Office. I'll admit that with your confession of living at the site of your grandniece's death *and* having visions, JD did call me for some clarification. But he's got an open mind. I've never known him to laugh at anything that will move a case forward. I think I've told you that he and I worked with a couple of psychics whose gifts proved helpful in more than one case."

He paused and reached for my hand. "Satisfied? You're sure? It sounds like you've been holding on to your questions for quite a while."

"I guess so. But you know I'm not a psychic. My concern is that I don't want to get in the middle of your relationship with John, working or personal."

"Hey, you should know him by now. He's easy going…at least until something really gets under his skin. Then, look out. You do not want to be on the receiving end when he's angry."

When John arrived, we moved into the kitchen. After each of us had a glass of tea in hand, we settled in with pen and paper at the ready, for a long session of brain storming. Keoni and I sat across from each other. John stood with his back to the sink, explaining how we would approach the task at hand.

"Since Miriam had no known family members, her attorney is serving as her personal representative. In that position, and as her friend of many years, he's granted HPD permission to share her autopsy report and anything else we choose, with anyone who can help solve her murder. I'm here to ask both of you to take a look at the results of our investigation to date, in case you see a lead we may have missed.

"I'm still waiting on toxicology reports, and input from the U.N., but you already know it's looking as though Samantha was the intended vic. I've sent out inquiries to the FBI and a couple of European agencies, but with such a clean scene, the case is not looking good. If we can't find a link to Luke Turner, we may never solve this case."

Glancing at Keoni's tablet, he said, "You know the drill. I'm going to ask you to look everything over, just like when we were partnered on a case. I'm glad to see you're prepared to track anything you question. From you, Natalie, I need something else. In addition to anything factual that pops out, I want you to tap into what I think is called a woman's 'feeling nature.' Does our reporting *feel* complete? And of course, the major question is whether we have described what you *saw* in your vision?"

Without further introduction, John opened his briefcase and began pulling out files. I was glad the kitchen's new lighting was excellent and that the small table allowed us to pass papers back and forth easily. With the images of Miriam's murder at the forefront of my memory, I tried not to think about the steps that had been taken by the Medical Examiner's Office to produce the report I was about to read. Surely it could not be worse than reading Ariel's. Lost in my thoughts for more than a couple of moments, my awareness slowly rejoined the conversation in the room.

"So, I think a dozen strippers would be the ideal entertainment for *your* next birthday, what do you think, Natalie?" asked Keoni.

"Uh, sure...*What* did you say?"

"Obviously you're lost in the clouds. What're you thinking about, dear?"

I licked my lips and thought of how to balance my fear of things gruesome with my desire to help. "I'm glad to share my perspective. But technically, I think *you're* going to have more to offer the investigation than I will, Keoni."

John smiled at my words and began handing files to Keoni. "Like I said, all input is appreciated. Just tell me if there's any discrepancy between what you envisioned and the words I'm putting in front of you. And remember, no detail is inconsequential. I don't expect you to understand all that you're going to read today, Natalie. But the last time we did this, you were able to verify there was an earring missing from your grandniece's effects. Maybe between the autopsy and CSI reports in Miriam's case, you'll notice something that's missing, out of place, or has been added to the mix."

As he picked up the multiple CSI report files, Keoni glanced at the title pages and began reordering them. Setting the stack of folders to his left, he began working slowly and methodically, making notes on his tablet. In turn, I received a single file containing an overview of what must be an exhaustive autopsy report. Fortunately, I had been promised it was *sans* photos. I sat staring at the folder for a moment, unable to face the cold words that would summarize the brutal murder of a gentle woman.

I sighed and opened the folder. With several crimps in the file fastener at the top, it looked like several pages had been removed. I was glad, because that meant John had indeed pared the material, leaving no disturbing images—except for the ones I personally brought to the table. The first page looked like Ariel's report had. It was a form with the abbreviated basics of the case: the victim's surname, given name, date of birth, age, and sex; the pathologist's accreditation, title, and identification number; date and time of death; date, time and identification number of the autopsy.

Following an assessment of Miriam's general heath that pointed out the ancillary finding of her intensive heart congestion, was the Final Diagnosis. It was presented in an outline form that was almost staccato in its verbiage. *Cause of Death: ligature strangulation...believed to be wire...1/16th to 1/8th of an inch in width and ranging in tinsel strength from 274 to 303 ksi...rust-colored abrasion-like furrow crosses the anterior midline of the neck, just below the laryngeal prominence, approximately at the level of the cricoid cartilage...almost completely horizontal, with slight upward deviation from the horizontal, towards the back of the neck...abrasions and petechial hemorrhages, anterior neck, and above and below the ligature furrow...petechia hemorrhages on face, upper eyelids bilaterally and conjunctiva of inner eyelids, circular in shape, 1 mm in circumference, resulting from bleeding of capillaries... cyanosis...venous engorgement...*

Perhaps it was not unusual that I best understood the beginning and end of the report. I certainly knew Miriam had been strangled by ligature—garroting by piano wire. And since she had discussed congestive heart failure, it was not surprising that Dr. Soli noted its presence in the autopsy. Beyond that, the interim discussion was too technical and gruesome for me to fully comprehend.

Between the material I had been reading and images that kept resurfacing from my vision, I was mentally and emotionally spent. Setting down the folder, I picked up my tea and drained half of the glass. I looked up to see that Keoni was already three quarters of the way through the folders in front of him. John was seated with his pen and notebook, patiently looking at me with an encouraging half smile.

"I'm sorry for your obvious discomfort, Natalie. I don't know if the technical details have put any aspects of your vision into perspective. But perhaps it will help if I answer any questions that may have occurred to you."

Stalling for time, I wiped my mouth with a napkin and tried to organize my thoughts. "I don't know that I understand the material well enough to formulate any questions. I guess the bottom line is that Miriam's murder was quickly accomplished. The man who killed her knew what he was doing.

With such a skill set, even I know he was a professional."

John nodded. "That sums it up."

Keoni looked up as John continued his summary of Miriam's death. "The perp was positioned at exactly the right distance and held the ligature at the precise angle to have the fastest impact. Sick as it is to say, that meant Miriam suffered no more than fifteen to twenty seconds. In about eight seconds, she suffered a brain hemorrhage from the lack of blood flow. Within a few more seconds, the pressure on her heart caused it to stop. We know this from the deeply imbedded imprint on the neck and the small amount of blood in the stomach."

Setting down the file he had been reading, Keoni reached across the table and squeezed my hand.

"If you're up to it," said John to me, "I'd now like you to look over the CSI reports, at least a couple of them."

I nodded bleakly as he separated three files from the pile Keoni had just read. "You'll find some pictures of the crime scene here. But, uh, Miriam is not in them."

"Okay, John." I opened the first. "Do you care about the order in which I look at them?"

"Not at all."

"In that case, I think I'll open all of them at once."

"Fine."

In the first file were photos of the room shot for overall context. I fanned them out and set them all to the right of the file. In the next were images of the room progressing from mid-range to close-up perspectives. Finally, there was a diagram of the entire room secured on the left side of the folder and a summation of contents on the right. As I paged through the photos and accompanying reports, I scanned the headings and major points.

"You know, Natalie, you're a visual person—no pun intended. Now that you've glanced through the ME and CSI summary reports, why don't you take a moment to close your eyes and put yourself back into the scene, *prior* to the crime…just as the perp was walking into the room. Are you with me?"

"Yes."

"Okay, you're standing in the doorway looking into the room. I want you to freeze that image in your mind."

He paused for a moment. "Now open your eyes and look through the photos of the crime scene."

I followed his directions and began sorting through the pictures, beginning with the long shots.

"With your vision at the forefront of your mind, think about *anything* in the photos, or inventory of the room's contents, that seems different, missing, or out of place."

I leafed through each image in the first two folders slowly. Then I closely examined the overall drawing in the third folder, before looking through the inventory of furniture and accessories. When I had completed that task, I looked up to find that John had turned on his voice recorder. "Good. Now I want you to close your eyes again and picture the room...this time as you saw it *after* the murder...as the perp has turned away from Miriam and is exiting the room. Are you there?

"Yes."

"Now open your eyes, and look at the first long shot of the room again. This time we're going to try an experiment." Reaching into his briefcase, he pulled out a tablet of paper and removed one sheet. "Take this and place it over the bottom half of the picture. Look across the top half, from left to right. Next, flip the process and put the paper over the top half and look at what's revealed on the bottom half. Now, place the paper over the right half of the image and look over the left side from top to bottom."

At each command, I carefully followed his instructions. During the third puzzle game, I finally saw an anomaly. "John," I cried out. "There *is* something different. Miriam's cane. I remember that the crook was facing the chair when the perp entered the room. After he killed Miriam, he put a couple of strands of her hair into a plastic bag and looked around the room. Then he bent over and picked up the cane which must have fallen during the murder. When he put it back against the wall, it was facing *away* from Miriam, like it is in the photo the CSI team shot. Joanne noticed it as well, but I forgot to tell you."

"Well done, Natalie. That's one thing we now know he touched in the room. And *that* is certainly worth a re-examination."

After my realization about Miriam's cane, Keoni raised a few questions for his former partner to run past his Interpol contacts. Although we invited him to stay for cocktails and appetizers, John rushed off to The Ladies' cottage to pick up the cane before returning to headquarters to intensify his efforts to bring the perpetrator to justice.

As we bid him farewell, I felt somewhat as I had the day before, as Izzy, Joanne and I bid Henri's cousin Juliette *adieu*. Although there was no animosity between us and our departing guest, I was glad to be at the end of the meeting.

Before leaving, John had repeated that while no direct links had been found between Luke Turner and Miriam, Luke was suspected of smuggling artifacts and drugs. As the man had once said to Samantha, "Whatever the client wants the client gets." From what John had discovered, the breadth of his international "transfer" business may have included the moving of people, as well illicit goods. His ties to drug trafficking meant there was a likely connection between him and people who possessed the necessary skills to kill Miriam by garroting.

No one wanted to think of her murderer going free and unidentified. But at least Miriam's desires for the use of her assets were coming to fruition. We already knew that her Ladies would live out their lives comfortably and that the bulk of her estate would be channeled through UNICEF. An interesting fact that had emerged was that Miriam had already disposed of Henri's family home in the south of France. The small manor house had been converted into a conference center for use by the United Nations and other agencies focused on strengthening communication among disparate peoples needing to reach accord...surely something that would have irritated cousin Juliette.

The next several days passed without requests for input from HPD. Keoni was able to install the security screens at Mokulua Hale. With Izzy and Joanne trained on the finer points of the hard-wired portion of their home's revised security system, the installation of the last solar lights in the yard was the only thing needed to complete the security overhaul.

My task of reading Miriam's journals was at a dead end, so I began researching day trips in windward O`ahu. Some mornings Izzy joined me on my morning walks on the beach—with or without the supervision of Miss Una. The police might be uncertain about the potential for solving Miriam's murder, but my fearsome feline remained on alert. Each evening I found her sitting tall and proud as she continued to monitor Miriam's Ladies from our *lānai* table.

Once Keoni finished his work for The Ladies, he turned to our last big project at White Sands Cottage—the hot tub. First he completed the concrete slab on which it would sit. By the afternoon of the spa's delivery, he had planted the cuttings Joanne had provided from the Hawaiian wedding flower vines that reached up to the windows of Miriam's suite. The following morning, I assisted him with the final phase of the project. My wardrobe for the occasion consisted of a one-piece swimsuit with purple orchids splashed across a black background, a sun hat and a liberal slathering of sun block on my chest and arms. While Keoni tested the chemistry of the water, I was supposed to adjust the jets for optimal impact on our backs and legs.

"You should join me, Keoni. In case you haven't noticed, I'm a lot shorter than you and I can't really set the jets for you."

"Well, honey, we're not always going to sit in the same places. We can't begin to guess the size of future guests. Simply position the jets mid-way for now and everyone can adjust them to their liking."

Standing back to evaluate his handiwork, Keoni shook his head. "I know what I forgot. Unless we want several tables around the spa, I think I should put in a small wall of interlocking pavers at the back, for our towels, beverages and other things."

"How about having a wall *and* a couple of tables? Maybe a set of stackable tables? And I think we need a couple more chairs for people who might not want to get in the tub, but want to sit near it."

"Sounds like another run to Costco."

"The Ladies should be getting a call to pick up the lights they ordered for their pathways and garden. Maybe I could tag along with them and see what we can use?"

"And just how are you going to get several tables and chairs for us, plus their purchases into the mini-van, Natalie?"

"Why don't we drive over in your truck the day they go? That way you can advise them if there's anything else they need to complete the lighting?"

"Good idea. Knowing you, our own list will have grown far beyond the tables and chairs."

In a few minutes, Keoni joined me in the spa with a bottle of Laurent-Perrier Brut Champagne. Soon we had other things to occupy us than discussing patio furnishings. After planning another romantic rendezvous at midnight, I beckoned for Miss Una to join us. Since she's comfortable sitting beside me when I'm in the whirlpool bathtub, I had hoped she would enjoy this new level of companionship. Sadly this form of familial togetherness was not to be. The intensity of the bubbles and jets were too much for her. She moved back to the edge of the patio, where she methodically washed the spray off her whiskers with her paw.

As we chuckled at the cat's disdain for our new outdoor activity, Joanne appeared at the gate between our properties. Trying to be polite, she waved broadly to make sure she was not interrupting anything too intimate.

"Come in and see our latest home improvement project," Keoni called out.

After wiping her hands on her gardening pinafore, she opened the gate and came across the grass with a small basket.

"A couple of goodies for you two," she said, setting the basket on the table before approaching us.

"You know me well, Joanne. I love goodies of all kinds," I replied, lifting my glass of bubbly.

As I motioned toward the wide rim of the hot tub, she sat down and ran her hand across the foam created by the jet closest to her.

"I'd offer you a glass," said Keoni, "But unfortunately, we just finished the bottle."

"Don't worry about it. After I freshen up, I'm going to enjoy some Beefeater gin and with a splash of tonic and a squeeze of Meyer lemon juice. Speaking of which, you'll find a couple of the lemons, a few heirloom tomatoes, and a cucumber in the basket."

"Oh, yum," I said with anticipation.

"In addition, I've got some wonderful news about Samantha. I don't know if you've heard, but John Dias just called me and it looks like Samantha can come out of protective custody."

"That's great," responded Keoni. "We've been out here for a while without any telephones."

"What happened?" I asked. "How can he be sure she'll be safe?"

"You know JD wouldn't be doing this if there were any question about Samantha's safety," countered Keoni.

"The big news is that Luke Turner's body was found at Diamond Head Beach Park last night. With him gone, JD sees no reason for Samantha to have to remain in hiding. Right now, I've got to go in and tell Izzy. We haven't done anything with the maid's quarters since she left. I'm going to put fresh sheets on the bed and towels in the bath…and maybe arrange some flowers to welcome her home."

With that, Joanne turned and strode purposely back to the Mokulua Hale. Keoni and I sat quietly for a couple of moments, digesting our individual responses to the update.

"Well, like you said, Keoni, John wouldn't be doing this if he was uncertain about Samantha's security."

"Mmhm. Nevertheless, I can't wait to hear the details of this new development," said Keoni with a serious look.

CHAPTER 19

Praising what is lost makes the remembrance dear.
William Shakespeare [1564 – 1616]

Later that day, John called to say he would be dropping in. Almost immediately thereafter, he showed up at the back door.

"Glad I caught you. I figured you'd like to know what's been going on the last couple of days," he said.

This time he accepted our offer of hospitality. Before we settled on the back *lānai*, Keoni grabbed a couple of bottles from his special stash of Weasel Boy Ale. I poured myself a glass of Sterling Pinot Grigio and plated some smoked salmon, fresh mozzarella cheese and garlic pita crackers.

"Mm, this is a *great* end to another busy day," said John with a broad smile.

"I agree. And think about the calories and alcohol content we're saving with this fine brew. It almost makes up for the rest of the calories we're consuming," added Keoni.

"With the miles showing on my pedometer during this case, I don't think I'm going to worry about today's little snack. Besides, look at all the meals I've been missing."

"Don't say we haven't offered," I interjected.

"So what's been happening? Since you haven't called, I figured you must have been busy keeping all the balls in the air," said Keoni with obvious curiosity.

"Well, there's been a lot of activity. But to be honest, we have no expectation of a resolution any time soon. About all I've been doing is dotting the "Is" and crossing the "Ts." The big news is that instead of our having one unexplained corpse, we've now got two. And, still no solid lead on the perp, *if* the same guy killed both Miriam and Luke Turner.

"It's probable that Samantha's husband put out a contract on her, and Miriam died by mistake. But thinking it and proving it are two different things. We've got nothing linking Luke Turner to Miriam's murder. Now that *he's* dead, I doubt we ever will. Since we found no sign of a conspiracy to kill Samantha, with Luke gone there's no reason for her to remain under wraps with us or go into witness protection. That's why I've dropped her back with The Ladies next door."

"So where did Luke's body show up?" asked Keoni.

"Two nights ago, a 911 operator got a call from a couple of kids who'd snuck out for a romantic midnight rendezvous at Diamond Head Beach. Instead of scooting around any cops who might discover their after-hours use of the park, they ended up calling the cops when the girl stumbled over Turner's corpse."

"Hardly what they expected from their clandestine date," I said.

"You're right about that. Although Ken`ichi and I had already pulled our regular day shift, we were called back in when Detective Sybil Carter realized there was a possible connection to Miriam Didión's death. So there we were, pumping java to keep our eyes and minds open enough to absorb the case at hand. And COD? There were no gunshot wounds, nor abrasions or other marks on the body that couldn't be attributed to his time in the ocean."

"That doesn't mean much in this age of clever murder," responded Keoni.

John nodded and continued. "Obviously we'll have to wait for the ME to tell us the cause of death, but we think he'd only been in the water a few hours. However, he'd departed from the home he was renting on Wai`alae Iki Ridge a day earlier. When we arrived at the house, we found no one on the premises, and no personal possessions. There was no food in the refrig or cupboards and no sign of habitation in the bedrooms or bathrooms. Just the shell of a high-end rental with basic furniture plus accessories, dishes, and cookware."

John paused to take a long sip of ale and eat a cracker piled with salmon and cheese. "We found some brochures and paperwork in a kitchen drawer, so we were able to track down the property broker. We learned that Luke had given an abrupt notice to vacate two days earlier. Evidently he had hired a cleaning company to put the place in pristine condition to minimize the ability of anyone to follow him. Everything was so highly polished, I doubt we would have found any forensic evidence."

"Sounds like Luke had been through the drill before," observed Keoni.

"Despite its condition, there were a few suspicious issues associated with the house. First, no one at the leasing agency had spoken to Luke personally. However, the correct lease number was cited in the nighttime call. But with executive lessees, it's common for underlings to make such notifications. Second, the groundskeeping contractor received an equally impersonal announcement of termination of service. Again, since the contract number was provided, there was no reason for the company to question the call or keep a copy of the voice message. Third, the servants Samantha told us about are nowhere to be found. We're checking airline manifests for the last couple of weeks, but who knows if we'll come up with anything. We know that at least two of them are Mexican nationals, and you know how slow Mexico is to extradite anyone to the U.S. in a capital offense case.

Keoni snorted and nodded knowingly.

"We found Luke's Merc Cabriolet parked on the road to the beach. His wallet and some miscellaneous papers were in the glove compartment, including a rental contract for a storage unit down on Wai`alae Avenue. When we checked that out, we found a ten by thirty-foot air conditioned space crammed floor to ceiling with antiques, high-end electronics, and the man's custom attire hung in several wardrobe boxes. Oh, and on one side were three huge boxes with Samantha's clothing crammed inside. He must have given her a pretty good allowance, because the designer labels I saw will justify the dry cleaning bill."

"Since she's his legal wife, all the stuff we found in storage will pass to Samantha, since Hawai`i is a community property state."

"That's good for her," I said. "Even if she doesn't want it all, she can probably sell everything for a nice amount of cash."

John nodded. "We interviewed the staff at the storage joint, and they said they'd seen a small van from the Kahala Home Services Company parked near the unit."

"Is that the same people who had Kahala Maids? Are they still in business?" questioned Keoni.

"Yeah, but they've changed their name and logo. Instead of a couple of Hilo Hattie types, they've got a hot chick in a miniskirt with a feather duster and a guy in a tux with a martini glass on a silver tray. Anyway, the storage folks said the van went in and out from about nine in the morning to closing at six the day before someone dropped off the house keys at the property leasing company.

"Oh, one other little detail. Once we got the car hauled in for analysis, we found a single item of interest—a recent CD by Carla Bruni."

"Isn't she that model-turned-singer who married French President Nicolas Sarkozy at the Elysée Palace in Paris?" I asked.

"That's the one. I asked Samantha about Luke's taste in music, and she said he didn't speak French and didn't listen to French music. When they entertained, he usually hired Hawaiian slack-key musicians. His own music library consisted of country western and classic rock and roll. His preferences were confirmed by the programmed FM radio stations in the car—KHCM for country and KDNN for Hawaiian music. That leaves us with the question of who put that CD in the van?

"Samantha's also been helping out with the names of Luke's colleagues. Some she's been able to confirm through her old day planners. So far we can't find any trace of the men she's named: no purchase or long-term leases for cars or property; no driver's licenses or auto registration; no records of them with national hotel chains; and no appearance on airline manifests. It's like they never existed.

"However, I've talked with Interpol. They'll be getting back to me about several things, including those illusive contacts. Before you ask, I'm not questioning Samantha's honesty. She turned over her day planners with a lot of sticky notes on memorable dates and people. Much of what she recorded through the last few years has proven to be on target—just not on the guys I was hoping to pin down.

"In spite of the gaps in evidence, several of the puzzle pieces point toward France. In addition to the CD in Luke's car, and Samantha's numerous trips to France, there's also the diving watch you described, Natalie."

"Another French connection?" I said laughing.

Reaching into his pocket, John presented a printout from a website for Swiss watches. "Beautiful, isn't it? It's a Blancpain SA. Each one is handcrafted by an individual watchmaker and only a few are made per year. The company's a couple hundred years old, but after going bankrupt, it ended up in the hands of the Swatch Company. The mechanism is very unique and those little points you noticed are quite distinctive. Jacques Cousteau had one and U.S. Navy divers used them back when they weren't quite so pricy."

"That's it! This is exactly what I saw in my vision. I didn't realize I was looking at something so specialized."

"I can't guess how far we're going to get with this lead, but I've got several agencies looking into it. You know, the first link to France was actually the technique used by Miriam's murderer. You see, death by garroting is typical of the underworld in Marseilles—especially done with the piano wire and dowels you described."

"Wow. That's a lot of pieces coming together," I said with a sigh.

"I wish there were more. It would sure help if one of the airlines or a hotel could confirm the arrival or departure of a single guy dropping in from France on the right dates. Also, there's no buzz about Luke, his business concerns, *or* Samantha anywhere on the street. I wondered if the perp's clever enough to travel with his own alibi, so we've been looking into the possibility of a couple, but so far *nada*."

"Maybe he *is* travelling with a woman, who may be unaware of what he does for a living. But instead of coming to Hawai`i from France, perhaps they came in from the mainland and the link to France isn't obvious," suggested Keoni.

"You may be right. Recognizing such a couple will be more difficult," responded John. "Anyone with the skills to pull these crimes off so cleanly is most likely mature in age and experience. If he's a European born after World War II, there's a good chance he's studied English. So he could be travelling on a fake ID that has *no* connection to France."

"Have you checked with the Līhu`e Airport? There are a lot of charter flights coming in there from Canada—since so many Canadians have condos or timeshares on Maui. You might want to run the pertinent manifests past Interpol to see if someone recognizes an alias," offered Keoni.

"Good idea. Despite the lack of evidence at either crime scene, we're glad to have a few leads to follow. And with Luke dead, none of his buddies in sight, and no sign of a personal property dispute, I feel we made the right decision about Samantha. Even so, I'd like you to keep an eye on things around the neighborhood, Keoni."

"That's a given."

Shortly after his departure, we got a call from Izzy, announcing Samantha was back. "If we'd had more time and Detective Dias wasn't concerned about safety, I would have hung yellow ribbons on the palm trees! Not all family is related by blood, and though she may not have been with us for very long, she's already part of our *`ohana*."

Izzy's joy at having Samantha returned was clear. Hopefully this time it would be permanent. I laughed and agreed with her recognition that Miriam had accepted the Hawaiian tradition of extended family.

The following afternoon, I looked across our backyard at Mokulua Hale and saw Samantha helping Joanne in the garden. The two of them were laughing during some well-deserved down time. A movement caught my eye at the edge of the scene and I glimpsed Miss Una frolicking with the leaves and petals that had fallen from a plumeria tree. I wondered if having all of Miriam's Ladies reunited would mean my ferocious feline could stand down from nightly guard duty.

Toward the end of the day, Samantha called my land line to announce The Ladies' order of solar garden lights had arrived. After a quick call to Keoni, I confirmed a mid-morning date for all of us to trek over to Costco and pick up their lights and some garden furniture for us. When we returned from our joint shopping expedition, we separated to position our new acquisitions.

Every once in a while, I heard laughter floating through the air as Samantha played with the branches of solar butterflies, hummingbirds and flowers that would turn The Ladies' cottage into a land of make believe after dark. It was as though the woman had lost two decades and rediscovered her childhood. This must be the shared joy that Miriam experienced whenever she helped someone find renewed strength and peace in their lives.

As sunset neared, Keoni completed stacking pavers at the back of the spa as I finished rearranging the *lānai* furniture. Pleased with our efforts, I glanced across our yard and toward what had been Miriam's home. Looking out from the kitchen, I saw Samantha standing with a basket of lemons and oranges balanced on the lip of the open Dutch door. Despite the shade of the roof, a shaft of sunlight bathed her freely flowing hair. With the *chiaroscuro* play of light and dark, the scene was reminiscent of a classic painting by a Parisian street artist.

After a day of playing house beautiful, Keoni and I decided all of Miriam's Ladies deserved some R and R and invited them to join us for a relaxing time in the hot tub. As I laid out towels for everyone and lit some bug-repellant candles, I saw the wisdom of Keoni's insisting that we purchase a spa that could accommodate eight comfortably.

With faces glowing with the anticipation of a good time, Joanne, Izzy and Samantha came across the lawn in a line that made me think of the seven dwarfs. Keoni played the perfect host, greeting each of our guests with a glass of Asti Spumante, which we knew Izzy especially enjoyed.

"Make yourselves comfortable," I said, gesturing toward the towels on Keoni's new wall.

"Gee, this is cozy back here," noted Samantha.

"Another of Keoni's successes in beautifying Auntie Carrie's home," I said with pride. "How did *your* projects turn out?"

"Perfectly," said Joanne succinctly.

"The lights are all so beautiful...the glass tulips, butterflies, and hummingbirds," enthused Samantha. "I'm sure Miriam would have enjoyed them all."

"I'm sure she *will* enjoy them as they shine across the yard tonight," added Izzy, pointing toward the clouds.

Once I had a glass of bubbly and Keoni a glass of cinnamon tea, we toasted both of the cottages and settled into the warm water of the spa.

"Each of you can adjust the jets behind your back for angle and intensity," instructed Keoni. "I hope the water's warm enough. With the heat of the sun, I didn't want to set the heating element too high.

"Mm, as Baby Bear would say, 'It's just right.' But since I'm short, I think I will adjust the jet at my back," said Izzy.

"Hey, I lucked out, there's a jet behind my ankle," crowed Joanne.

"That's the inflow of warmed water," explained Keoni.

"It's just so wonderful to be back at Mokulua Hale with all of you. This may not be where I grew up, but you've made me feel so welcome," declared Samantha.

"Remember, Mokulua Hale is your home for as long as you wish," affirmed Joanne.

It was plain to me that Miriam's Ladies were as pleased to have Samantha back as families who've had a loved one come home from any absence. For Joanne and Izzy, the woman's return signified their own nightmare was lessening.

"So what have you decided to do, Samantha? We heard you were thinking of going back to school," I queried.

"I'm going to take some classes at Windward Community College. Joanne is going to help me review for the placement tests."

"I'm happy to help. It's so wonderful that we live at a time when everyone can benefit from continuing their education," affirmed Joanne.

"Tell them what you're going to study," prodded Izzy.

"Since I already know Spanish quite well and have learned a bit of French, I'm thinking about getting a degree in European languages."

"That sounds wonderful. You never know when John Dias might have a need for those skills every once in a while," Keoni observed.

"*I* might even have a need for your assistance. You know that although I'm officially retired, I still take on writing and research projects. And today I accepted a new assignment for *Windward O`ahu Journeys*, writing a little piece on that new chef school," I announced.

"Congratulations," said Keoni, lifting his glass toward me. "Is there any chance you might hang around long enough to pick up some ideas for putting all those pots and pans you've been un-boxing to good use?"

Everyone laughed at the image of me executing even the simplest of menus.

"I'll have you know, I've been saving those pans for this very opportunity. I'm officially putting you on notice Izzy. I might learn to cook something you have yet to try."

"I'm really a very plain cook. Mainly a baker, you know."

"Whatever you want to call yourself doesn't matter. Just call me when it's time to eat!" said Samantha with a smile.

"Now you two should share *your* news. Joanne has spoken to a rabbi and she and Izzy are planning several ways to celebrate Miriam's life."

"Oh, please tell us what you've decided to do," I said encouragingly.

Joanne paused for a quick swallow of wine. "I spoke to the rabbi of a Reform Jewish synagogue about Jewish funeral customs. It seems that since Miriam did not practice the faith and had no children, we are not bound by Jewish traditions.

"For example, although Jewish custom calls for burial of the body within twenty-four hours if possible, many religious as well as non-religious Jews like Miriam opt for cremation. That simplifies things. For instance, performing *tahara*, the ritual washing and purifying of a body, would only be done if she were being buried."

"I had spoken to my friend Abby at Hale Malolo who's studying estitology...about doing makeup for Miriam. But then we learned that isn't appropriate for a cremation and it's not something you'd do for a traditional Jewish burial anyway," added Samantha.

At that point, Izzy broke into the discussion. "We also read some Internet articles. If Miriam was to be buried traditionally, her body should be turned east, toward Jerusalem."

I paused to absorb what I had heard. "It's good that you're honoring Miriam's wish to be cremated. Since she only has a handful of friends here, are you going to have a memorial service or other ceremony?"

"Oh, yes. And we're going to include the most important Jewish tradition, the saying of the *Mourners' Kaddish*. That's a hymn of praise to God that's said by a group of ten adult Jews," said Joanne.

"It's called a *minyan*. Originally, only men could be part of the group. Now, at least in Reform Judaism, a *minyan* can have women in it," said Izzy enthusiastically.

Looking somewhat serious, Joanne said, "Beyond the memorial, we've decided to take Miriam and Henri's ashes to his family's home in France. Even though it has been turned into a conference center, there's an old family cemetery, and a beautiful crypt where we can put their urns. Since there's no need for a graveside funeral here in Hawai`i, we've decided to have

Miriam's memorial service at the cottage."

"And we'll serve a celebration buffet afterwards," said Izzy. "There'll probably be just a few friends and neighbors coming, so there'll be plenty of room on the lānai for the members of the *minyan* we've invited to join us if they want to," said Izzy.

"I know there's no need to be concerned about the food, but would you like some musicians? A couple of Ariel's friend's played music at her life celebration. I could call and see if they are available for Miriam's," I suggested.

"That would be lovely. But we'd insist on giving them a stipend to help out with paying for their music, clothing or classes," said Joanne resolutely.

"I'm sure they'd be grateful for anything you offer. I'll go ahead check to see who's free to play on that evening. Most of them play stringed instruments...violin, viola, and guitar."

"That sounds wonderful," said Samantha. "I used to coordinate Luke's parties, so maybe I could call the maid service we used."

"That would be a big help," nodded Izzy. "It would mean we can be with our guests instead of being stuck in the kitchen."

"It sounds like you've thought of everything," said Keoni. I don't think you'll require it, but if there's any need for crowd control, I can handle it."

Joanne glanced at Keoni. "Speaking of public safety, could you call John Dias and invite him and Sergeant Ken`ichi. They've both done so much and I know how badly they feel that there has been no resolution to Miriam's case," said Joanne.

"Unless they get called into work, I'm sure they'd like to come," Keoni replied.

"What did you decide to do about the people who can't come to the celebration here?" I asked.

"We're going to follow through on suggestions you made, Natalie. I've already started a website in memoriam to Miriam, as well as Henri," replied Joanne.

"We have a lot of photos from the albums they kept

through the years. And Joanne will put in some of her pictures of the house and the beach," added Izzy.

"I'll order some blowups for displays at the memorial," explained Samantha. "Later we can add photos of the celebration to the website, so people who didn't come will feel they have been part of the festivities."

"It doesn't sound like you need anything from me, but please let me know if something comes up," I said.

"Well, there is one area we could really use your help with," said Joanne. "Could you write Miriam's obituary and maybe a summary of both of their lives? You were right to suggest we place notices in newspapers in major cities where there may be people who knew them."

"I'd be honored to do that, Joanne. I'm afraid there will be some expense in doing this," I said hesitantly.

"Not a problem. I would pay for it myself, if needed. But Curtis Leighton has already said that there are ample funds for whatever we plan. When I told him my idea of taking both of their ashes to France, he thought it was a fitting tribute to their lives," Joanne concluded.

After that conversation, we shared stories of unusual trips we had taken during our lives. Our neighborly R and R session ended with Keoni and me agreeing to join The Ladies for a tour of their newly-lit yard that night.

In the interim, Keoni and I lazed in the spa a while longer. Having already discussed our wills and durable powers of attorney, we spoke briefly of our own eventual funerals.

"It sounds as if you gave The Ladies some excellent advice," said Keoni.

"I didn't suggest all that much. I just asked several questions. There were only a couple of issues for them to consider. It looks like they've addressed the Didión's foreign friends and former co-workers. And I think it's awfully nice that they're going to have a *minyan* say the *Kaddish* for Miriam," I replied.

"Everything they're planning sounds like a perfect send-off to me!" Keoni declared.

CHAPTER 20

If ignorant both of your enemy and yourself,
you are certain to be in peril.
Sun Tzu [c. 544 BCE – c. 496 BCE]

Later that night, we toured Mokulua Hale's grounds with Miriam's Ladies. Before we set out, Izzy provided each of us with a delicious Meyer's lemon slushy. Despite the cloudy sky, the solar lights highlighting the walkways, flower beds and gateways, made the old cottage and its grounds seem like a fairyland made for Hansel and Gretel.

In the midst of our adventure, Keoni got the call he had awaited since his birthday party. Master craftsman Makoa Pane invited him to help harvest a fallen *alahe'e* tree up in *Maunawili* on the edge of Kawai Nui Marsh. The tree but may be small in circumference, but it can grow to thirty or even forty feet tall. Until the men saw it, there was no way of knowing how many board feet of wood it would yield.

During his work on White Sands Cottage, Keoni's woodworking skills have expanded considerably. At this point, he didn't care whether he would be shaping a mantle, cornice pieces for porch posts, or accents for the cottage's built-in cabinetry. He was just thrilled to have the opportunity to advance his knowledge.

"This is great news! I recently cut out a newspaper article about tours of the marsh. Are you all game for a tour? I'll see if I can schedule an outing for us at the same time the men are harvesting the tree?" I offered.

The Ladies nodded enthusiastically.

"We could take a picnic and you and Makoa could join us for a mid-day break," Izzy suggested to Keoni.

"Sounds good. But I can't make any decisions without checking with Makoa, but I doubt he's going to want to schedule anything in the middle of harvesting a tree."

"Well, no matter how lunch works out, this is a great chance to get to know my new neighborhood," said Samantha.

"The area offers many things to do. Amateur archeologists and artists often find inspiration there. And there's a variety of hiking trails. Some are easy paths on the flatland. Above that, are some of the toughest uphill hikes in windward O`ahu," I added.

"I don't know that I'll be up to that much walking, but let's check it out," responded Joanne, whose weight gain since retirement presented several challenges.

Within a couple of days, everything was in place. Although tours of historic sites in *Maunawili* are generally held once a month, a special one had been booked to accommodate Chinese students visiting the University of Hawai`i. Luckily, there were enough vacancies to allow us to join in the fun. So while Keoni and his new friend Makoa felled the tree that had been struck by lightning, the rest of us would tour part of the 830-acre marsh that is the largest remaining wetland in Hawai`i.

Keoni and I kissed goodbye early in the morning, so he could follow Makoa to the Marsh. We had agreed I would call him when the tour ended to see whether the men were free to attend the picnic. Since our party had grown to include Larry Smith and his nine-year old grandson Joey, we decided to take my Optima, as well as The Ladies' mini-van.

Besides having ample seating, we were prepared for several scenarios that might develop. The key question was whether everyone would want to remain in the marsh for the entire day. While Joey and Samantha were young and strong, I was fairly certain that Izzy and Joanne would want to return home after lunch. I wasn't even sure if the General or I would be prepared for a hike following a tour lasting three hours.

I really appreciated the tour guide squeezing us into an

outing with his Chinese guests. Unsure of the number of people participating in the day's events, Izzy and I planned a flexible picnic menu. Although the tour was on a schedule, Keoni and Makoa's work would be subject to unknown factors, so we did not expect them for lunch.

Larry and Joey met me outside my garage on the morning of our outing. As always, I tried to plan for unforeseen occurrences. Accordingly, I had packed metal bottles of water, some *mochi* and energy bars to snack on, plus sun block and bug spray. Joey might not like the rice cakes filled with sweet red bean paste, but I figured they would add to the report he would give mainland friends about his adventures in Hawai`i.

As we buckled our seatbelts, I was already anticipating the stories we would hear about Kawai Nui Marsh—especially those of Queen Lili`uokalani as a young woman. Having researched the latter days of her life a year ago, I was intrigued to learn more about the lively princess who had interacted so rigorously with her land and people.

With the tour broken into several segments, it was good we arrived *en masse* with only a few vehicles. Miriam's Ladies arrived in their mini-van. The Chinese students arrived in two commercial vans. The Chinese professors and a Canadian couple arrived in rental cars.

The first part of the tour was conducted by a community volunteer who was helping with the restoration of wetlands located in more than twenty acres below Castle Hospital. The project was overseen by the U. S. Army Corps of Engineers and the Hawai'i State Department of Land and Natural Resources, with the support of many Hawaiian civic organizations. It was designed to provide flood control and sediment filtration to benefit the entire Kailua Bay ecosystem.

By terracing shallow ponds and removing invasive vegetation, native plants and endangered species were flourishing in the renewed habitat. We were all impressed to learn that the marsh is recognized as a Ramsar Wetland of International Importance. And although Joey was young, it was encouraging to see him demonstrate particular interest in the native

Hawaiian water birds benefitting from the improvements.

Next we had an opportunity to visit sites that are sacred to native Hawaiian culture, including ancient settlements, a large fishpond, a temple, and several terraces used for farming. The man who was guiding us was so personable that his data-filled presentation held our attention. One of the most enthusiastic members of our tour was Joanne, who was busily taking long-distance and close-up shots by interchanging lenses on her new camera.

"When you look down from the Pali Lookout, you'll see that one of the highest points of visual interest is Olomana—comprised of *Mount Olomana* and two lesser peaks: *Pāku'i* and *Ahiki*. Between there and the ocean is Maunawili Valley and natural springs that feed a network of streams in the Marsh. Later today, if you choose to go on a long hike, you may find a swimming pond and waterfall at the end of your trail. In addition to nature lovers, anthropology buffs, and hikers, the area attracts artists who can choose from a variety of subjects for their drawing and painting.

"Archeological evidence from 1400 C.E. abounds, with numerous petroglyphs and several Hawaiian temple sites, called *heiau*. This, the *Ulupō Heiau*, is the largest on `Oahu, with a stone platform measuring 140 by 180 feet and having outer walls up to 30 feet in height. Like other sacred sites and objects for daily living (including fishponds, roads, canoes and houses), the *heiau* is associated with the *menehune*. This is a diminutive race of remarkable craftspeople traditionally considered legendary, but whose presence in the Islands may actually predate the arrival of the Polynesians.

"In addition to the temple site, you'll note the *lo`i*, has been restored. Once farmed by the *maka'ainana*, these terraces traditionally grew the dietary staple *kalo* to make *poi*, along with *ki* plants and the flowering herb *pōpolo*, used in Hawaiian rituals. Later, with the availability of ample water, rice was grown on some *lo`i*. You have already seen restoration of some of the fishponds that were carefully tended to assure thriving supplies of mullet, *awa*, and *o'opu*.

"This was the seat of political power for the Ko'olau Poko District in 1750. With the abundant fishing in the bay and excellent landings for canoes, Kailua was a favorite recreational area for the *ali`i*, their families, and retainers. When royalty visited, the meadow land within the rain forest was decorated with banners and the food and entertainment of a *lū`au* were enjoyed during sunny days and evenings lit with hillside bonfires."

Since our tour was connected to the Kailua Historical Society, we had been granted permission to visit the old Maunawili Ranch. As we moved toward one of the decrepit homes on the property, I was filled with the expectation of learning more about the life of Queen Lili`uokalani.

"In the nineteenth and early twentieth century, success through mercantile enterprise, cattle ranching, and intermarriage between the Boyd family and royalty of the Hawaiian Kingdom made the Maunawili Ranch a gathering place for leaders of government and business. It was also a popular destination for artists and writers of international renown, such as Mark Twain.

"There isn't much to see today. The original Boyd home is gone, but we can view other historical features of the Boyd Irwin Estate. This includes a couple of period homes like this one, and a carriage way with a few remaining royal palms lining its course. Another remaining feature is an outdoor bath believed to have been built for *Queen Lili`uokalani*, the last monarch of the Kingdom of Hawai`i.

"Throughout her adult life, she made frequent trips to the area. As the heir-apparent, Princess Lili`uokalani often made horseback tours in windward O`ahu, including visits to the *Maunawili* home of the Boyd family. The Queen was a noted writer of prose, as well as lyrics. A visit in 1877 may have provided the inspiration for her writing the famous song, *Aloha `Oe*.

"It is said that when the future queen rode off toward Honolulu, she looked back to observe Edwin Boyd receiving a *lei* from a young Hawaiian woman, whom he then kissed tenderly. While the song is commonly associated with personal farewells, or allegorically as political commentary on the lost Kingdom of Hawai`i, the Queen reportedly said it was based on her memory of the two lovers bidding farewell to each other.

"Since its early days of ranching, crops of coffee, sugar, and rice, plus orchards of fruit trees [including orange, papaya, cherry, and apple], as well as mangosteen, avocado, and kola nuts have been grown here. Today there are few agricultural products harvested from this land. But its overall contributions to the community remain vibrant. I'm sure the ancient Hawaiians would be pleased to see its wildlife flourishing and appreciated by locals and tourists alike. Artisans in woodworking eagerly await permission to harvest the wood of endangered trees which are damaged or have fallen."

I chuckled at this reference to the work Keoni and Makoa were undertaking at that moment. I had not meant to interrupt the presentation with my laughter, but evidently the comments on creative usage of the marsh were the conclusion of the tour. After encouraging us to make the most of the opportunities afforded by our unique access to this part of Maunawili, our leader departed for another lecture. Then, after conferring with their instructors, the Chinese students left for an event with American students who were preparing to visit Beijing the following semester.

I looked around and counted heads for lunch. Our tour group had dwindled to the three Chinese professors, two Canadians, and the seven of us from Mokulua Drive. While Izzy was inviting the tourists to join us for lunch, I called Keoni to see if he and Makoa could take a break. He declined, saying they were at a crucial point in their work, which they were trying to finish before the day got much warmer. I said I would call back when we finished eating. By then I would know if I was going on a hike and the men might know when they would have completed their task.

Izzy and I carefully selected a spot to lay out a couple of blankets in accordance with the instructions we had been given for keeping the land around us pristine. Beckoning everyone to be seated, Izzy started pulling out plastic food containers and serving utensils. The twelve of us settled down in an uneven circle. As Joanne scooted back a bit to take a group shot, her camera's battery gave out. Fortunately, my smart phone takes excellent pictures, so I handed it to her to continue capturing images of our continuing adventure.

We were all hungry, so conversation was at a minimum initially. As always, Izzy's guests were pleased with her menu. The majority of skewered *teriyaki* chicken, potato-macaroni salad, *sushi* with cucumber, and dried papaya were eaten quickly. Our first real conversation centered on Izzy sharing her *teriyaki* recipe and Joanne's revelation of her secret drop of Dijon mustard in the salad.

Once he was through with lunch, Joey became absorbed in the life surrounding us. He took delight in teaching the older tourists a few of the Hawaiian words he had learned in summer school. "Look, there's a *poloka*. That's the wrinkled frog. He's not native to Hawai`i. There are so many of them now that they're becoming a danger to the environment. And that's a *Mo'o'alā*, a gecko. They're little, but they can change colors, so they're protected from being eaten by something bigger." Proud of the knowledge he'd shared, Joey turned to offering the lizard a long piece of marsh grass.

Meanwhile, the rest of us shared perspectives on the morning's activities. It was good that the Chinese were fluent, if a bit stilted, in English. Although reserved in manner, they were interested in everything we had to say, and offered keen analysis of potential benefits from similar environmental projects in China. Next, we enjoyed hearing travel anecdotes from all of the tourists. Most of their encounters with local life had been benign, but Canadian Andre Chambre had had an unpleasant interchange with a Portuguese man-of-war, and sported a red bite from the stinging jelly fish. I enjoyed listening to his sexy French accent and was pleased when he and his girlfriend Monique decided to stay for at least a short hike.

The numbers in our party declined rapidly after lunch. The Chinese scholars expressed their gratitude for being included in the picnic and departed for a tour of the University's libraries. Izzy and Joanne then announced they would be going home for a rest. I wasn't sure how long I would last, but I decided to join Samantha, the General, Joey and the Canadians for at least the first part of the hike. But before linking up with them, I walked The Ladies back to their van with some of our leftovers and a couple of bags of trash.

Waving them off, I turned back to join the hikers. On the way to the trail head, I called Keoni to see how he and Makoa were progressing. In case they needed some quick nourishment before the end of the day, I had held back some of the papaya and sports water. As we were chatting, I sent Keoni a picture Joanne had taken. It showed our feast in the foreground with passing hikers behind.

"It's really been a great day. I think I told you Larry Smith and his grandson Joey came today. And there were a couple of tourists from Quebec. Boy, is he sexy, with a lean body and French accent. Too bad he's with his girlfriend, since Samantha could use a fresh start in the romance department."

"From Quebec?" Keoni asked.

"Yes. As he and his young girlfriend began describing the city, I remembered how much it reminded me of parts of Paris the first time I traveled there. It's a good alternative for those who can't afford a trip to Europe," I said envisioning the time when Keoni and I would begin taking trips of our own.

"The picture you sent has me thinking. Would you send me all the pictures you have? I'm hoping you might have one at the picnic and another of the hiking party setting off?"

"Sure Keoni. But they aren't very good images. In the picture of the picnic, the Chinese profs were chatting among themselves and Andre and Monique were looking down at their food. When the hikers left, nobody was looking our way."

"That's doesn't matter, just send me the pics."

As I tried to pull up the images he wanted, Keoni began asking me for a detailed description of Andre. "Well, he's a bit younger than we are. I'd say he's about your height. Slimmer, no offence intended. Kind of blah brown hair. But his eyes are very unusual. They're gray, sort of like silver or steel…but not sparkly, like yours."

I sent the pictures he wanted and within a minute, he sent back an enlarged image of Monique and Andre. In the center was Andre's left hand, with the sun glancing off of four points of steel framing the face of his watch.

Everything around me stopped…including my breathing. I thought of the man's slim build and penetrating gray eyes. Then I gasped.

"Oh, my God, Keoni. If you're right and he's…he's the man who killed Miriam, then…"

"Never mind God at this point. Say a prayer if you want, but get moving toward that hiking party. You can bet your tourist friend Andre did *not* come along to learn about the romantic doings of Princess Lili`u. And by the way, he's probably the one who offed Samantha's husband.

"The main thing is that two people are already dead, so don't get too close. With the skills that man has honed, he's probably been responsible for many deaths through the decades. If you see anything odd taking place, hurry and call 911. Okay?

"Yes, Keoni. How long will it take for you to get here?"

"We should be near you within five minutes. Makoa took a call about a downed monkeypod tree over your way, so we decided to have a quick look at it. We're in my truck since Makoa's is full of the *alahe`e* tree and was blocked by mine. We stopped a couple of minutes ago so Makoa could take the wheel and I could edit the photos you sent. I've already sent them to JD with a text for him to join us. Lucky for us, he's on the windward side of the island enjoying another golf day at the Kāne`ohe Bay Marine Corps Base. Where are *you* now?"

"I'm almost at the fork where everyone agreed to take the path on the left. It goes into the trees a bit, but remains on flat land."

"Okay, our ETA is now about three minutes from where you had your picnic. Try to get close enough that you can see the hiking party, then pull back and call to keep me in the loop."

I hurried as fast as I could without chancing a fall onto the softened ground. I did not know if it was my nerves playing tricks, but it seemed the temperature had dropped and the wind was starting to gust. I was hoping the combination of a soggy pathway and Andre's ignorance that a pair of strong men were on their way would give the righteous side a chance for success. But what would I do if I *did* catch up with the hikers? I had a delicate hip and no strength in my hands or arms. Even if I had a weapon, what good would I be against a successful hit man and a mysterious female companion who might be a criminal herself?

Just as I was approaching the fork in the path, I saw Monique walking slowly toward me. I put on a smile and greeted her as though I knew nothing about her companion. "Well, hi. Aren't you going the wrong way?" I asked.

"I slipped and my knee is too sore to go all the way to the end of the trail, so Andre suggested I start back slowly."

"I see. How thoughtful of him."

"You are so right. I've only known Andre for two weeks, and he's always very polite.

"Is everyone else still up ahead,…on this path?" I asked.

"Yes. They're only a little bit behind me. You should be able to catch up with them in a couple of minutes."

"That's good. You take it easy. I'm sure the hike won't last much longer," I concluded, knowing there was more than one reason to predict an early end to the day's events."

I waved to her as we parted and watched as she walked around the bend. Then I hit number one on my phone and updated Keoni on both the short-term relationship between Andre and Monique, as well as my proximity to the hiking party. "So what's your ETA?" I asked anxiously.

"We're parking right now. I've got my Glock and Makoa's got an axe. Can you see the hikers?"

"No, but I must be close."

We hung up and I began moving toward the hikers as fast as I could. Although the path had been packed down through the years, summer rains the day before had left puddles and slick spots. With my hip to remind me of the consequences if I took a wrong step, I moved steadily but carefully.

Between the rapid walking and talking, I was getting tired. Moving into thicker shrubs, I caught sight of Larry's red cap passing a tree several yards ahead of me. How close could I get without being visible? Would I be heard approaching? Would I be able to hear *their* conversation?

My head was overflowing with questions. Would Andre really be willing to kill an old man and little boy just to get Samantha? Why did Andre even care about Samantha? She had not seen him. And Luke was dead. Maybe Andre followed some kind of twisted ethical code of honor that decreed he had to complete every contract. I wondered how he would feel about someone who tried to prevent him from completing his task?

CHAPTER 21

Come at once if convenient — if inconvenient come all the same.
Sir Arthur Conan Doyle [1859 – 1930]

Soon I was at the fork in the road. Monique had said I would find our party of hikers on the path to the left. As I moved in that direction, I saw a family of four coming toward me. They greeted me with smiles and I had to decide whether to say anything about my predicament. They looked so happy and chatted about making it to the end of the trail, where they had found the swimming hole our tour guide had mentioned. They had even seen a waterfall spurting uphill because of recent rains and the wind that had risen in the last half hour. Looking at the boy and girl who appeared to be about six and seven, I decided to go it alone for safety's sake—theirs that is. After they confirmed having seen *my* group, I waved goodbye. I hoped I was not dooming myself, or those I cared about.

Knowing I had paused long enough for my party of hikers to move out of hearing range, I called Keoni. In a whisper, I confirmed that I was about three minutes behind Andre and his intended victim or victims. Keoni said he and Makoa were moving rapidly and should catch-up with me before I got to Andre.

"Be careful of the paths, Keoni. There's been some rain you know, and that ankle of yours isn't up to another battle with Mother Earth."

"Never mind me, honey. You just take care of *yourself.* I don't think our perp will try anything in the open. He'll be looking for an opportunity to get Samantha alone. If he can take her out without collateral damage, he will. But if he thinks *his* survival is on the line, he won't hesitate to kill you all. And don't be expecting another scenario of death by piano wire. He knew he was coming to a group outing today. That means he'll have a firearm. And with his background, he's undoubtedly an excellent shot."

On that note we cut off our connection. I stood there for a moment, rocking from side to side to ease my hips. Then I inhaled deeply and continued my trek, contemplating how I would handle myself when I caught up with Andre. Within a couple of minutes I caught sight of Joey. He was standing on tip-toe looking up at a tree. I didn't mean to startle him, but he was in conversation with something or someone I could not see.

"Hi, Joey" I called out softly. "What are you doing?"

"I think I see a mynah bird. I thought he might answer if I talked to him," he replied. Does it look like a mynah to you?"

"I'm not sure. It looks black. That's about as much as I know about mynah birds," I admitted. "I saw Monique a few minutes ago, but where is everyone else?"

"It's too bad Monique got hurt. Andre told her to go back to the car. Grandpa is kind of tired. He's right behind me, resting on a big rock. Andre and Samantha are going on to the end. There's a pond for swimming, but I didn't bring my swim suit and Grandpa needs me to stay with him.

"I see," I answered. That took care of one issue; I would not have to worry about Joey or Larry becoming targets. "I have a surprise for you. Keoni and a friend are coming to join us in a couple of minutes. It would help if you would point them to where I've gone. Can you do that for me?"

"Sure, Natalie."

"After that, I want you stay with your Grandpa until we all come back. Okay?"

"Okay," he said, turning back to look up into the trees.

I continued on a few yards until I spotted Larry Smith seated on a tall stone. "You look very regal, Larry."

"I can assure you I feel nothing like the royals who used to cavort in these marshes. I'm feeling every one of my years right now."

He smiled ruefully. "Maybe I shouldn't have let Joey out of my sight, but he's kept his promise to call out to me every few minutes."

"With all the scientific knowledge he's demonstrated today, I'm surprised he hasn't told us its Latin name."

We laughed and I wondered how much I should reveal about Andre and Monique. "I guess Samantha and Andre have gone on?"

"Yes. They aren't very far ahead. Samantha said even she was tiring and won't be going very fast. You should catch them in a couple of minutes," said the General.

"That's good. Keoni and his friend Makoa are right behind me. They've uh, got some questions for Andre, so please tell them how far ahead I am," I requested, trying not to sound too anxious. "Oh, I told Joey to make sure he stays with you after the guys arrive."

"That's good."

I tried to smile cheerfully and departed. When I was out of sight of Larry, I pulled out my phone and texted Keoni that I had not told Joey or Larry about the situation and that I must be close to Andre and Samantha. He replied that he had caught sight of Joey. That confirmed that he and Makoa were closing in quickly. I just hoped we were all being quiet enough to be able to approach Andre without inviting a violent response.

Just then I heard laughter from Samantha. "You seem right at home in the wild, Andre."

"You could say I've had some experience in survival with nature," he replied. "But I think my age is speaking to me. Why don't you go on ahead and let me catch my breath for a moment. I'll be right with you."

"If you're sure. I seem to be getting a second wind," she said.

I crept forward slowly and watched Samantha moving away from the small clearing where she had been standing beside Andre. At that moment, he reached toward his waist and I had no illusions about what he was preparing to do. As expected, he made a quiet movement with his left hand and reached down into his pocket.

Suddenly I remembered the end of my dream about the attack on the U.S. Embassy in Nairobi. I had seen Samantha. Standing in a forest. Just like now. I knew that Andre was about to pull out a semi-automatic handgun. He did. Then he drew a cylindrical object from his breast pocket. ~~In this case, putting one and one together would equal a lot more than two.~~ I knew what it was, and what it would do. The silencer I watched him screw onto the barrel of the gun would allow Andre to easily take out Samantha...and anyone else who got in his way.

Just then I heard a slight rustling behind me and looked up to see Makoa placing a finger to his lips as he moved past me quickly. Coming on his heels was Keoni, with his Glock already drawn. He briefly squeezed my shoulder and moved forward as stealthily as Makoa had.

The next few moments were a blur of action. First I watched Andre position himself to take aim at Samantha who had continued moving forward, oblivious to the nearing danger. I watched in horror as Andre raised his weapon. Then I heard a tree branch snap and there was a slicing of the air beside my head.

For a second there was nothing. No sound. No movement.

And then I watched Andre fall on his side. As I rushed forward, I realized Makoa had thrown his axe to halt Andre. The man lay still, crumpled at the foot of a small monkeypod tree. Blood was oozing from the side of his head.

A single-edged axe was embedded beyond him in a tree limb lying on the ground. Although the incident had been short and nearly silent, I saw that Samantha had stopped and turned around. As I hurried to apprise her of the situation, I passed Makoa who had kneeled to wrap Andre's head with a T-shirt. Meanwhile, Keoni stood to the side making a call, presumably to John Dias.

Within a few moments we had all gathered around the

man who had been determined to commit one final crime in Hawai`i. Distracted by the call of a bird, I glanced up. It seemed ironic that the axe that felled the murderer was fragrant with the small white flowers of an endangered *alahe'e* tree.

* * * * *

Much had happened in the few days between the harrowing incident in Kawai nui Marsh and Miriam's memorial. With an unidentified perpetrator in medical lockdown, I knew that some issues might never be resolved in the deaths of Miriam Didión and Luke Turner. We might have to live with such questions, but I was not resigned to accepting the fact that a premeditated murder resulted in the death of the wrong person.

As I thought about Miriam, I was conscious that the roots of my connections to her predated her killing in many ways. In addition to being my neighbor for a short while, she had lived next to my Auntie Carrie for over two decades. My vision of her escape from Denmark to Sweden in early childhood had introduced her personally—even if I did not recognize her as the central figure in the sepia scenes I had seen. Then, following her death, I had read her private thoughts in journals spanning most of her adult life.

It seemed like more than a couple of months since I had had that vision of Miriam's family escaping from the Nazis. I wondered about the other experiences that had filled the months, if not years, she and her family had lived on the road. For her there had been no home, no Teddy bear beckoning from a rocking horse, or candles to light on *Chanukah*.

And companionship? There had been no neighbor with whom to share dolls, no schoolyard adventures, no outings with friends to the zoo on a lazy Sunday afternoon. She had had a single possession to call her own—a necklace that had to be hidden from authorities who should have been dedicated to keeping all children safe. Beyond that, she had survived on handouts of clothing and food, when she was lucky. On the cold nights when there was nothing to eat, there might have been a single cup of warm water to fill her empty stomach.

And what of the parents who saved her? I could only imagine what they had given up for her. I could almost hear the whispered sorrows they had kept from the ears of their precious daughter. Surely if those who have passed beyond can see the loved ones they leave behind, Rose and Samuel Reznik must have found joy and pride in seeing the life their Miriam lived.

As to the man who had probably shortened that life, his own end might arrive quite soon. Although a craniotomy to relief pressure was scheduled, the brain surgeon had said he did not expect his patient to regain consciousness. And with no identification, let alone next of kin, I wondered if he would be disconnected from the technology that was keeping his lungs aerated and his heart pumping.

* * * * *

Completing plans for Miriam's memorial service was fairly simple. Izzy and Samantha had pulled images from Miriam and Henri's photo albums and scrapbooks, which Joanne digitalized for the memorial website. She then added shots of Mokulua Hale and its surroundings to provide visitors to the site a sense of the couple's life in Lanikai.

While I was helping with captions for the images on the website, Joanne lamented her poor skills in digital picture editing. "It's too bad we can't groom nature," she said, referring to strips of seaweed interspersed with bits of trash strewn on the beach.

"It isn't like you're shooting an ad for the Hawai`i visitors Bureau," I countered.

"I think everything you've put together is beautiful, Joanne," said Samantha.

Before Izzy could express her opinion, Joanne held up a hand. "Thank you for your encouragement. I do recognize that this isn't a photo contest. These pictures are for friends of Miriam's who will be happy to feel like they're seeing the life Miriam enjoyed here."

Borrowing from her journal, I sprinkled Miriam's words

throughout the site....*both my personal and professional life here has been fully satisfying...as full of joy as I or any other human being could possibly expect within a single lifetime... through Henri's camera lens and the writing and personal consulting that I provided, we passed our years together in personal peace and harmony.*

The previous day, Izzy had filled me in on some of the other preparations for the memorial. "Thank you so much for the obituary you wrote. We've put it in newspapers in New York, London and Paris."

"I'm honored to participate," I said.

The day of Miriam's memorial dawned like most in the Islands: The skies were clear, the temperature moderate, and there was a light breeze. After enjoying our usual early morning at the beach, Keoni and I tidied the house and patio for the guests we knew might float by that evening. A couple of hours before the event, John Dias dropped by to catch us up on the results of his continuing investigation. As usual, we ended up around the kitchen table. As he began, we sipped glasses of mint tea since we would be having champagne later.

"You know, Keoni, I'm seeing you just about as often as when you were on the job. It seems like you and your sweetheart here are magnets for homicide. Three deaths per year is simply too high a rate for a private investigator. Do you think you two can take it easy for a while?" John requested.

"Well, at least the cases we've been involved with have been unusual," retorted Keoni.

"That's true. Regarding Miriam's murder by mistake, it looks like Luke Turner did put out a contract on his wife. Unfortunately, he's not alive to explain his motive or to straighten out the crazy things that have been happening in his financial portfolio. There may be some odd pockets of cash for Samantha to inherit, but there's been some mysterious electronic emptying of his larger accounts. If we didn't have the body at the Morgue, I'd suspect he'd staged a fake death."

"As to the apparent murderer, he's not available to answer questions about the details of any instructions he may have been given. Even the woman who accompanied him to Hawai`i couldn't provide much information. Monique Davis is a legitimate model from Quebec. She has no criminal record, no connection to anyone in this case, nor any criminal activity in Quebec or Vancouver. She works occasionally as a companion to wealthy businessmen. She said she'd been booked for this gig because of her height, weight and fluency in both written and spoken Parisian French and knowledge of French cuisine. The agency representing her seems legit. They quickly provided records of the deal that had been brokered by email with the guy they ID'd as Andre Chambre. Except for a dummy website, we can't find any record of the man prior to the last couple of months."

"Sounds like you're nearing the end of the line on him," commented Keoni.

The Lieutenant snorted and continued. "Andre wasn't known to the agency before this transaction, but his references from Vancouver were impeccable—personally, professionally and financially. Said he was taking a vacation before and after a business consultation he had. While the pair shared a suite at the Hilton Hawaiian Village Hotel, they had separate bedrooms and bathrooms.

"Well, at least that means she didn't catch any diseases from him," I noted.

"Now there's an acclamation for the perfect date," laughed Keoni.

"She had never met the man before and knew nothing about what he was doing when he was not with her. She was just along for a good time," said John summarizing the relationship between the two would-be tourists. "And that's what she experienced. Monique was booked on a first class roundtrip ticket to Vancouver, British Columbia, where she met Andre. Almost immediately, they boarded a corporate jet on a junket to Maui. With all their travel arrangements made in advance and him paying cash for everything else, she never saw any ID, checks, credit cards, or anything to make her question his story. Although there were periods when Andre was gone each day, he had reasonable excuses for his absences."

"So what were the two of them doing?" I asked.

"Typical tourist stuff. They drove around the island, visiting most of the popular beach parks and shopping centers."

"Good cover for checking out Kailua, Lanikai, and Diamond Head Beach Park," said Keoni.

"Yep. I'd say 'planning' was one of his greatest talents. Saying he needed to see clients, the man scheduled an amazing number of appointments for her: hair styling and mani-pedis; massages; and hula classes. Monique said she never saw him with a briefcase or talking to anyone unrelated to whatever they were doing. He didn't seem to have any electronic toys, except a complicated smart phone. He never left it anywhere and never placed a call in her presence. And no, we never found that device. Monique admitted to peeking in his suitcase, but said there was nothing special in it. Every day he sent his clothing out to be cleaned and his shoes polished, so she had never had an opportunity to look through his pockets.

"Guess he was pretty generous and quite the gentleman. They never had sex and he didn't even try to kiss her. She said he purchased clothing and trinkets whenever she expressed an interest. Whatever the price, Andre produced cash for everything. Pulled out chairs, opened doors, and selected the best food and wines. Helped her with her shawls if the wind came up...even rubbed on sunblock."

"What a prince...if you discount a couple of murders," joked Keoni.

"Yeah," smiled John. "The ideal escort. On top of the pleasure of the trip, Monique had been paid a high fee for a month of her time. With no family, boyfriend or kids, she would be an ideal candidate for a hit man seeking a temporary companion as his cover. Knowing that no one would report her missing for a while, he probably figured he could easily murder her at the end, ensuring there were no loose ends in his mid-Pacific crime spree."

Keoni and I shook our heads.

"I'm waiting for some follow-up reports from the Royal

Canadian Mounted Police, but I don't think anything of substance will be revealed. Not with the guy's attention to detail! We've also been checking on Luke Turner's staff. We've identified the older married couple who served as his housekeeper and gardener. According to them, Luke paid all the remaining staff for three months of service and provided one-way tickets to San Diego for those wanting to go to the mainland. That couple was thrilled; it's where they have a home. They didn't know why they were being released from their annual contract and didn't care.

"Once Samantha moved out, there were no parties and there was little work to be done at the house. As to the collateral staff, we've hit dead ends with all three of them. They probably gave false names to everyone they dealt with, so we can't even trace them to flights to San Diego."

"What about Andre? You said he's in a coma. What's the prognosis?" Keoni asked.

Reaching into his briefcase, John said, "Funny you ask. I just received a report from the hospital. Doesn't look like our friend Andre will be with us very long. Look for yourselves. Since the docs did a CT scan, there's almost as much detail as an autopsy."

Keoni accepted the sheet of paper John handed him and I looked over his shoulder.

The patient is in a vegetative condition due to Traumatic Brain Injury caused by a compound skull fracture. A single sharp-force transverse wound caused by a frontal/parietal blow....the anteriomedial upper left forehead within the hairline...measuring 4 inches in length and .35 inch in depth...pierced the skull...damaging...dura membrane and brain tissue...resulting in significant cerebral injury...Edges of the wound were smooth, free of abrasion or tissue bridging and consistent with the blade of a straight edged single-bit axe found at the scene of the injury...To relieve the swelling of brain tissue against the inflexible bone, a ventriculostomy drain was inserted to remove cerebrospinal fluid. Further neurological exams revealed the unlikelihood of the patient's recovery due to the severe damage caused by a subarachnoid hemorrhage....

The final description of minor injuries caught my attention immediately.

...dusky purple discoloration...two blisters and one ulcer from Portuguese man-of-war stings...sustained within the last two weeks.

"Andre complained about his battle with Portuguese men-of-war during our picnic. Now that I think about it, there was quite a swarm of them in Lanikai the week Miriam died," I commented.

"Another bit of evidence linking the man to the neighborhood around the time of Miriam's murder," observed Keoni.

"If he's in a coma, who will make the decision to disconnect him from life support?" I inquired.

"With no ID, there are no known relatives. So, he's basically a ward of the State," said John. "The docs have said there's little likelihood of recovery no matter what they do. Who wants to foot the bill for a man who's probably killed two people here, and who knows how many elsewhere through the years. It's not like he's a Nelson Mandela that the world didn't want to lose.

"Looks like the man was a pro for a long time. With that tan, he hasn't been inside the walls of a prison any time recently, if ever. That means there's little likelihood of finding a match for his DNA. And with those burned off fingertips, it doesn't look like he'll ever be identified. That's the why the State of Hawai`i has become his personal representative. They've got to follow a set protocol, but eventually someone will sign the papers to get him disconnected. And unless authorities on one continent or another come up with something, another John Doe will go into a county grave. And Miriam's case will end up in the cold case files."

* * * * *

Despite our disappointment over the disposition of Miriam's case, everything about her memorial was as lovely as the weather. Keoni was positioned at the side gate of Mokulua

Hale to direct everyone into the back yard. At five fifteen, a van pulled up with the *minyan* of ten adult Jews. I was surprised to see that they were all young and mostly women. A few minutes later, the Smiths, the Ho family and several other neighbors arrived. Behind them were John Dias, Ken`ichi Nakamura and Miriam's attorney, Curtis Leighton. Except for members of the *minyan,* Izzy greeted each guest with a fresh *lei* of white carnations and lavender. Then her niece Malia escorted them to chairs set in a wide semi-circle, facing ten chairs set in a line for the *minyan* who would recite the *Mourners' Kaddish*. As I watched the procession, I looked up into the trees and noticed Miss Una perched on a branch where she could enjoy the event at a safe distance.

Despite notices in foreign newspapers and within international organizations, we had not expected anyone to come from outside of Hawai`i. To share the day with those who could not attend personally, Joanne had set up a video camera to record the gathering for the memorial website. Miriam might have departed this plane, but her Ladies proudly shared her home and life with both those in attendance and those who would participate online. The site suggested that people across the globe lift a glass of champagne in honor of Miriam and Henri at the time of the memorial in Hawai`i.

Just before five-thirty, Keoni closed the gate and came to sit beside me. Surrounded by the scent of Miriam's lavender bushes and the blooming plumeria trees, I could imagine the romance of Miriam's first year in the cottage with her beloved husband. After welcoming everyone, Joanne explained the significance of the Hebrew hymn that would be recited and we all stood with the *minyan* to hear the words of praise Miriam's ancestors had chanted for unknown generations.

After that, The Ladies shared their stories of becoming Miriam's housemates. Then several of us read from letters and emails that had come from afar. One surprising element was that several arrived with only the senders' initials and a postmark to indicate their cities of origin. Many of these messages shared a common theme—had it not been for Miriam, it was unlikely the writers could have fulfilled their goals for education and career...or even survived their former circumstances.

CHAPTER 22

By mutual confidence and mutual aid —
great deeds are done, and great discoveries made.
Homer [c. Eighth - Ninth Century BCE]

After the memorial, most people, including members of the *minyan,* remained to learn more about the woman we were honoring. By the end of the buffet dinner, many of us had expressed a desire to set new goals for our own lives. Samantha confirmed her desire to get a degree in European languages, while Joanne was going to look into volunteering at the local high school's newspaper to help students develop their photographic skills. Without concern for survival on her limited income, Izzy wanted to augment the education of her grandchildren and great grandchildren by taking them abroad after graduation from high school.

Thinking of the challenges faced by people with physical injuries like that to his ankle, Keoni was considering teaching self-defense to women and children at Hale Malolo. I was thinking of volunteering in the shelter's literacy and workforce re-entry programs.

The day after the memorial, elegant envelopes arrived at the doors of White Sands Cottage and Mokulua Hale simultaneously. Ken`ichi personally delivered one to The Ladies. Keoni and I received ours from John.

"The reason this is being hand-delivered is so you know it's legit," said John. "I'm not going to say any more than that. Just be there, at the Moana Surfrider Hotel in Waikīkī tomorrow at eleven a.m. Okay?"

Keoni looked at me. I nodded. "Okay...but how about we get together for a drink after this mysterious meeting!"

"Sure thing. I can't wait to hear what you're going to learn at your little tea party."

"What do you mean by what *we're* going to learn? Aren't you're going to be there?" I asked.

"Maybe someone forgot to include me on the VIP list. I haven't a clue about what's going on. But Captain Makani said to make it happen. So that's why I'm here instead of using up some of my comp time on the golf course. You may recall that's where I was the last time you called to report murder and mayhem."

As we laughed at the weak joke, Keoni opened the ivory linen envelope. As I looked at what he held in his hand, I was impressed by the quality of the raised print in gold foil.

M. Keoni Burgess Hewitt and
Mme. Natalie Harriman Seachrist
Are cordially invited to a private tea
Honoring Miriam Sophia Reznik Didión
Tomorrow morning at eleven o`clock ante meridian
In the Lanikai Room of the Moana Surfrider Hotel
2365 Kalākaua Avenue
Honolulu, Hawai`i

I have attended some elite functions before, but never had I received such a distinctive invitation to an event intended for so few attendees. By the abbreviations preceding our names, I guessed that our host or hostess must be French. For such an elegant affair, perhaps the most fitting attire would be what we wore to Keoni's birthday party, the night before Miriam died.

While Keoni walked John to his car, I rushed to call The Ladies to see their reactions to the invitation. We were all curious about the identity of the man or woman who had invited us to the mysterious event. Not knowing how long we would be in Waikīkī, we decided to take two vehicles. Given the formality of the invitation, I doubted that we would need to stop for lunch, but perhaps Keoni and I would decide to stay and play in town following our meeting with John Dias.

Driving toward Waikīkī the next morning, I thought about Miriam and how her life had impacted so many people. I think that my favorite quote from her last public speech was, "When we stand in righteousness, with the law behind our words and actions, we answer and undermine the narrative of the terrorist." The truth of her words had certainly been shown in the strength of the people of Boston in the aftermath of the attack on that city's marathon. It was especially sickening to think that although Miriam had been killed by mistake, the method of her murder, garroting, reflected the silencing of her voice.

Due to Keoni's concern for punctuality, our two-vehicle caravan arrived at the Moana Surfrider fifteen minutes prior to our appointment. With its distinctive white colonnade and *porte cochère* entrance, the First Lady of Waikīkī has often been mislabeled a classic Victorian since her opening in 1901. Her architecture is actually of Beaux-arts design, with features added that were inspired by the Italian Renaissance, Art Déco and Bauhaus movements. Once the home of the old *Hawai`i Calls* radio show, today she usually hosts events that range from outrageously expensive weddings and honeymoons to formal balls and political fundraisers attended by Island elites.

Today's invitation gave no hint of where the tea would fall in the scheme of special events being held at the Moana Hotel. As we entered the lobby, John Dias came forward to greet us. With few words, he escorted us to a ballroom located on the *makai*, or ocean side, of the lovely old building. When he opened the doors to usher us in, the room appeared to be set up to *fête* a wedding party of over one hundred, with its tables featuring a purple and ivory theme, and a multi-tiered cake sitting on a table by itself.

In the back near a service entry, one of the tables was laden with food, beverages and settings of china, silver and crystal. Facing us from the far side, sat a diminutive elderly man with an impeccable goatee. As we neared him, I saw a boutonniere of Lily of the Valley in the lapel of his grey pinstriped suit. Leaning against the table beside him was a cane topped by a griffin carved in gold. Before him were a tea service as well as a crystal decanter and stemware. Taken as a whole, the vignette looked drawn from a spectacular spy or gangster film set in the 1970s.

"Ah, Monsieurs, Mesdames, et Mademoiselle, please be seated. I may now call you Mademoiselle, I believe, Samantha? Do come and join me.

As Keoni seated Joanne and Izzy, Samantha stared across the table at the man who played host.

"I've seen you before," she said, as Keoni moved to seat her.

"You are correct, my dear Samantha. While we did not meet formally, I was just departing when you arrived for dinner with Quinton Duval, an associate of mine in Paris. It was the night after you had delivered my goddaughter to her school in Switzerland."

"You're Naomi's godfather?"

"Yes, indeed. Before we continue, I wish to thank you, former detective Hewitt, for watching over Miriam's Ladies, as you rightly call them.

"And now, it is time for some refreshment. Please help yourselves from our simple menu: Champagne grapes; sliced Fuji apples; warmed brie cheese; mini baguettes; and *petits fours glacé* with *liliko`i* fruit syrup. And allow me to pour from a selection of beverages. There is your mellow Kona coffee, Darjeeling tea, and my personal choice, Armagnac from the Gascony region of France."

Keoni gave a small nod for me to make a selection for both of us and then, as usual, remained a silent observer. The other women chose to drink tea with clotted cream in fine china. I selected to partake of the Armagnac in goblets of a unique crystal pattern. While pouring our drinks, Monsieur again gestured for us to help ourselves to the delicious looking food. China, silverware, and glassware clinked as we began eating and chatting about other significant teas we had attended. Gradually, the pauses in conversation lengthened as we readied ourselves to learn the reason for this meeting.

As Samantha completed stirring sugar into a second cup of tea, she looked up at the man she must have realized was an important element in the landscape of Luke Turner's European operations. When her curiosity finally overcame her timidity, she cleared her throat and asked, "When did you learn I'd married Luke?"

"Oh, my dear, I have followed most every aspect of Luke's life, since long before you appeared in his inner circle. You see, not only was Naomi my godchild, but her mother and father were as well.

"But isn't Naomi Luke's daughter?"

"No. Luke was not her father. My nephew was. Unfortunately he died in a less-than-ideal business transaction, after which Luke Turner burrowed his way into the heart of my family. After he married Renée, we had to accept her decision to join him in your beautiful Hawai`i. As you can imagine, we were delighted when Naomi was sent to school in Switzerland. And, after her mother died, we were pleased that Naomi decided to remain with our family in France.

"There were many reasons why I initially watched you from a distance. As you may imagine, our family's business concerns are very complex. Each person who enters into the picture must be, shall we say, evaluated for their appropriateness. While we live in an age of 24/7 connectivity, certain events and personages must be considered within the framework of a longer view."

Throughout this soliloquy, Joanne and Izzy quietly sipped tea and nibbled cake. This did not prevent them from watching Samantha as closely as they did our host, who remained unidentified. And although Keoni had barely touched his drink, I had no qualms about accepting a second glass of the king of French brandies.

Continuing his story, the small man said, "Sadly, several items under review were incomplete at the time we became aware of Luke's intention to marry *you*. In fact, the nuptials had already been performed and you were his wife. It was only *after* your wedding that we finally had confirmation that Renée's death was *not* an accident. With the many intricacies our family faced, it was decided that we would remain in the background and watch what unfolded from a distance. But, once the death of Miriam Didión fully demonstrated the maniacal machinations of Luke Turner, several of my associates felt the time had come to halt his unseemly mayhem before anyone else we cared about was harmed."

At this point, movement stopped and all eyes were riveted on the smoothly-spoken man. While I was fascinated to hear his story completed, I could not wait to hear John Dias explain how this obvious scion of the Marseilles underworld had been allow to enter the United States.

"Ah, now I have the full attention of everyone. How, you may be wondering, does all of this connect with your beloved Miriam? To explain these complexities, I shall have to move our story to an earlier time. As you know, Miriam and her parents escaped across multiple borders to find safety in Sweden during the Second World War. Clearly the impact of her rescue from the Nazis never left her. While she did not have to endure the atrocities faced by others, the fear of knocks on the door at night, and whispered conversations by fear-filled loved ones remained in her memories—and, I believe, also in her nervous system. I never entered a room without announcing myself, and tried never to whisper to others in her presence.

"Like most of the world, I am sure you know her for the research positions she held in her youth, and later, from the articulate speeches and first-person stories she wrote to accompany the photo journalism of her dear Henri. But I knew her, and Henri, from the time before anyone in the public knew of their work. Henri was older than Miriam. By ten years. While she was a toddler in the latter days of the war, Henri was a young teen, helping the underground in France. Beyond that, the details of how we knew one another in our youth are not relevant to this conversation.

"When Henri and I met years later, I was charmed by his lovely bride and impressed with the skill and artistry with which the duo combined their talents to present gruesome scenes in a way that stirred a world-wide audience to action. The years passed, and sometimes we met in ways not unlike those of our youth. You see, while Miriam and Henri were working publically against human trafficking, sometimes they were using the same methods to move women, children, and others across borders with the same networks as the white slavers against whom they were battling."

The room had been quiet before this pronouncement. It now radiated the heavy silence of a courtroom in which a verdict in a capital case was about to be announced.

"The difference, of course, was that Miriam and Henri were putting all their resources and even their lives on the line to help such people escape from absolute hells on earth. From their years in this work, it is possible to picture someone emerging from the shadows to punish anyone who interfered with criminal profit-making or a twisted honor killing.

"My friends may have seemed high-minded about the causes they served. However, when it came to ensuring that the helpless escaped from horrific circumstances, there was nothing Miriam and Henri would not do. That meant that they would deal with anyone they had to in order to accomplish their goals.

"Many of the networks they tapped into had been utilized during World War II. The reawakening of these cells and organizations for aiding persons in need was not difficult for those who knew how to inspire passion. Some of these people had been members of *La Résistance Française*, what you call the French Resistance. You may know of their work to render collaborators of the Germans ineffective and their brave acts of sabotage. They also helped Jews, Gypsies, and Allied soldiers elude the Nazis.

"Unfortunately, by the late Forties, altruism had given way to profiteering for some French patriots—many of whom were simply returning to the lives they had led before the war."

"Are you speaking of the *Unione Corse*?" asked Keoni, finally breaking his silence.

Showing considerable emotion, Monsieur responded heatedly, "Now you are crossing into a dialogue we shall not have. There are, and have always been, many individuals and organizations who involve themselves in the moving of goods and persons for the benefit of themselves. In such matters, there is a code of ethics you may not understand or appreciate. It is not my purpose today to explore the underworld of my city, or my country.

"It is enough to say that Miriam and Henri knew who could help them accomplish any task at hand. And, with their focused view, they ignored activities irrelevant to their own endeavors. With this background, let me turn to more recent events. As you may have surmised, Luke was associated with manipulations of people, as well as the moving of all manner of portable objects and substances. His bywords were, 'whatever the client wants, the client gets.' As I eventually learned, these words also expressed what he demanded of those who served him. "The complicated dissolution of Luke and Renée's estate in Playa de Carmen masked many details of her death. It took considerable time for my associates to uncover the fact that my dear goddaughter had been 'assisted' in the fall that caused her death. Then, at almost the exact moment that truth was presented to me, I learned what had happened to Miriam."

After a prolonged pause and glance at Keoni, Monsieur continued. "The reason I am able to sit here with you for this little *tête-à-tête*, is that despite my intentions, I had nothing to do with the events of these last weeks. As you know, the man with whom Luke contracted to remove you from this planet, Samantha, became incapacitated in the marshes of your beautiful island. Prior to that incident, the man had already dispatched your husband. Whatever reason he may have had for so doing has not been uncovered by the authorities, and I doubt that anything *I* might do would reveal his reasoning. At least there is one less case in which your authorities need to invest further time, effort or funds.

"As much as I wish I could turn the clock back, there is nothing we can do but look forward. When we examine the work that Miriam and her friends accomplished, the effects are innumerable. Although the *number* of people they were able to help may be small, the *impact* has been great—and not merely for those individuals and their families. Every life is precious, and each person who is saved may one day help someone else in need. This is the 'pay it forward concept,' I believe. Was there not a popular American film that reflected what Miriam and countless others have done, and will continue to do in their own ways?"

We looked at each other and again nodded in reply.

"I must repeat that there is no way to measure the eventual fruits of Miriam's labors. As you know, when Miriam spoke of her "Ladies," she was like a gardener speaking poetry to her flowers—each blossom so different, yet blending together in a profusion of beauty. I would like to think that when you hear a story in the media of a woman or girl in dire straits who has suddenly disappeared in the dark of a moonless night, you can smile and wonder if this is the blooming of another seed planted by Miriam and Henri."

"And what about you?" I could not help asking.

"Me? Oh, no. Do not confuse me with the noble ones. Rather, my family and I have been in positions to help repay kindnesses shown us in our own times of challenge."

At the pronouncement of those words, the service door swayed open slightly.

"Before I leave you, let me share one of Miriam's last communications with me. We had both been alone for several years since the passing of our spouses. She had come to Paris to join me in attending a fundraising event in Paris featuring a great diva retiring from the opera. I shall not recount the tale of how we had all become acquainted. I will say that the woman had used her talent and resources to help Miriam over the decades of their acquaintanceship. As a final homage to our mutual friend's work, the diva was donating her country home as a refuge for women and children gathering strength to begin their lives anew.

"It was an event that had been fulfilling in many ways. As we left the concert hall, the evening's vibrant music echoed through our minds, while the taste of fine wine and food lingered on our palettes. We were waiting for our limousines when Miriam leaned in to me and whispered something I have tried to live by since. She suggested that I should remember the words of Henry David Thoreau who advised that, 'We must live in the present, launch ourselves on every wave, and find our eternity in each moment.'"

His words lingered in the air for a moment. Then, after looking down at his watch, Monsieur rose, leaning heavily on his cane. Stepping back from his chair, he bid us *adieu* and safe passage in our lives and slowly walked out of the room.

As we departed, I looked up at a sign appropriately naming the space we had just left as the *Lanikai Room*.

Lanikai. That was where the denouement of Miriam's life had begun and ended. What we had learned from our French connection had only added to our awareness of the stature of Miriam Didión—and to the sorrow we felt at her loss. The little girl of my vision had traversed a long and complex journey to become the gracious woman of world renown who openly welcomed me into her community. I may not have needed her help, but she had touched the core of my being. I knew that I would consider the light of her life in steering my way through many of the future choices I would face.

EPILOGUE

...Dance like a wave of the sea.
William Butler Yeats [1865-1939]

Two days later I dropped Izzy and Joanne off at the airport. Theirs was a heavily laden trip for many reasons. Urns containing the ashes of both Henri and Miriam accompanied them under provisions governing the shipping of human remains. As they were going on a Mediterranean cruise after visiting the Didión Center in southern France, they were taking two large suitcases apiece. In the cargo bay, there were also three cartons of Miriam's journals that I had packed for donation to the Center's library.

The airport was busy that morning and it took several passes before I could find space at the curb to let The Ladies off. As we drove around, I looked at arriving passengers streaming out of the terminal with *leis* around their necks and thought of the first time I landed at the old Honolulu Airport. Nathan and I were young children that chilly winter in San Diego. When we arrived in Hawai`i, what impressed me the most was the beauty of the ocean as our plane came in low over Pearl Harbor. As we walked from the plane to the old terminal building, the warmth of the moist air bathed my face. As we approached the fence where people stood waiting to greet those who had deplaned, I was struck by the heady fragrance of many kinds of fresh *leis*. Once within the gate, we were welcomed by our Auntie Carrie who had held a block party for her neighbors to help make the extensive number of plumeria *leis* with which she greeted us.

Scent and color can be so evocative of distant times and places. That must have been why Miriam loved her lavender bushes so much. Every time she looked at the depth of their color, she must have remembered the lilacs of Henri's family home. In addition to the thrill of meeting his parents, it must have been a heavenly break from the smog-filled air of post-war London. I could imagine the young woman delighting in the plentiful food and wine of the rich French countryside.

Once The Ladies were on their way, I contemplated what I would do. With Keoni meeting a client for a working breakfast, I was in no rush to return home. Departing from the airport, I was filled with such a sense of contentment that I wanted to do something special. For the first time on my own, I drove up to the Pali Lookout above the Nu'uanu Pali tunnels leading to and from the windward side of the island.

It was still early morning and the tourist buses hadn't arrived, so I had the viewing space almost to myself. The only people present were a young family of four sporting matching baseball caps featuring the insignia of the Hawai`i National Guard and a very senior couple who chatted about their first visit to the Islands thirty years earlier. Standing at the lava rock wall, I looked out on a panorama framed by cumulus clouds floating across the sky. Vast expanses of green flowed from the volcanic Ko`olau Mountains down to the sea. It is amazing how much beauty life can bring us, in the midst of great joy as well as sorrow-filled times.

I closed my eyes for a moment and turned my mind to that inner space I sometimes visit at will.

* * * * *

I look downward through a dull sky at a dark gray sea. Dawn is approaching as the waves lap against a wooden hull. I see a small hand reach out, as though to touch the green foam dancing across the top of the icy water. The scene then freezes and dims.

Warm air envelops me with a hint of rain to come. A new vista emerges in a color palette that brightens from shades of mauve to full color. I look up at fluffy clouds floating through a sky that shimmers beneath a full moon. In front of me, a youthful Miriam Didión leans against a gazebo of white wrought iron. The lattice work is covered in lilacs reminiscent of the jasmine vines climbing up the side of Mokulua Hale. She wears a vintage ecru lace dress that looks as though it had been taken from a trunk at the top of the attic of the gracious French manor house. She is focused on swans swimming on a placid lake a few yards in front of her.

A door at the back of the home opens. I hear strains of Richard Rogers' Some Enchanted Evening *floating from what appears to be a conservatory. A man comes out onto the verandah with two glasses of red wine. It is Henri Didión dressed in a longish ivory dinner jacket from the late 1950s. He walks down a broad flight of stone stairs and crosses to the gazebo. I hear no dialogue, but as he nears Miriam, she turns with a smile and accepts the glass he offers. I stand below them on a sloping well-manicured lawn. He slips his arm around her waist and pulls her close to him. The couple sips their wine for a while and then sets their glasses on the bannister beside them.*

Henri then reaches beyond the gazebo's fence, then plucks a flower from the fragrant lilac hedge. Startled, a chocolate and ivory Birman cat appears and runs down toward the edge of a pond. After whispering something to Miriam, Henri entwines the flower in the hair above her ear. He gathers her into his arms and they slowly dance around the gazebo, her long, blond hair flowing around her shoulders.

NOTES AND ACKNOWLEDGMENTS

In this second book of the continuing Natalie Seachrist series, I have drawn again on my years as a long-term resident of Hawai`i. As other authors have observed in their own work, my characters have grown larger than my original conceptions. Wherever possible, I have presented factual information about the historical individuals and incidents described.

During approximately twenty-eight days in the fall of 1942, Danish seamen and their supporters transported ninety-eight percent of the Jews then present in Denmark to safety in Sweden. Lady Marie Ogilvie served as principal of St. Anne's College at Oxford from 1952-1966. Noted for bold and expansive leadership, she established the first nursery for the children of staff members at Oxford. She also fought against co-education at women's colleges, fearing women might lose their equal footing with men and their percentage of teaching positions at Oxford, which was high compared to the national average.

Serving porridge on Christmas Eve, often as a first course, is a true Danish tradition. There is a ceremony when the porridge is almost cooked: everyone watches as a single blanched almond is dropped into the pot. The lucky person who finds the almond in their bowl wins a small gift, sometimes a figure of chocolate or marzipan.

Many stories are told of Queen Lili`uokalani, the last monarch of the Kingdom of Hawai`i. Many are true, but some are merely wishful thinking. It is reported that the Queen said that she drew inspiration for writing the lyrics to *Aloha `Oe* from a visit to the home of the Boyd Family at Maunawili Ranch in windward O`ahu.

I am grateful to several people have assisted with verifying information included in this work and refining the storyline and text. Again, I wish to acknowledge Tim Littlejohn, a State of Hawai`i library manager, for his weekly commitment to my oral reading of each Natalie Seachrist mystery. As the series has developed, Tim's input has been invaluable in encouraging my attention to cultural sensitivity and the harmonizing of plotline elements.

For her specialized knowledge of unique reference holdings, I also wish to express my gratitude to Gina Vergara-Bautista, who previously served as an archivist at The Hawai`i State Archives. Vital input in areas of technical expertise in various areas has been provided by poet Bill Black and geologist Kevin C. Horstman, PhD. I also thank the intrepid librarians of the Kirk-Bear Canyon branch of Pima County Library for their interest in and support of local authors.

Fellow writers in a weekly literary salon have provided unending support and inspiration for several years, including: Kay Lesh, psychologist and mystery writer; Larry Sakin, green energy entrepreneur, political writer and radio host; memoirist Margherita Gale Harris.

Special thanks go to long-term friends and supporters who provided close review: Viki Gillespie, bookworm and bookman; the Reverend Patricia Noble, a resolute author, lecturer and philosopher; and, Susan and Bob Shrager, retired entrepreneurs.

Finally, I thank my husband John Burrows-Johnson for his patience and continuing support.

Errors, of course, are my responsibility and I regret any you may uncover. Please contact me about egregious flaws you may find, as I dislike the idea of repeating them. I would also like to hear your suggestions regarding historical or cultural themes that might be appropriate to the Natalie Seachrist series. You may contact me through my author website at JeanneBurrows-Johnson.com or my author email at JBurrowsJohnson@gmail.com.

A BRIEF OVERVIEW OF THE HAWAIIAN LANGUAGE

The Hawaiian language was unwritten until 1826, when Christian missionaries transcribed the sounds of the language into a thirteen-letter alphabet. Hawaiian consonants are pronounced as in standard American English. They include **H, K, L, M, N, P, W**, and the `okina [ `]. Often, the "W" is pronounced like an English "V." As there is no "S" in the Hawaiian language, plurals are determined by the preceding article. Each vowel is sounded in Hawaiian; they are similar in pronunciation to those in Spanish, and other Latin-based European languages:

A	=	***Ah*, as in above**
E	=	***Eh*, as in let**
I	=	***Ee*, as in eel**
O	=	***Oh*, as in open**
U	=	***Oo*, as in soon**

Diphthongs are expressed as common English sounds. The "au" transliteration is pronounced as "ow" in "How." Diacritical marks indicate emphasis and syllable separation. A ***kahak*** [-] placed over vowels, indicates a need to hold the vowel sound slightly longer, as seen in the "a" in the word "card." The ***`okina,*** [ `] is both a consonant and a diacritical mark; it dictates indicates that the preceding vowel should be pronounced more loudly.

Please note, that in accordance with standard practices, foreign words included in this work are subject to the grammatical rules of English.

GLOSSARY OF NON-ENGLISH & SPECIALIZED VOCABULARY

The definitions within this glossary reflect the meanings used within the text of this book. Please note that many Hawaiian words have multiple spellings and (with or without diacritical marks) may have multiple meanings. Also be aware that Hawaiian words, especially names, have ambiguous, layered, and sometimes hidden meanings.

A

Adobo — *Dressing, sauce.* [Spanish] Filipino dish with vegetables or protein marinated in vinegar-and-garlic sauce, often served with rice.

Adieu — [Middle English; from the Old French *a dieu, I commend you to God*]. A farewell.

`Ahí — *Tuna;* often yellow fin tuna. [scientific name, *Thunnus albacares*]

Ahiki — See **Olomana.** [Hawaiian]

Alahe`e — Native Hawaiian shrub and tree growing to 20 to 30 feet, featuring green glossy leaves and clusters of small, white, fragrant flowers. [*Psydrax odorata*]

Ali`i — *Chief, ruler, officer, aristocrat, commander.* [Hawaiian]

Aloha — *Love, affection, compassion, loved one.* [Hawaiian] Traditional term for greeting and farewell, expressing love, friendship and mercy.

Aloha `Oe** — *May you be loved.* [Hawaiian] Popular song by **Queen Lili`uokalani.

Ashkenazi — Subgroup of the Jewish people. Approximately ninety percent of world Jewry, that settled in

	Eastern Europe after the Muslim conquest of Palestine in the seventh century Common Era.
Auwē	*Alas, too bad*, or *oh, dear*. [Hawaiian]
Awa	*Milkfish.* Tropical fish found widely in Pacific and Indian Oceans. [*Chanos chanos*]

B—D

Bruschetta	[From Italian *bruscare, to toast or roast*] Toasted bread appetizer with seasoned oil and assorted toppings, or tomato based toppings.
Caro senhor	*Dear Lord.* [Portuguese]
Chanukah	*Dedication*. [Hebrew] Festival of Lights, an eight-day Jewish holiday beginning on the twenty-fifth day of Kislev, the ninth month of the year. Commemorates Maccabees' vanquishing of Syrian-Greek invaders in second century B.C.E.. Following rededication of the Holy Temple and altar in Jerusalem, oil judged sufficient to provide light for one night, lasted for eight nights. The holiday is especially enjoyed by children who receive a gift each evening after recitation of prayers and the lighting of candles on a special nine-candle **menorah**.
Cheongsam	Anglicized word from Southern Chinese Wu dialect. Mandarin *Qípáo* is now more often used. Tight-fitting Chinese dress with slit skirt and mandarin collar. Originated in the Qing Dynasty [1644–1911]. A modern version emerged in 1920s Shànghăi.
Derrière	*From behind.* [Old French] Buttocks.
Didión	*Desire, longing.* [from Latin *desideratum*] Diminutive form of the name Didier.
Du jour	*Of the day.* [French] Term usually used to describe restaurant specialties being offered on a given day, as in "the soup du jour."

E—G

E komo mai	*Welcome; enter and be refreshed.* [Hawaiian] A traditional greeting.
En masse	*In one group or body.* [French]
En Suite	*Immediately attached.* [French]
Entourage	From *entourer, to surround* [French]. Companions of, or a body of people surrounding a usually important person.
Entrée	[French] Course preceding or between main courses in a meal.
Et cetera	[Latin] *And so forth; f*rom et, *and*, plus cetera *the rest.* Expression indicating the conclusion of a lengthy list of similar items.
Fête	[French] As a verb*, to entertain lavishly or honor someone.*
Graças a Deus	*Thanks be to God.* [Portuguese]

H

Ha`ikū	*To speak abruptly; a sharp break.* [Hawaiian] Land section in **Kāne`ohe** on the island of O`ahu, containing a popular garden by that name.
Hale	*House*. [Hawaiian]
Hale`iwa	*House of the frigate bird*. [Hawaiian] Surfing beach and town on the north shore of **O`ahu**.
Haole	*Foreigner, of foreign origin*. [Hawaiian] Current usage, *American, Englishman, or Caucasian*.
Haupia	[Hawaiian] A pudding made from the milk of the coconut palm.
Hawai`i	Fiftieth state of the United States of America and the name of the largest Hawaiian island. The Kingdom of Hawai`i was established by **Kamehameha the Great** between 1795 and 1810. The Kingdom was overthrown between 1893 and 1894, when it was replaced by the short-lived Republic of Hawai`i. Instituted in 1898, the Territory of Hawai`i became a U. S. state in 1959.

Heiau *Temple.* [Hawaiian]

Honolulu *Protected Bay.* [Hawaiian] Located on **O`ahu**, it is the largest city in, and the capital of, the state of **Hawai`i**.

Hors d'oeuvres *Outside of work.* [French] Originally food partaken after working hours. Now refers to appetizers served before a meal.

K

Kaddish *Kaddish ahar Hakk'vura* [Kaddish after a burial] Jewish funeral hymn of praise to God. Traditionally chanted by a **minyan** of ten adult Jews, which may now include women.

Kahakō *Macron.* [Hawaiian] A diacritical mark, [—] A dash placed over a vowel to extend pronunciation of its sound.

Kailua *Two seas.* [Hawaiian] A bay, beach, and town on the northeast end of the windward side of **O`ahu**.

Kaimukī *The oven of the kī.* [Hawaiian] Ti plant. [*Cordyline terminalis*] A neighborhood in east **Honolulu**.

Ka`iulani, Princess** *The royal or sacred one.* [Hawaiian] The beloved niece of **Queen Lili`uokalani, she was the last princess of Hawai`i [1875-1899]. Also a **Waikīkī** hotel and upscale clothing line.

Kalo *Taro.* [Hawaiian] A staple of the traditional Hawaiian diet used to make **poi**. [*Colocasia esculenta*]

**Kama`aina** *Native-born.* [Hawaiian] Designation extended to non-Hawaiians who are long-time residents of Hawai`i.

Kamehameha *Hushed silence.* [Hawaiian] Dynasty of Hawaiian Kings, founded by King Kamehameha the First [1758-1819] of the island of Hawai`i. He fully unified the Kingdom of Hawai`i by 1810. He sought alliances with European nations that ensured the independence and economic growth of his kingdom. He was also noted for transforming the legal system, including enactment *of the Māmalahoe Kānāwai* [*Law of the Splintered Paddle*], which provided human rights to non-combatants in wartime.

Kāne`ohe** *Man of Bamboo*. [Hawaiian] Town in windward **O`ahu, west of **Kailua**.

Kapahulu *Worn out soil*. [Hawaiian] Subdivision of **Kaimukī** neighborhood on **O`ahu**.

Kapi`olani, Queen** *The heavenly or royal arch*. Princess Esther Julia Kapiolani Napelakapuokaka`e. [1834-1899] married King Kalākau and reigned as Queen Consort. Her philanthropic works included the foundation of a maternity home that evolved into The Kapiolani Medical Center for Women and Children. Also a **Waikīkī neighborhood, major boulevard, and community college.

Kawaiaha`o** *The water used by Hao*. [Hawaiian] A high chiefess or chief, believed to have used an area spring for ritual bathing. The **Honolulu** Kawaiaha`o Church was built on land deeded to Congregational missionaries by **King Kamehameha III. It was constructed with coral reef rock and logs from **Kāne`ohe**. Sometimes called the Westminster Abbey of **Hawai`i**, it was the Hawaiian Kingdom's national church and site of royal christenings, coronations, and funerals.

Kawai Nui *The big water*. [Hawaiian] Refers to a swamp, marsh, fishpond or canal. A windward marsh and stream, once **O`ahu's** largest inland pond.

Keiki *Child, offspring*. [Hawaiian]

Keoni Diminutive form of "John." [Hawaiian]

Kī The ti plant. [Hawaiian] [*Cordyline terminalis*]

Kiawe A tropical mesquite tree [*Prosopis pallida*]. [Hawaiian]

Koa Acacia tree. [Hawaiian] An endangered species of acacia tree known for its fine grained wood. [*Acacia koa*]

Ko`olau** *Windward.* [Hawaiian] One of two volcanic mountain ranges dividing **O`ahu.

Kūka`iau** *Current appearing.* [Hawaiian] A gulch, village, and ranch located on the island of **Hawai`i.

Kūlia *Stand upright or strive; lucky*. [Hawaiian]

Ku`uipo *Sweetheart.* [Hawaiian]

L

Lānai *Porch, balcony*. [Hawaiian]

Lanikai Community on the southern edge of **Kailua** in windward **O`ahu**. [Hawaiian]

Lebensraum *Living space.* [German] A philosophical excuse used by the National Socialist [Nazi] Party of Germany to justify their 1939 invasion of Poland that initiated World War II.

Lehua Flower of the **`Ōhi`a** tree. [Hawaiian] The red variety is the official flower of the island of **Hawai`i**. [*Metrosideros polymorpha*].

Lei *Garland* of flowers, leaves, shells, candy, or other decorations. [Hawaiian]

Liliko`i *Passion fruit.* [Hawaiian] [*Passiflora edulis*]

**Lili`uokalani, Queen** [1838-1917] Last reigning monarch of Hawai`i and the only woman. Her name is sometimes translated as, *scorching pain of the royal chiefess.* She may have been named in reference to the eye pain of her foster mother's aunt at the time she was born. Her birth name was, Lydia Lili`u Loloku Walania Wewehi Kamaka`eha; her married name, Lydia K. Dominis; her chosen royal name, Lili`uokalani. She authored numerous poems, chants, lyrics, and the book *Hawaii's*

	*Story By Hawai`i's Queen*. Also an accomplished musician and composer of songs, including the popular ***Aloha `Oe*** [*Farewell to Thee*].
Lokelani	Common red rose. [Hawaiian] Now the official flower of **Maui.**
Lo`i	*Terrace,* often irrigated. [Hawaiian]
Lū`au	***Kalo*** **[**taro] *tops*. [Hawaiian] Modern name for a Hawaiian feast.

M

Mahalo	*Thank you*. [Hawaiian] Often printed on public garbage cans to encourage respect for the environment.
Maile	Flowering tree shrub in the dogbane family. Its fragrant leaves are used for making a long, open **lei**. [Hawaiian] [*Lyxia oliviformis*]
Maka'ainana	*Commoners*. [Hawaiian]
Makai	*Toward the ocean; ocean side.* [Hawaiian]
Makiki	*To peck.* [Hawaiian] A type of volcanic stone used as a fishing weight or adze. A neighborhood northeast of downtown **Honolulu**.
Makoa	*Fearless, courageous, aggressive.* [Hawaiian]
Malasada	[Portuguese] Deep-fried doughnut.
Malia	*Mary*. [Hawaiian]
Māmaki	*Flowering nettle plant.* [Hawaiian] Used as a tea. [*Pipturus albidus*]
Mānoa	*Thick, solid, vast, deep*. [Hawaiian] Valley and neighborhood northeast of downtown **Honolulu**. Location of the main campus of the University of **Hawai`i**.
Maui	Second largest Hawaiian Island, named for the demi-god Māui. [Hawaiian]
Mauka	*Inland, toward the mountain.* [Hawaiian]
Maunawili	*Twisted mountain.* [Hawaiian] A stream, valley, and ranch in **Kailua**.
Menehune	A people of small stature whose legendary presence in the Hawaiian Islands may actually

predate arrival of the Polynesians. They are credited with exceptional craftsmanship that fabricated sacred sites and common objects like fishponds, roads, canoes and houses. Tales of the nocturnal *menehune* center on their building massive stone objects within a single night. [Hawaiian]

Menorah *Candelabrum.* [Hebrew] A seven-branch menorah is used in Jewish temples; it is also the emblem of the modern state of Israel. Also, a nine-branch menorah used for celebrating Chanukah.

Michling *Half breed.* [German] A deprecating term used by the Nazi Party to describe individuals of mixed races.

Minyan A group of ten adult Jews. [Hebrew] The traditional minimum required to conduct a communal religious service.

Mo`ai Monolithic statues of past Rapa Nui chiefs of Polynesian Easter Island. Carved in a flat-planed minimalist style between 1250 and 1500 BCE, they feature oversized heads. Most were carved from tuff, a compressed volcanic ash. Varying in size, they average thirteen feet in height and fourteen tons in weight.

Mochi Molded Japanese rice cake made from glutinous rice paste.

Mokulua *Two adjacent islets*, as those off the **Lanikai** shoreline. [Hawaiian]

Mo`o`alā Gecko or lizard. [Hawaiian] [*Lepidodactylus lugubris*].

Mu`umu`u *Cut short, maimed, amputated.* [Hawaiian] Dress adapted from the garb of nineteenth-century Protestant Christian missionary women, often having short sleeves and no yoke.

N

Nada *Nothing, not anything.* [Spanish]

Natatorium *Swimming* Place. [Late Latin] Natatoriums are usually indoors, but the **Waikīkī War Memorial Natatorium** is beach side. It was built to honor the 101 men of Hawai`i who died in World War I military service. It opened on August 24, 1927, the birthday of surfer and Olympic Gold Medalist swimmer Duke Kahanamoku, who dove in for the first ceremonial swim. Redesigned to comply with the Americans with Disabilities Act, the 100 X 40 meter salt water pool's lifts accommodate wheelchair-bound swimmers.

Niçoise *In the style of Nice, France.* [French] Dressed with vinaigrette, this salad includes mixed lettuce, tomatoes and green beans, and is topped with anchovies and sometimes tuna.

Nu`uanu *Cool heights.* [Hawaiian] Valley, stream, and neighborhood north of downtown **Honolulu**.

O

O`ahu *The Gathering place.* [Hawaiian] The third largest Hawaiian island; location of **Honolulu**.

`Ohana *Family, relative, kinship group, clan, extended family.* [Hawaiian]

`Ōhi`a Two varieties of trees, including evergreen myrtle that produces the *lehua* flower [Hawaiian] [*Metrosideros polymorpha*] The red *`ōhi`a* is the official flower of the island of **Hawai`i**.

`Okika *Orchid.* [Hawaiian]

**`Okina** *Glottal stop.* [Hawaiian] Diacritical mark [`] indicating a break in consonantal sounds, like that separating an interjection's syllables like "oh-oh."

Olomana *Forked hill.* [Hawaiian] A stream, peak, and ridge in windward **O`ahu**. The ridge is comprised of Mount Olomana and two smaller peaks, **Pāku'i**

	[*swift runner*] and **Ahiki** [named for an area overseer].
`Ono	*Delicious.* [Hawaiian]
O'opu	General name for several species of marine and fresh water fishes [including *Eleotridae, Gobidae,* and *Bennidae*]. [Hawaiian] The term is most often used to identify five species of freshwater fish native to the Hawaiian archipelago, four of which are found nowhere else in the world.
`Opihi	*Limpets* of the gastropod family. Measuring one to two inches in diameter, they resemble a classic Chinese field-hand's straw hat and are found only on the volcanic shores of the Hawaiian Islands, Popular item on **lū`au** menus. [Hawaiian]
`Ōpū	*Stomach, belly.* [Hawaiian]

P

Pā`ina	Ancient word for Hawaiian *feast.* Now, a *meal* or *dinner party.* [Hawaiian]
Pāku'i	See **Olomana.** [Hawaiian]
Pali	*Cliff or craggy hill.* [Hawaiian]
Pālolo	*Valley, stream.* [Hawaiian] An avenue and neighborhood northeast of downtown **Honolulu**.
Pane	*Answer, reply, response; to answer or speak.* [Hawaiian]
Peignoir	*Gown worn while combing hair.* [French] Woman's long negligee or dressing gown often made of chiffon or other translucent fabric.
Petits Four Glacé	*Small oven.* [*French*] Bite-sized tea cake covered with icing or fondant glaze.
Pīkake	*Peacock.* [Hawaiian] An Asian jasmine shrub or vine in the evergreen olive family that produces fragrant white flowers. [*Jasminum sambac*]
Plate Lunch	Island meal with Asian style protein often served on a bed of shredded cabbage. Accompanied by two scoops of white steamed rice, a

	scoop of macaroni salad, and sometimes pickled vegetables.
Plumeria	Flowering and fragrant tropical tree including the frangipani, a genus of flowering tree in the dogbane family. [*Plumeria*]
Poi	Thinned paste of pounded **kalo** root [taro] that is the staple food of the traditional Hawaiian diet. [Hawaiian] [*Colocasia esculental*]
Poloka	*Frog or toad.* [Hawaiian] Wrinkled frog [*Glandirana rugosa*].
Pōpolo	*Flowering nightshade.* [Hawaiian] A flowering herb used in native Hawaiian rituals. [*Solanum nigrum*]
Porte cochère	*Door for Coaches.* [French] A roofed driveway at a building's entrance, intended to shield vehicular passengers from the weather.
Punalu`u	*Coral that is dived for.* [Hawaiian] A rural community and beach park on the northeast shore of O`ahu in the Ko`olauloa District.
Pūne`e	*Sofa, couch, pew.* [Hawaiian]
Pūpū	*Marine and land shell; circular motif; appetizer.* [Hawaiian]
Purim	*Lots.* [Hebrew] Originally, plural of ancient Persian *pur*. Reference to the lottery used by Persian Prime Minister Haman in the fifth century B.C.E. to select a date to massacre Jews within the Empire. The holiday of Purim is a joyous celebration of the delivery of the Jews from annihilation. It centers on reading the *Megillat Esther* [*the Scroll of Esther*]. Rowdy remarks from audience members punctuate mention of Haman in relaying Queen Esther's ploys that saved the Jewish people. With children often dressed in colorful costumes, *Purim* is mistaken sometimes as a Jewish "Halloween."

R

Ramsar Convention — Named for the Iranian city of Ramsar, this 1971 global environmental treaty provides a framework for international cooperation for conserving and wisely using wetlands and their resources.

Rassenhygiene — *Racial hygiene.* [German] A concept utilized by the Nazis to justify their attempts to attain and maintain a "pure" Aryan race.

Rassenschande — *Racial defilement.* [German] Crime delineated by the Nazis for a German citizen who marries or has sexual relations with a person of "impure" racial background.

S

Sans — *Without.* [Middle English and French]

Sashimi — *Pierced body.* [Japanese] Thinly sliced raw saltwater fish, served with varied garnishes and sauces.

Shànghǎi — City at the mouth of the Yangtze River in the center of the coast of the People's Republic of China [PRC]. With the largest population of any city in China, or the world, it is classified as a province.

Staccato — *Disjointed, clipped* [from the Italian *staccare,* to detach]. Words or music presented in short, sharp bursts.

Sushi — *Sour tasting.* [Japanese] Cylindrical dish of hand-rolled sheets of *nori* [edible seaweed] or thin omellete, soy paper, cucumber, or perilla leaves, layered with rice cooked with vinegar and a filling. *Kappa maki sushi* is named for a cucumber-eating monster.

T

Tableau — *Living picture.* [French, short for *tableau vivant*]

	Artistic grouping or scene with silent and immobile figures.
Tahara	Ritual washing of a corpse. [Hebrew] The simple and dignified ritual of purification includes cleansing, washing, and dressing of the deceased's body. The act is performed by volunteer members of a *chevra kadisha* [burial society], with women attending to deceased women, and men to men. Prayers are offered to raise the soul into eternal rest in the Heavens.
Teriyaki	"Teri," *glaze* plus "yaki" *to broil.* [Japanese] Cooking process that usually features meat marinated in a soy-base prior to broiling.
Tête-à-tête	*Head to head.* [French] Private conversation, often of two people.
Tūtū	*Grandmother or grandfather.* [Hawaiian] Title of respect often for an older unrelated person.

U

Ulupō	*Night Inspiration.* [Hawaiian] Ancient **heiau** near **Kailua** on **O`ahu**. Building of the large open platform is attributed to the **menehune**.
Una	*Tortoise shell.* [Hawaiian]
Unione Corse	Founded in the 1920s, the secret society and criminal organization operates in Marseille, France and Corsica. Members sometimes - wear a pendant or watch fob with the symbol of a *Maure* (*Moor's Head*), consisting of a black human head with a rag tied around its forehead on a white field.

W

Wahine	*Girl, woman, lady*. [Hawaiian] Something reflecting femininity.
Wai`alae	*Rippling water*. [Hawaiian] Avenue, beach, neighborhood in southeast **O`ahu**. **Wai`alae Iki** A ridge above **Wai`alae**; a neighborhood of

	exclusive homes.
Waikīkī	*Spouting water.* [Hawaiian] A Hawaiian chiefess; famous **O`ahu** beach
Wauke	*Paper mulberry tree.* [Hawaiian] [*Broussonetia papyrifera*]